Mario III

Risky Business

This book is intended for adults. Violence and sexual antics are not intended for minors or sensitive readers. Mario is a work of fiction. Fortunately, all the people in the book lived and died only in my imagination. Any resemblance to actual people should be apparent in your imagination too, when you read the book. The story is purely a product of long, boring plane flights leading to flights of fantasy, the wild goose-chasing of a caffeine-fueled imagination, and a dull foundation of years of experience in wrongful death cases. Like Mario, I am no lawyer. Unlike Mario, I do not employ nubile sex groupies, or toss people out of high rise buildings when they get on my nerves.

One of the guys, a new one I hadn't seen before, whooped and said, "Fresh meat." The bustle stopped like they'd all been frozen. I thought the eyes were going to come out of Jo's head.

"No, Hamilton Burgette," she said. "No and no and no."

"Excuse me?" He looked around, mystified. The cluster of people around Burgette inched away, as if he'd contracted leprosy, body odor and bad breath, all in one fell swoop. "What's up?"

"Your job, if I have any say about it," Jo said tersely.

"He doesn't understand," I said.

"He should. He shouldn't have to be told," Jo said. "If you have to be told, you're in the wrong profession."

Jo took a step toward him. If it had been me, I'd have been poking him as I talked. Not Jo though.

"Never for an instant forget that every case is a tragedy. Even if no one dies, it is a tragedy. But here, this case, this so called fresh meat, this man who died is not some statistic. He is not some raise for you. He was not meat. He had a wife. Her name was Betty. Did you know that? Did you know that Betty was so broken up when he died that they found her wandering the neighborhood in the middle of the night, looking for him? They took her to the psych ward. She's in shock, maybe even a fugue state, and she's got amnesia, doesn't remember who she is because as long as she can't remember, maybe he's not dead. What about the kids? There are two kids who now may have to go to relatives, or might end up in foster care. That's your fresh meat, you son of a bitch."

Works by George Hatcher
One Wilshire

Fiction by George Hatcher

Ambulance Chaser Series
I. Mario: Woman in Jeopardy
II. Mario: Coming of Age
III. Mario: Risky Business
IV. Ambulance Chaser (2017)
V. Jack the Banker (2017)
VI. Flyboy (2017)

Independent Titles
Arabe (2018)
Pretty Face (2018)

CasaHatcherPress Pasadena

George and Molly 1968

To My One And Only
Molly
I love you

My assistant and also my proofreader, Jody Clinker.
Once again, you have come to the rescue.

If it were up to my collaborator and editor, Allie Bates, this book would still be in edits. It would be in edits for the next hundred years. I had to pry it out of her grip while she was still marking it up with her yellow pencil. Even after it was in print, she came running after the publisher's delivery truck, yelling, "Wait, let me change that period to a semi-colon. Delete that exclamation point." That's not how I tell a story. However, without her, I'd be lost, for sure. Thank you, Allie.

Chapter 1
November 4, 1972
Morning

The candy apple red Camaro in the right lane raced toward the intersection, veered directly in front of me and screeched to a stop underneath the yellow traffic light. I was boxed in. Cat Stevens sang 'Morning Has Broken' from a tinny car radio in the VW bug to my right. A pick-up was tight on my ass. I was in no mood to be the meat in a scrap metal sandwich. I stomped my brakes, swerved right into the lane just vacated by the Camaro, nearly took out the beatnik flower-painted Volkswagen bug, but managed to dodge it as I successfully crossed his lane and nailed a sudden and unexpected right turn. Something slid from the seat to my floorboard with the crunch of breaking glass. I heard the pickup behind me screeching tires before it smashed right through where I would have been and into the bug, which went squealing across the sidewalk. A front tire from the pickup rolled down the street under its own steam. I slowed, staring at my rear view mirror. On this unusually warm November day, my top was down. Cat Stevens got louder when the beatnik got out of his mangled bug. The pickup driver swore impressively in Spanish at the beatnik or me, nothing I hadn't heard a thousand times before in the old neighborhood. The way he looked in my direction gave me the distinct impression that he had been gunning for me.

You never know when you need pictures. I reached into my passenger seat for the Polaroid, and discovered that's what had fallen off the seat. I picked it up. The flash bulb was broken. Otherwise, no harm done. I turned in my seat, and used up the end of a pack, snapping five shots of the accident behind me before driving off. I considered exchanging business cards, but I was late for a meeting, and had to let it pass.

My name is Mario Luna, not Mario Andretti. The near-accident broke me out into a sweat. I am not a race car driver. I am what some people call an ambulance chaser, though I've never chased an ambulance in my life. I'm not a lawyer. I don't work for anybody. When I say I'm with a lawyer named Jake, I mean I'm a hired gun for Jake in the ambulance chaser sense. I don't get paid by people named Guido, or plant people in concrete. My job is to do what I do best. You might call it client development.

I wouldn't be telling Jake about today's close call. He'd just be perturbed I hadn't picked up the case.

My assistant sits behind a door at Jake's law firm in a terrific downtown Los Angeles office building on 3rd and Broadway. If she had to sit in the office for very long, she'd hate me. Most of her time now is spent in the field. The great location is a healthy walk from the state courts at the Hall of Justice, the criminal courts, and the Federal Court House where Federal district court lifetime-appointed judges preside over their courtrooms. For the five minutes a day I am in the office, I don't need a room, desk, door, or even a chair that is uniquely mine. Jake's digs are not far from Grand Central Market at 317 S Broadway, across from Angels Flight. Juice bars and street food vendors are plentiful in the huge open marketplace. That's all very convenient for him, and his herd of legal eagles. My actual work station is my car.

By anybody's standards, Jake is rich. He lives in a huge mansion off Wilshire Boulevard in Hancock Park, about a fifteen minute drive from his office. His high-end office is paneled wall-to-wall with enough beautiful furniture to make an interior decorator delirious with envy, but, if you look for Jake at lunch time, you'll find him rubbing elbows with the regular folks at Grand Central Market. About two in the afternoon, Jake hits a juice bar at Grand Central, and sometimes drops in at another favorite juice bar right before five. His office officially closes at six.

Back in '66 when I was eighteen, and Jake had defended me, he had spotted my business potential, so here I am. I had been charged with possession of marijuana for sale, and tax evasion for not having filed tax returns. At that age, I started working with him, and thought of him as my boss, though I am more of a subcontractor. I hadn't understood such nuances then. The IRS is a harsh teacher. I got a cruel slap on the wrist for the drug charges, and no pass on tax evasion. Jake had warned me that Zachary Kasprzak, the federal judge we were in front of was a real bad egg. I don't think he knew about Kasprzak's penchant for creative sentencing. Kasprzak did not follow the probation report recommendation that my debt be satisfied entirely by every penny I had, plus community service. No, not only did I forfeit all the money I had in the bank, forfeit the proceeds of my beautiful Corvette, and get assigned community service; I endured backbreaking debt it took me four years to pay off.

At the time of the arrest, although I was just eighteen, I'd been working for Harry since I was fourteen and a half. I didn't want to leave Harry's practice and work for Jake. We had a good thing going. Harry got excited like a kid over every case I brought him. He paid me well. I had never filed a tax return. But what kid of my age actually filed a tax return?

The Jake I met when I was eighteen was cool. When I was eighteen, his hair was brownish with no hint of gray, but I had no idea of his age. He had a pair of glasses that he wore to court, but court was the first place I'd seen them. He wore contacts the rest of the time, but he told me privately, the glasses added five years, and an air of scholarliness. I didn't see it. I just hoped the glasses would help.

The arrangement was for Jake to represent me in the criminal case in exchange for my working for him. At the time I thought the job was finite, that I could work for Jake till my IRS debt was paid off and then I could go back to Harry, and somewhere in there, Jake would be paid off. I'd have been happier to pay Jake a flat fee for representing me but Jake wouldn't have it. I wasn't green or innocent, but no one had warned me about the IRS, or how to handle when my best friend Pélon got sent to the big house for murder and running a gang.

When I got charged, since I was out on bail, I really figured I would not do any time. Jake assured me I'd just get probation. Even the prosecutor had not pushed for jail time. Everyone was convinced that a fresh young guy like me with no arrest record would walk, or at the worst, get probation.

Too bad the judge didn't see it that way.

I could remember sitting in the courtroom. I faced the judge, but sometimes turned to see friendly faces. It looked formal, and like it meant business, with armed policemen standing around in crisp uniforms, lots of polished wood paneling, tube lights flickering and buzzing behind opaque yellowed ceiling panels. Perched a yard or more above everyone else, the judge was formidable and gray and grim on his bench. I was grateful for the table in front of me because it made me feel less exposed. I could feel the eyes of the audience on the back of my neck. The air stank of pine cleanser, sweat, fear, and cigarette smoke and was accompanied by the dull commotion of creaking chairs and restless people in the rows in back. Jake had gone on and on explaining what a good kid I was. The prosecutor recommended the judge follow the probation officer recommendations. Not even the prosecutor had pushed for jail time. I was so anxious, I hardly know what I heard, or even much of what I said. I was pretty good at assessing people, and could tell that the judge's mind was somewhere else.

I tried to follow Jake's advice to keep it short and humble, and that whatever I said should sound like I was really sorry. How could I be sorry for something I didn't do? No one cared that the drugs in my car were not mine, or that Carson, the asshole, had framed me. I was fucked, fucked, fucked. And something else really pissed me off. I'm not even sure that Jake believed me that I didn't know anything about the marijuana bag in my car. At least Aunt Carmen believed me. As far as anyone else was concerned, truth didn't matter. The investigation was crap. The broken passenger window on my car where the drugs were probably pushed through didn't even raise an eyebrow in my favor. They were convinced the money in the bank, my new car, and the house I bought for my aunt must have been purchased from drug sale proceeds. It wasn't. I earned it getting cases for Harry. I never gave Harry up. The buck stopped with me.

Jake got the prosecutor to agree not to move against my aunt or take the house. That was the deal.

My aunt is emotional. In the meeting, Aunt Carmen was passionate and fragile-looking. Five minutes later in the courtroom, she appeared calm, unworried, supportive of me in every way. She'd gotten a seat as close as possible, so I could see her out of the corner of my eye if I turned my head a fraction. I never really realized how much her support meant to me until I was sitting in jail looking back. Jail provides way too much time to think.

The judge had been somber. He must have just been middle-aged, but to my eyes, at the time, he looked ancient, stern, and at the risk of sounding redundant, judgmental.

"Mr. Luna, do you have anything to say to this court before I pronounce sentence?"

"Sir, I'm very sorry for the crimes I have committed. I was not raised like this. I know better. My Aunt Carmen didn't raise me to become a criminal, and I'm ashamed and embarrassed to be here before you. I feel terrible that my aunt has to be here feeling hurt and humiliated for my behavior. I promise you, sir, that this is the first and last time I will ever come before a judge in a criminal case. I will never, ever, commit a criminal wrong again."

I felt my throat go tight, and refused to break down. Having my aunt in the courtroom hearing me confess to doing something I hadn't done was doubly disturbing. Having Harry and Cosmo in the courtroom was shameful and troubling, but the smattering of kind faces felt like some kind of life raft, before I got tossed into shark-infested waters. The only thing I was really guilty of was the tax thing. I know they say ignorance is no excuse, but I had no concept of taxes and filing tax returns. I had earned the money fair and square getting cases for a lawyer named Harry, but he would get in trouble if I said so. He was like a father to me, and he had kept my aunt and me afloat for years. I owed that lawyer more than I can ever repay, so I wasn't saying. The probation officer and everyone in this room full of strangers believed I had made the cash selling drugs, so my remorse when I spoke was just good business. I was screwed. Jake had told me at least a dozen times that judges want to hear remorse. I focused on the friendly face of my aunt, but I knew she was shaken. I was frustrated, but couldn't rat on Harry about the cases. Realistically though, even if I had, would they have believed me? I was just a kid. What kid would have the skills to do what I did, finding cases for Harry? It was easier to believe that a kid could sell drugs.

The judge locked his dead eyes on me. The hypocrite. He spoke in a fatherly manner, as if he were not pronouncing my doom.

"You will be remanded to the custody of the US Attorney General to serve two years in a federal correctional institution. I see from the probation report that you and your aunt are very close. I am recommending that you serve that time at Terminal Island so your aunt is nearby and can visit you. Upon release, you will remain on probation for a period of two years. During that time, you will gain lawful employment, and be required to pay the Internal Revenue Service whatever sum is still owing after the application of the money that has been attached from the bank, and the sale of the car. If you violate probation..." It went on. I don't believe I blinked once. I could see the judge's eyes and his lips moving, but my ears quit on me. He slammed me real good. I consoled myself thinking of all the years my friend Pélon was doing, but he was in for murder.

At Terminal Island, I went right in to a dorm. The only good thing I can say is that it was better than the cell they threw me in when I was arrested. I had a top bunk. Because the bunks were designed for a shorter man, I had to plan what was going to hang off the edge: my head or my feet. When I was on it, all I could think about was how I would get Carson for doing this to me. He had destroyed my life.

This was federal prison. My bros like Pélon were doing time in state prison. Most of the inmates at TI were older than me. I found no one there from the neighborhood. And though TI was supposed to be a country club compared to any state or federal prison, that's just a comparison. It was serious, with gun towers, and mean guards with batons. They put me to work in the mattress factory, where I made about two dollars a week to use for canteen. I started reading some paperback novels, and played chess with some of the inmates I got close to. Some were mob figures that the LA Times and the Herald Examiner had featured on the front page.

I missed my Cosmo classes, which I had been taking since I was ten. Cosmo had been my first boss. He had a karate studio, and I got him business. He paid me for clients and insisted I study karate. At every opportunity, I worked out with weights in the inmate gym. In the yard, I practiced karate moves. No one messed with me because I was tall, husky, strong, and lucky to stand six and a half feet tall in my bare feet, but still it was agonizing to be there. On top of being demeaning, there's something awful about all those doors you can't open, knowing how deep into the maze you are, knowing you can't get out, and having to do what the guards say. After exercise and books, chess and work, there was still way too much time to lie in my bunk getting increasingly pissed off at Carson. I actually thought about killing him slowly somehow and without using my karate expertise. While I was out on bail awaiting court, I was tempted to pay Carson a visit. I didn't want to chance it. I figured I was being watched by the cops. It was stupid of me to think that. I was just a young punk who got caught with a bag of weed for sale. The law didn't really want me. I had no sales connections. I had no drug connections. Nonetheless, I worried every day I was out on bail. With each second that ticked by, I hated Carson more. There was no question in my head that he had planted the bag in my car then called the cops. Why did I think that? Timing. The day before I was arrested, we'd had a fight. I punched him out. Framing me was Carson's payback.

Nine days after I had arrived, I would not say I had settled in, but I wasn't expecting a visit from Jake. I had gotten almost accustomed to the crappy food. It reminded me a whole lot of what they used to feed us in public school, except that in public school, you could get by not eating it because there'd be something better at home. Here, I saw men threaten to shank lightweights for mystery meat my old neighbor wouldn't have fed his dog. I'd even started liking the peanut butter sandwiches we got sometimes. Peanut butter wasn't something Aunt Carmen ever had in her cupboard.

It wasn't a visiting hour, but lawyer visits are permissible at almost any time of day or night. They pulled me from the mattress job, and I was escorted to the attorney visiting room.

"Hey man," I said, sitting down. "Anything that is a break from routine is good, but I hope this is important. Every meeting means a strip search." My tone wasn't friendly. I realized it and didn't care. I was disgusted with the entire justice system, especially my attorney who had said I would not do any jail time.

"Mario, you're getting out."

I hopped up. "What? What did you say?"

"I said, you're getting out. Right now. The two years you don't serve will extend your probation. Unless you prefer to stay here." He winked.

"No shit?" I asked.

Jake put one hand over his heart, and the other in the air over an imaginary bible. He wasn't kidding.

There was a table in front of me, and my top half just fell forward on it. I felt like I was going to cry and laugh at the same time. I'm lucky I didn't have a heart attack and a stroke simultaneously. A freight train of blood was rushing between my ears, and my heart pounded like a jackhammer. I didn't know how resigned I'd been to my fate, but my body felt getting those two years back, all at once. The whole light of life flicked on. It was like that scene in *Wizard of Oz* when everything goes from black and white to Technicolor.

I was escorted back to the dorm to roll-up my bedding and pack my personal belongings that amounted to toiletry items and some pictures. I had a deck of cards and a book which I left for the guys in my dorm. The guard waited for me, and I wrapped it up in less than five minutes. Everyone was at work, so when I left I didn't see anyone. I wasn't looking back. I had no clue what Jake had done to get me out. He hadn't told me yet.

Carson's folly put me behind bars, cost me everything I owned, including my self-respect, and put my aunt through more grief than I could measure, but when I got out of Terminal Island Prison, I was so happy to be done with it that going after Carson was the last thing on my mind. The first thing on my mind was never going back.

There were some formalities. Some more signings. They handed me the contact information for my probation officer with instruction to make contact within twenty-four hours. I sat through a lecture that impressed on me that I better not screw up, because if I did, the probation officer had the power to revoke my freedom and send me back to prison to serve out my suspended sentence minus one day in jail and nine days I had served in Terminal Island. As long as I kept my nose clean, there would be no more prison. Judge Kasprzak was an advocate of a "Scared Straight" program that had been going on in New Jersey prisons, and thought that 10 days in real prison would do me good. While it was happening, I thought Kasprzak was a major asshole to make me a guinea pig for his private experiment. Later, it occurred to me I should be thanking the man for picking me for his experiment.

The good feeling, the relief of not having to do time faded as I put in four hard years working like a dog, and watching a big chunk of my income go to fines and the IRS. By the time I paid it off, I was twenty-two. I lived with the fear that if my probation officer had a bad day, he would use his power to send me back to prison for the rest of my suspended sentence. I avoided Carson even when I got to a case after he did, which was a rare thing. When mutual friends from the old neighborhood told me Carson was a living ball of frustration because most of the time, by the time he got to a case, I had already signed it, it did my heart good.

The first thing I did after I had gotten out of jail was Pixie. I got her to a hotel and we fucked our brains out. The second thing I did was to get a big jar of peanut butter. Now, it's a staple wherever I am. Protein you don't have to cook. Not bad. Somewhere down the line of first things I did was take a hot shower in a room that had a door I could open and close.

I had patience. I waited four years, until the probation was done before confronting Carson. I was twenty-two when I received my discharge letter from probation in 1970. It was time to handle unfinished business. I didn't have to do any research to find him. The mothers of my old friends still met with my aunt. Old friends kept me up to date on all the news, especially all the news about Carson, my former friend, now my nemesis. Carson's rental house was not far from where we had grown up in the old neighborhood. He was living with three girls he called his assistants who ran around with him signing up cases. In five years, he had moved through six lawyers. I didn't know the details behind the changes, and I didn't give a damn. I didn't hide, either. I parked behind his '62 Chevy on the driveway.

It was just getting dark when I banged on Carson's front door. No one answered, but I knew they were there. I put my shoulder to the door, and knocked it down. No one was in the living room, so I ran toward the sounds coming from a bedroom. The television was on at full blast. The occupants of the bed were laughing and talking loud, and, no doubt, high. They weren't smoking, but I could smell weed. They were so engrossed or doped up they didn't even turn to see me when I stormed in. Carson was centered in the bed, up against the headboard, a girl on each side. There wasn't a stich of clothing on any of them.

I reached for Carson, grabbed him by his greasy hair and threw him on the floor.

The girls were high as shit. There was a good long delay before they noticed something was going on. They screamed.

So did Carson.

"Shut the fuck up," I said.

The screams stopped.

Carson flopped around like a rag doll. I propped him up, ready to punch him out. He crumbled like the shit he was, crying on the floor on his knees. I never threw a punch.

"Mario, bro," he cried at me like a girl.

"Get up and fight me like a man, you stupid son of a bitch. I should beat your face in. You put that shit in my car. You cost me my car, my beautiful car, and a fortune in fines and all the money I had in the bank. Took me four years to finish paying the IRS. You set me up."

"It wasn't me," he wailed.

Carson was a liar. He hadn't told the truth in his life, if there had been an opportunity to lie. There was no reason to think he spoke the truth now. His denials fell on my deaf ears.

I looked down at him sobbing on the dirty carpet and felt only disgust. My rage was a lost cause. My plan for revenge was circling the drain. I couldn't beat him down. He was barely a man. I walked out, leaving him to his pathetic, miserable life. I had only one thought: he'd better not ever get in my way. His dopey girls ignored me and went down to the floor to comfort him where he was curled, coiled like a snake, except snakes don't sob. As far as I am concerned, Carson is a ghost from my past. He is old news. I had learned to live with the knowledge that my ex-friend, Carson, was a lying backstabbing chiseling cheat who did his best to ruin my life. The dude denies framing me. I know he did it. If I had kicked his ass the day I got out of jail, he may have confessed. Good riddance motherfucker. Though it is all water under the LA River bridges, that betrayal still pains me. I'll hold the grudge for the rest of my life. Friends don't do what he did to me.

My conviction was for not filing tax returns, tax evasion from when I was fourteen, so believe me, I learned my lesson. You don't mess with Uncle Sam. He has to get his, just like the body shops and others who send me business. Now I have Felix Billingsly to handle my IRS math. I pay him way too much money to handle my tax affairs. I make sure he gets the best gift basket every year.

I am in and out of Jake's office like a jack-in-the-box, but since it is Los Angeles, like a Mario in the smog box. I spend more time working from my car than in any office, but that's okay with me. I'm no desk jockey. Every dude from the Beatles to Sonny Bono is wearing his hair long and in a shag. I usually have it longer than this, but thanks to the LA weather and an overly enthusiastic barber, my hair is currently like the fuzz on a tennis ball, and my head frequently sun-burned, because I succumbed to the allure of a convertible. Ah, the car. It is a 1970 fire engine red GT. Nice cars are my passion, and my ride is sweet, but in the summer, the sun bakes the top of my head crispy. It's just into November now, and there's no burn, but I still put down the top when it is warm and sunny enough like today. I've got a couple of sport coats in the back seat, flapping a little in the wind as I spin across town to visit a potential client, but I usually have jeans on. If my closet is in the back seat, my portable office is hidden in the trunk: boxes of contracts, and papers to be filed, staplers, and scissors. I even have a portable typewriter back there for when I drive around with my gal Friday. My shirt is cotton and light, and for the time being, my tie is looped around the rear view mirror. I'd have to make better time in this paper-packed car on these car-packed streets to work up enough of a breeze to cool down.

Thanks to being mentored from fourteen to eighteen by Harry the lawyer, at the tender age of seventeen I bought a house for my Aunt Carmen, but ever since Jake repped me in court, it's been Jake who has been keeping me busy. My aunt wasn't thrilled last month at the move into my own apartment, but she's not far, and I frequently show up for dinner. Ever since her madam kicked her out, my ex, Pixie, a former hooker, lives with my aunt, and she's having a second childhood along with her little girl, Lainey, under Aunt Carmen's wing. How she got there is a really long story.

Everybody there is in school. I'm all for education, but school has never been my thing. Aunt Carmen knows how important my work is to me, but she's asking me to come over all the time. Even if I hit her up for dinner every night, Aunt Carmen would still want me there on the weekends too. Truth is, I count myself lucky that she took Pixie and Lainey in as family a couple of years ago. They keep her busy.

All my stuff is still in boxes. I've only been out of the nest for a month or so. And why not, since I bought the house my aunt is living in. The apartment is kind of crappy. It's not the kind of place a guy can bring a woman home to, but a man has to have his space. I'm casually looking for an apartment that is better than this place I have to crash in. I don't plan to stay in this crappy place for long. I could rent a great big house somewhere in the expensive districts of Los Angeles. But what would I do living in Beverly Hills? My contacts that send me business are not in that area. I really don't want to live over there, but I'm just saying, I could.

When I was a kid, I was raking money in hand over fist. I'm still a kid to some people, but I'm talking about how I started working at age ten. At fourteen, I became a marketing person for a lawyer named Harry. You would not believe how many auto accident cases I got for Harry over the next four years. I still get paid right away for initial services, but my deal with another lawyer, Jake, has changes in the works. My deal with Jake was practically the same as I had with Harry when I was fourteen. How much I get paid depended on how successful I was in steering business to the law firm. Jake recently sweetened my deal. Now there's a so-called bonus that comes if the case settles for more than three grand. The bonus is not a percentage of attorney fees, because I'm no lawyer, but a "bonus" passes some legal smell test to keep it from seeming like I'm sharing in attorney fees that Jake makes on a case.

Aunt Carmen used to be an off-the-books accountant for a small sewing factory, and also she used to be a nurse, and also a part-time midwife. Now that she's got her nursing creds back, she dumped accounting, and is just a working midwife. The whole midwife thing has come back into style in a big way, but like it or not, I give her five hundred a month so she's got no worries. I don't know how she stood accounting for as long as she did.

It's not only Aunt Carmen, Pixie, and Lainey at the house. It's also the soon-to-be moms dropping in all the time. On any given day, there's more estrogen in that house in an hour than one man should have to deal with in a single lifetime.

I don't spend much time in my apartment with my feet up either. It was available, centrally located, convenient, has covered parking, and it's dirt cheap. My bread and butter is a generous working relationship with ambulance drivers, doctors, nurses, therapists, body shop owners, messengers, funeral directors, embalmers, casket salesmen, priests, restaurateurs, car wash workers, and the million paper pushers and day jobbers who work in all areas that come across accidents and the survivors of accidents. Some of these people are, or at some time were, my neighbors or clients. I keep their palms oiled, and they keep me informed when there's an accident in their venue. A great number of these people are pretty girls with questionable morals. So sue me.

This morning, after checking the rear-view mirror a hundred times, I pulled up to a greasy spoon on Soto, three minutes from Lincoln Hospital. I sat in the car for a couple of minutes, just looking around. I tried to look like I wasn't looking, but I was checking out people on the sidewalk, cars, everything. There wasn't anything suspicious to be seen. It's not like I'm afraid. I am confident I can handle whatever comes up. I guess I'm getting paranoid. Maybe it was the fault of that accident I was almost in this morning. But no, I think this feeling started earlier than that. I've had a feeling for the past few days that I am being followed. I keep seeing someone out of the corner of my eye, and when I look, he's gone. If it happens again, I'm going to get real serious about catching him or her.

I ordered some burgers, fries, and coffees. The table I always take is in the back, because it gives me a good view of the door, so I can see who is coming in. They might have a case for me. But now there's an extra layer of watchfulness. There's nothing suspicious I can put a finger on. I know how paranoid that sounds. I've walked the worst streets in Los Angeles and never had a worry. Why would anyone be following me? I guess that everyone thinks that they are being followed at some time.

I did notice a guy standing by the register. He was medium tall, black hair cut a little long for a lawyer type, but too short for a beatnik. He was wearing the cheap suit of an aspiring businessman who maybe didn't aspire too high. The hair rose on the back of my neck. I leaned forward, and realized who it was. As if he could feel my eyes on him, the pseudo-businessman turned, confirming my hunch.

It was Carson.

Right after he turned, I saw a sleek brunette in a nurse's uniform enter, drawing the admiring glances of every male in the place, including Carson.

Tanis was exactly on schedule. She walked to me, and bent, giving me a kiss on the top of my head, and ruffling my short-cut hair.

"Mario." Her smile was contagious, a flash of perfect white teeth. She saw my expression, and looked over her shoulder, where Carson now was. She stood upright, and stepped behind my chair. She's got good instincts, does my Tanis.

"I don't believe I've had the pleasure," she said.

"It's no pleasure," I told her, rising to my feet. I put my hand out to shake hands, and Carson did his old move, and pulled back from the handshake. His hand went to slick back imaginary bangs.

"Still the same old shit," I said.

"Long time no see," Carson said to me, but his eyes were on Tanis, giving her the once-over.

We weren't eighteen any more, but he looked the same as ever. A little older. The hair was a lot shorter than it had been a couple of years ago, and maybe his hairline was going up. I wasn't sure. He had a couple of scars I didn't remember. They could be scars I gave him. He's still half a foot shorter than I am, and built along smaller, softer lines. I doubt that he worked out. His siblings were all sisters, and maybe that was why he always seemed a little effeminate to me. Back then, he did take good care of his clothes, and looked like he still did. Of course he did. It was part of his con. When we were kids, he always swore he had only one pair of pants. It was possible. Money was tight.

Carson put his arm back down, reached out and took my hand. He forced a handshake. He was a genius of bad timing. When we were kids, it had been funny. Not so funny now.

"Let bygones be bygones, eh, man?"

It wasn't likely I'd forget his faked accidents, or that he'd forget my beating his ass and knocking out a tooth or two. I sure wasn't forgetting his planting drugs in my car. I let the comment pass.

A beeper went off. Tanis and I both checked, but it wasn't ours. With his left hand, Carson pulled a beeper out of his pocket, and glanced at the number. It was a strange moment, all of us with our beepers out.

He let go of my hand, and tipped an imaginary hat.

"Good to see you Mario." He tipped the imaginary hat toward Tanis. "Good to meet you." He gestured to me. "Dude taught me everything I know."

He left. I decided to ignore his intrusion. Tanis, however, was curious.

"Is he an ambulance chaser?"

"He's an asshole," I said. "He's nobody. He's history."

"You all right? How come you're the color of the salsa on the table?"

"I'm fine. The last time I actually exchanged words with Carson was a couple of years ago. It had not been a social call."

Carson was best forgotten, so I pushed him to the back of my mind. "How's my best girl?"

"Counting the minutes till we go to our spot."

She laughed. She had a husky, velvety, sultry laugh that brought every male cell in my body standing at attention. She wasn't exclusively mine, but lately I've been thinking about changing that. She was an emergency room nurse. We were free spirits. We usually met up only when she had a case for me, about once a week.

"You wouldn't believe what I had to do to soften this dude up for you. The fucker wanted to fuck me."

"Who doesn't?" I grinned. "And?"

Her eyes laughed. Tanis, not yet sitting, noticed she had drawn attention. All the people at nearby tables were looking at her. Next to us, the elderly couple nursing their coffee and doughnuts had frozen at the turn of Tanis's conversation. The old grandpa was grinning. The woman next to him was frowning like a carp. Playing to the crowd, Tanis whispered in my ear.

"I told him, maybe, just maybe, I'd give him a hand job, but that was it."

We both laughed.

She sat across from me.

"I'm going to wash your mouth out with soap. You're scaring the vicar and his wife." I whispered across the table, reaching for her hand. It wasn't much of a whisper.

"Don't mind me," Grandpa said, "I'm not a vicar, I'm a postman." I thought there was a good chance his wife was going to slap him with her cruller.

"The things I have to do to get you a case," Tanis said, grinning. "I'm kidding." She looked the postman up and down and told him, "I'm kidding."

"You're not kidding," I accused. I wondered how far she'd really go to get a good case for me. She got a lot of cases. My guess was pretty far.

Her response was another big smile and a promise.

"Save the soap until you come in my mouth."

The old lady's glare frosted over. "Well, I never!" she huffed, shoved her chair from her table, and stomped to the door.

The mailman stood. He pulled out a couple of dollars and dropped them on the table. He wrapped the rest of their doughnuts in a paper napkin. His wife had already slammed out.

"It's true," he said in our direction. "She never did." He was laughing.

Tanis giggled, and I laughed.

"I think we embarrassed him. He seems like a nice guy. Maybe we shouldn't have."

Tanis brushed me off with a hand. "He loved it."

Here's the thing with Tanis. I can't always tell when she's kidding. It occurs to me that I am better off not knowing how she gets the cases she brings me. But she is profoundly competitive.

"So, about this case?"

When Tanis had a case for me, she would call, as she had earlier, to tell me we needed to meet. She could get fired for referring a lawyer to a patient, but Tanis was careful-smart. I never saw her in action, but by the time I met with the prospective client whether that day or in the future, the sell was done, especially if it was a male. And most of her cases were male. I came in for the signature.

The waitress arrived with her full tray.

"Good! You ordered," Tanis said.

"Of course. Cheddar cheese, spicy mustard, tomatoes and lettuce. Coffee, black." The waitress also brought a third burger to go.

"You're a life-saver, Mario. I'm ravenous. And you know how bad the hospital cafeteria is."

"What about the case?"

"Mr. One-Track Mind."

She took a bite and chewed, making me wait.

"You're the one who called me," I reminded her.

She was so pretty I could hardly tear my eyes away. I felt lucky to have her on my side. Tanis wasn't just a pretty face; she was a highly motivated person who oozed with smarts, and had a gift of gab that injured men could not resist. She had mouths to feed—not just her own kids, but her kid sister with two kids of her own—and not quite enough money to provide for them. Her ex was a jerk who had taken off with a hooker and ended up dead of an overdose of heroin. Tanis hated him for leaving her, but insisted that he was not an addict so the overdose had to be a fluke. Fluke or not, he had been dead for more than two years.

"A milk truck hit this guy at the crosswalk on Whittier and Soto. His leg is broken. He's perfect for you. I haven't been home since Friday. There's a flu going 'round, and the ER has been packed. I caught a cat nap in an empty room." She bit into her burger and juice ran down her face. "Ambrosia." She laughed. Her husky laugh rolled over my senses, and made me regret we weren't somewhere private.

As an emergency room nurse at Lincoln Hospital in East Los Angeles, Tanis is exactly the kind of contact I like best, working in the trenches, rubbing shoulders with a constant stream of accident victims and their families. To say that I am very grateful for being on the receiving end of her seventies-era anything-goes Free Love sexuality is putting it mildly. I love many girls, including this one. That she introduced me to great clients is the cherry on the frosting on the cake. She gets me in the door before the insurance adjuster swoops in. I haven't talked about insurance adjusters. I don't want to say they're the enemy. But they are the spawn of the devil.

"How is life treating you?" I asked her, "How are your kids?"

"They're fine," she said. "It's a good thing Niley is my live-in housekeeper, or else I'd be up shit creek."

Tanis was ten years older than me, had two kids, a boy and a girl. Niley, her little sister, had two boys with no daddy around. The arrangement for her little sister to take care of Tanis's kids and live at Tanis's apartment was a good deal for both of them.

"So tell me about the client."

Between bites, she filled me in on her patient's details.

"Married. He works construction. Wife also works. Weather was perfect. Driver was in a rush, ticketed. I told our guy you aren't a lawyer. He understands that you're an investigator working for a law office. He's expecting your call. They released him about an hour ago. He was going straight home."

When my beeper went off, I glanced at the number. It was Jake's office, which could mean anything.

"Is it important?" she asked.

"It depends on you."

"I have to get back. We're short-handed, otherwise I'd have met you at our spot."

Our spot was a motel near the hospital. The hours she worked were as crazy as mine, but I didn't have a time clock to deal with. She took all the overtime the hospital would give her. When we could sneak away, we whiled away every available hour in athletic sex. I was a little disappointed that this lunch date wasn't turning into something more, but we were both busy and loved it.

I scarfed down my meal. I'm not a gourmet, and I spend way too much time in diners, eating fast, a la carte, and on the run.

Jake beeped me again. Tanis watched me look at the beeper and stow it in my pocket.

"You'd better call him back."

"I will, but I'm not wasting a minute of my time with you on the phone with Jake."

"Charmer." She stood up. "Gotta run."

She gave me a folded sheet of paper with all the information on it about the milk truck accident. I pocketed it, and handed her four new hundred dollar bills, more than a week's wages at the hospital.

She gave me a quick peck on the lips and sailed back to the hospital. I still felt uneasy, and walked to the door to gaze out, watching Tanis disappear into a typical sidewalk crowd. Nothing seemed out of the ordinary.

I headed for the phone booth to call Jake.

"Why didn't you call back? Why did I have to call you twice?"

"I was in a meeting."

He paused. I could feel him smiling on the other end of the line. He knew and liked that clients always took precedence. He wanted to know if I was coming in today.

"I just got a great case. Milk truck versus pedestrian. Big injuries."

"I'll talk to you when you get here," Jake said.

Before I left the greasy spoon, Jake put my assistant on the phone.

"I got a couple of referrals coming to the office." I told her, "I want to shoot up to Oakland on Pacheco, and the other case that you have details on. Please prepare retainers. We can fill in the blanks later. Book me a flight, today, if you can. I'll be there ASAP. Book yourself a seat, too." I hung up the pay phone, and headed in.

My assistant is Jo Friday. Yes, Jo, just like the character Jack Webb played on Dragnet, except she's a chick. Her full name is Jolanthe Webb, but she is more of a Jo than a Jolanthe. She's married to her childhood sweetheart, a guy named 'Nando Webb. 'Nando is former military, a decorated hero. He is a good guy, but his career left him in a wheelchair. Now he paints and is a live-in dad. Jo manages two kids, and all of my shit. She's about seven years older than I am, and an organizational wonder. She picked it up mostly from being a military wife. (The organized part, not the age.) When Jake got the idea that I needed an assistant, I cut a deal with him. For the past six years, he's paid half of her salary, but she works entirely for me. For five years, she sat in the office and did paperwork. She came to me not too long ago and said she wanted to do more. I've started her going out signing up cases. She explains to clients if their cases are good, and how they should get medical treatment, telling them to go to doctors to get their personal injuries tracked. She explains about the medical bills. Those are called specials, and specials add to the value of the case. At one time I personally signed every single case I was referred. Having Jo signing cases has been a real load off of me. I trained her, and she is good at her job. It is rare that she comes back without a signature on a retainer. Phone calls, I handle. When the exchange beeps me, I call back as soon as I am by a phone.

Recently I bought a phone for my car but it is almost worthless. Everyone who has a car phone shares one or at most, two lines, to receive and make a call. To make a call you have to monitor who's talking. As soon as the conversation ends, you say "Mobile Operator, Hello," and hope that it's you who gets through and not some other anxious caller. Consequently, pay phones are very important to my livelihood. Without my beeper, I'd have very little business.

Chapter 2
November 4, 1972
Afternoon

Jo had two retainers and one police report for me to check out before she turned it over to Jake's people. I don't usually need a police report, but sometimes it can clarify what happened in an accident, or identify a responsible party. Jake had signed off on an investigator to look into the elusive defendant where the client had paid cash for a used car that blew up on him. All the used car lot assets were smoke and mirrors. Jake felt sure there was money there somewhere, but it was hidden in a quagmire of dummy corporations and liens, so we were trying out this forensic account investigator. Then there was a personal injury case where a penniless driver in a borrowed car injured a passenger, and there was no insurance. Our client was the injured passenger, who had a stack of hospital bills, but without insurance or assets, there was just nothing anyone could do. No driver assets to pursue, no thirty-three percent for Jake, nothing for me. But we were still holding out hope that the court would go after the guy who loaned out his car to his drunken friend.

I handed over the food, signed the papers, and exchanged them with Jo for three messages that had come in on the office phone. She had begun typing out forms for our Robert Pacheco meeting. I rifled through the messages. She stuck her nose in the paper bag and inhaled a whiff of the grilled burger on buttered-toasted bun that I had brought her, and set it aside.

"I'm sorry it's cold," I told her, "I can run down the street and get you a hot one."

Jo replied, "Cold is good. No worries."

She was still filling out papers. Her fingers paused at the typewriter.

"Referred by?"

"Cecile Pacheco."

"And Cecile is...?"

"The grandmother and mother-in-law of the victims."

Cecile Pacheco had called me early that morning and sobbed out her whole sad story, ending with "It's time for my son Robby to speak to you about your recommendation about getting a lawyer. He's ready to come to LA or to receive you up at his home."

Her son was drowning in grief, struggling with bills, and just realizing he was in over his head.

Jo scooted her wheeled task chair off to a filing cabinet, and glanced over Cecile's history. Here at Jake's, we'd handled two car accident cases for her. Before I had read to the end of the first page, Jo scooted back to the typewriter, filled in some more blanks, whipped out the page, and dropped it into the new Pacheco file folder I was looking over.

"Do you need to stop by your place?" I asked her. "We have just enough time to make it there and to the airport."

"No need," Jo shook her head, and lifted her enormous purse. "I got it covered."

All the way to the airport, Jo was fussing at me like a mother hen. She was a nitpicker, a valuable characteristic in her line of work. The very most important thing about Jo is that I trust her. She is a heck of a personal assistant. Today, as always, she looked the part.

"What's this?" she said, picking up a photograph off the floorboard.

"You tell me," I said. "My eyes are on the traffic."

"Looks like an accident. A pickup and a VW bug." She squinted at the picture. "I don't remember the case."

"Oh yeah," I said, "That's the guy who almost rear-ended me this morning. I got out of his way, and he rammed the bug."

"And you didn't sign the case?" she asked. "That's not you."

"I was late meeting Tanis."

Jo picked up the other four pictures and put them all in the glove box. "You can see the plates of both cars, and both the drivers' faces. We can follow up."

Over a plain white button-down shirt, she wore a woman's business suit that managed to be sexy to me, and, I think, non-threatening to other women. Aunt Carmen always said she liked Jo's style, and tried to get Pixie to dress that way. The jacket and skirt she had on looked expensive—a dark pinstripe. She even had a silk handkerchief in her pocket. Today's panty hose had a stripe down the back. The dress wasn't short, but it was slim, with a cut along the side that emphasized her fantastic legs. If I didn't know better, I'd be fantasizing stockings and garters, but Jo wasn't one for fuss. I knew she'd have panty hose on under there. Lately, Jo wore her hair no-nonsense, cut at about chin length. It was straight as a board, and when she wore heels, swung when she walked. It was usually a shade of brown, but sometimes there were highlights. I'm not one to notice make-up, but Jo did wear bright red lipstick. Her lips were wide, and expressive.

"You haven't slept in two days. I'll go to San Francisco solo on this one. Get some rest," Jo urged.

I don't know where the energy came from. All I knew is that I wasn't done yet.

"Can't. This one is personal. The referral of this case is solid, and she's a friend."

"These people are all your friends."

I didn't argue that. Sometimes they started out as strangers, but almost always ended up as friends. It was true.

"Besides, the main reason I'm bringing you is there's another case in Oakland I want you to sign while I'm chatting up Pacheco."

She nodded.

I continued, "You got us the flight. I'll sleep for an hour on the plane." I thought about mentioning my feeling of unease to Jo, but it might frighten her. She had a history of being superstitious. It had come up before.

With Jo along, I didn't have to keep track of anything. She did the organizing, and I would be free to sleep. I thought I saw a car shadowing me, but slowed down and speeded up, and took a turn to make an unnecessary block. They didn't follow. I looked over my shoulder a couple of times. Still had the feeling.

She noticed the detour. "What was that about?"

"Nothing, really. I've just had this feeling for a couple of days that I was being followed."

She rolled her eyes at me. I had worried needlessly about her being superstitious.

"A couple of days ago, I was walking to the courthouse. There were a couple of punk ass gangies behind me, and later a low rider and a pickup followed me from North Hollywood to Culver City. This morning, a pickup almost railroaded me into a wreck. You saw the pictures."

She shook her head. "You watch too much Columbo."

In no time, the car was parked, we were situated in our seats, and the plane was underway. The biggest problem I had was stepping in something gooey in the parking lot. It made my soles tacky. I felt lingering stupidity for telling Jo about my paranoia.

Jo said, "Give me your shoes."

I handed them over.

I reached into my pocket, pulled out my knife, snapped it open, and handed it over to her.

"You can use this for scraping," I said.

"Holy felony, Batman," she said, "You never do anything half-way, do you?"

"It's not a crime. Every man worth his salt carries a knife," I told her.

"You must be worth your weight in salt," she said. "Trust you to find a knife made by Smith & Wesson."

I looked to my right. There's no privacy on a plane. The guy across the aisle grinned at me in camaraderie and pulled out his Swiss Army knife. So did the guy next to him. A couple of boy scouts. The guys in rows in front of and behind us pulled out theirs, and they ranged from harmless looking single blades to a badass switchblade that probably was illegal. The women with them looked embarrassed. It was a testosterone moment. I think all of us guys were one gene away from beating our chests.

"Nuff said," I said, a little complacently.

"What is that smell?" Jo asked, ignoring the testosterone in the air. She looked toward my feet.

"You *told* me to take off my shoes."

"I also said to stick with cotton socks," Jo said. "I think you're allergic to that polyester material. You know they put formaldehyde in those."

"Fine," I said. I think she was right, and I didn't like it. I was going to have to throw out all my new socks. Everything these days was made out of polyester, and polyester didn't absorb anything.

She dug a handful of pre-packaged Crab Shack towelettes from the deep reaches of her massive purse.

I folded my foot up on my knee and pried off my sock, first one, then the other. She handed me a vomit bag to put them in, a handful of lemon-scented wipes for my feet, and from somewhere in her magic bag, produced a new pair of men's designer cotton socks before anyone in the cabin was overcome by the toxic fumes.

"Go to sleep," she commanded.

The last thing I remember of the flight was being enveloped in the pleasant smell of lemon, and seeing Jo vigorously using the knife and the last fish restaurant wipe to clean off the bottoms of our shoes. When we landed in Oakland, the lemon scent had dissipated. Jo had a paper cup of cold airline coffee for me to gulp down.

By the time we hailed a cab in the well-lit taxi zone in front of Oakland International Airport, I was wide awake. The airport is south of downtown Oakland in Alameda County. After dark, the airport is a forest of light, but outside of the airport, it is as dark as it can be at seven in the evening in November in California. It gets dark early. I hate that. I prefer light. I like how it stays light so long in the summer. Dark is so gloomy.

Usually I'd have rented a car, but that can be time-consuming. It was going to be a quick trip, so I settled for a taxi. I took one look at the cramped back seat and sat in the front.

The driver was cool about it.

"Hey man," he said. "The name's Tim."

I scooted the seat back as far as it would go. I'm a big guy. I need room.

"You look a lot like John Lennon," Jo told the taxi driver as soon as she saw him. This taxi smelled of smoke, but not cigarettes. It was San Francisco, after all.

"It's the glasses. If only I could sing," he said, and gave us a sample.

"Please stop," Jo said. "If only you could."

He had John Lennon's hair, and John Lennon's glasses and face, but sounded like Sesame Street's Big Bird. Tim told us he was attending San Francisco City College, and just moonlighting as a driver. He was a big fan of Lennon, and told us John Lennon had been in the paper a lot lately in his fight to remain in the United States. We made a deal with him. He promised to ferry Jo to our potential client, victim of a hit and run, and then come back to get me when she was done. I promised him a big tip. He promised not to sing.

The cab pulled up to Pacheco's house. The porch light was on, illuminating a small, wood frame house, in a neighborhood of nearly identical small wood frame houses. There was a carport visible from the street, and an old sedan parked under it. It was time for me to go to work.

The information I had on Robert Pacheco was fresh in my head. Thirty years old. Ninety-seven days ago, his wife and four year old daughter were in the back yard when a power line had dropped down into their lawn. His daughter, Maylene, was four years old. She picked up one end of the wire and was immediately electrocuted.

The taxi discharged me on to the short front lawn and sped off with Jo in it, off to sign another case. I walked up the steps to the porch and rang the bell.

Robert Pacheco answered the door. He was a middle-sized man, a couple of years older than me, but looked twenty years older. His hair was long, unkempt, and his eyes held too many sleepless nights. His button-down shirt was as wrinkled as if he'd been sleeping in it. I took off my coat and hung it on the metal coat tree in his foyer.

We shook hands.

"Thanks for coming," Pacheco said. "My mother recommends you highly."

"How is she?" I asked. Of course, I had talked to her early that morning. She had been overwrought. The accident had happened three months before, but telling the story always brings buried feelings to light. I had also talked to

Pacheco on the phone, and answered his few questions. I could tell from our conversation that he was still in the throes of grief, and did not have much energy to muster interest. He'd admitted he was signing because his mother had been nagging at him, and he'd do anything just to get her to let him be.

"We're all terrible," Pacheco said. "Nothing will ever be right again." We all sat down. There was a long silence.

Pacheco stirred himself, as if he'd forgotten I was there. "Can I get you some coffee? Tea? A beer?"

I accepted tea because he had a teapot out, and a plate of Oreo cookies. He bustled off to the kitchen and came back with an extra tea cup for himself.

"I don't usually drink tea," he admitted, "But my wife used to. It reminds me of her."

Everything he said was punctuated with deep sighs. He saw me glance at a framed photo of a woman and child. He picked it up from the table, and handed it to me. I looked at it for a moment.

"They are lovely," I said, handing it back to Pacheco.

It was a candid shot, not very clear, but brightly lit and very colorful, probably taken by an instamatic. A brunette woman was squinting into the sunlight, her hand curved over her forehead in a salute to the sun, shading her eyes. She was hanging on to a little girl with hair of the same hue. The child was tugging hard, with an eager, determined expression. They looked like they were dressed for church. The only indication of Pacheco's presence was his shadow across the sidewalk.

As we exchanged a few more pleasantries, he did not put the frame back on the table, but held it as he told me about his daughter. He told me about his wife.

I had heard some of this from his mother. He spoke in more detail of when his little girl had gotten electrocuted. It had been a hot September afternoon. No rain. Mom and daughter were outside spending time together. His wife had run to her daughter's side. When she tried to pull Maylene away from the sparking wire, she got stuck there with her. A neighbor out mowing his lawn had seen the whole thing. Screams and crackling caught the attention of other neighbors and passing cars. By the time Robert rushed home, the fire engines were already parked in front of his house. His wife and daughter were ready for transport by the coroner.

Pacheco slumped as he talked, getting lower and lower in a recliner that had seen better days. He was bent over the photo, and as the minutes passed, he curled closer around it like a leaf drying up. He had that same frail look, as if he'd crumble if touched.

I took out the typed retainer Jo had prepared at the office, put a pen on it, and slid it in front of him.

"I can go over the contract with you line by line," I offered. "The attorney will get thirty-three and a third percent if the case is settled before a lawsuit is filed, or forty percent if the case is settled after the case is filed in a court."

Pacheco raised his right hand. "My mother trusts you, and that's good enough for me."

"Thank you, but, are you sure you don't want to go over this before you sign?"

Pacheco signed before I finished my sentence.

"Put this with a lawyer you trust. One who kicks the ass of the utility company responsible. That's all I ask."

I had been there about an hour and a half when the horn outside squawked.

"I'm sorry. That's my taxi," I said.

Pacheco did not complain about the taxi, the noise late at night, or the abrupt end to our meeting. He was shutting down inside himself.

I offered to stay in touch with him even though the lawyers would be doing the work on his case. He gave me a big hug that was vibrating with emotion. I have been through this many times; the emotion is contagious. I never got used to it. I felt my eyes tear up as he pulled away. We shook hands.

As soon as I got in the cab, Jo handed me a file.

"I got the case," she said.

"Of course."

I squirrelled the pages away in my briefcase.

In a couple of hours, we were back in LA. I dropped Jo off at the office parking lot where she had her car.

I should have gone to bed when I got home, but first I showered. For the time being, I live in a duplex that used to be one old house. How I ended up here is a random thing. In October, I'd had a day like today, one of those days that was really two days long with a flight in and out of Las Vegas, plus a court date for an important case, two meetings with clients, and an afternoon spent listening to Jo drone on about math. When all that was done, I was beat. If I'd been thinking straight, I'd have crashed with a friendly girl who had a pad close by, or pampered myself in a nice hotel, but as luck would have it, the traffic was bad. I took a shortcut around it, heading for the Monterey house, and saw this fully furnished place for rent close by in City Terrace. As luck would have it, the landlord was out mowing the lawn about three seconds before I passed out from exhaustion. Okay, to split hairs, he wasn't mowing; he was drinking a six-pack, and sprawled in an aluminum lawn chair, a lawn mower beside him on the dead grass. I glanced at the sign, pulled up, and when I heard the month's rent was less than the hotel overnight, I handed over the cash, walked in, and went to sleep. I woke up with an achy back, hoping it had been a nightmare. It wasn't. I decided to make a go of it. A trial month, just to see if life was better living in my own place. I'd have to break it to Aunt Carmen that I was moving out. She really did not want me to move.

The apartment has a tiny entry parlor with a lumpy short bed in it, the original kitchen, a big room that I use as my everything room, an old claw tub too short to lie down in, and a showerhead hung low enough for a midget. The rent is dirt cheap. It's a place where I only intended to sleep, but I am coming to realize that I could use my own office to work from, and it might as well be somewhere I live. I don't cook a whole lot, but I have a couple of jars of good peanut butter on the shelf. You'd be surprised how great peanut butter can be. Nothing beats a couple slices off a loaf of fresh real bread—not that grocery store stuff mind you, but good bakery bread—with nothing but a knife full of room-temperature peanut butter swiped across it. It can't be refrigerated. If you refrigerate peanut butter, it turns into a hard wad that rips up the bread. I don't always opt for the bread. Most times I make do with peanut butter straight from the spoon. It's not like I spend much time cooking, but if I do say so my-self, I make a mean peanut butter sandwich. And the occasional steak.

I had only ever brought one girl to the duplex. Her name was Patricia. She was a blonde knockout, a cashier I knew from a car wash I visited at least three times a week. I gave Patricia my card every week, and told her to let me know about any auto accidents she came across, and that I'd make it worth her while.

"I don't have a car accident," she said. "I just wondered if you might want to go out for a drink."

I'd been over to her apartment once. It was tiny, shabby, and she had a roommate. If I hadn't seen her place, I'd never have invited her to mine. She suggested we meet at a bar. Casey's Irish Pub on Grand in downtown Los An-geles was a busy place, packed with office workers and business people. It wasn't somewhere I went often, but the ambiance was great. We ate and drank, and left Casey's, and went to my duplex.

"Not bad," she said. "I love how these old places have such high ceilings."

"Call me a snob," I told her. "I really don't like this place, but it's conven-ient."

"Well, you tell me when you move, and I'll snap it up. I see its potential," she said. And then we did calisthenics and all kinds of nasty things that proved she was indeed a real blonde.

Anyway, the apartment leaves a lot to be desired. The biggest drawback is that washing my hair means standing like an arthritic vulture to soap and rinse. The whole procedure reminds me of karate moves I learned when I was a kid. By the time I stepped out of the tub on to a stack of laundry on the tile floor, I felt like a contortionist. I reminded myself to find a maid. There's no time for cleaning up this place. I had to dig around a clothes basket to find a clean towel. I started drying off. There wasn't much of me to make out in the low-hung, flakey, steamy mirror, but in it, I saw something blinking.

"What the hell?"

I turned around, and saw the blinking was coming from the reflection of the light on the answering machine. I walked out of the dinky bathroom, passed the open door to the kitchen that was much bigger than I needed, with an ancient refrigerator that moaned and groaned all night. In my everything room were some Salvation Army caliber couches, end tables, and stacks of boxes I have never unpacked. The solitary table held some files from work, breakfast dishes from a few days ago, a stack of unopened mail, and the answering machine. I flicked it on, and headed to the bedroom, listening as I vigorously dried off.

"What do I do? There's a lawyer calling me. I put him off but he keeps calling back." He hadn't left his name, but I recognized the voice as Robert Pacheco, the electrocution case I had just signed hours ago in Oakland. The tape had captured a few hang-ups, probably Pacheco trying again. It was late but it was important to him, so the time did not matter.

I opened my briefcase to get Pacheco's phone number.

"Robert, it's like I told you, you have something to say to this attorney who keeps calling and other attorneys will keep calling you and knocking on your door, just as they have since the tragedy. Now that you have us, scream if you have to 'I have a lawyer, stop calling me!' And if they come to the door, slam it shut after telling the intruder you have an attorney already. If that doesn't work, let me know, and we'll start collecting names and business cards."

"Mario, thank you for calling me back. I'm sorry to bother you so late."

"Call me any time. I will always return your call. It's my pleasure to have your back. Don't worry about anything."

"My mother is right," Robert said in the low, scratchy, nasal voice of someone who had been crying. "You are an angel."

After I hung up, I listened to Jake's messages.

I thought about Robert's angel comment. I was not even close to being perfect when it came to getting a case I wanted, but harassment is a line I don't cross. If I get hung up on or turned away at the door, I don't keep calling. I never go back without an invitation to return. I did cheat a little. Sometimes, I'd have Jo call. A female voice could make a difference if the victim is a male. Other times, I might send Jo to a door to offer to help. I always insisted that I never knocked on doors in my attempt to get a case, so I lied, but only a little. I might knock on a door, but only once. I didn't canvass door to door. Also, what I didn't do is bother the family, at all, if there was a death and the funeral had not taken place yet. The exception was when I got a referral that the family needed help with funeral expenses, and wanted to talk about hiring a lawyer. You'd be surprised how many calls I get from a desperate family unable to afford a funeral.

"How did it go? Tell me."

Jake was always impatient. He'd left the same message several times, and I got the same message from his secretary. Now it was past midnight, too late to call back. He was not a client in distress. I would respect his sleep time.

The tape ran through some more calls. It had been a long day, and I could hear my bed calling me. I tossed the towel aside, and threw my naked self on the rumpled sheets. The bed just about filled the room, and I stretched out, and shut my eyes. The tape ran through a few more calls, then there was this smoky, husky voice. The voice brought me straight upright, and I don't mean I sat up.

"Hey, sucker," Tanis said. "I got off early, and I don't plan on going home till morning. You know where to find me."

Chapter 3
November 5, 1972
Dawn's Break

Tanis was a siren call I'd be stupid to miss, and I'm not stupid.

I threw on clothes.

Who the hell needs sleep when there's Tanis to be had? There was only one place she'd be.

I parked next to Tanis's car and went into the office. It wasn't anything fancy, just a cheap city motel that was nearly always full. The hall was open air, the parking lot surrounded on three sides by three floors of rooms. The guy at the desk recognized me. He was close to my own age. He was in his mid-twenties, hair all the way down his back, in faded Levis, a tie-dyed t-shirt, and wearing a plastic tag that said ROGERS. I know from my afternoons with Tanis that his wife had the day shift and wore a similar tag, or maybe they shared one. I don't know. I did know they lived in a room at the motel, and had a kid. It was one of those couple jobs. I got a kick out of calling him Mr. Rogers like the TV guy. He gave me a knowing grin, and tossed me the key.

I got the door open, and held it that way for a second, appreciating the view.

Tanis had the lights on, knowing I prefer it that way; and she was as naked as the day she was born. She was tall and curved, with tawny skin, and generous breasts. I know she had kids, but the only effect it had had was to make her body more lush. To be honest, I'd been hard since I heard her voice on the machine, and by now, I could have battered down that door without a key.

We rolled onto that bed. Tanis was ripping my clothes right off.

"I got two hours sleep waiting on you," she warned, "So watch out, I am totally charged!"

If I'd been home, I'd be dead asleep by now, but I was so sexually charged, I was buzzing at peak voltage.

The first time was pretty quick. Tanis made a lot of noise. I bet Mr. Rogers heard us in the office, through two sets of closed doors and across the concrete lot.

The second time...well, I took my time. We started off head to feet, and ended up face-to-face. We were both dripping with sweat. It was cold outside, but we were steaming. She flopped against the pillow, panting. I got up, grabbed a stack of towels from the john, and turned on the air conditioning. I wouldn't be needing to do any sit-ups this morning. The bed creaked as I sat down, and dried off. The air conditioning kicked in, smelling of smoke and motel. The mattress gave with my weight, and she rolled slightly toward me. We were both on our sides. She smelled so fresh.

"I love you Mario," she said. "I love your face."

She clicked off the light. The room went dim, but not quite dark. Dawn was starting to lighten the sky. I could make out her features as we lay in the bed, facing each other.

"I love you Mario," she said, and kissed my lips, tongued me deeply, then made a face. I felt her whole body twitch. She pulled back, reached her finger into my mouth, and pulled out a hair.

"Sorry," I said. "Guess I got a little enthusiastic."

"No complaints," she said, laughing deeply. She ran her hand over my chest and arms. "I can't believe you get all this from karate." She slid down a few inches. I knew what was coming, and was hard again. She noticed.

"I love your body," she sighed.

Her mouth caressed my stomach, and moved lower. The room was chilly now, but her mouth was soft and sleek and wet, and her tongue left little flashes of fire in her wake.

"And I love you, Papi Grande." At least that's what I think she said. I'm not sure. Her mouth was full, and I wasn't listening, just feeling.

The fireworks were over, and we were enjoying the aftermath. Most people would be sleeping, but not us. The crack of dawn found us in furious competition. When Tanis would do sit-ups, she hit the bar around two hundred or so, which is about my halfway point. Still, she never gave up. It was one of her charms. The air conditioning was off now and we needed to warm up a bit.

I had done about two hundred fifty sit-ups and switched to push ups.

"Show off," she said, struggling somewhere in the one nineties.

I laughed. My arms were burning, but I kept on going.

"Babe, you're so good. You're absolutely the best at what you do. I don't understand why you won't go to law school."

The question hurt a little. I shot back at her, "Why aren't you a doctor?"

"I would be, if I could have afforded the schooling."

"I hate school," I said.

"Not. A. Good. Reason." She panted out a word at a time, not between moves, but each sit-up was taking longer and longer. She abandoned the effort, sat up, and reached for a towel. Her body was covered in a sheen of sweat. "I mean it, Mario. The world of law needs you. Just think of all you could do."

She worked the towel over herself, dabbing up the moisture. I watched.

"I'm doing all I can, Tanis. You know I can't be a lawyer. I'm an ex-con."

She turned toward me. "That drug charge was bogus. If you wanted, your attorney could fix it for you to go back to school."

"I don't want to. Can you see me doing eight years of school, then worrying about passing the tests to get a license? Thanks, but no thanks."

"I just think you'd be gifted that way. I accept you for what you are, babe. This would be for your benefit. You know the way it is is better for me. I'm making money and get to fuck you."

"Right on," I said. "I give you permission to keep on fucking me, no matter what."

She started to protest, and I interrupted. "The drug charge was bogus. The tax thing was not. I was guilty of not filing tax returns on the money I made from the attorney I was working with at that time."

"Money you made as a minor. The law is so stupid. They should forgive a fourteen year old kid for tax screw ups. Who says to a kid, put up or else?"

"Very convincing," I said, "You're the one who should be a lawyer. But fuck it. That's behind me."

She tossed the towel aside and stood up. The sun-blocking curtains were drawn, but she moved into a ray of morning light that snuck around the curtain's edge, outlining her beautiful body in a halo of light. She stretched like a cat. I perked up. So sue me. I'm a guy.

"I guess I should head for the shower. Good thing we have a mountain of towels."

She sighed, looking in my direction, and noticed Mr. Happy, or as she had nicknamed me, Papi Grande. She bent over, and gave me a teasing little lick.

"Remember that for next time." Before she disappeared into the bathroom, she stopped, and repeated it again. "That whole drug thing was a load of bullshit. Start to finish, that was just wrong."

Tanis came out of the shower. She was wet, and slick and accessible, and I was inspired yet again. What can I say? She never should have given me that lick on the way to the shower. We had another interlude, then life intruded. A beeper went off. It wasn't mine. I'd left it in the car.

Tanis was always on call. She carried her beeper, and never ignored it. As a nurse, she felt that lives might depend on her responding.

I hit the shower. I let the endless supply of hot water flow over me, and lathered like mad, using up the remaining sliver of motel soap. I made do with what was left of the damp towels, and dressed. When I came out of the bathroom, Tanis was ready for work. I was going to have to go home and change. I had early meetings.

"We have to do this again some time," Tanis said.

"I thought you were taking a few days off."

"The beep was the hospital. They're shorthanded. I didn't have to say I'd be there, but I can use the money."

Tanis hugged me tightly then kissed me. "Let's do this more often, please," she whispered.

"The ball is in your court. When's the next client?" She knew that's when we tend to meet.

"What a jerk you are." She pounded my chest with both fists. "I gotta come up with a client, or I don't get to see you. Prick!" She grabbed me between the legs.

"I'm kidding. You know I love being with you. Call me anytime. Even if it's not a new case, I'll come running."

"More like it, love," she said, licking my lips with her tongue. The fragrance of Joy teased the air.

The door opened inward. We stepped outside into the gray of a November morning on to the concrete passageway of the second floor. The unpainted black iron railing wrapped around the outside of the building. City noises intruded on our idyll: the clatter of traffic, sirens, hushed voices from inside the rooms, slamming doors, slamming trunks, droning newscasters rattling off morning traffic reports, radio, footsteps on pavement. The odor of traffic fumes fought with coffee and breakfast from nearby shops. I ignored it all. Didn't want to waste these last few minutes. She was irresistible, and I didn't try. She tugged my head down, sidestepped, pushed *me* against the door aggressively, and kissed me. I flipped our positions, and pushed her against the door, my back to the parking lot.

Tanis kissed me. Fourteen years of karate, but my guard was dropped. Our eyes were open, my eyes on hers. She looked up, beyond me, surprised. I caught her alarm. First clue.

The second clue was the gun pressed in my back.

"Turn the fuck around."

Chapter 4
November 5, 1972
Emergency

I turned in one motion, shoving Tanis farther from the weapon. She was a solid weight behind me. The hood gestured with his gun for me to step away. I concentrated on my breathing, and felt a huge rush of adrenaline. I tried to move smoothly as I assessed our assailant. A guy in a jacket. Long hair. His face was shadowed in a hood, but I recognized the quality of the crude jail tattoos. I'd recognize him if I saw him again. He was a gangie. But I didn't know him by name.

"Wallet," he said, "Now, or I shoot."

"I'm getting it," I said, reaching into my pocket. He didn't wait. The punk fired one shot, two, three.

I felt something. Impact. Heat. Liquid.

Behind me, Tanis melted to the pavement.

I sent a kick, jabbed at his throat. A reflex. I went a little wild, my leg melting under me. Shock registered on his face. He was thrown back, falling over the railing to the cars below. Windshield crashing. The gun fell with him, clattering. Time moved in slow motion. I caught flashes of visuals. No thinking. Tanis was down in a pool of blood. Her eyes were blank. I dropped to my knees, realized the blood was not all hers, and knew no more.

A greenish light was glaring. I could see it through closed lids. Cleanser, bleach, and rubbing alcohol filled my nose. Burning in my arm. I was poked, and poked, and poked again.

"That's not an orange you're injecting. That's my nephew. Be careful, idiot."

That could only be Aunt Carmen on a tirade. My head was full of fog and dreams, but I was aware enough to be glad it wasn't me she was correcting. A passionate Aunt Carmen is a tiger on the rampage. Her target was some faulty nurse. Aunt Carmen wasn't always talking, but she had parked herself close by, and I could feel her there, a constant presence. Pixie's voice came and went. I could feel lips on my ear, hear Pixie whispering.

"I'm going to suck you dry, so hurry up and get well. I'm going to do it just the way you like it. I was so worried about you, but the doctor says you will be fine soon. Baby, hurry back to us."

Some of my brain was working. I knew exactly what I liked Pixie to do to me, but not with the fresh memory of Tanis's blood on my body. I could see her slumped on the motel walkway. Eyes staring. She was dead. I knew it. Felt it. My eyes were closed, but filled with tears. I felt one drip down the side of my face.

Pixie whispered in my ear again.

"I'm sorry if I said something to upset you like this. Just be okay."

I was still processing what happened to Tanis, and the mother-fucker that shot her. I phased in and out of consciousness. I had no beef with the world, and the world's only beef with me was Carson. I was sure Carson was connected to the gunman. I had a dream sequence involving catching up to the rat bastard Carson and leaving him lying dead. I killed him a dozen different ways. Karate.

Strangulation. After he confessed, begging on his knees for his life, I'd kill him anyway.

At one time I heard a voice that had to be Cosmo, then Jake from some distance away. He had come in, frantic. I'd heard a nurse questioning him, and dragging him out of the room. He'd been back of course. He'd come with Harry, the lawyer who had been my mentor when I was a kid. A little thing like visiting hours and a cavalry of nurses couldn't keep them out. We had talked a little, but I'm not too sure about what. They were there, and my body was there, but my brain was somewhere on the backside of the moon. I remembered that I had showered at the motel, where the water pressure sucked, but at least the shower head was high enough; I'd planned to go home to change into fresh clothes for work. I had not planned to be shot. My visitors' voices carried over a softer background of hushed whispers, rings, buzzes and clicks of machinery. I knew I was at Lincoln Hospital. I heard more voices, and blinked in and out of awareness. Doctors were keeping me heavily medicated. A doctor told Aunt Carmen I was lucky that no blood vessels were nicked, and it was only a nine mm. He said that this kind of wound takes a month to heal, but I was healing at a remarkable rate. She was a fixture by my side. When Pixie took her place, I always knew. Pixie would whisper about sex.

I remembered flashes of the ambulance. I remembered that Tanis hadn't moved as they rolled her on to a stretcher and into another vehicle. I remembered when they'd covered her face up with the sheet. They had rolled me into the Lincoln emergency room for an IV, and a blood transfusion, and a dark nap while they dug metal out of me. I wanted to ask what was happening, but it was hard to move. Whatever they'd given me hadn't worn off yet. When my head was finally clear, my sense of time was fragmented, like a puzzle with missing pieces. I was in a hospital room that had become familiar, so I concluded I must have been here for a while.

"Do you need anything?" Aunt Carmen asked.

"Just to get out of here." I struggled to a sitting position.

"Don't do that," a nurse said. "You'll tear your stitches." I hadn't noticed her standing there. She tried pushing me back on to the pillows. Surprised at the resistance I gave, she backed off. Karate has its rewards. She was a small bit of a thing, fair hair, not hard on the eyes. A good Santa Ana wind would blow her across Beach Drive.

"I'm fine." My voice came out weaker than it should have. I took a deep breath, winced, and repeated it louder, deeper. "I am fine."

"Linda, he'd say that if you were chewing his arm off. Mario would never admit being in pain."

Little nurse Linda didn't say anything, but started doing something with the IV.

Trust my aunt to be on a first name basis with the nursing staff. She knows me pretty well. It hurt like hell, but I have never been about lazing around like a grilled sea bass on a hot plate. I am about getting things done. My first action needed to be to get out of this room and figure out if the shooting had been an accident or if someone had targeted me on purpose.

"I already know, but I need confirmation." I was looking at my aunt. "Did Tanis make it? Tell me I'm wrong. Tell me that she made it."

I could tell by her hug that Tanis was gone. My eyes filled with tears.

"She's in a better place, I promise you. She's with God."

I closed my eyes, and everything went black again.

I don't know how much time passed till I woke up again. Aunt Carmen was next to the bed. My focus was better. She looked haggard. Her hair was down, and her dress was wrinkled. She probably hadn't slept for however long I'd been here. By the stack of neatly folded hospital bedding on the metal couch under the window, I knew where she'd been passing her nights. There was a huge tub of peanut butter on the bedside table, and a plastic spoon in a wrapper. Trust Aunt Carmen to keep my favorite snack on hand, even when I was unconscious.

"Auntie, I got to get out of this place. What day is it? How long have I been here?"

"You're recovering really well," she replied, ignoring my question. "You need to listen to your doctor. He'll discharge you when it's time. Let me get you something from the cafeteria."

She stood up, and shoved the peanut butter in my direction without telling me to save my appetite for real food. She must really be worried about me.

"Nevermind cafeteria food. I'll call Jo and have her bring me something with protein." I loved steak. One side of my brain flashed Tanis beneath me at the motel, and abruptly, the thought of eating made me want to puke. My face must have showed my reaction. My aunt returned to the bed, and tried to comfort me. She assumed I was in pain. I was, but not from the gunshots.

I couldn't remember a time in my life when I cried so freely. It was embarrassing to cry. I had not cried when the judge shipped my ass to prison for what I thought would be two years. But this was Tanis. My Tanis. I'd never lost anyone before, and it hurt like hell.

"I'll go see if I can find something good for you."

"They've got you on a bland diet," Nurse Linda said. Her voice quivered a little as if she were nervous at the possibility of being alone with me.

"Okay, I want an ice cream shake, a malt. Can you do that?"

"You bet I can," Linda said. "We have a big assortment of ice cream. You can have malts as part of your bland diet."

While I waited for my aunt to return from the cafeteria, and the nurse with my malt, I closed my eyes.

Tanis. My heart hurt, suddenly.

Unreeling like a movie, the events at the motel were suddenly very clear in my head. I knew my Tanis was gone. She had been dead at the motel, along with the *pendejo* I'd kicked off the balcony. I felt a sharp pang with no relation to the path bullets had gnawed through my guts. What would be happening to her kids? Their father was dead, and now their mom. I had been raised by my aunt; and now I could not help but feel responsible for Tanis's orphaned kids. I would have to talk to Tanis's sister that took care of the kids, and find out if she could handle it. I'd only met her one time. Niley was younger than Tanis, but had two kids of her own. A single mom.

Aunt Carmen brought me a bowl of soup. I didn't want real food. Linda brought me the malt which I finished. I could have downed another two of them, but I could barely keep my eyes open.

Linda was watching me closely. As if attuned to my mood, she walked back to me, and under the guise of adjusting blankets, she patted me on the shoulder as if I were a small puppy in need of comfort. I recognized her touch, which could not be more gentle. I had a vague impression of another nurse before her, a big, rough one that Aunt Carmen had chased out. Don't remember exactly when. But maybe I had dreamed that.

When I woke up, Pixie was there. My aunt was gone.

"You're smiling," she said, moving close to me, her face right up to mine. "I can tell you're so much better, babe."

"I need you to hand me the phone," I said, "I can't reach it. I feel like it's been years since I used a phone. How long have I been here?"

"Not long enough," she said. She hesitated, then held the phone while I dialed the office. Jo picked up on the first ring.

"I need food."

"Hey boss. You sound awful chipper for a guy who was dead to the world this morning when I came by."

"They're pumping me full of shit," I said, looking at the IV bag. "I'm starving. But I don't want meat."

"You don't want a steak from PDC? Are you kidding me?"

"No, I'm not kidding you. Here's what I'd like: a full stack of pancakes from the Pantry, two orders of bacon, real crispy, and a bottle of syrup. Try and get here fast, but don't get in an accident."

Pixie was all smiles as she took the phone back.

"What if I blow you while we wait for your order?"

Her smile bared a tiny separation between her two upper front teeth.

"Don't make me laugh right now. Besides, I'd never get hard." But I admit I thought about it. "Is Aunt Carmen out of the hospital and back home?"

Pixie giggled. "Yes, it's my shift. She's gone. The coast is clear."

She reached her hand under the blanket. Her very knowing hand.

"Feels hard to me."

I knew by my response that I must be getting better. A nurse walked in to change my bandages, and interrupted Pixie who shifted from what she was doing into straightening my blankets.

Jo arrived. Linda adjusted my bed so I could sit up, and then checked the food to make sure it was bland. She made some noise about the bacon, but let it pass. I poured syrup on the tall stack of pancakes and dug in under Jo and Pixie's watchful eyes.

"How long have I been here?" I asked again.

"Seven days," Jo informed me.

I stopped eating. "Has there been a funeral yet?"

"Yes."

"Take the flowers home," I told the girls. It looked like a fucking flower shop.

Whatever was in that IV was kicking my ass. I felt out of it, so messed up, tired, filled with fatigue, unlike myself. I dozed off, unsure if I finished the pancakes or touched any of the bacon.

Tanis was next to me, a warm pressure running the whole length of my body. I had a sense of something being wrong. We were together on that motel bed, too exhausted to move. My bones had melted into the mattress. An annoying buzzer kept going off. Tanis was next to me, lying still, ignoring the buzzer. She was exhausted, too.

The alarm was persistent.

"Ignore it."

She sat up, naked. She was going to answer the door. I saw she had been shot.

"Wait," I told her. "Don't open the door." I knew who was behind it. It was urgent that I stop her. I tried to get up but couldn't move.

"It's too late, Mario."

She pointed to her gunshot wound. "You gotta see to my kids. I don't want them to end up in a foster home or to get split up. My sister is a good mom. Help her so she can take care of my children. Please do that for me Papi Grande."

I woke up uncertain of what had happened and what had not. I was in jail instead of the hospital. I was eighteen, and Carson was there visiting, pissed because I had knocked out some of his teeth. I'd been pretty savage when I found out he'd been faking accidents, jeopardizing Harry, the lawyer who was kind enough (and needy enough) to teach me the ropes before I was even old enough to have a driver's license. I couldn't figure out why my body hurt everywhere except the hand I punched him out with. We were just kids at the time but Carson was jealous that I had the sports car, and the money in the bank, and a pretty girl who was crazy about me. He couldn't get it together. The one good thing was that I had learned my lesson, to watch my back. But I looked closer, and this wasn't eighteen year-old Carson. This was Carson in his mid-twenties, the Carson I saw the day of the accident. I wanted to be dreaming. I wanted to wake up. I hated Carson.

"Man," he said, furiously, "You can't get all the cases. I wanted this one, bad. You piss me off. You piss me off every time I see your Red GT, every time I go to sign somebody, and they've already got your fucking name on the dotted line; every time I chew." I heard his voice, loud and clear but whispered, like in a confessional.

Then I wasn't in the hospital; I was in church, and Carson was walking down the aisle with a phone in his hand, yelling at me over another case. And then on the sidewalk, a bright summer day, not a cloud in the sky, no sound but Carson still going on, pissed off about being mistreated, not getting clients because I was there first. Then I was back in Harry's office, Pixie was still pregnant, and Carson was yelling over some case—a car full of Mexican teenagers. That had been a real case, only everyone in the car had been fake. Carson had staged the whole thing, and it put all the cases I had brought to Harry in question, and endangered Harry, the lawyer I had been working for. That was when we'd had our falling out. My dream flashed to a recent case, only months ago. In less than twenty-four hours, I signed the family of Carlitos and fourteen injured passengers aboard a bus. The accident had been bad, but signing the case had been easy. Carlitos's family attended my aunt's church and they knew I knew lawyers, and the crash had been in spitting distance of Jake's office. The women of the family had gone to my aunt, who came to me. Even Carson's own mom came to me. Signing the family members had been a done deal. Usually, I have to work harder for it. Of course it was a tragedy, but that wasn't the nightmare. The nightmare was the angry call from Carson. Carson was the nightmare. And when I woke up, he was there in the flesh.

"Carson?" I said. I knew it was his voice that had wakened me, but it didn't seem possible. I didn't know if I was still wandering a delirium of cases.

"Man, you sleep like the dead." The loud, whispery voice I knew all too well. How long, exactly, had he been here?

The room was almost dark, but hospital rooms never get fully dark. In the hall, medical noises continued. Loudspeaker voices. Squeaking machinery.

Carts rolling, footsteps, hushed voices. The central air was set too high, in November when the heat should be on. The thin blanket did nothing to warm me. Aunt Carmen was asleep on the couch. I reached for the blanket, to pull it higher. Someone stood at the foot of my bed. I knew who it was.

"I've been here a while," the voice said, "You look like death warmed over. I didn't feel right waking you."

"Yeah? How come you were talking, then?"

I froze, my hand still groping for the end of the blanket.

"There's an extra blanket on the table." Carson reached for it, shook it out, as if he gave a shit. It floated down over me. It was a piece of shit blanket. A hospital blanket, no warmer than a sheet.

"Here to shoot me in the back?"

"Come on, man," Carson said. "We were buds. I heard you were here. Had to come and see. I even brought flowers. If you're okay enough to be pissed off at me, then you're okay."

"You've seen me," I said. "Now you can go."

I saw Carson smile. He didn't say anything, just that fucking smile.

Then Aunt Carmen was standing by me, shaking me awake.

"I called the nurse. You were having a nightmare, and pulled out your IV." She was holding a bloody napkin to my arm.

"What were you dreaming about?" Aunt Carmen was wearing bright polyester sweats. Her hair was trimmed in one of those short shag cuts that look better rumpled than brushed. She had a lot of hair. A big jar of peanut butter was on the end table. I'd downed a good portion of it, a spoon at a time.

She clicked a dim light on the lamp beside her. Even in the shadows, I could see she looked rested. I must be getting better. Judging by the date on the folded newspaper beside her, I had been here a week. While I was in a stupor, on November seventh, Nixon had beat out George McGovern to win the 1972 election.

"Who are you dreaming of?"

I looked at the foot of the hospital bed. No extra blanket. No flowers. Had Carson been here? I hoped so. I hope I hadn't dreamed him. That's the last bastard I'd ever want in my head.

"Dream's gone. Sorry I woke you."

A nurse came in and put in the IV. Aunt Carmen fussed around the bed, moving pillows, and trying to make me comfortable. I had to pretend to get mad to get her to lie down. Funny though, even if it was a pretense, I have a lot of rage nobody knows about. I do a good job keeping it under wraps. I grew up in a tough neighborhood, and saw how uncontrolled anger can bring you down faster than anything else. Maybe I had it easy, thanks to karate, thanks to my being a pretty big guy, but more than anything else, having some good bad associations like Pélon. I was proud of being Aunt Carmen's boy. She was great, but also there was a cool factor that so many of the superstitious types in the old stomping ground thought she was an old school *bruja*. Who knows? Maybe she was, maybe she wasn't. She says the midwife thing goes back centuries in our family. Real or not, I didn't mind letting some of that power of hers rub off on me.

She fell asleep on that uncomfortable looking hospital couch. She sleeps like a baby, with a clear conscience. When I was a kid, she used to keep me in line by saying she had secrets, but looking at her sleeping the sleep of the innocent, I knew she's never done a thing in her life to keep her up nights. I felt like I still had to keep all the bad stuff away from her. Would I ever sleep like that again? Tanis's shooting stirred up a lot of things in me that I had thought were dead and gone. Ghosts and demons walk my hall of dreams.

Back when I was a stupid kid, drowning in trouble, facing a court case and a mountain of debt, I had fended off Aunt Carmen then. She had tried to get me to tell her who had framed me. I knew it was Carson. Not being a rat, I was going to handle it myself so I never let it slip. Before the trial, I remember being stuck in a car between my lawyer Jake, and Aunt Carmen.

"Tell me who put that marijuana in your car," Aunt Carmen pleaded.

"I told you a million times, I don't know for sure."

"Then tell me who you think it is."

I shrugged.

"Promise me you won't go near him. Promise that you won't accidentally run into him."

"How can I promise not to see or run into somebody when I don't know who it is?"

She insisted until I agreed that I would not go near anybody from the old neighborhood till this was cleared up. I promised that I would do my best to avoid running into this unknown evil-doer.

Before the screwed-up trial on bogus drug charges, I drove by Carson's house every chance I got. Sometimes in a borrowed car. Sometimes in the beat up junker I bought to get around in after my beautiful Corvette was impounded. I cruised his house during free moments day and night, watching for his royal blue 1964 Chevy Impala. Sometimes it was there, and sometimes not. Sometimes I even snuck to his window and watched him sleeping off whatever he'd gotten drunk on. Tequila, or imported beer to impress some girl. I didn't confront the asshole. He'd snitch me off to the cops and they'd forfeit my bail.

Back when we were kids, we were like the three musketeers. Carson and Pélon and me. Carson was the plotter, but his plots came to nothing. Pélon was the killer, who managed most of the time not to get in trouble. I was the talker. Maybe my silver tongue opened some doors, but there was a lot of work, too. People saw me as the one who had a knack for playing the system to get things done, but there was more than that. Maybe I had a little of both of them in my head. I knew Pélon would never turn on me. Carson already had. His betrayal enraged me.

I didn't have any enemies. There was only Carson who had derailed my life when I was eighteen, and now he had done it again. Coming after me was one thing, but going after Tanis was something else. There was going to be payback.

I thought about the dream of Tanis. I wasn't superstitious like Aunt Carmen and Jo. I don't know if it was my own head talking, or if I'd been visited by a ghost. All I know is that I would have to do something for her kids. As soon as the sun was up, I called Jo.

"I need to check on Tanis's family. Ever since her kid was sick, they've been living paycheck to paycheck. Her sister watches them, and doesn't have a job. There's probably not even food in the house."

"I'll go by there and get a full rundown on what's happening, and I'll be back with a report."

"Get someone to buddy up with, and drive my car here. I promise, I'm not using it until they release me. But the instant they say I can go, I'm out of here."

I spent two days in emergency, was admitted two days after I was shot; and ten days after I was admitted, my doctor released me. The only medication I would be taking was antibiotics. The stitches were out. Everything hurt, but it wasn't pain I couldn't handle. With all the kicks and bumps and slams I had undergone in karate, living with pain was not new. You can imagine how excited I was to know I was free at last.

Aunt Carmen and I had it out when she saw me with my keys.

"What do you think you're doing? You're not driving yourself. Where did you get those keys?"

"Nevermind that. The point is I have them, and I am driving home."

Aunt Carmen glared at me as only she could.

"When you say home, do you mean home, or the rat trap you're renting?"

I stared at her, and thought about the cruddy shower, and the old house smell. I thought about the piles of laundry and the creaky refrigerator, and how nothing was in it but a few beers and some spoiled milk. I thought about how much 'fun' I'd have trying to feed myself, including shopping, and carrying groceries up the stairs when it was still damn uncomfortable to stand up straight, much less in front of a frying pan. Most of my home cooking was a steak on a little hibachi grill on my kitchen counter, and now the thought of steak made me queasy.

"Hey, I'll let you cook for me for a week. I can go to your place without injuring my dignity."

"Good then, I'll order a hospital bed right now." She reached for the hospital phone. I put my hand over hers and stopped her.

"Whoa Nellie." I put my other hand up like a traffic cop signaling stop. "No hospital bed. If there's a hospital bed, the deal is off."

She glared at me, but agreed. The argument would have gone on longer except that my aunt knows how stubborn I am. She cut it short because she got what she wanted, which was me back under her roof. For a while, anyway.

The physical therapist showed up.

"It's part of the exit protocol," she explained to Aunt Carmen, who went downstairs for an hour.

The therapist ran me through some stretches. I could barely do them.

"Don't let that stop you," she encouraged. "It's going to hurt a little. Just push a little more every day." It hurt more than a little, but I took her words to heart.

"How much is too much?"

She frowned. "Don't open up your stitches. Use common sense. If you start bleeding, you've gone too far."

It had been a challenge to dress myself, but I managed, then packed my stuff in paper grocery bags and gazed around the hospital room. It was painted a dingy, nausea-inducing shade of green, and overlooked the rooftop air conditioners of a shorter part of the building, a view I would not miss. I sat back down on the hospital bed, fully dressed, waiting for them to bring me the final papers and wheel me out. I'd thought I was already home free. There was a knock on the door, and it opened. I was expecting the floor nurse to come in, but instead, it was three strangers.

There was one guy in a cheap suit with a couple of police officers.

"Mario Luna?" asked the guy in the suit.

"That's me. Who are you?"

"Detective Mike Sanchez. I'm here about the murder investigation." He flashed his badge.

Chapter 5
November 15, 1972
Recuperation

The badge looked way too real.

"Tanis," I said, closing my eyes. Saying her name was like punching a bruise in my heart.

"We know who was shot. You killed the shooter. We have questions," Sanchez said. "This case is going to stay open as a robbery homicide. We still have zero leads and no better motive than robbery. Do you have anything to tell me?"

I answered his questions. I told him everything I knew. He took notes. He was still asking questions when a nurse came in to wheel me out.

The argument behind us, Aunt Carmen pushed me in a wheelchair to my car.

At my aunt's, I knew I would recover quickly. I'd think about the rental, later. The place was cheap by any standards. It was no permanent solution, but had shown me that I was ready to be on my own—at least, I was before I was hurt.

Aunt Carmen watched while I pried my car door open, and managed to squirm in. I gave a thumbs-up to the orderly who had walked us out, and he took the chair. Instead of going to her car, she stood with her hands on her hips, watching. I did my best not to wince. I won't lie and say that it didn't hurt to get behind the wheel. My aunt was alert to every wince and grimace. I pasted a smile on my face.

"Want a ride to your parking space?"

She ignored my question.

"You look like death," she said. "Are you sure you don't want to ride with me? You can stretch out in the back seat."

"As tempting as that offer is, no thanks."

She was still standing there when I drove off. I went straight from the hospital to Cosmo's with every intention of working out. Cosmo wasn't there, and I walked to the back of the studio, passed a working class, going into the bathroom. I still had the idea I was going to work out. I put my hands against the wall, leaning forward, and made it successfully halfway through a stretch. I sat down on the john for a good five minutes to recover before I splashed water in my face, toweled off, and left.

The cemetery wasn't on the way, but I made the detour, after I stopped at a florist's shop to pick up a bouquet. I parked and went into the guard house, where there was a small desk with a man behind it. On the wall behind glass was a grid map of the property. The man was on the phone, an open yellow pages in front of him, as well as a portable radio that was playing Neil Young's "Heart of Gold." He was a jolly sort, looking more like a burly Santa than a crypt keeper. I guess I'd been expecting some funeral director dressed in a tux and tail. This brown-bearded flower child in a tie-dyed purple t-shirt and jeans was not what I expected. He put down the phone when I came in.

"I need directions to a grave," I said.

He introduced himself as Melvin. It took under a minute for him to find Tanis's name in a big book, and he pointed out the location on the map. I looked out the window and got my bearings, then headed out the door. He grabbed the radio and followed me. The song switched to Neil Diamond's "Song Sung Blue."

"No need to walk," he said, heading outside where a golf cart waited. I hadn't noticed it, parked behind bushes. It was plugged into a socket on the back of the gatehouse. Melvin unplugged the long cable. He looped the radio's cord over a hook on the dash.

"It gets too quiet here," Melvin said. "I can only play the radio when there's not a funeral going on."

I shrugged. Normally, I'd have passed on the ride, but today I appreciated it.

I stepped in the passenger side, and Melvin took the golf cart's wheel.

"This is what attracted me to the job," he admitted. "Hang on tight."

He turned the key, and the engine hummed. He gunned the accelerator. The cart bumped forward, bouncing over the curb, across the lot, and down a winding asphalt path. Every bounce was agonizing. After a few minutes, he pulled up, and pointed.

"I'll wait here," he said. "She's over there, third on the right, the one with no stone."

Her grave was easy to find. It was the only one on that row with no marker, and the ground was raw.

"I miss you, Tanis," I said. There was nowhere to put the bouquet. I jammed the stalks into the soft earth. The bouquet looked puny and inadequate. I wished I'd brought armfuls of flowers.

I heard Roberta Flack's "The First Time Ever I Saw Your Face," and it was the last straw. I broke. I went down on my knees in the dried mud, and cried until there were no more tears in me. I talked to her about how much I missed her, and how I would do everything I knew to do to help her sister and kids.

That damn song. I remembered the first time I'd seen Tanis's face, and the memory cut like a knife. She'd been in her white nurse's uniform, so tall and slim that even the clunky nurse's shoes looked elegant on her. Her thick, straight hair was not quite black. It was the darkest brown, with a few strands of gold on one side, gift of the sun. Her brows were dark, straight and uncompromising, her skin a shade somewhere between whipped cream and liquid gold. Under the small nurse's cap, her hair had been pulled back into some kind of chignon. She had perfect features, bedroom eyes, lips like strawberries. I'd noticed her instantly. We had met years ago, when I'd been chasing one of Harry's potential clients to finagle a meeting in the emergency room. I barely remember the client now, even though I'd signed him. When I gave her my card, as I did with all potential sources, I asked about the bruise on her cheek. She never said where it had come from. Her husband had been alive then, a mean brute with a meaner drug habit. Eventually, he'd left her to live with another junkie. He had been dead for two years. I looked on either side of the grave, glad to see she'd been laid to rest in a family plot beside her parents. I don't know where her ex-husband's body was, but it gladdened my heart to see he was not here.

I might have been able to get a grip on myself faster if the radio hadn't played Bill Withers' "Lean on Me."

"Hey man, I've got a funeral in an hour," Melvin yelled. "Are you done here? Because I have some prep work to arrange." Across the paved path, and up a hill, I saw a crew of grave diggers working around some kind of large machine.

Using Tanis's father's headstone, I pushed myself up from the ground. The exercise of the day was getting to me, but I was learning how to move to keep from waking irritable nerves. The new grave was unmanicured, pathetically small. The ground was spongy. It hardly seemed possible that the spot was large enough to be a final resting place for such a vibrant woman. The dirt beneath my feet was nothing but a wound in the earth, far from healing. I felt quite as raw myself. I dragged myself back to the golf cart.

"What's the fee for landscaping?"

"It's part of the deal."

"So what about the grass?" I said. "She needs grass."

"Write down her name," he said, "and I'll put her on the list to get turf. We're scheduled to be laying Bermuda sod, soon as it comes in."

I gave him a twenty, and one of my cards with Tanis's name scrawled on the back.

Gilbert O'Sullivan's "Alone Again, Naturally" was playing. It was too much to hear, and I switched it off. Melvin reached for the controls to turn it back on.

"Touch it, and you lose a hand." I wasn't kidding. If I had to listen to one more depressing fucking song, I was going to explode, and take him with me.

"Okay bro," he said, putting both hands up in a gesture of surrender.

We rode back to the gates in silence.

On the drive to my aunt's, I had plenty of time to think of how, if the shot had been an inch in any direction, I could be dead right now. A close call like that changes a man. It made me think about what I wanted my life to be. It made me think of what and who was important. I've already said how I started my client development career at Cosmo's karate studio at ten and had moved on to work for Harry, the attorney across the street at fourteen. I don't often reflect on how valuable these relationships have been. In fact, those two men were there for me when I was a kid. Cosmo and Harry were more than friends. They had been my mentors. There was no denying I cared for them like a couple of fathers, not just because they had always been there for me since the day I knocked on their doors looking for employment, but they were friends, too. I'd worked for Jake since I was eighteen. In these past six years, I'd learned so much. Jake claimed to care about me. I had to wonder if he would love me so much if I weren't bringing in cases.

I had a little money in the bank, which would go to Aunt Carmen if anything happened to me. Knowing her, she would just give it to the church. It would have been such a waste, when all I wanted was to make up to her for the sacrifices she made for me when I was a kid. There were so many things that I wanted to do, I found it hard to think she was content. What a shame it would be that I never did them, never really lived it up the way I could. Even when I was on probation and paying the IRS the debt I was ordered to pay, I always made enough to have pocket money over and above my expenses. As a precaution against future hardship, I had always saved whatever was over and beyond the bills. I didn't exactly live like a pauper, but having to pay off the IRS had certainly made me live conservatively. Plus, that was the influence of Aunt Carmen, and Cosmo, and certainly Harry. This near death experience taught me I should change my standards. I thought about Jake's mansion, and his fantastic vacations, even his pampered family and their luxurious lifestyle. I compared it to my workaholic habits and shabby apartment, and shuddered. The rest of the drive, I daydreamed of the kind of beautiful women who were attracted to wealthy men, of traveling to exotic locations, of living in great houses with spacious rooms with big windows that didn't look on to an alley with trash cans, tall showers with hearty water pressure, refrigerators that didn't leak and knock, and baseboards without mouse holes.

Before too long, I was home and tucked in the extra long bed that had been mine since we moved into the new house I bought at seventeen. I could close my eyes, and feel as if I were still a kid, with only three years under my belt of working for Harry. It was Harry who had suggested I invest in a house.

I hadn't wanted to leave the old neighborhood, but it had been the right investment. Some of my things were in the attic, and some still at the place I was renting. Lainey had left some of her toys on my old desk, but she was a careful kid and had left my stuff alone. Essentially it was the room I had left behind. Despite the clothes and items I had taken with me, in spite of Lainey using it while I was gone, the room was intact. Aunt Carmen had kept it essentially as a shrine to me. Pixie and Lainey didn't mind sharing the third bedroom.

The week I'd planned to stay at Aunt Carmen's stretched out longer than I'd intended. It was all Pixie's fault. She was the only treat I'd been allowing myself. I was focused on getting back in shape. I developed a routine of simple stretches, mostly leaning against the wall, all concentrating on the affected areas, and combined that with a couple of low impact calisthenics that didn't jar where the bullet had cut a path through me. I did these in front of the bedroom mirror, and learned to control my expressions, which were pretty scary, if I do say so myself.

Aunt Carmen had only made the mistake of fixing me a tray once. That gesture is okay if I'm working, but I refused to be fragile and bed-bound.

After about a week, I mentioned I was planning on going to Cosmo's.

"It's too soon," Aunt Carmen objected. "Boy, you can't sit up without looking like someone's trying to pull your arm off with a pair of sharp tweezers."

"I was shot on the 5th, in my hospital room on the seventh, here on the seventeenth. That was last Friday. I gotta go work out. I'll lose my edge."

I was glad I'd never mentioned to her going to Cosmos after I left the hospital. At least I wouldn't have her throwing that day's stupidity up in my face.

Pixie, who had been testing my edge every chance she got, snorted green peas all over the table, and diverted Aunt Carmen's wrath.

On the 22nd, I turned up at the eight a.m. class at Cosmo's. I'd been home for five days. He was glad to see me until he realized I intended to work out.

In the eleven or so years I'd known Cosmo, he hadn't changed. Sometimes he wore a gi, and occasionally, a business suit. He had been an adult already when the jeans and t-shirt generation came up, but he embraced it like it was his own. He'd been a tiny, graying Oriental man when I'd first met him, and he looked exactly the same all the years I've known him. His face was smooth, his expression placid and inscrutable, but now, I could read him like a book. He only came to the middle of my chest, weighed as much as my left leg, and even on my best day, he could still take me down in ten seconds flat.

"You're a glutton for punishment. It's only days since you were shot," Cosmo complained.

"Almost three weeks," I said, exaggerating a little.

It was an easy class of beginners. Right away, reality struck like a toe-stub at midnight. Moves I'd handled since I was ten were killing me. The mirror helped me keep my expression under control so that my face was not giving away the knife-stabs that shot through me every time I twisted raw muscle fibers trying to grow back together. Usually I watch my whole body in the mirror. It's a good way to get visual feedback, and keep movement smooth and balanced, or see faults. But now I just stared at my face, with sweat dripping down into my eyes, keeping the pain-grimace from appearing.

I felt myself cutting off some moves because if I extended, the killing pain was going to streak across my torso. Cosmo stepped down the class because I was there, but I didn't bother to say anything to him about it. It was an effort to keep up. I doubt I could have managed to muster out a word, much less the usual banter. Every muscle hurt, but the more I concentrated on each move, the more I felt I deserved the pain. Tanis had died because she was with me. I had failed to protect her. I had gotten away with a gun shot wound, but she had lost her life. Her kids had lost their mom. Fuck it. Tanis was gone forever, and this pain was my penance. I was a kid again, in St.Mary's Church with Aunt Carmen passing judgment on me, making me crawl through the church on my knees all the way to the altar. That was penance then. So is this, now.

I was relieved when the class quit a little early. I toweled off, and as casually as was humanly possible, I turned and tried to get a good look at my back. The physical therapist had said to stop before it was bleeding. I was so sweaty, I couldn't tell by feel. At least, I could see that no red had seeped through the back or front of my gi. My curiosity would have to be satisfied, until I got home to get a good look.

Cosmo had bitten his tongue during the class, but after everyone left, he had his say.

"You should go home, and wait another week."

"I managed today. I will manage tomorrow, better."

Cosmo's face, a cool, inscrutable mask, normally betrayed no hint of emotion. The outer edges of his mouth turned down the merest fraction. For him, it was an expression of extreme displeasure.

"You were as jerky as a three-year-old out there."

"Was not. Maybe a four-year-old." I had not been watching anything except my facial control. I did not confess how glad I was that I had come for the eight a.m. beginner classes instead of the usual six a.m. expert classes that had sparring and routines that were strenuous.

"Sometimes I think you're a masochist."

"That's hardly fair," I told him, "when you're the one who taught me how to push myself to the limit. I'm not a masochist. I'm just ready to be done with being injured and babied. And the doctor said he'd never seen anyone heal so fast."

That wasn't quite what the doctor told me. What he said was more along the lines of saying that sure I could leave the hospital, and if it killed me doing it, he was washing his hands of me. He didn't put it in writing though. If I died, Jake would get Aunt Carmen to sue the doctor's shorts off. But I didn't die. I felt almost normal except that I still woke up barmy after dreaming of the shooting, and seeing dream-Tanis crumbled and bloody.

I won't lie and tell you that that first week, I was badass. I felt like I was moving like an old woman. I was hurting, but either each day was less intense, or I was getting used to pain. My skin and muscles remembered precisely how it had felt right after I was shot, and there was no comparison. I survived the gunshot. I would survive the workouts. I knew working out would help me get over the bullet wounds faster. By the end of the week, the rest of the class was pushing to keep up. I didn't consider it great progress, as they were beginners. I was aiming to get where I was before this shooting, but not even Cosmo would be able to see how far from that I was.

There was a mouth moving up between my legs. I was nestled in a billow of pillows, the blankets up to my neck, and only a slight ache throbbed vaguely in my shoulder area. At first I was disoriented because of the dark. Darker than the hospital. Darker than the apartment. There was a faint fragrance of chiles, cumin, limes, and cilantro scenting the air that clued me in to where I was. The ceiling fan was buzzing slightly, and the quiet drift of air whispered from the central heat. But it was the mouth that woke me. Even when I didn't know where I was, waking disoriented, my body did not care. My body was taut like a fiddler's bow, singing "wahoo!" and giving me a world class thumbs-up. Soft lips fastened on my hard cock, and I forced back a groan. Then I knew where I was. This was home. Aunt Carmen's house. This was the room I'd lived in since I finished out my teens, and the hot, wet sweetness enveloping me was Pixie. She took her time, teasing and drawing it out, until I thought I would scream, or drag her under me for a thorough fucking.

I didn't need to have the light on to see Pixie's face; it was rounded, heart-shaped without a hint of cheekbones, but the slightest cleft in her chin. There was a narrow uptilt to her eyes that was like some forbear of hers might have been oriental. Her lips were full and soft. Before the baby, she'd been all legs and bones. She was an adult my own age. The baby she'd had at seventeen had given her breasts that made most men look twice. Of course she was still tall but the leanness had been replaced with the kind of full-blown curviness that begged to be undressed. Her waist was small, and all the clothes she wore emphasized the tiny waist, and the contrast between her hips and chest. Aunt Carmen said she could have looked like an angel, but her clothes were always too tight, too loud, and she wore way too much make-up. I had no objection to what she wore, but it was probably true. Pixie always dressed to attract men. And she tended to do crazy things with her hair. In 1971, she'd cut bangs and dyed her hair red like Fonda in Klute. In 1972, she died her hair pitch black and hacked it short to be like Sally Bowles as played by Liza Minelli. Come to think of it, Sally Bowles was pretty close to Pixie's personality. Pixie's whole philosophy of life was what's the point if it's not fun? Her hair was back to brown now, and growing out but there was no telling what she'd do to it next.

I fought to keep from moaning or thrashing around. The bed was a solid platform with only a mattress and no creaky box springs, but I knew from experience, there's only so much you can do to keep it quiet enough not to wake anyone. One of my arms was in a sling to keep me from jarring the healing muscles, and I found myself curling my fingers around the fabric to keep from moving, but with the other, I reached and buried my fingers in Pixie's hair, giving myself up to the sensation.

It was the first of many nights that blended into each other. Like she had years ago when everyone went to sleep, Pixie would sneak in my room, lock the door, spend hours with me, and sneak out before Aunt Carmen or Lainey awoke. Maybe it was all physical, but she was a tremendous help in numbing the pain of Tanis's loss.

On the second night, I woke in pitch black, Pixie's mouth working around me.

On the third night, I woke, and found her face, pulling her up so we were lip to lip.

"You don't have to do this," I whispered to her, "I can't take advantage of you."

"Hush, big boy," she whispered back in a breath of spearmint gum. "I'm the one taking advantage of you. Sucking and licking your big cock gets me hot; and I love it when you fuck me. Stop worrying and let me get back to what I was doing before you so rudely interrupted me."

On Sunday, when my aunt went off to church, I revisited the graveyard. Melvin and his golf cart were not there, but I was able to find the grave. Melvin, or one of his staff had put down a patch of turf, but there was still no stone.

Pixie insisted that I had saved her life years ago when I brought her home to my Aunt Carmen to have her baby, and maybe it is true. Back when we'd been growing up, she was a hooker, and also my girlfriend. After she moved in here, Aunt Carmen took a shine to her. She never left. Now that Tanis is gone, Pixie's my only regular sexual partner. It's no sweet, romantic thing. I guess you'd say we were using each other because we both love sex. When I wasn't around, there wasn't much activity for her in that department, or at least none that I knew about. She probably made some bed buddies at that steak place where she waited tables at night, but living at my aunt's house with her daughter would put a damper on that sort of activity at home. I loved her, but like a long-time friend. It was a unique relationship. We never led each other on. We never had relationship expectations of each other. She was young, and pretty, and hot, and Latina; and there was no visible sign that she had grown up hooking to survive. Truth be told, in the neighborhood where I grew up, it wasn't that unusual.

I had a desk and a phone in my bedroom. When I needed privacy, I shut the door. The door was shut frequently, especially when Aunt Carmen was holding one of her Lamaze classes. The truth was that with my aunt, Pixie, Lainey, my work, and me under one roof, I needed more space than I was getting. I kept threatening to pack up and go back to my apartment, not that I much wanted to go back there in particular, but the threat was handy to make them back off.

I stayed on at my aunt's. My beeper buzzed off the hook, and kept me busy with work. With this new thing of working in the field, Jo's presence at Jake's office became a rare thing. She was busy doing my job, meeting up with victims and signing them on as clients. People called daily to refer a case, or to check on the progress of their case. For progress calls, I checked with the office to get an update, then called the client back. It was about service. It had always been that way. It was never about dropping the case off with the attorney and walking away. I suppose that's why I was in demand.

All my life I've been terrible at math, but it's funny how I remember phone numbers. I got beeped. I knew the number when that LAPD Detective named Mike Sanchez called. He was the one handling Tanis's murder.

"What do you need, Detective? I already told you everything I know."

"There was another shooting at the motel," the detective said. "We were thinking the shootings were related to gang activity. Yours and Tanis's included."

I sat on the phone, waiting for him to say more.

He had called me a couple of times. I remembered him from just before I was going to be discharged from the hospital. When he came to see me with two other cops, I told them everything I knew. Now he had looked into my history, and wanted to know about my gang connections.

"I've never been the member of a gang." It was the truth, though my childhood friend Pélon ran a gang, and was in prison for murder.

He was persistent. He had a lot of questions, and I could tell he was trying to pin the shootings on some gang connection I had. I can't deny that I thought about mentioning Carson, but the thing between Carson and me was personal. It didn't involve cops. He finally hung up. While I had been on the line, I got a beep from Pete.

Pete and I went back all the way to when I was a kid breaking in to the business. Once I had given him ten dollars a case. Later it was twenty for each head in the car. I paid whether or not the case was good. Everyone else only paid when a case was good. I had figured out long ago what kind of relationship kept the contact alive and with me no matter what. I made a call to Jo to check with Pete, and get on whatever case he was giving us. My beeper went off again. I was still in my room at my aunt's, and immediately called the number displayed. I didn't recognize the number, but when he picked up, I recognized the voice.

"Mario, long time. You know who this is?"

It was Johnny Rodriguez, a tow truck driver. He was an independent contractor, and owned his own truck.

"Johnny, asshole, who you giving your cases to? I never hear from you anymore."

I heard traffic noises.

"Speak up man, I'm in a phone booth."

We talked for a few minutes. I ribbed him for not calling me.

"No way Mario. I just haven't had anything good. You the man. I never send a case to anyone but you."

"I was kidding, Johnny. What you got for me?"

"Left turn broadsides a car in oncoming traffic. Both cars are totaled. Idiot made the left. Wronged party refused to go to the hospital so I took her home. The fool at fault went over to ELA Hospital. He'll be okay. This gal is pissed. She asked me if I knew an attorney."

I took down the information, and promised Johnny that Jo would catch up to him with a gift for thinking of me. Then I called the number Johnny had given me.

"Jan, so sorry about the accident. Hope you are okay. Are you okay? Your car was totaled, so why didn't you go to the hospital?" I said all this in one breath, presumably to the woman who was the wronged party.

"Who the hell is this?"

I introduced myself as a mutual acquaintance of Johnny. After a fifteen minute talk, Jan admitted she was not feeling well. She promised to go to the ER, and later would visit a doctor we would refer her to since she didn't have a doctor who handled personal injury.

My next call was to Jo. I gave her Jan's information, and told her to go sign her up, then meet up with Johnny and take care of him. Jo would go to the impound lot and take pictures of the car.

As I set the phone down, everything appeared almost back to normal, but it was a lie. Inside my head, I carried the burden of Tanis's death, and of my own injury. I might have been semi-conscious when I had first thought of Carson and his machinations, but I was not just getting back to normal. I was preparing myself to meet Carson face-to-face, some time when he was sober, not hiding behind a couple of girls. My gut told me he was responsible for Tanis's death. Vengeance was a huge weight on my shoulders. I had a fierce need to make him pay for what he had done. I kept this rage against Carson hidden inside me. No one knew what was on my mind. Even I wasn't sure what I would do. If Pélon had been around, he would have been making plans to deal with Carson, and I'd have been the one urging caution. But Pélon was in prison. I was left to stew in my own juices, simmering like a pot about to boil over.

Jo came over to see me at my aunt's, and stayed for lunch. Then we went over the cases she'd signed in the past few days. There were a lot of them, and that meant a lot of paperwork. We filled up my desk, and expanded to the table in the dining room. Retainers, questionnaires, injury pictures, police reports on older accidents just being signed were spread all over. Once I finished with this preliminary work, Jake's office would open up a case file for each new client.

"It's hard to keep up to speed without you in the field," Jo said. "I'm not complaining, but if I could cut back to twelve-hour days, it would feel like a vacation."

"You know there's no such thing as twelve-hour days," I said. "Enlisting is 24/7."

"You know what I mean," she said. "I love the money. I could make more of it if I had extra hands. I dropped in to Liberty Hospital Emergency Room for a look-see, and guess who I saw?" As she talked, she sorted papers.

"No telling."

"Hugo. He was working a couple. When he saw me, he left them and bought me a Coke out of a vending machine."

Hugo Pliego is also an ambulance chaser. I'd never actually seen him close a deal, which is just to say he's never stolen a client from under my nose; but I occasionally run into him. He drives a beat-up Impala. He's a friendly enough guy, and mild to the point of being invisible, which works in his favor. He can haunt emergency rooms and no one notices. He is of middle height, and has medium colored hair, and brownish greenish grayish eyes. He's the kind who fades into the woodwork, so he can get in places where someone else would stick out. I feel sorry for him, but he seems to like Jo.

"Next time you see him, tell him 'Hi' from me."

Jo looked up from the papers, and nodded.

"Remember those pictures in your glove box? I called Pedra about the tags on the pickup and the bug. I got the bug and owner but the pick up turned out to be stolen. The pick up driver got out of there before the police arrived, but you got a couple good pictures of him. There was also a red Camaro."

Pixie ambled out of the kitchen carrying a sandwich. She saw Jo intent on work, and glanced at the papers with some curiosity, and maybe a little envy. Her attention fixated on a particularly gruesome account of an accident. She picked it up, and her brow furrowed as she concentrated on the words. She looked at me over the top of the page, quirking an eyebrow in my direction, which probably meant she wanted to meet me in the broom closet in ten minutes. We don't actually have a broom closet, but that's the code we use when her daughter's listening.

When Pixie had moved in six years ago, she had been practically illiterate. She'd never gone to school that I knew of. She'd lived at Nana's, an old whore who had a house down the street from our apartment. I had always presumed her mother had been one of Nana's girls. I'd always known she'd been young for a hooker, but in high school, I thought she was way older than me. Under all that make-up, I never realized she was a couple of months younger. Aunt Carmen had been a determined teacher, and as Pixie's foster auntie, had spent these years teaching her to read, and the basics of numbers. Pixie's progress seemed really crucial now, because I had the beginnings of a brilliant idea.

"Okay, Jo," I said, "If you need some help…" I looked at Pixie.

Pixie stopped fiddling with the report she'd been reading. She saw me watching her.

"What? What is it?"

Jo is pretty intuitive. She's used to how I work, and how I think. She started looking at Pixie too. Pixie looked from Jo to me, and back again, knowing there was communication whizzing around her head that was going entirely past her. "You guys are freaking me out."

"Pixie, what if you put in some time with Jo learning how to sign up cases?"

Pixie hesitated.

"Me?" She shook her head. "I'm not like you. I didn't go to college. I'm such a dummy. I wouldn't know what to do."

"I didn't go to college," I reminded her.

"But you know stuff. You always did, even when we were snot-nosed kids."

A determined expression crossed Jo's face. She really did need help and was immediately on board with the idea.

"Pixie, I'll teach you," Jo said. "You ride along with me, and you'll get the hang of it."

"You really think I could do this?"

"Of course you can. It's not brain surgery."

"Yeah, but I'm so dumb, you'd hate me after a while."

"Nonsense," Jo said.

"Can I do it just when Lainey is in school? Hours are from eight to three, and I wait tables in the evening."

"You could make enough doing this that you could lose that waitressing job," Jo said. "And I'll drill you, and get you to pass that GED."

The GED comment almost chased her off. Pixie was apprehensive but I knew Jo would have her up to speed in no time.

Since I had been out of the hospital, I'd been loading her up with too much work. Before getting shot, I had been employing a new strategy, and handing Jo all the fender benders and small cases, the kind of cases that would end up settling for peanuts. Fender benders have been my bread and butter for a long time. I'm not turning my nose up, but I've been thinking about bigger cases. Except for the sheer number of cases, I wasn't giving Jo anything she couldn't handle. And as for Pixie, I trusted that she would rise to the occasion. I'd help her get a driver's license and a car. I'd help her get whatever she needed to do the job. Jo could send her around to the body shops that required foot service. The guys would love her. The owners of the body shops were like family. I just don't have time to run over to a shop to meet a client at the drop of a hat, the way I did when I was fourteen. Business from body shops formed the foundation of my work, but who has the time? If we trained Pixie, then Jo could step back from those, and have Pixie handle it.

"If you think I can do it, then I think I can," Pixie said. "If I disappoint, I can always fuck, suck, or jerk off the person you want to sign. I know I can do that with no problem."

"Not all prospects are guys," Jo said.

"No matter. Girls are easy."

Pixie turned out to be a good student of Jo's; and Jo and I turned out to be good students of Pixie. I had never been involved in a threesome before. Pixie sure knew where to place the bodies and how to direct the action. I guess her former calling paid off. The distraction of sex blocked Carson out of my mind. For a little while, at least, I didn't think of Tanis lying there dead. She still visited my dreams, though. Pixie had no limits, but she reminded me of how I used to wonder how far Tanis would go to get me a case. Tanis had been out there, but now, the place Tanis had held in my life was a void. I carried the void around with me. Everything reminded me of her; and at every thought of her, I became more convinced that Carson was behind the shooting that caused her death. Every single day was one less day to count before I stormed his house to get even. For a couple hundred bucks, I could have a homey from my old barrio wipe that sucker from this planet. That was the coward's way, a path I'd never take.

East Los Angeles, unlike areas nearby such as Alhambra, South Pasadena, Pasadena and San Marino, doesn't Christmas-decorate the city's trees. Home-owners go all out to put up lights and decorations outside the small homes, but that's it. ELA had beautiful palm trees and many other trees but no lighting. Los Angeles does Christmas pretty well, even without snow. It wasn't cold like it gets in the Northeast, but the convertible's top was definitely secured, and the car's heating system was blasting. Gold bells, and red and white Santas abounded outside, especially in department store parking lots. The bell ringers with their collection cans were out and about. Jo had been where we were going back in November. It was time for me to make a showing. I'm no Santa, but I had a pocket full of cheer. The car was full of my team members. Pixie had been working a couple of weeks, but never alone.

"Jo tells me you've been doing a good job."

"It's fun," Pixie said. "It's just like hooking, without having to take your panties off."

I laughed. Pixie thought everything was just like hooking. But then, that's where she gets her abundant street smarts. She'd been off the street for more than six years and still used that lingo. I guess you can take the girl off the street, but it's not so easy to take the street out of the girl.

Pixie had pulled out a compact, and an eyeliner wand, and was examining her face. On her own, she preferred the heavy make-up, bright colors and long, loose hair, like a Hispanic Peggy Lipton, if Peggy Lipton had been a stripper instead of on Mod Squad.

"So where are we going now, boss?"

From the back seat, while arranging papers in my briefcase, Jo answered for me.

"We're on the way to Niley's house. I told Mario you'd be good to have along to visit a woman who is divorced, has a couple of toddler boys and is also raising her niece and nephew. You'll probably get along great with her as long as you don't mention your former profession."

Pixie angled the mirror to include Jo's face, and stuck her tongue out at her.

In the rear view mirror, I could see the interplay between Jo and Pixie. Two women could not be more different. Jo was all work. Pixie was all play. If they could be put together, they'd make the perfect woman.

"Ease up on the eye liner, Twiggy, the sixties are over," she said. "Seriously, don't screw up the make-up. I put some effort into making you look like you're not wearing any."

"I look like a nun."

"You do not look like a nun."

Pixie made another face, then returned the compact back in her purse. Buckled in the passenger seat, she looked like a respectable young secretary. Her A-line dress, stockings and heels weren't fancy, but they could have come out of a Sears or JCPenney's catalogue. Left to her own devices, her wardrobe choices were risqué, but these days, Pixie allowed my aunt to direct what was in her closet. She hadn't always been so malleable. When I'd first brought her home to Monterey Park, she fought for her old working clothes. It took a while for her to figure out how the other half lived.

"Here's the deal," I said. "Niley's sister Tanis was a friend of mine."

Both of the women in the car knew Tanis had been killed the day I'd been shot. "Tanis left a couple of kids. The father is dead, and the only family is the girl you will be meeting today. Harry is handling the legwork to make her guardian of her sister's kids to keep them out of foster care. She's divorced, unemployed, and Tanis was the household's only means of support. I've never met her, but Jo has."

"What do I say to her? I'm not so good with women not in the business." Pixie asked.

Jo sighed, and said, patiently, "Just say her name. Say it's pretty, or something complimentary. Don't worry. The conversation will come as long as you don't reminisce about hooking up with guys."

Jo had met Tanis plenty of times to sign up a case that couldn't wait when I wasn't available. I doubt they'd ever had a personal conversation lasting over a minute. While I had been in the hospital, Jo had done the due diligence on Niley. She'd been my eyes and ears, meeting Niley for coffee, checking out the family circumstances, meeting the kids, dropping in several times, and bringing cash on more than one occasion. The situation was far from unresolved.

I turned into the neighborhood not far from Lincoln Hospital. Tanis had lived in an apartment in a low rent district. The ugly brick building was constructed to house people, and that's all. There were no frills, no playgrounds, no pools, no bells and whistles. I knew from memory that Tanis had a three bedroom unit. She had the master bedroom, her sister had another, and all the kids shared the third bedroom. It was not the best situation, but they had a roof over their heads.

I pulled into the parking lot. At this time of day, there were plenty of spaces, because most of the tenants were out earning a living. Jo, Pixie and I headed up to the third floor apartment.

I knocked on the door.

It was opened by a slim young woman close to my own age. In spite of the short haircut and the glasses, I'd have known her for Tanis's sister immediately. She was a smaller, paler version of the vibrant woman who still visited my dreams.

She looked a little frightened, but the fear didn't seem to stand in her way.

"Mr. Luna," she put her hand out to me. "I've been expecting you. It's so nice to meet at last. I heard so much about you from Tanis before...." Her voice faded away.

"I heard a lot about you too, Miss Niley," I said, wondering if she was going to faint or something, "Mister is not necessary. Everyone calls me Mario."

"Me too." She blushed. "I mean, everyone calls me Niley. No Miss needed."

I refrained from saying she looked too young to be called ma'am and moved on to the introductions.

"This is Pixie. She's a member of my team. And of course, you've met Jo before."

"Niley," Pixie repeated, "That's an unusual name."

"My father was from Egypt," she explained. "He didn't want my sister or me to forget it, so we got named for places."

The apartment door opened into a main room with a large couch that had seen better days. A tiny galley kitchen was visible through an open door at one end opposite a short hall. The hall led off to several closed doors. Lots of furniture was packed in the small room, including a rickety dining table with eight mismatched chairs crammed around it. I recognized the look of a merged household, of different sets of furniture, hand-me-downs, and odds and ends aimed at a black and white TV on a collapsible TV table. On the corner of an entry table, I saw a stack of mail. The top letter was open, and protruding from it was a pamphlet from Sun City Stones. Jo and Pixie had moved so that I was standing behind Niley. I snatched the brochure to sneak a look at the memorials, but Niley turned, unexpectedly. Jo looked alarmed, and grabbed both of Niley's hands, squeezing them, using her grip to keep Niley facing her direction.

"I'm so glad to see you again." Over Niley's shoulder, I saw Jo's gaze move from the stack of mail to my pocket, and she frowned at me. She might be mad I was sorting through the mail, but she didn't rat me out. I shrugged. I had the best of intentions, so I wasn't worried. Jo released her grip and took a small step toward a framed picture, and looked it over, admiringly. Niley looked a little confused at the abrupt change, but at least she hadn't noticed the brochure and a couple of bills go into my pocket.

Pixie plopped down on an easy chair by the couch, and Jo took the one next to it. That left me with limited choices: a chair from under the dining table, an ottoman that smelled of feet, or several short, stuffed chairs that might not hold me. I opted for the low couch, which creaked as I sank into it, pulled back into an awkward, nearly reclining position. The back and the underpinning of the couch was broken. Niley offered to bring us water, which we all declined, and then she sat on the couch also, a cushion's width apart from me. To be polite, I stood, and sat again, this time sitting on the edge so I didn't get sucked in. To say it was awkward is an understatement. My knees were around my ears.

As Jo had predicted, Niley and Pixie hit it off. They fell easily into a conversation about their children.

"Do you plan to stay here after the judge grants you custody?" I asked Niley.

"If I must. It's tough to move when you have four kids."

"How are you getting by?"

"I'll get aid for Tanis's kids. The kids will get Social Security because Tanis had always worked. I already get a little monthly aid, and medical for me and my kids. By the way, thank you so very much for referring me to the attorney. He's just wonderful."

"No thanks needed," I said.

Pixie had run out of conversation. Jo was sitting primly with a briefcase on her lap.

Niley sat quietly for a long time, struggling to say something.

"We all depended on Tanis. I don't have the job skills she did. I'm just a glorified housekeeper, and not even a good one. With her gone, I didn't know how we were going to make it. Then Jo showed up. And now you. Tanis talked about you frequently. I know she cared about you. Now I know why."

She didn't know the half of it.

"I miss her too," I said.

Niley's eyes brimmed over. I heard a sob, and she launched herself at me. She cried, and mumbled unintelligibly into my collar for what seemed to be a very long time. I patted her on the back and felt awkward. Jo looked on compassionately. Pixie stared at the peeling wallpaper, embarrassed. In the distance, pipes creaked, and traffic noises rose and fell. The apartment had thin walls.

"We are here for you. Just think of us as family."

Jo left her chair, and walked over toward us, motioning to Pixie. A moment later she was in the embrace. Pixie hung back a little, and rather than hear it, I saw her silently mouth, "What the hell," and dive into the huddle.

Niley gave us a tour of the apartment. Tanis's room was locked.

"We need the space but I can't bear to use it," she admitted to us. "It's her room."

"It's a room, not a shrine. It's not like she's coming back," Pixie said.

Niley looked at her in horror.

"I didn't mean it the way it sounded. I'm sorry."

"Pixie doesn't have sisters," Jo said. "Pixie was an orphan. She never had to lose anybody, so she really doesn't understand. She never had anybody to lose, not that she remembers."

"I do too understand," Pixie said. "I lost Nana."

"Who was Nana? Your grandma?" Niley asked.

"No. She was the old whore who raised me."

When Jo's alarmed eyes met mine, I realized Pixie was going to take more polishing before we could let her loose in the field.

To Niley's credit, she only looked shocked for a minute, then she said, "You poor thing."

Niley reached up, and grabbed a little copper skeleton key from over the door, and let us inside. It was squeaky clean, but even more crowded than the front room. From atop the mirrored dresser, I picked up a small bottle of Joy.

She had always said Joy was the only fragrance for her.

I looked at the neatly made bed, the pretty comforter, the matching shams. I could feel her presence. For a moment, I almost lost it. I felt an overpowering urge to lie on the bed, to bury my face in the sheets, to see if I could smell my girl. That Tanis was gone was a continuing nightmare for me. Somehow, I pulled myself together, grateful no one could tell what was going on in my thoughts. When Niley was showing the other rooms, I snuck a look at the kitchen, pantry, and in the refrigerator. It was slim pickings for a woman with four mouths to feed.

"You can count on five hundred [1]a month from me, and more if that doesn't cut it," I assured her, when I joined the others. I handed her a small envelope.

Niley started crying again.

What a fucking tragedy this was, and so needless. I felt the familiar rage building. I wanted to focus it on whoever had sent that gunman after me. I knew in my gut that it wasn't a random mugging. I knew I was going to kill the person behind all of this. I guess I must have gotten flushed. Whatever the tell was, it was noticeable enough that Jo took my hand and whispered at me.

"Take it easy," she said.

In the parking lot, Pixie said, "I didn't even know her, and I feel fucking terrible."

In the car leaving Niley's, the only sound was from the cassette player. I had put in the Neil Diamond album, 'Moods'.

"What was that letter?" Jo asked, raising her voice over the music.

I dug the brochure out of my pocket and tossed it to her. "Sun City Stones. Check up on this."

Jo's beeper went off. I pulled into the parking lot of the greasy spoon close to Lincoln Hospital. Jo got out and answered her call from a booth.

Pixie was looking bored. "I can't wait to get home and take off these shoes."

"Already?"

"We did the thing," she said.

"You think that's all it takes to call it a day?"

"Well, sure."

I pointed at Jo. "Look."

---

[1] $500.00 in 1972 had the same buying power as $2,877.43 in 2016

Jo was having an animated conversation with someone on the other end of the line. She had paper and a pen out, and was writing something down. She knew I was watching, and gave me a thumbs-up.

I shrugged.

She pantomimed with her fingers: walking, slipping, falling.

"Jo's got a slip and fall on the phone right now."

"What's that?"

"It's a kind of case Jake hates, but they can get really interesting."

"Does interesting mean money?"

"Sometimes."

Jo returned to the car, and handed me the sheet of paper. I started up the car, and pulled into traffic. I recognized the street address. It wasn't far, and I knew a short-cut.

"Gomez called back," Jo said.

"Who's Gomez?"

"Gomez—the wife—took a fall at the market. They drove her to the emergency room in an ambulance, but she was released right after she was checked. I don't think she broke anything."

"Jake hates slip and falls," Pixie said.

Jo looked at Pixie, not needing to ask where she'd gotten her information. Pixie wasn't so much a quick study. She was more like a parrot.

"Yes he does, but not all slip and falls are losers. We've had some hella good cases."

"Jo's right on the money."

Jo explained, "Even if it's a loser, we sign her up. We let her know in advance that a slip and fall is one of the most difficult cases to get any money on unless the fall breaks you up pretty bad."

"And what are you going to do about it?" Pixie asked.

"We're dropping you off, and going to talk to Gomez."

"She's coming with us."

"In that case," Jo said, "Pixie, listen up. You can't go talking about sex like you always do, or talking about Nana, or your former profession, or her profession, or anything like that. People just don't understand. We got lucky with Niley, but Niley is not a client we're courting. She's a friend. For clients, you've got to be on your best behavior. We go in, and get their signature on a piece of paper. We don't alienate them, or piss them off, or push any hot buttons if they're deeply religious. All you have to do is pay attention, not talk about sex, and look prim and proper. Can you do that?"

"No shit, Mama," she said, then belatedly, "Who are these people?"

"Slip and fall case, or they will be after we sign them. They've been to the emergency room, and they've got an appointment with orthopedics."

"So, we're like coyotes," Pixie said.

Jo repeated something I had told her a long time ago. "We are not coyotes. We're not looking to swallow them up at a time they are desperate. We want to help. We level with them. They will be better off with us than without us. If all goes well, we're going to get paid by the attorneys if the case settles. If something goes wrong, they pay nothing. You know that is not what coyotes do. They take everything they can. The only issue we have is having to be extremely careful not to solicit and hand out cards."

The Gomezes lived in a cramped cottage with a pocket-sized front yard full of toys and balls, and bicycles, boxed in by a decorative wire fence about two feet high. The back yard was concrete, and full of vehicles in various stages of repair.

In due course, one of the Gomez kids let us in.

"Are you the lawyer guys I'm supposed to be waiting for?" the boy asked. He looked about fourteen.

"We're not lawyers, but we are here to help. I've talked to your mother. She phoned me from the emergency room. Is she home?"

"Yeah, she's laid up in the den, wiped out on painkillers."

He led us around the corner to a paneled den. Mrs. Gomez was stretched out on the couch with her foot on a pillow. She was an attractive woman with a mess of dark hair and heavy make-up that was slightly smeared. She had on a lemon-colored polyester leisure suit, with the hem of one pants leg hiked up to a slim thigh. Several buttons of the top were undone, revealing a lot of undisciplined cleavage resisting containment by a black bra. She was chasing whatever medication she'd been dosed with by a bottle of beer, and fiddling with an ice pack wrapped in a kitchen towel. On the end of that slender leg, her foot looked like someone had pumped it up with a tire inflating machine to about forty psi, and it was about to pop any second.

I had talked to her, but Jo handled the introductions. She had a battery operated tape recorder with her, and with the family's permission, she set it on the table to record the description of the accident. We talked for a good ten minutes about her obvious injury, and made arrangements for our getting a copy of the doctor's report. Pixie was on her best behavior. She could have been an Avon Lady, or Welcome Wagon, or maybe a kindergarten teacher. I was proud of her.

We got through the explanations without making any promises, which was good. The client understood that the outcome hinged on whether the case was good. Thanks to the drugs, Mrs. Gomez looked like she wasn't feeling any pain but her condition made me think we might need one of her family members handy. I sent Carlos out back to get his father.

Jo nudged Pixie toward the camera, and pulled a questionnaire from her briefcase.

"Mrs. Gomez, if you don't mind, we need some pictures of that swelling. Gotta have a record to show how bad you are hurt." Pixie snapped pictures. Jo asked questions. The recorder recorded. As our new client gave Jo the answers, she jotted them down.

She took great care in recording Mrs. Gomez's description of how she slipped on a soda spill. As she adjusted the retainer description from auto accident to slip and fall at Safeway Market, Jo explained what she was doing. Mrs. Gomez dismissed the explanation about the retainer, and signed where a signature was required.

A door slammed at the back of the house. We heard water running in a bathroom somewhere, then the man of the house stepped in. His hands and arms were half lathered up as he worked a head of dark soapy foam.

"Mr. Gomez." Disregarding the soap, I put my hand out. It's never right to be discourteous to a client. Plus I knew that oily, soapy handshake could mean something a regular handshake would not.

Gomez smiled, and made an apologetic gesture, and avoided me. "Maybe after I get this '68 Chevy washed off," he said. "You're here about my wife's little spill?"

I explained about the slip and fall case, and Jake. I did not mention that Jake didn't like "slip and falls" and saw Pixie catch herself from saying it aloud. I saw Jo's eyes roll skyward, in a brief prayer of thanks.

The swelling looked horrible. I figured this case was much better than most. The pictures would help, but so would the bills for ongoing therapy. It could become a good payday for the client and for Jake.

Mr. Gomez seemed concerned, like any good husband, and said how he was glad that there was a possibility his wife might have some recourse. He complained to great length about the cost of medicine.

"They get you on the hook. Them hospitals, and them doctors. Doctors are just highway robbers in white coats," he said.

"Actually, Jo can make copies of the bills. They support the case, if these were from the slip and fall."

Mr. Gomez opened a drawer in a small desk, and pulled out a packet of envelopes held together by rubber bands.

"Yeah, they were. And look at that paperwork we had to fill out just to get into the emergency room. It was longer than the last book I read."

He turned as if he were going to go rinse off his soap, but stopped. He gestured politely toward Jo and Pixie, with a kind of salute, then froze in his tracks. His color dropped two shades, and he did a double take. He stared at Pixie like she'd grown a third head. His arms dropped to his sides, dripping oily foam on to the carpet.

Pixie raised her hand up parallel to her face and wiggled her fingers in a little wave.

He squinted at her, got even paler, if that is possible, and then disappeared into the bathroom, closing the door very softly.

Pixie shrugged.

Jo and I looked at her.

"Hey, we're right in the old neighborhood," she whispered in my ear. "So? I had regulars."

"Carlos!" Mrs. Gomez yelled for her son. "Turn down the TV."

"I can get it," Jo said, turning down the TV, and positioning herself between Mrs. Gomez and Pixie.

"Thank you so much," Mrs. Gomez said. Her eyes were at half mast before we left the room. Considering Mr. Gomez's relationship with Pixie, I was now seeing Mrs. Gomez's dopey condition as a happy accident.

We were on the way to the car when Mr. Gomez came around from the back of the house. Jo was in the middle of opening the car door, and blurted out something cautionary about mixing meds and beer. I followed it up with what was probably an unnecessary explanation that I'm an equal opportunity employer. Pixie hung back, an arm's length from Gomez.

"I'm not a churchy man," Gomez said. "But my wife...she got her heart set on heaven. Seems like a dull place, but I don't want to rock the boat." His eyes were fixed on Pixie. "You ain't rocking the boat, are you?" he asked, hopefully.

"I've never been on a boat," Pixie said. "Is that an invitation?"

She smiled. It wasn't an ambulance chaser smile. It was a shameless full-on come-hither flat-out lip-puckering invitation.

Gomez took a step forward.

Jo left the car door open, and dashed to Pixie's side, whispering something into her ear. She tugged her toward the car.

"Oh," Pixie said, "I'm not telling your wife about my former profession. I don't do that stuff anymore."

If ever a man managed to look happy and miserable at the same time, it was in that moment. Pixie has a look and body that is not easy to forget. The poor stiff.

Clearly, Gomez wasn't worried about Pixie in any moral sense. As soon as he knew the secret was safe, he had moved on to the tantalizing possibility of making more secrets.

We piled in the car. Jo sat in the back seat, her head leaning on to her hand. Pixie waved at her former client again through the window. As upset as he was that she showed up on his doorstep, I could see Mr. Gomez's mind whizzing. He was probably wondering if he could get Pixie to make house calls.

"You can't blame this one on me," she said, "I didn't say one word about sex. You'd think that after six or seven years, the fucker wouldn't remember me."

Jake didn't trust phones and neither did I. It wasn't as if we had real 007 shit going on, but Jake warned me that people are impulsive. Stress and emotions could make people do things out of the ordinary. We didn't discuss important things over the phone. Jake and I met almost daily. It was rare that I didn't bring a new case or cases with me every meeting; and when I didn't bring the paperwork, Jo did. I crashed occasionally at the apartment, just because I had paid for December. In fact, the end of December was my mental deadline for finding another pad. I just hadn't spent any time looking for alternatives.

Jake met me at the juice stand at Grand Central Market, a few minutes walk from his office. Jake always wore a suit and tie, and usually ordered for me. Today, a large glass of fresh carrot juice was waiting across from him. The newspaper he had already read lay open on the table. I handed Jake three cases that had been signed the day before.

Jake smiled broadly, showing his teeth. He had regular lawyer hair, cut short by an expensive barber. His hair was darker than it used to be. It might have been an illusion because of the silver touching his sideburns, but he wasn't beyond getting his hair dyed. He'd given up contacts and now wore glasses all the time, not just to court. He was probably in his fifties, a little on the heavy side. I'd never asked his age but I knew he had grown children. He had to be twenty years younger than Harry though. Harry was old, a grandfather. Probably a great-grandfather.

"You are the best." He glanced through the pages, beaming. In the distance, I could hear the screeches of tires and rumbling traffic. I was always listening for the telltale sounds of a crash.

"Aww," I said, then read aloud, "Berry Oakley, bass guitarist of the Allman Brothers died while I was in the hospital back on November eleventh, in a motorcycle accident in Macon, Georgia." I put the paper down and folded it. "That's depressing. I liked the Allman Brothers Band but they're dropping like flies. Duane Allman died last year."

"Who? Berry who?" Jake said. "Someone you know? Did you miss another funeral?"

I stared at Jake. How tactful of him, deliberately or not, to remind me I'd missed Tanis's funeral. I thought I might go by the cemetery again and pay another visit.

"Is that supposed to be funny Jake, or do you want me to punch you in the face?"

Jake put down his cup, and set aside a magazine he'd gotten from a vendor but hadn't opened. It lay atop a section of the newspaper.

"You're no hothead. What's up?"

"Did you hear what you just said? You think my good friend lying in a grave is something to joke about?"

"I didn't mean that at all. I'm sorry. I'm not taking her shooting, or your shooting lightly. It didn't come out the way I meant it to."

I stared across the table at him, and realized we might as well be a million miles apart. He might be one of the most effective lawyers in the county, and have perfect vision where courtrooms were concerned, but there were just some things Jake didn't get.

"Are we good?"

I didn't answer immediately, but finally nodded.

To cover the awkwardness, he did the one thing he did best—talked about a case.

"The electrocution case in Oakland will be huge," Jake said as he patted the top of my hand from across the table.

He was referring to the Pacheco case that I had signed the night before the shooting.

"Good to hear. How's the milk truck case that Tanis gave me?"

"That's a good case, kiddo."

I thought of Tanis. I remembered the four hundred I had given her the day she gave me the details about the accident at the restaurant.

"I've been thinking I need to go for the big cases. There must be something I can do to draw big cases," I downed the carrot juice.

"You're doing great. There isn't a lawyer in this business that wouldn't give one of their nuts to get twenty percent of the business you bring me. No one comes close to having our volume. You're a champ. No question." Jake said this with a great big chuckle. He had great looking teeth. "I was really worried about you when I saw you in the hospital. You looked bad. Not like the Mario I know."

"You were just worried about losing the business I bring in for you."

"How can you say that! You're like a son to me. Surely you know that."

"Maybe I do. Thanks for being there for me."

A moment passed. Jake was a serious person for sure, but he tried to joke around with me. I'd seen him use humor to control a courtroom. I wasn't going to let his making light of the situation change my focus.

"I'm serious, Jake. Where do I look for big cases in volume? I'm tired of the same routine. I have Jo with Pixie working the signups unless the client insists I be there. In the past, I would never have allowed anyone to sign a case for me."

Maybe that was a hangover from working with Carson. He used to bring me cases for Harry way back when. I learned after the fact that his cases were phony. I guess that would make anybody shy of working with a partner.

"You are not going to find an electrocution case every day," Jake said, "and you are asking the wrong person about where you need to look. You're the magician." Jake looked a little alarmed. "Don't burn any bridges. Don't walk away from the cases that made you, and still feed all of us."

"I'll never refuse a small case, if that's what you mean." He wasn't telling me anything I didn't already know. I decided to drop it.

Jake was looking his age. It made me worry a bit. I hoped he lived to be two hundred, not just to protect my deal with him but because I really cared about the man. Maybe not as much as I love Harry and Cosmo, but he's one of the big three who changed my life.

I have been terrible at math my whole life, but good enough to know how much money I had in my pocket, in the bank, and how much I was owed. I got paid for services rendered for every case I worked on, but if a case promises to bring in more than three thousand dollars [2]in attorney fees, I am promised a bonus when it settles. I made a mental note to sit down some time soon with Jo, an adding machine, and a pot of coffee to project what I might have coming if every pie my finger is in settled even in a mediocre fashion. Predicting the value of a case was nearly impossible. Not only for me. Lawyers never knew either until the case settled or went to court to let a judge or a jury decide the value. I would use a low number on the list of cases that were pending just to get an idea of what I'd have coming if I brought no more cases and just waited for each case to either blow away because it was no good or settle for a reasonable sum.

I would be young for a lawyer, but if I were a lawyer, I'd be new. This is a job I've been doing with Harry since I was fourteen, and eighteen with Jake. I knew enough about the law that I realized if something happened to Jake, the handshake agreement I have with him is not legally binding on anyone. He has no partners, just attorneys who he has working there. A lawyer can't partner up with a non-lawyer and split attorney fees, so our arrangement is a bond of honor instead of law. I trust Jake, but what will happen if Jake is not around? I might have thousands coming. I might have a million. I wouldn't know till I sat down with Jo. I knew this coming in. It is what it is. If Jake is around, I will get every penny due me, no question.

Maybe it was the winter temperatures that had invaded my head. It started to drizzle, amplifying the chill from brisk to glacial. I was probably more susceptible than usual to the weather, after my time on ice at Lincoln Hospital. I fastened the top button on the wool sweater I was wearing and turned to look toward the traffic on Hill Street which was buzzing along as usual. They'd better slow down. My fender bender antennae were up. It was definitely accident season. A lot of water causes hydroplaning, but a little causes the oil in the pavement to float up, making tires float on a thin sheen of lube. Desert city dwellers

---

[2] $3,000.00 in 1972 had the same buying power as $17,264.60 in 2016

are less skilled in rainy day driving than, say, Seattle drivers. I watched the light change.

A little red Fiat pulled up to the light and stopped. It was a sporty little car with a cloth top, just the kind of car that would catch my eye. The driver was idling patiently. I heard a screech, and a shiny new pickup slid directly forward, wheels locked, knocking the Fiat into traffic.

"You call it in," I said to Jake. Without another thought in my head, I was up and running. Behind me, I heard Jake chuckle. "Go for it, boy!"

I was first on the scene, running past the pickup, whose driver was sitting in his vehicle looking stupefied. Through the window, I got a pretty good glimpse. His western-styled rusty-colored suede jacket had seen better days. He looked a year or two younger than me, and had the shoulder-length hair of Mick Jagger. I instantly wrote him off as a student. Other than a scratch across his front bumper, his vehicle looked fresh off the dealer's lot.

My concern was for the victim. I've seen too many accidents to be blasé about them; and these cases are never about law. They are about people. Someone inside that car had been bounced around pretty good. I wasn't sure they'd survived. While I had been sprinting toward it, the Fiat had skid catty-corner into traffic. A succession of braking cars on the cross street had screeched, and banged, bounced it around until it ended up on the sidewalk across the way.

When I made it to the street, gridlock opened the way for me to run through a tangle of disabled, trapped, and wrecked cars and rubberneckers. Several car doors down, a big guy in a cop uniform was getting out of an Oldsmobile. I saw two things about him right away. He was about my age, maybe younger, and he probably liked doughnuts a lot. There was some powdered sugar on his shirt. His name badge said *Wilson*.

"I'm gonna be late punching in," he said, walking up. "What's going on? I couldn't see from back there."

"Looks self-explanatory to me," I said, walking so that he had to walk with me. "The roadster was rear-ended into traffic by that pick up. Don't you have some kind of protocol for off-duty emergencies? Get these people out of here before that car blows up, call in, direct traffic, whatever," I said. "I'm checking the car."

"Who's the cop here, you or me?" he barked out, but I had already given him my back. He jumped to it though, and started herding people out of the danger zone. A street pole had been struck and now it leaned at a crazy angle. The wires were still attached, but every so often sent a stream of shooting sparks like the Fourth of July. I thought about Pacheco's wife and daughter, and moved faster.

The Spider was badly banged up, the rear smashed in hard enough that the frame crumpled. The door was squashed. There'd be no opening it. The odor of gasoline hung in the air. My knife was already out. I snagged the fabric top of the convertible where it was already ripped, dropped the knife, grabbed with both hands and jerked the tear wider. Only one person inside. I reached in, turned off the engine, and put my hand on the girl's shoulder. Her head lolled back, but she was awake, and breathing. She was twisted trying to get the driver's door open with her right hand. It wasn't working. She looked at me with eyes so brown they appeared black. She opened her mouth to speak, and when her voice came out, it was small.

"Help."

She had her left arm bent over her chest, and gave up on trying to get the door handle to function. It clearly wasn't going to work ever again. She covered her bloody fingers protectively by her right hand. She was shaking.

"I can't get the door."

"I see that. It's pretty much banged up on this side." She tried to crane her head to see and her head thumped against the glass in her window. I thought there was a good chance she was in shock.

I took off my sweater, tossed it several feet away on the pavement, reached through the rip, and locked my hands under her armpits.

"You okay? Anything broken?"

"Just get me out, get me out!"

I knew I should wait for the ambulance. If she had a back injury, picking her up would make it worse. But there was a chance the car would be on fire before help arrived. I tugged.

She made a little moan.

I hesitated.

"No, I'm fine, out, get me out!"

She wasn't wedged in. She didn't weigh anything to speak of. In seconds I had her down on the sidewalk, on my sweater. As I lowered her down, she hooked her right arm around my neck, and wouldn't let go.

"You're so strong," she said, "Like Superman."

I thought she might be delirious.

I could already hear the ambulance, though I can't imagine how they got there with traffic so boxed up. We were close to the hospital. I tried to stand but she was clinging like a baby monkey.

"It's okay, I'm not going anywhere. But I was going to see if I could reach your purse."

She released me reluctantly, her hand lingering. I got to the car, grabbed the leather loop of her handbag, and my knife, and set off at a run. The bag was fairly small, certainly not in Jo's league, but it was surprisingly heavy. No time to look. I didn't need to sniff twice to notice the car smelled like straight gasoline.

I went back to the pavement, scooped the girl and my sweater up, and took us a safer distance from the vehicle. There were tiny droplets on her pretty face. It was still cold, but now the drizzle had lessened to a fine mist. The cop had enlisted the help of a couple of guys, and they were all herding people away from the Spider. The red and white ambulance pulled up. I caught the attention of one of the paramedics. A fire truck that had been inching through traffic blared it's horn. Cars and drivers tried to make way. I saw paramedics and called out for them.

"Guys, over here."

I approached with the victim in my arms. We met in the middle.

"They'll get you to the hospital," I told her.

Some distance behind us there was a whooshing noise, and her car burst into flames. She looked from her burning car to me, her eyes big as cups.

"Superman, you saved my life. What's your name?"

"Mario. What's yours?"

A couple of the paramedics interrupted, asking about her body parts and condition. They slid a gurney directly underneath, and I eased her down. With her uninjured hand, she was hanging on like a monkey. I bent over and because I knew jarring her to get loose was bound to hurt, I got stuck in that position while she gazed up at me. I was transfixed by her eyes. Then it occurred to me what she reminded me of—Lainey's dog, one of those aristocratic toy breeds with delicate bones and huge brown eyes. I was standing carefully motionless, as the paramedics buzzed around like worker bees. That's not to say she was a dog. She was gorgeous.

The cop tapped me on the shoulder. As I turned my head, a paramedic was splinting the broken hand.

"Hey Wilson," I said, still bent over.

"We gotta talk," he said.

The gurney rolled away.

I straightened, turned from the ambulance and answered all his questions. I gave my contact information. He looked over my identification, stared at it, and looked back at me. He held my drivers license between his thumb and fore-finger, and gestured with it.

"Now where do I know you from, Mr. Luna?"

"Call me Mario," I said pointing to where we'd been standing when we'd first exchanged words. "We met back there, about ten minutes ago."

Damn cops always probing. How could he know me way down here in downtown Los Angeles?

He stuck my card on his clipboard as he continued working on the accident report. By now, other cops had arrived, and were talking to the pickup driver who was getting loud. He was some distance away, yelling about how he was going to be late to class. With a weird sense of déjà vu, I could hear cop radio chatter on various frequencies. It hadn't been that long ago since I had been the one carted off in an ambulance. One of the cops escorted the driver to a patrol car and stuck him inside to cool off. Three Los Angeles County Fire trucks had arrived with sirens blasting and were starting their fire control dance. The cop and I scooted out of reach of the hard jet pulsing from the fire hose.

"Now I remember," he said. "You're the guy that got shot up at the motel out on the East Side some weeks back, I read about it in the paper."

"Bingo."

"Did you really get shot, or was that some fiction put in by the reporter?"

"Real shot," I assured him, "Real 9 mm."

"Not real bad shot," he said, "if you're up to pulling girls out of burning cars."

"You want to see the scabs?"

Cop laughed, looking up at me. He was younger than me, a little shorter, and I could tell he liked his doughnuts. "Nah, I believe you. You're a big boy. You should play football."

"No time." When you work from age ten on, there is little room for sport. Besides, if I had one, karate would be my sport.

"You were real lucky. This young lady you just saved was lucky. You got her out of that car. Now you're a hero!" He was laughing but not mocking. I figured he would have gotten her out had I not been ahead of him. He wasn't taking any credit at all.

"The car wasn't burning when I pulled her out," I reminded him. "But I smelled gas. The most recent articles were out last week, but they've been yammering on about it since I was shot back on November fifth. We're in December, now. They really need to let it go."

"I know what month it is." He looked me over. "You some kind of weight lifter or something?"

"Nah. Just a little karate."

He perked up. "Like David Carradine? In that new series?" I didn't disagree or differentiate between Kung Fu and karate. I didn't tell him how karate was developed in Okinawa as empty hand movements called "Ti" or "Te." Okinawan karate uses the whole body.

I had years in, but my sensei Cosmo always said to be humble, never brag about ability on the mat or off.

"You interested? I can get you lessons on the cheap. I know a guy." I gave him a Cosmo card. I didn't really push Cosmo these days, but it goes against my grain to ignore opportunity. You never know when a potential connection is going to come in handy. "I bet it would help with the whole being-a-cop thing."

"Far out."

I glanced at his clipboard. "Is that going on the report?"

"No, man, I just wanted to know." He started writing again, and after a few minutes, said we were done. He gave me back my driver's license.

"You always carry a purse?" he asked.

I shook my head, no.

He laughed again, conferred with the other cops, got in his Oldsmobile, and inched into a lane of redirected traffic.

As I made my way back toward the lot Jake's office used for parking, I glanced at the strap over my shoulder. The girl's handbag. No wonder he was laughing. But it was my ticket in to this case. Let him laugh.

All emergency rooms have an air of dingy desperation, and Queen of Angels is no exception. I had rushed straight there, but the desk nurse said I had to wait till the patient was in a room. Ten hours later, I was back. I walked past rooms packed full of full chairs of waiting people. It's not always easy to tell who is the person seeking treatment, and who are the families in waiting. A line had formed in front of the nurses' station. If Jo had been here, I'd have had her in it, but I was alone. I looked around the room to see if there was anyone I knew, hoping to see a helpful nurse. I thought I saw that ambulance chaser, Hugo, but when I looked again, he was gone or faded into the woodwork. The girl's wallet was small, and blue, and made of hand-tooled leather. I dug it out to get her name. I was examining the delicate stitches when I heard someone say "Hey Mario."

I recognized the speaker instantly. His son had been in a bad wreck a few years before. I had signed him, and Jake had handled the case. Sometimes I feel like I know half the city.

"Mario, I hope you are well? Not shot again, I hope."

"I'm waiting on someone, Dr. Mendoza," I said, shaking the man's hand.

"In that case, I'm glad to see you." He was in the standard issue hospital coat but judging by the blue jeans on his lower half, I had caught him coming or going. He was paler than I remembered, and looked exhausted. I knew from Tanis how difficult an emergency room rotation could be.

"How is your boy? Miguel Angel, if I remember correctly."

The boy been one of several kids being driven to his kindergarten class and they'd been struck by a school bus. The families had settled out of court for less money then than they would get now, but at least it had been enough to cover medical expenses for the little boy, who had had some broken bones. Mendoza's English was better than mine. He was Mexican but had graduated from medical school here in the States. His wife and son had been new to Los Angeles, and didn't speak the language yet. During their case, most of the time he had been tied up with school and doctoring. I pitched in to translate so I was pretty close to the family for a while. That had been when I was twenty, about four years ago.

"He goes by Gio now. He's all of ten years old." He looked at his watch. "I have to run pick him up. He's got a Cub Scout meeting. But let me fetch one of the sisters for you."

"That would be kind of you."

"Kindness has nothing to do with it. We owe you so much. Don't be a stranger! Drop by for dinner some time." He fished around in his pocket, and handed me his card before disappearing behind a door marked "Authorized Personnel Only."

Not sixty seconds passed before a husky older woman emerged. A score of waiting people converged on her, but she looked past them and fixed her gaze on me. Mendoza must have given her my description.

"Mr. Luna?"

I apologized, and squeezed through the crowd surrounding her. When I was close enough, I saw her name tag and responded in kind.

"Sister Margaret Mary."

She led me past endless rows of offices and filing cabinets in a series of low ceilinged narrow halls not meant for patients. We emerged behind the front nurses' desk. Busy nurses bustled past, eyeing me curiously. Right away, I recognized two of them from unconnected cases. They were both nuns too, but of the modern kind who didn't always wear habits. They waved surreptitiously and continued on their way.

"So who are you here with?" Sister Margaret Mary asked.

I folded open the wallet still in my hand and showed her the name. She nodded, and turned to an open loose leaf binder that had to be a foot thick. She ran her finger down the top page, down the patient list looking for the girl's name and location. While her back was to me, I snuck a look at the name on the driver's license, and put it away.

"This way," she said. She led me down a corridor, and made a turn. We went into an elevator and up several floors. She stopped at a closed door. The sounds of an argument came from within, loud enough that I thought about handing over the purse and making my escape. But she was a possible client. The sister knocked and we entered.

An older nun who looked like she might have known St. Peter personally, was seated in a metal folding chair that was backed up against the wall. Two middle-aged nuns were beside the bed. They were holding their patient down and giving her a shot from an angry looking syringe. Their patient, the girl I recognized from the accident, was agitated, resisting their attention. I had vivid memories of something similar happening a few weeks ago, and wondered if I had looked that crazy. It had taken a room full of people and big doses of sleeping potions to keep me in bed. But this was a slim, pretty girl, and didn't seem quite fair.

"I have to go home now," she was saying, her voice at a high pitch. "I've been here long enough. I've been to x-ray, and you tore up my favorite jeans, and that jerk of an intern yanked my leg all around and nothing hurt too bad till he got a hold of me. I have put up with all the poking and fussing I can stand. I am ready to go."

"The doctor is coming back in," the nun said. "We've got you scheduled for surgery in the morning, and then there's a bed waiting for you in post-op."

"No way, José! I have had enough of you. I have had enough of this entire scenario." She struggled with the nurses, gazed in my direction then stopped dead. Every woman in that room froze and looked at me.

The nun in the chair got up. I heard her bones creak from across the room.

"If there's family here, I won't need to sit with you. Nobody's allowed back here but family members." She teetered in shoes that looked fifty years old. "See that she stays in that bed!"

She fixed an eagle eye on me. Years and years of catechism enforced by nuns with rulers kicked in.

"Yes ma'am."

"Family?" the patient said. "*Cousin* Mario?"

The girl was quick-tempered, but she was quick, too. I probably shouldn't call her a girl. She was older than me. No idea how much older. I'm not good with ages.

Her expression brightened. She was still in her street clothes, but one of her bell-bottom pants legs had been cut away. Her left hand was done up in a bandage, heavily wrapped up in gauze and immobilized in a sling. Her leg was splinted and wrapped as well.

"Mario!" she said, "I am so glad you came!" She hissed at one of the nuns. "Let go of me, Hoss."

"Down, Melina, they're just trying to help," I said, using her name for the first time, ever. "What's the diagnosis?"

"Some busted bones in my hand, and a broken leg."

Hospital personnel usually grills you on your relationship to the patient, but none of these nuns did that, nor did Margaret Mary. I wondered what family relationship Dr. Mendoza had told her that had gotten me the personal escort to the room.

"Dr. Bono is coming in, then you stay put till your surgery." Margaret Mary said, reading from a chart that she stuck in a slot on the wall.

"You stay put," she said to Melina.

"You," she said. "Keep her here."

The nuns filed out in a big hurry and left the door open. I pulled it closed, and before I crossed the room to get to the chair by the bed, Margaret Mary opened it again. She poked her head in, and wagged her finger at me.

Nuns.

Melina made a face like she'd eaten a lemon.

"Thank God they've gone." She flopped back angrily against the pillows, and jarred something that was supposed to be still. It made her whimper a little. She turned a hazy smile in my direction. "How did you know my name? The ambulance took me before I said what it is. *Cousin* Mario."

"It's on your chart. And you forgot something, Miss Marron," I said.

"I liked it better when you called me Melina," she pouted.

"An unusual name."

"Not to me."

I laughed, thinking she'd made a joke. She seemed to have forgotten her desire to leave the bed.

I held out her purse.

She didn't reach for it, so I dropped it in the paper grocery bag on the nightstand.

"Your purse is heavy. You always carry a gun? You got papers for that? Most girls carry cosmetics."

"It's for protection," she said. Her eyes shut.

"I know that look. They gave you something for the pain."

"Mmhmm," she nodded. "I think it just kicked in. I'm so glad you're here."

"I just came to make sure you got here safely, and to bring back your purse."

I looked at my watch. It was late. The accident had been maybe a dozen hours ago.

"Well, if the sisters have everything well in hand..."

"But they don't," Melina said, fighting a yawn. I saw her eyes shift to the grocery bag that held her shoes, and where I had dropped her purse. "When I know you better, ask again about the gun." That was the end of her consciousness.

I thought about the "when I know you better." She planned to get to know me better. Good news.

On my way out of the hospital, I stepped into a phone booth in the lobby, and rang Jo.

"So you checked on the headstone?"

"As you expected, it's for Tanis," Jo said. "Niley put down a deposit on it, but it'll be years before it's done. They won't start on carving it until it's paid for. Judging by Niley's income, those kids will be out of college before there's a headstone up."

"So pay for it. Pay it off, and tell them to get it installed as soon as possible. Make sure they carve the right thing, whatever it is. I went by the grave." I stopped talking for a moment, remembering how sad it looked. Nothing but a small patch of muddy ground.

"There's more," Jo said.

"Yeah, you gifted the tow truck driver."

"No. I mean, yes, I gifted him, but that's not what I was going to say," she said, clearing her throat, "When I got to that last fender bender call, someone had been there in front of me. They had already signed with Carson."

I felt my whole body get hot.

"We're seeing entirely too much of him lately," I said, trying to give the impression of a cool head.

"I knew this would upset you especially because it's Carson. It's just a case. Not even a big case. We have so many others. Relax, Mario."

Before I said anything, Jo added, "What is it with you and Carson? Is it really just him beating you out of a case from time to time, or is it something else?"

After a long pause, I lied. "It's just a case. No big deal." Then I was out the door. I was going straight to Cosmo's to work off this steam. It would be dark, and no one else would be there this time of day, but I could let myself in. It was better than the alternative.

Yesterday had been a short day. Jo and I worked half a dozen callbacks before I called it a night. That was because I went from the hospital to Cosmo's and spent the entire night sweating out my rage. I cycled a hundred reps of pushups, kicks, lunges, and ten minute runs of jumping rope before I switched to shadow boxing. Then the six a.m. early class got there, and I sparred everyone there, one at a time, for an hour, while the rest of the class did its group thing. I was leaving puddles of sweat wherever I stood. I went from there to my ratty apartment, showered, and straight to Jake's office. Timed it just right, too, because Jo pulled into parking lot before I got out of the car.

"You look like hell," Jo said into the window. "Have you been to bed?"

"I'll sleep when I'm dead," I told her.

"Go to bed," she said.

"Who's the boss here?" I asked her.

She glared at me stubbornly. "Are you forgetting you were shot a month ago?"

"More than a month," I said, "But I remember it every time I twist my torso." Or stand. Or turn. Or push-up. And now I was stiff from that hell night of exercise—but it was a good kind of ache, the familiar kind from after a thorough work-out. I was over the hump.

From the briefcase sitting open on the passenger side, I grabbed a couple of folders and held them out to her.

She glanced down, and crossed her arms. "I'm not touching a thing unless you promise you'll quit early, and go rest."

"Deal," I agreed.

I popped my portable Sony recorder and handed her the tape I'd recorded on the way here. "Those are notes on the Pacheco case, and a couple of letters. And I want to send a gift basket to Dr. Mendoza. His kid likes baseball, so tickets would be a good addition. Kid's name is Gio now. Throw in some baseball tickets for the kid. 'Thanks for getting me in to see Cousin Melina.'"

Back when my cases went to Harry, the adorable Monica Chavez first became his client. Hers had been a small case. She'd been hurt but had nothing broken. I was still very young, and I catered to Monica. I even drove her to the doctor three or four times because her car was still in the shop after her accident.

It didn't vex me at all to cater to her. She lived with her parents who worked during the day. On my second visit to the house, we fell on her bed and made each other very happy. She was in her third year at LA State College, and now shared an apartment with a friend near the school. She worked part-time and was actively dating guys from school and others she met at work. She didn't hide that she liked me, and loved having sex with me. Aside from the good sex, Monica was a great source of business. Her referrals were never big cases, but that didn't matter. She sent me business. I gave her gifts of money when she did. She buzzed me that day with a couple of cases.

I followed up on Monica's cases. By four p.m., I was bone tired. I hit the Pacific Dining Car for the biggest steak on the menu, brought most of it home to my apartment wrapped in foil, then fell into bed. I did go looking for Carson, but only in my dreams.

The apartment is a little better than it was. After I had spent a couple of weeks at Aunt Carmen's, I'd hired a girl to come in once a week here and clean. There's not a lot of cleaning to do, but my aunt donated a ton of linens and blankets, so the bed, at least, is comfortable as hell. Still, when I get a spare minute, I'm going to find somewhere that's not a rat hole.

First thing I did when I woke up was run the machine. First were several messages from Aunt Carmen to call her, then two messages from Jo. Jo's not one of those people who says "Call me" on a message. She actually leaves complete messages so you don't have to call her back. She explained that we got the autopsy report on Pacheco's wife and daughter.

No surprise there. The cause of death was electrocution.

"The investigation work is being handled by Jake's staff, but Jake wants to keep you in the loop."

There was a message from Pixie. "I miss when you were sleeping here, and being able to sneak in to your room. Just say the word, and I can run over to your apartment."

The message from my aunt, again, was "Call me."

Even though she hadn't said it, I knew what my aunt wanted. Me, at Sunday dinner.

A few days went by with work as usual. I was home on a weeknight when the phone rang. I sipped a late coffee, and figured to let the machine handle Jake, if it wasn't anything urgent. I thought I might go somewhere for brunch.

"Hey Mario. I don't know if you remember me."

I recognized the voice immediately. I spilled the coffee leaping to grab the phone before she could hang up.

"Speak of the devil, Melina. I was just thinking of you," I said, "Have they released you from the hospital yet?"

"You need to come by. I have something to show you. I'm in my apartment."

Chapter 6
December 6, 1972
Melina

Thirty minutes later, I was at her pad on Figueroa Street. She lived in a nineteen story apartment tower in a convenient neighborhood for someone who worked downtown. Jake's office was minutes away. I passed this building every time I went to Jake's but had never made the turn. I'd never even pulled in for a close look of the entrance. I was surprised to see a doorman and a security guard, amenities not found everywhere in Los Angeles. I parked. Even the fresh pavement was like a gift, especially when I compared it to the cruddy garage at my rental. Before I went through the doors, I saw some guy in a suit toss his keys to the doorman, who took the car and parked it.

"That's the life," I said to myself. I'd had it up to here with parking my car in my half-ass garage, and having to get it detailed every other day to keep tree crap off of it. I fucking loved the idea of calling downstairs to have my shiny, clean car driven to the door, waiting for me. I loved the place instantly, before I even looked inside at an apartment.

The building still felt brand new. I passed a dry cleaners, and signs pointing to a laundry room, on site grocery, and work-out room. There was a line at the two elevators so I took the stairs up ten flights to Melina's floor. I didn't get winded, and the stairs didn't provoke my healing wounds, so I just found my real workout, at least until my karate is up to speed.

I knocked.

Melina yelled for me to come right in. I don't know what I was expecting, but I was surprised her place didn't look lived in. Just inside, I found her foyer to be an obstacle course of trunks, and bags, garment bags, and suitcases. A couple of rubber banded rolled up blueprints leaned in the corner beside the door. A yellow hard hat was sitting on a spindly looking entry table that looked barely able to hold its own weight. I swiped the hard hat and put it on my head.

She was stretched out on a long, orange plaid Herculon sofa, a TV dinner beside her on a TV tray. She rolled her eyes at me wearing her hard hat, and I dropped it on her coffee table next to my briefcase.

"Cousin," she said, "Good to see you. Stick a TV dinner in the oven for yourself and join me."

"Pass, Cousin," I said. I guess cousins were our thing, now. "Maybe we can order in."

I gave her a quick spiel about the accident, asked if she'd retained anyone, and dropped the retainer by the hard hat.

"This is what you do? Are you a lawyer?"

"No." I started to go into the explanation, but she waved it away. She signed the retainer, chuckling to herself.

Behind her, the windows provided a sweeping, tenth-floor view of Los Angeles.

"Nice place you've got here."

"Thanks."

"You know, I'm looking for a place."

"There are plenty of apartments open," she said. "Go talk to Flo, downstairs. She'll fix you up."

I bent down to upright a travel kit that was on its side. The hard surface was covered in stickers. Raffles Hotel, Singapore. A blue and red and white rectangle announcing Les Acascias Hotel, Paris Etiole, 47 rue des Acalas. A red oval with big white letters proclaiming Hotel Weisses, St. Wolfgang, the White Horse Inn. There were dozens more, covering all the luggage. I felt a little envy. I'd hardly ever been out of LA, certainly never out of the country. I didn't even own a passport.

"I didn't know I was in the presence of a world traveler."

"I left for Europe after law school," she said. "Eight years of school, in fact."

I couldn't help it. I groaned in sympathy. "I'd never survive eight years of school." It made her smile.

"When I was done with classrooms, I didn't know what to do next. I sold the house, sold almost everything. I got a lease on this place, and moved this stuff here. Something to come home to, you know. Then I locked the doors and went off to travel. I haven't been back long enough to unpack."

She stuck her fork into the mashed potatoes on her tray, and took a bite.

"You said you had something to show me?"

She pointed toward a table with a newspaper on it.

"You're a hero."

Today's copy of the LA Times was folded and sitting atop a small glass coffee table. I sank into a recliner, picked up the Times, and read about Melina's rescue from a burning car. I stood up again. It didn't matter how often I kept telling everyone, no one seemed to remember that the car hadn't been burning when I got her out. The facts didn't seem to matter. I turned the newspaper face down.

The last thing I want is to have my name and face on a newspaper. I'm plenty happy to have lots of friends all over town sending me cases, but I keep low key, and function under the radar. The media had jumped all over the news of the shooting and Tanis's death. Now this.

"They got your name wrong," she said. "They didn't put down there how you're really Superman."

I laughed. "I guess that makes you Lois Lane, since no one else calls me that."

I walked to the window and looked out. "Hell of a view you've got here. Looks like all of downtown is laid out for you like a banquet. How's the building during an earthquake?"

"Dunno. I haven't been here during a shaker. The building's only three years old."

"As long as you don't expect me to actually fly to the rescue. This is a seriously nice place."

"Take a look around," Melina said. "Give me a second, and I'll come with you."

"No need to get up. " I looked at that stack of pillows. "You're probably supposed to keep that foot raised higher than your heart."

"I am," she admitted. "You look around. I'll just sit here and keep the couch warm."

I looked at her, stuck on the couch. "But first, I have to do something." I filled my arms with her baggage, and took it all into the master bedroom. She had a king-sized brass bed, clearly an antique, with linens and a comforter that ranged in hues of gold to cream. For an instant, I pictured her there in the bed, naked, waiting for me. I got my mind out of her panties, and fetched the rest of the baggage.

"You got enough luggage, lady?" I yelled.

I returned to the couch.

"Why don't you give me the guided tour?"

She looked a little dismayed, then started to get up. "If you want."

"No, you don't have to get up." I took a few steps over to a room abutting the end of the kitchen.

"Ah," she nodded. "Go straight, and you're in the dining room. To your right, there's all of Los Angeles. To your left, through the doors, and you're in my kitchen. Gas stove. Frigidaire refrigerator-freezer. Dishwasher beside the sink. Closet for the washer and dryer if you want to buy one, but they have a laundry downstairs, too. Go through the other door back into the den."

I opened the door. A round tube of oatmeal fell on the floor. I returned it to the shelf.

"Wrong door," I yelled.

"That's the pantry. Try the other other door."

I did as she directed, and poked my head in. She saw me.

"Hi," she said.

I waved.

"Nice trip?"

"Not done yet."

"Ah. The bedrooms are off the hall," she said, "The hall is that way. The master bedroom is at the end, but you've already seen it."

"That's ok."

I pulled a dime out of my pocket, and dropped it in her hand.

"Oh, you want the ten cent tour." She pointed. "Hall, that-a-way. Linen closet. Bathroom. Bedroom. Master bedroom." The second bedroom was set up like a closet, double racks lining the walls. They were all empty.

It seemed strange.

It practically sold itself to me. Two bedrooms. Two full baths. One half bath. Open den big enough to work out in. Separate dining room.

The leasing manager was downstairs, as Melina said. She was a strange girl named Flo who said she lived in the building. I rode the elevator with Flo back up to the tenth floor. She led me in to a vacant apartment a few doors down from Melina's. It looked as if it had never been lived in. It was love at first sight.

Flo went back down to the office while I wandered around, convinced that I'd found the place for me. I checked out every room. I stepped in the tub and saw I fit below the high showerhead. I locked up, and when I found a line at the elevator, broke all land-speed records hightailing it to ask Flo, "Where do I sign?" I handed over the deposit check that included first and last month's rent, and a security deposit. I caught my breath for a second, wondering if I was doing the right thing. A whole year is a long time to be in one place. I put away the doubt because I was so hot for the apartment. It was great, and I could easily afford it. I gave Flo my beeper number, and promised her an extra fifty[3] if she nailed me a place on the tenth floor by Saturday. She refused the fifty, and told me that I could expect it to take two weeks. I couldn't hold back my disappointment. I told myself that two weeks wasn't that long. Talk about mixed feelings. I'd paid the cash, and I was still in my cruddy apartment. The wait was murder.

I'd been taking Cosmo's early class. On one Friday in December while I was still waiting for confirmation, Harry showed up in the middle of the class. He brought doughnuts for us, though he'd eaten a good many before we got to them. We finished the workout first.

"Just seeing you work that hard wears me out," Harry said. "You look good as new. Healing fast, my boy. Congratulations. I heard you moved into a high-rise."

"Still waiting for the keys, actually, but I'm looking forward to the move. If I get it, they're prorating December because I didn't want to wait until January. My first apartment came furnished by Goodwill. I'll be glad to be out of there." I picked up a doughnut, and told Harry what I was thinking, "This is early for you to be out and about, Harry."

I polished off a couple of glazed right off the bat.

---

[3] $50.00 in 1972 had the same buying power as $287.74 in 2016

"It's still early for me. But I have a little something for you." Harry pulled out a check and dropped it in my shirt pocket. He gave me a careful hug. I know he was still worried about the stitches.

I was touched by the hug. He didn't grab like most of the dudes I know, to whom everything is a feat of competitive strength. Maybe he was gentle because he was getting older, and was a little fragile, but it was hard for me to see Harry that way.

As I walked to the car, I don't know why I didn't think much about the check. Harry had never paid by check. Harry had never paid bonuses, and he really did not owe me anything. Maybe it was because I was on this street. I thought about how much of my life had gone down here, from when I had gone door to door begging for work when I thought my aunt had been arrested, to the day Pixie came to me crying that she was pregnant and homeless. I was a block from the parking lot my car had been in when Carson planted the dope to frame me. I was on the sidewalk where I had punched Carson out for putting Harry in danger by committing fraud.

 I got in to my car, trying to shake off the peculiar mood.

All these years, Harry paid me fifty dollars, or a small multiple of fifty, always in cash. Our arrangement had been simple. Fifty dollars per client. As I got older and bigger, the amount was the same, but seemed smaller and smaller. I guess that was inflation, or just my growing up. I was in the car in traffic before I pulled the check from my pocket, and glanced at it, expecting to see something like a fifty or a hundred. It was much more. I was flabbergasted.

I wheeled the car around, pulled into a restaurant parking lot, and sprinted back to Harry's office.

Barbara the receptionist was thrilled to see me. His whole staff was thrilled.

Everybody was in a celebratory frame of mind. More than a dozen people who were working there had jobs now because years ago, I'd bumped up Harry's business. I was glad to see it was as busy as ever, and it was great to see every-body. They had all dropped in to the hospital to see me last month.

Even before that, I wasn't a stranger. Not only did I still do the occasional job for Harry, there'd been a few cases Harry brought me to give to Jake. So I don't know what was up with everyone having to come over and act like I'd come back from the dead. Maybe I'd been worse off than I thought, and that stream of friends had been a stream of people who were expecting me to keel over.

I finally made it into Harry's office, and shut the door behind me. The old place had been refurbished when it should have been torn down. They couldn't take the sow's ear out of the silk purse. Now that I was living somewhere new, Harry's office felt dark and cramped. Harry's office was pretty much the same, except the paper clutter was now safely stowed away in file cabinets. That was a massive improvement. His furniture was pretty nice.

"New desk?"

"Same one I had." Harry chuckled.

Could have fooled me. Of course, there'd always been so much junk piled on it, it was impossible to tell if there had been a desk, a picnic table, or a Model T Ford parked underneath it all.

"I see you looked at the check," Harry said, still chuckling.

"What the hell is this for? This isn't our agreement. You always just gave me a per-client fee. I could get you clients from now to kingdom come and not earn all that."

"Jake's not paying you fifty dollars a case. You're a big boy now. I can pay you like one of the big boys."

I put the check face up on the shiny, polished surface of the desk and slid it in front of him.

"Seriously, Harry, why would you write me a check with that many zeroes? You're going to bankrupt yourself."

"Thanks to you I've made a hell of a lot of money from four years worth of cases you sent me. One case alone settled for a million dollars. I can afford to give you two hundred fifty thousand[4] as a thank you if that's what I want to do."

"Are you kidding me? What case? No case settles for that much."

He chuckled. "I will get to that. Let me explain the check. When you got arrested six or seven years ago, when you were still a kid, you could have ruined me."

"Never," I said.

"Let me finish," Harry said, "You're still so impatient. Instead, you said nothing. You were facing several years in jail if that judge hadn't given you a break. I felt sick over the charges when they put you away for the week. Several times I started to tell the prosecutor that it was all my fault, but Cosmo stopped me. He said that my confession wouldn't get you out; it would just get me in. Still, it makes me sick. I know you were under terrible stress, and your aunt was in agony. There is no money in this world that can pay you for that. I have felt years of guilt that I never thought to counsel you about the IRS. I should have walked you through what you needed to report on what I was paying you, or paid my own accountant to handle your taxes, especially when you bought the house and the car. I feel like it is my fault that you became a target. Even if someone hadn't planted drugs in your car, sooner or later Uncle Sam would have knocked at your door.

Anyway, I owe you, Mario. I wish I had been able to pay you like this when you were eighteen, and they released you from your week in prison. Six years ago, I carried too much debt to be able to be generous. This is my way to show you how much I love you, and respect you. If you are as smart as I think you are, this two hundred fifty thousand will open up a bright future for you. Believe me, I can afford it. Unfortunately you will have to report this on your

---

[4] $250,000.00 in 1972 had the same buying power as $1,438,716.55 in 2016

taxes, and no doubt will be hit with having to pay a chunk of it to Uncle Sam. As long as you pay off Uncle Sam and follow your heart, you can do no wrong."

I wanted to object but I was in shock.

"I don't know what to say. Thank you? And...thank you."

I never run out of words, but I couldn't find any.

Harry looked directly at me as he spoke.

"Kid, I'm thinking of retiring. Not sure when, but it's coming."

It wasn't like me to run out of words. I was getting soft. I got myself together.

"It doesn't have to be this much. Give me less. You can—"

Harry came around his desk. I am so damn tall that when he hugged me I had to bend down. Is it ironic that the man I most look up to, I had to look down to? He wasn't short, but he felt frail.

"Take the money and run to your accountant." Harry chuckled. "You deserve every penny of that check and then some. I love you, kid. Go turn the capital into the thing that's in your head." His eyes were bloodshot, and glistening with tears. His nose was red. He let go of me, grabbed a Kleenex and dashed it across his face.

I heard myself say, "I love you too, Harry."

We were hugging again. Maybe it was in that moment, I felt in my gut that he was the father I never had. I remembered the hundred dollar bill he had given me when I first met him. If he hadn't hired me, I'd have had a very different life. I'd probably be in jail beside Pélon. The tears rolled down my face. I didn't try to cover up my emotions.

"Go start a real life, son," Harry said, "I am so proud of you."

Early Saturday morning, Flo notified me via my beeper. When I arrived in person, she gave me a cheerful smile, and handed over the keys.

How often in life do you have the resources to do whatever you want? I felt like a million bucks. I liked the spaciousness of the apartment building, but it was a good thing because I was feeling bigger than myself, and needed the elbow room. Smaller rooms might not have contained me. Harry's gift was safely in the bank, and it's impossible to say how relieved I felt. I hadn't even realized how stressed I had been. Now that the stress was gone, I felt like I'd spent my whole life trapped in a tiny box, and now I was free.

The rooms had height and depth. Everything felt shiny and new. The extra features were bitching, especially in comparison to my old digs. It seemed flat out amazing to have a little market downstairs. It was convenient to Jake's. Melina living there was a nice perk.

Moving in was a piece of cake; it meant filling my car with boxes full of clothes, and making all of two trips. Pixie and Jo provided the extra hands, but I didn't let them upstairs yet. I told them to work out of Jake's until I called them to come in. I didn't want to go back to the crappy place to sleep, so I ordered a new king sized mattress and box spring from a shop that offered same-day delivery service. I went out to make a final sweep of the old unit to make sure I wasn't leaving anything I wanted to keep. I was gone when the mattress arrived, and Flo handled the delivery guys. I wasn't sure where I wanted it yet. That first night, I just threw a comforter on top of the plastic, and went to sleep. It's funny how sleeping in new places can be so exciting.

I hadn't bothered to furnish the place. Other than the new mattress in my front room, the only furniture I had was an oriental lacquered cupboard Cosmo had given me when I was eighteen.

Two weeks out of the hospital, Melina was still not one hundred percent, but she hobbled down the hall with a brown paper bag and paid me a visit on my first morning, before breakfast. I had been practicing moves and answered the door.

"Gorgeous piece," she said, looking at my weapon cabinet, and me in my shorts.

I unlocked the cabinet with a key and put away the heavy sword I had been using. She got a glimpse of my collection of martial arts weapons as I locked it back up.

"Are those real?"

"I use them when I work out." I had Escrima sticks, knives, nunchaku, and a couple of swords that I practiced with.

"Most of the men I know just play golf," she said. "So that's why you're so sweaty."

"I was about to take a shower," I said.

I walked back over to her. She handed me a paper bag, and braced herself on her crutch, before running her hand down my abdomen. "That's not from golf."

"I'm a little hooked on the workout," I admitted. "I've been doing karate since I was ten."

She hobbled over to the bed.

"Excuse me."

I went through my empty bedroom, tossed the shorts, and took a quick shower.

The apartments weren't side by side, but had the same view. It was pretty scenic from my uncurtained windows. I was sitting beside her when Melina unpacked her paper bag. It had bagels, cream cheese, and a tin of coffee. It was like a picnic.

"Would you prefer coffee or orange juice?" I asked.

"How about both?"

"Sounds good," she said, "I like it strong."

I went into the kitchen and rattled around. I started the coffee, poured juice, and made some more noise signifying my return with juice and coffee.

"You could use a table," Melina said, as I walked in. "Also, are you planning to leave your bed in the den? Most people actually put the bed in the bed-room."

"So the pretty girl is a little sarcastic. I like a girl who has grit."

She grinned.

"No, I don't plan on sleeping in the den. I just haven't decided yet if I'm going to use the Master bedroom as a bedroom or my office."

"The Master bedroom should be the Master bedroom," she said, "because the bathroom is en suite."

"If you say so. I don't really think much about things like that."

"It's just like my place," she said.

"Almost," I agreed.

The only difference was that Melina's place was full of heirlooms and furniture from her family's house; all I had was a bed, and a closet with some clothes. I didn't have anything in my bathroom or kitchen cabinets, and the rest of the closets were empty too.

"You need to go shopping."

I was reluctant. Shopping is not my favorite thing. I put up some resistance. Shopping conjured up pictures of wandering around Los Angeles wasting working hours and shoe leather wandering around department stores. I remembered when I was a kid, Aunt Carmen had loved to go to Dearden's and window-shop for furniture she'd never buy. Once I had surprised her with a new house, full of furniture she'd picked out. It was a satisfying memory. I thought maybe shopping wouldn't be so bad when there was enough money around to cover the bill.

"What's wrong? Can't you afford it?" Melina looked concerned.

"Of course I can." If anything, that was a challenge I could not resist. I barely managed to keep from whooping about how much I could afford after Harry's gift, even if I'd had to hand half of it to my accountant for the IRS.

"I can get anything I want."

"I know right where to go. Okay then, it's a date." She went out the door, wielding that crutch of hers like a manic jouster. I was still reeling a little that I somehow wrangled myself a date to go furniture shopping .

I called downstairs for my car, and when we came out of the elevator, the doorman had it waiting. Melina wasn't impressed since she's been in the building a while, but I'm still jazzed by it. I tried to look sophisticated, like I'm used to luxuries like doormen and security guards.

Once I had her stowed in the passenger seat, she all but took the wheel.

"Turn right."

"Who's driving here, you or me?"

"I know where to go. Trust me," she said.

"Never trust anyone who says 'Trust me,'" I told her, as I turned right.

Five minutes later, we were stuck in traffic. Melina was tapping her foot, impatiently, craning her head out the window, trying to see what was holding us up.

"Looks like an accident up ahead," I told her. It's almost funny how I had given myself some days off but now work seemed to be following me around. I didn't feel like I could drive past an accident without making some kind of connection with it.

I had a pen in my pocket, and a business card ready, in case the wreck looked promising. I'd been planning to write down the car's license plate number. There's a girl we call, Pedra, from the old neighborhood who can check up on the numbers. She works at the police department. She'd been a friend of one of Carson's sisters. More importantly, she'd married an immigrant, and had brought him to me to bring to Harry to get his immigration status straightened out. The plan to call Pedra went out the window when traffic blocked my view of the plates. Then I saw Johnny Rodriguez in his tow truck hauling a demolished station wagon. He pulled into traffic not too far ahead of me. After our recent doings together, I was waiting for his call.

A few hours later, my beeper went off.

"Wholesale is the way to go," Melina told me. We were in a tall building not far from our apartments. I was only paying half-attention to Melina, distracted by the pager. It had indeed been Johnny who had called. Outside of the public restroom on the third floor, I found a store phone booth where I called him back, and then called to get Jo on the case. Jo wasn't at her phone; she was already out on a case, so I left Johnny's number and information on the machine. Then I was back to shopping. I felt like a kid playing hookey. The showrooms were laid out wholesale-style for furniture store owners and decorators. I have no idea how Melina managed to get us a guest pass, but there we were. Just Melina and me, a couple of commercial buying agents, and fifteen floors of every kind of furniture you could imagine.

In addition to being nosy as hell, Melina was turning out to be a control freak. She dictated the order of floors we were shopping in, not from the top down, with some logic, but following the path of some drummer in her head. At least her control was in an area that bores me. You'd have to put me in a pink polka-dot room before I'd object to someone else doing the decorating. I took no joy in picking out tufted leather sofas and chairs.

"All I want is for it to be comfortable," I said.

She seemed to be in heaven. I picked out an entire suite, with everything matching. She insisted I lose all the matching pieces, and go eclectic. She picked some alternative pieces for me to choose from.

"Look at that!" I pointed out the round bed, which was something of a curiosity. I'd never seen one in person. The next thing I knew, I was replacing the king I'd just bought with a round bed with a mirrored headboard. I admit it was flat-out badass. I got a couple of big television sets, a stereo, and kitchen full of dishes and gadgets that would never see the light of day. The truth is that while Melina had wandered into the kitchen showroom, I snuck off and from a pay phone at the showroom, I called to schedule the return of the king-sized mattress later in the week. Then I found the floor with office furniture, and was measuring a spectacular, masculine, solid wooden desk to make sure it would fit through the door. It was a thing of beauty, with tooled brass handles and fretwork. Not only did I get the best desk and chair I could find, I found the perfect sofa for the office. I lay down on it to make sure it was comfortable. I found a couple of captain's chairs to flank the desk, and a comfortable leather recliner that Archie Bunker (or Jake) would kill for. I chose a couple of drop leaf tables to use as desks when the girls came over to work, and got shelves to organize the walk-in closet in the office as a supply room. The second bedroom was going to be a killer office.

Melina called around and found round bed linens at the May Company. They were a rare commodity. When I saw they were available, I got sets in flannel for winter, cotton for day to day, and satin for when I was feeling adventurous.

As we shopped for me, I kept a running list of things Melina seemed to want for herself. I actually scribbled notes about her choices on the back of business cards. I always have business cards handy. Before we left, I handed the sales clerk the list of things Melina had liked, and I paid for them. It was supposed to be a secret. I didn't tell her.

I admit that while we were there, I had a flashback of Dearden's Furniture where my aunt bought our furniture for that tiny apartment where we lived in ELA. Dearden's was the farthest thing from this. When we'd lived off of Hollenbeck Park, window-shopping at Dearden's had been a regular event for my aunt. We were poor, not that I realized it as a child. Dearden's furnishings were utilitarian and affordable rather than fine or fashionable; but even that cheap stuff was more than we could afford. Window-shopping had been dreaming. We started with a black and white television, and soon after that, my aunt bought a color set. None of my friends had a color television. I remember the television being taken away from us because a payment had not been made. It had been a key motivator behind why I started working at ten years old, along with Carson telling me my aunt had been arrested, and that I had to post bail. (It hadn't been true. She'd been off being a midwife and delivering a baby.) With my first week's wages in hand, I took a streetcar to downtown LA, went in to the furniture store and settled out the past due balance. That night our color television was back. Aunt Carmen gave me a terrible scold after Dearden's brought back the TV, but I caught her watching it after she'd sent me to bed. The memory brings a smile to my face, even now.

The reality of shopping was not what it would have been if I could have made a quick trip back in time to give myself a couple hundred dollars. I was excited over having all this fine new stuff, but a small part of me resented that actual shopping had taken hours out of my day. I was resigned that it was a necessary evil, even the rushed same-day delivery that was an expensive extra. Melina said that the seven thousand I'd paid for everything was a fraction of what I would have paid at a regular commercial furniture store.

I tipped the two hefty delivery guys extra. They were a couple of dudes named Norman and Santiago. With a little incentive, they were happy to moonlight as movers. They were in on my secret surprise for Melina, and didn't let on that her stuff was at the back of their delivery van. They were supposed to hang around after we were done with my place, and then surprise her with her stuff. The three of us danced furniture around the apartment, with Melina conducting. My beeper went off six times, and I gritted my teeth and kept hauling furniture around. She was a perfectionist, so we moved and arranged and re-arranged, until finally all the rooms lived up to the ideal she saw in her head. The pair of Joe Six-Packs left, happy as clams with a couple of new twenty dollar bills [5]and a six-pack each. Melina and I shared a glass of red wine before she went home to crash.

To be honest, I rushed her out. I walked her back to her apartment, and

---

[5] $20.00 in 1972 had the same buying power as $115.10 in 2016

held the door for her. As soon as she was inside, I hotfooted it down the hall back to my place and hit the phone to make up for the lost day. First I ran through the beeper calls; a couple were confirmations from Jo, but a couple were cases. I took notes, and promised call-backs, made appointments, wrote out details. I handled some other calls that I had not returned at the showroom, or that had rung while Melina and I were drinking wine on the new couch. I touched base with Jo, then made my routine calls. There are sources I normally stay in touch with, just because they are low key types who need hand-holding to keep them primed, or they, for various reasons, will just stop sending me new cases. You might say my work haunted me, but it is just what I do. I felt guilty when I slowed down or stopped, even for a good reason like moving and setting up my new place. I had to find a way to have a life, without having life get in the way of my work. I needed to figure a way to have it all without one costing the other.

About fifteen minutes into my calls, I heard a knock and a muffled squeal, and knew that Melina's furniture had arrived. I sat just inside my door, grinning to myself, then fell back into work.

"Johnny's case was good," Jo said, over the phone. "We got them signed."

I scratched Johnny off the list, and was about to go on to the next item when there was a knock at the door.

"I'll call back in the morning," I said. "Sounds like I have company." I had expected Melina to come by after the furniture had been brought up to her place, but I didn't know her well enough to guess how she would respond.

It was Melina at the door.

I had some quip on my lips, but Melina knocked it out of my head as she walked in. She handed me a check.

"What's this for?" I asked.

I followed her as she hobbled to my living room and sank into my new sofa.

"Sweetie, thank you for getting all that stuff for me, but I can pay my way."

"I just wanted to thank you," I said. "I bet what I got for you was less than I'd have to pay a decorator to do what you did today. I had the cash so I paid for the stuff you liked along with mine. What's the harm?"

We ended up playing hot potato with the check for a couple of minutes. It went back and forth.

"You keep it," I said.

"No, really, you keep it," she replied.

Eventually I folded it and stuck it in her pocket.

She gave up and kissed me on the cheek. "You're so sweet."

"So now what?" I said, "Wanna do something?" Like roll around in my new bed.

"I'm tired," she said. "I can't stay."

It was a little awkward as she left. I had some sense that we were going to kiss, and some sense that we weren't going to. But she didn't even want me to walk her down the hall to her place. I just stood in my open doorway, and watched as she traversed the hall. She waved at me as she went in her place. Her door shut with a definite click. I followed suit. When I turned around, and headed back to my phone, I found the check I'd given her on my coffee table.

I ran into Melina daily. Our meetings occurred when I was heading in or out, or going somewhere in the building. She was more or less homebound, but still got out of her place around noon, and went to the downstairs market. Even though it was just in passing, she started feeling very familiar.

I had been spending money like crazy, but I had not touched the money from Harry. I considered it my nest egg. Business was good. Jake paid me every couple of days. He said he wanted to keep my cash flow healthy. He'd been a lawyer for a long time, so maybe he thought he knew from experience what it cost me to produce the flow of business I streamed in his direction. He had no clue how much I actually paid out to some of my sources. It wasn't cheap, but at least we were kicking ass with new cases.

I was on the phone with Jo and Pixie constantly. I had to beep them. Most of the time, they were out somewhere and they had to stop at a pay phone to call me back. I kept them working. With two phone lines connected, I kept them busy in the field. We were using Jake's as a temporary home base, but busy means out in the field, driving somewhere or at someone's home.

"I'm dead curious about your place," Jo said.

From Pixie, it was a steady stream of "Can we come over?"

"Not yet," I told them both. I didn't want them over until everything was ready.

Melina was growing on me, but neither of us made sexual advances. Melina was a little strange. Maybe it was the age difference, her being ten years older than me.

Fuck it, I figured. If I had to get my rocks off, I'll go find some girl with the hots for me and we'd have a little mutual get-together. I had a feeling she'd come around. Meanwhile, I was settling in. I'd knock on her door and say something like "I'm making a run for office supplies." We'd go on an epic spree. I'd haul everything up and spend the rest of the day organizing. One day it was groceries. Another, it was cleaning supplies. I don't know why I did it when going out with Melina was an exercise in jealousy. I'm not usually a jealous guy, and she's not mine to be jealous over. She wore short skirts, and flirted constantly. The hand cast and that cast on her foot didn't slow her down one iota. She was so hot that I could hardly take my eyes off of her. Everywhere we went, from office supply to grocery, she caught and played the attention of the males. In the hospital on the day we met, Melina and I had started the cousin thing. Now there was no reason for it, but it had stuck. We introduced each other as cousins. She was no Tanis, but she reminded me of her in many ways. Like Tanis, she was a professional, even if she was a lawyer instead of a nurse. Like

Tanis, she was ten years older, and confident. Like Tanis, she drew men's eyes. Unlike Tanis, Melina was a mystery, to me anyway. All the flirting she did made her seem like a nympho, but we hadn't gotten close to doing it. I didn't try to figure it out. Instead of making out, we talked and talked. Melina talked of her travels through Europe, of places I'd never heard of. I enjoyed hearing her tell her stories and watched her as she spoke.

After hitting Cosmo's six a.m. class, I met Jo and Pixie at Jake's every morning. That was when we made our daily updates. We went over notes, and I looked over cases they signed. Sometimes I got beeped and responded immediately from Jake's, but most of the referrals came when I was at home by the phone.

I was impressed at how well they signed new cases, and told them so.

"Sweet," I said. "I should retire. You guys are fucking wonderful."

"Don't kid yourself, sport," Jo said. "The regulars are no cakewalk. They've been dealing with you for years. They don't want to give it up for me to handle. By comparison, the new sources are a piece of cake." Jo said. "Your sources are pretty protective of you."

"Starting tonight, I will call everyone you sign that day to give them some feedback. Give me a list of everyone we signed since I moved. I'll make contact with them all. By tomorrow, I'll have reassured everyone."

"That should do it," Jo said. "I think they know you're back on your feet, and knee deep in the business again."

"From now on, if you can tell that old clients or contacts prefer I come out, let me know. I'll go out and sign the case."

The boxes were gone, the clothes hung, the furniture where I wanted it to be, curtains installed, and the office was a thing of beauty. I invited the girls to have dinner, and check out the pad. I have a modern kitchen, a dishwasher, and enough cooking gadgets to give Julia Child a wet dream, but no actual food to make into a meal. The girls brought over four bags filled with Mexican food from Barragan's Restaurant on Sunset Boulevard, about ten minutes from my apartment. When they got to the door, I opened it, bowed, and said, "Welcome to Casa Luna." I gave them the grand tour. It was just supposed to be a social evening, but Jo said the office made her fingers itch, and she disappeared in there like an organizing whirlwind.

An hour later, Melina joined us. Jo and Pixie, and Melina and I sat at my new dining room table, and ate like the four little pigs.

Melina fit in as if she'd known Pixie and Jo her whole life. The swinging sixties might be over, but the dinner was all very democratic and jealousy-free. Melina showed up in a weird get-up of her yellow hard hat and matching bright yellow coveralls. No one said anything about it which meant Jo and Pixie were on their rare good behavior.

Pixie and I go back to our early teens when we'd hit every position in the Kama Sutra on a regular basis. Our intimacy never got more possessive than a handshake. I'd had a tight, professional working relationship with Jo for six years but we'd done it a bunch of times and recently even had a threesome with Pixie. Jo was in a special situation. She was devoted to her husband and kids. She wasn't so much a swinger, but her husband was disabled and in a wheelchair. She never talked about his condition. I don't know how or even if they managed sex, and it wasn't like it would be something I would ask about. All I did know is that Jo was a delight I adored in my own way.

Melina was a whole new element that I hadn't figured out yet.

We spent two hours talking after the food was gone, then Jo and Pixie picked up. Both girls gave me a wet kiss on the lips right before Melina's eyes.

Melina stayed after they left.

The forced air furnace obediently maintained the pleasant temperature that I had set on the thermostat, and the machinery gave off a hum of white noise. We both wore sweats, socks, and no shoes although it was cold outside. That round bed in my bedroom was there just waiting for anything, but we were in the living room. The lights were dim, and the gas log burned colorfully in the fireplace. This was my first fireplace in any place I had ever lived. Instead of romance, we were talking about our past. Today, it wasn't about her travels.

Melina was easy to engage. I don't know if it was her personality or the red wine we'd been sharing, but before I knew it, I had opened up and told her about the shooting. She knew I had been injured, but she never read about it. I think it had happened before she was back in the country. I had not gone to bed with her, so she had not seen my scars. I found myself baring the scars you can't see.

I turned away when I got to the heart of it.

"I lost Tanis," I said, feeling deeply emotional. "She wasn't really my girl-friend. I didn't see her every day, but I saw her enough, and we were close. We were great in bed and out. We would meet for lunch or breakfast and most times it was business that brought us together. I never took her to a movie or even to dinner. But losing her just crushed me."

Melina moved closer. She put one arm around me, and caressed my face with the other hand. "Poor baby," she said. "I'm so sorry."

Her face was close to mine. I felt her tears. Maybe they were mine, or both of ours. We were silent for a long time. Then I talked about the two children Tanis had left behind with her sister.

Melina asked about Niley, and so I told her. She asked like she really needed to know, as though she was concerned about Tanis, about the kids, even about the sister left behind to carry the burden. Melina asked questions as if she were painting a picture of my life with Tanis, and Tanis's life with her children and sister.

"I took my team to their apartment. Jo and Pixie and I walked through it. I almost broke down when we went through her room. It smelled like her fragrance."

Melina asked, "What fragrance was it?"

"Joy."

I felt good talking about Tanis. Maybe it was the lawyer inside Melina that made her so inquisitive, but the reasons didn't matter. It was a relief. I felt good unburdening myself to her. All this time I've had this grief about Tanis buried inside me. Maybe I was finally getting it out of my system. By the time I stopped, the only thing I had not opened up about was Carson, and my suspicions. I even told her about the criminal charges that cost me everything, the prison sentence that was supposed to be two years and turned out to be a little over a week, the probation/parole I had to serve, the fines I had to pay, the IRS money I had to pay after I got credited for the money they had confiscated from my bank account, and the forfeiture of my Corvette. I told her about my relationship with my Aunt Carmen. I didn't tell her about Pixie's past, but I did tell her how I brought her to my aunt six years ago when she was a pregnant kid, and that she was family to me.

"Is she your girl?"

"That's hard to explain," I said. "Maybe she was once, when we were in our teens."

"But you still have sex with her."

"Yes," I heard myself say. "My aunt would not approve, but we sneaked around that for years. I don't want to give up how she makes me feel. I don't mean just because of the sex." I took a deep breath. "And then there's Jo."

"So you are in love with both of them?"

"Pixie and Jo are my treasures. I guess we all love each other, but we're not in love. It's not the kind of love you are asking me about. Pixie is free to do whatever she wants, and Jo has a husband in a wheelchair."

"Is it all about you?" Melina said. "Or you're some kind of swinger."

"That's just a word," I said. "Are you mocking me?" Melina would have no idea, but sex was not all about me. Pixie and I had started fooling around at fourteen. We had called it my sex lessons, and she had been a very good teacher. If she had a thought in her head, it came out of her mouth. She held nothing back. She'd been a hooker, and knew more about sex than anyone. I hadn't known for years that she was my own age. But she had been very clear about what I needed to do to make a girl happy.

"No." Melina laughed, but only a little laugh. "You are friends. They work for you. From what you said, there are no catches. You're all free. Every man that has ever come near me wants to control everything about me."

"You need to tell me about that," I said.

"Maybe I will someday."

"You have me at a disadvantage. I've spent half the night baring my soul, and you've said nothing at all."

"I'm telling you now, I'm not looking for a relationship. I just want a friend."

"Okay, Cousin. So dish."

She laughed. "Where do I start?"

"Start where you like."

She got up. I followed her to my bedroom where we lay on the bed facing each other, fully clothed.

"I hope you don't mind," she said, "but I need you close in order to share this with you."

She was very serious. We lay there in the dark face-to-face. I concentrated on ignoring the tremendous hard-on I had pushing through my sweats. I wondered what all the drama was about, why she wanted to be close in the dark. I wondered if the story she was going to tell was embarrassing, or if some son of a bitch raped her.

"Tell me."

She was quiet for a while; then she began talking in a low, emotionless voice that was all the more terrible for its silence.

She told me about her parents' Mexican Foods Market in Echo Park. The store included a meat department, and sold cooked meals to go that included menudo and tamales. The family lived in a home behind the store. Many times they were so busy, they all went home together late, after closing the store. Melina grew up in the store. She loved it, and spent every waking moment there, when she wasn't in school. She learned everything about running the market. She knew every job, from sweeping up, to green grocery, even to the butchering. She worked elbow to elbow with her father's fourteen employees, who were like an extended family to her. She spoke of how her mother could single-handedly manage everything when her dad went out to buy supplies or to the bank. She loved being around the shoppers. She organized shelves. She pushed for her father to buy new food products that she found in catalogues. Then her mother died of cancer, and her father ran the business.

"I was always mad at my mother," Melina said. "She left me. As an adult, I know she didn't choose to die. I was young when she died, and she was just gone. It was like she just left. I know she died, and it wasn't on purpose, but I felt betrayed. All I could think was how could she? Have you ever felt that kind of betrayal?"

"Actually, I have. But it wasn't accidental. It was intentional. And nobody died."

"Explain," she said.

"It's nothing big like your mother dying. I mean, my mother died like yours but not when I was a kid. She died when I was born. I never knew her. My aunt raised me. I never knew my mother, but I never missed her, either. But I had some friends growing up. We were close, like brothers. The three of us would have done anything for each other. Anything. One of them betrayed me." Thinking about Carson ruined my mood.

"So who was this paragon?"

"His name was Carson," I said.

"Carson," she repeated. She had a funny look on her face. I had no clue what was going on in her head. "Introduce me to him."

"No, and hell no," I said, staring. "Why would you ask such a thing?"

"I'm good at reading people. If I meet him, I can get a feel for him. I want to know your friends."

"If you think we're friends, you have not been paying attention. We are not friends. I used to trust him, maybe, when I was six. When we were teenagers, I taught him the ropes of the kind of work I do. P.I. really."

"Private Eye?"

"No," I laughed. "Personal injury."

She laughed too. "I should have caught that, being a lawyer. I don't know that much about personal injury cases, though."

It took some more coaxing on her part, but I told her how at eighteen, Carson had been faking cases and handing them over to Harry, the honest lawyer who was like a father to me.

She asked a lot of questions. The whole time, I felt like I was on the witness stand, and I was trying to convict Carson, while she was his defense attorney. I told her how I'd kicked his ass for putting Harry in danger. I told her how the very next day, the police had found a stash of pot planted in my car, which caused the shit storm in my life when I was eighteen, that I had already told her about. "Carson was always something of a con artist. It was like my own brother turning on me. I still see him around sometimes, chasing my cases, but I avoid him like the plague."

Melina told me how after her mother had passed away, her aunt had come from Mexico and stayed to attend to the house and to Melina. Two months before she graduated from high school, she was at the store later than usual. She was in the living area on the phone with a girlfriend.

"I heard my father shouting. I couldn't make out exactly what he was saying. He handed over all the paper money in the main register. He told the two *pendejos* to take the money and leave."

I could feel Melina's heart racing against my chest, even through the sweats. She trembled and began to cry. I held her tight. Her tears pressed against my face.

"I heard a shot, then a second shot. I heard screams, not knowing whose they were. I grabbed the shotgun my dad kept in the back room, and ran through the open door to the store. I was holding the shotgun straight in front of me, and found myself facing two masked men. They saw me. I hadn't been quiet. Both men raised their guns to shoot me, but I managed to fire. It threw me to the floor. It wasn't until I was down that I saw my father in a pool of blood. I shouldn't be telling you this."

"Go ahead, Melina. I'm so sorry this happened to you."

She sobbed. I held her close.

I thought about the rage I had toward Carson. I wondered if she was living with that kind of anger. No wonder she carried a gun in her purse.

"Did they get away?"

She shook her head. "The pellets hit them both. One died. The other was sent to prison for murder. They were brothers. Can you believe it?"

We lay in silence for what seemed a long time. I realized that Melina had shot and killed one of those assholes. I wondered how she felt about it. I wasn't going to ask.

"Remember at the hospital, you noticed the gun in my purse?"

"I can understand why you carry it."

"No," she said. "You don't. One of those brothers survived. One of them is in prison, waiting to get out, waiting to come after me."

"He won't get out," I said.

"He'll get out. The dead brother is the one who killed my father. This one was younger, a juvie. He keeps trying for parole, and one of these days, he'll get it." She sat up and hugged herself.

I thought about Pélon. He would know what to do about this, but I hadn't known Melina long enough to talk about him. I could be proactive here, and take care of this. She didn't need to know.

"How about some tea?"

Tea was the last thing on my mind, but I agreed.

She got up. I followed her out of the bedroom to the kitchen. She put the teapot on the stove.

Because I'd done some shopping in the market downstairs with Melina, we had coffee (me), and tea (Melina), peanut butter and jelly spread on regular white bread.

"You make the sandwiches," she said. She poured hot water in a teacup, and dropped a tea bag in.

While I popped a couple of slices of bread into the toaster, and took out the peanut butter and some of Aunt Carmen's homemade red pepper jelly, Melina shook out the tablecloth, and wafted it over the little dinette in the kitchen. She set the table as if it were some kind of dinner party, with glasses for water, and juice, and our respective cups of coffee and tea. It seemed very strange and adult to me. The eastern edge of the sky was brightening, and I realized it was closer to daybreak than bedtime. We had talked through the night. I don't remember doing that with anyone before.

"I'll be right back," Melina said, heading through the front door.

I scraped peanut butter on the first two pieces of toast while the second slices turned brown and got fragrant. I spread the jelly, and cut the sandwiches into halves, diagonally, and set them on the dinette on a couple of mid-sized salad plates from my new set of dishes. Melina returned with a carafe of orange juice. She poured orange juice into my new wine glasses, and iced water in my new water glasses.

"Fancy," I said.

I pulled the seat out for her, and she sat. She stirred two spoons of sugar into her hot tea, and waited until I was sitting to her right. I drowned my coffee in cream and sugar.

She bit off one corner of the sandwich, chewed a couple of times and made a face.

"Spicy!" She grabbed her water and finished it in one long gulp. I fetched her more and sat down again. She peeled opened the sandwich and looked at it. She dipped her fingertip in the red jelly, touched it to her tongue, and put the bread back over the sandwich.

"So, not strawberry," she said, "What is this?"

"Aunt Carmen's jalapeño jelly. Red pepper jelly."

"That was a surprise."

"If it's too hot, I—" I scooted the chair back, planning to fix her a plain peanut butter, but she stopped me.

"No, I like this. I was just taken by surprise."

"I guess I like it spicy," I told her.

"Me too," she said. "I admire anyone who can cook like this. I learned to do lots of stuff, but never spent any time in a kitchen."

"I'm no cook either," I said. "I guess I'm pretty lucky Aunt Carmen can cook. I can't wait to bring her here to take a look at the place."

I wondered if Melina had any family still living, but that would be a hard question to ask. Instead, I said, "Do you have any other family here?"

"There's some family in Mexico, but I don't really know them."

I saw that her tea was gone, and got up. I replaced the teabag, and poured in more hot water, and sat down.

"Thanks," she said, dunking the teabag, and adding some spoons of sugar.

"What did you do? After the robbery, I mean."

"Three days after the funeral I graduated from high school. My aunt was the only family I knew, and she stayed with me. I had lots of friends, kids from high school, everyone from work. My friends were kind to me, all very sympathetic to the tragedy. I appreciated the concern but hated the attention. I told you already how everybody at the store was like an extended family."

"What happened to the store?"

She sipped her tea and finished off her sandwich.

"Before the funeral, Angel showed up. Angel Lara. He was my father's friend, and an insurance agent. He had advised my dad from way back when my parents came from Mexico. To me, he was a real angel. He told me how my mom and dad had life insurance. I was eighteen, so Angel helped me take over my father's bank accounts, and did the paperwork so I was the named beneficiary at the bank on all the accounts."

She poured me more coffee.

"Are you sure you want to hear this?" she asked.

"Sure."

"I was doing all this stuff at the bank, and my father was still at the morgue waiting for an autopsy. It was tearing me up, but I know he would have wanted me to put all the affairs in order. I had cried so much the night it happened, you'd think there were no tears left. I was overwhelmed. I wouldn't have had any idea what to do, if not for Angel. Angel took me to see another of my father's friends, a lawyer named Carlos Munoz, on Sunset. I knew him as a customer at the market, and he had known my parents for years. Carlos got me a probate attorney, and we shut down the store. It was one of the hardest decisions I ever made, because it meant breaking up that big family, you know? I just didn't think I was up to running it by myself. Angel had handled the payroll before for my father, so he had the contact information, made all the announcements, and arranged severance pay. I sold all the merchandise to a wholesaler who bought out everything when a store went broke. My father had mortgage insurance on the building where the market was and also insurance on our home. The insurance paid off the mortgages, and soon after my graduation when the death certificate was issued, the insurance paid me the death benefits. I didn't have to work."

She told me how she had enrolled at USC, and how, during her sophomore year, her aunt died of a heart attack.

"I found her on the kitchen floor," she said.

"I'm so sorry," I told her.

"It was a long time ago," she said. "I moved out of there the same day. I arranged to live on campus. A couple that I knew from the store asked to lease the house, and they moved in and lived there for a couple of years. After they moved out, I didn't bother leasing it out again. Then after I graduated from college, I went straight into law school. I passed the bar. That's when I rented the apartment here. I kept what I wanted, sold everything else except the land. The market building was in bad shape, so I sold off the parts for surplus building materials, and razed what was left. I had plans for a new market. You know I took off for Europe. I had just gotten back when I was in the accident. I hadn't even unpacked yet."

"You grew up fast," I said.

We were sitting shoulder to shoulder at the corner of the table. I put one hand over hers, leaned over and kissed her softly on the cheek.

"Cuz, I feel like I've known you for a long time."

"Thank you for letting me unload all this on you."

We cleared the table, rinsed off the dishes, and put everything except the wine glasses in the dishwasher. It was the first time it had been loaded in this apartment.

"I wish I had pancakes or something else to offer you," I said.

Melina had opened the freezer for more ice, and noticed what was in there.

"Let's live dangerously," she said, pulling out the ice cream.

We chased this early morning feast with samples of the three different flavors of ice cream that were in my freezer. I know the philosophy of karate is one of balance, and maybe I was the only karate master who was a sugar junkie; but then my teacher, Cosmo, had a weakness for doughnuts.

"Sorry," I said, "I don't normally keep groceries to speak of—just whatever condiments I wanted to add to my usual diet of take-out food."

After a couple of spoons of ice cream, we were both yawning. It wasn't quite sunrise yet.

"You want to lie down again?" I asked.

Melina nodded.

We returned to the bedroom. The instant we hit the bed, we were out like a light bulb.

In the morning, I woke up alone.

I sent Jo to the library to dig up everything she could about Melina's history. She came back with photocopies of several articles. One of them talked about Melina's father's shooting by one of the Vicario brothers. The one in prison was called Bruno. I filed the information away for future reference. Much later that same day, I went out in the field with Jo and Pixie. I had a couple of cases of tequila in the trunk, and we were making a run on the body shops. Just a little reminder that I was still kicking and in the game.

Jo said, "Melina is beautiful, isn't she?"

"Sure is," I agreed.

"So is it serious?"

Pixie, at her own insistence, was driving, chauffeur-style. I was with Jo in the back seat of my car, but that didn't stop her looking back at us.

"Keep your eyes on the road," Jo scolded.

"Mario, is it serious?" Pixie repeated.

"No way, serious. Melina is a good friend, that's it."

"She's awful pretty," Pixie said.

"You two are awful pretty too, and I managed not to be serious with either of you."

"How many times have you had Melina?" Jo asked.

"Yeah, how many times?"

"I haven't had sex of any kind with her."

"I'm not buying that," Jo said.

Pixie looked back, and opened her mouth. Jo interrupted.

"If you look back here one more time, pull over. I'm driving."

"Speaking of sex," Pixie said, "I want to try out that round bed of yours."

She didn't turn around, but flipped down the sun visor, and used that mirror to look into the back seat. She took off her sunglasses, snapped them shut and tapped them impatiently against her lip.

Jo looked at me. I could see the question in her eyes.

"How about we have a little celebration after we deliver the baskets? That bed of mine hasn't been christened yet."

Jo reached up and tapped Pixie, "Do I hear a yes or a no?"

"That's a yes from me," Pixie said.

By February, Pixie was good enough at signing cases that I got her a car. Lainey was in full-day kindergarten. Pixie worked mostly from eight till four on weekdays. Aunt Carmen pitched in evenings and weekends watching Lainey when the day ran over, because my policy was that we worked 24/7. Pixie quickly got hooked on the income, and gave up her piddling restaurant job. Pixie's work eased some of the pressure off Jo, but not much as I expected. We were that busy with new business. Always when it rained, even a little, it became crazy busy. I never had enough hands, and wasn't able to be in two places at once. Now, it wasn't only me out there. Since I was back out in the field, that was three of us. Jake was delighted. It was triple the cases.

Daily, and sometimes twice daily, the three of us met up either at Jake's or my apartment to go over cases. Our organized approach meant we didn't only get the retainers; we got authorizations to get medical records and police reports. These were documents that the clients signed over to Jake. This enabled his people to work right away. While I hated the idea of signing and dropping off, we were so busy that that was the most efficient way to handle it.

Ever since Jo had started signing on her own, I called back everyone she signed. Now I did the same for Pixie. It was more than touching base with clients. I made myself available to answer any questions they had. I developed the client relationship, even when I didn't know them from before. We kept files on the families, so we could look on a card, and keep personal details straight. I had this giant Rolodex where I kept all personal details about the clients on a card. I wrote them longhand, but when Jo had time, she'd pull out the card and type it. It was like a rolling bible with hundreds and hundreds of clients I had signed over the years.

Jo got to my place first.

"Pixie is signing a case," Jo said. "She's a half hour behind me."

I offered her peanut butter from the jar I was spooning, but she got a Coke from the refrigerator instead.

"Are you pooped out?" I asked.

"No more than you are," she replied with a smile. Jo always smiled. If she was stressed she seldom showed it.

"Are you cool with all this work?"

"It's so much better than being a desk jockey. I should have nagged you to put me in the field years ago," she laughed. "I love the money, and so do my kids and husband. They don't seem to care I'm not around very much."

"Aww," I said, "Let me console you. Come sit next to Papa." I gave up the peanut jar. We sat on the couch.

"I love working for you, Mario," she said, giving me a kiss on the lips. "Can't beat the perks."

"What perks?"

"This," she said.

"Is that all you got?" I said, as if she hadn't given me a mind-blowing kiss.

She smiled and put both arms around my neck and gave me a long deep kiss that gave me an instant hard on.

"Want a quickie?"

In under a minute, I was on my back, and Jo was on top.

"You're on the top of my list of things to do tonight, hot mama," I said, kissing her.

"Shut up. You talk entirely too much," she said in to my open mouth. "Just fuck me."

Pixie never knocked. She found us sitting at the dining room table eating ice cream smothered in Hershey's chocolate syrup. Her path to the kitchen brought her past the couch, where she stopped and sniffed. She crossed her arms, and looked at me irritably.

"Did you leave any for me?" Pixie said.

"Two tubs," Jo said, pointing out the obvious.

"Gotta have some of that," Pixie, said running for a spoon. "But I wasn't talking about the Angelfood." She sat down and did her damage to the ice cream.

"Did you do it once or twice? Like I said, any leftovers? Did you leave any for me?"

Jo stuck her tongue out at Pixie, and laughed a little. "So nosey."

I had put away more than my share of ice cream, and was thinking of all the calories I would have to burn the next morning at Cosmo's. I patted my stomach. "Next time baby. Jo drained me."

"Bitch!" Pixie said. "I guess I'll have to do with ice cream. If I get fat, it's your fault, Jo."

"Okay, let's look at the cases," I said, interrupting their game. "Let's get through this so you can scat out of here to get some rest before the next wave."

We finished in record time. I was soon in my shorts falling asleep in front of the television in the den. I had been asleep for a couple of hours when Melina waltzed in. By now she didn't knock either.

"What's that smell in the living room?" Melina asked, sniffing. "Did my Cuz score when I wasn't around?" She kissed me lightly on the cheek and sat down. She lay her hand casually on my shoulder, moving it absently over my chest, though her attention appeared to be on the TV.

After three months, I still hadn't scored with Melina.

"So what did Miss Melina do today besides sit on that fine ass all day?"

Melina made a face. "You're getting pretty fresh with your cousin, referring to my ass as ass."

I got up, walked in a half circle and looked at her backside. I made a square with my thumbs the way you see photographers do, framing their shot, and looked at different angles, then returned to my place on the sofa. "It's a hot ass."

Melina kissed me on the nose. "You wish you could take my fine ass to bed, eh?"

"We've been to bed many times."

"Yeah, we have, but never bare-ass!" Melina slapped my shoulder. "I know Pixie and Jo now," Melina said. "When are you going to introduce me to Carson?"

"Why the fuck would you ask that?"

"I told you, I want to know your friends."

"Carson is not my fucking friend. I have no proof, but my gut tells me he's behind the shooting that killed Tanis."

"Did you tell that to the detectives working the case?"

"I'm not a snitch."

"You plan on taking care of it yourself?"

"Stop the questions regarding this asshole." I meant business. I caught her eye and held it until she had to look away.

She kissed me lightly. "Okay, no more questions. Sorry I didn't know how sensitive a topic this is for you."

My return kiss was as light as hers.

"You'd like to fuck this fine ass of mine?"

"You're the only lawyer I know that has such a dirty mouth."

"You ain't heard nothing yet," she warned, then said, "My clit's not in my throat like Linda Lovelace, but you want me to throat you?"

"I thought you haven't seen it."

"I lied." Melina said.

I didn't know if she was teasing or not. Melina teased all the time. She seemed to get off on being a tease.

Last year the movie *Deep Throat* came out. Pixie had seen it the day it was released. Jo had gotten a babysitter and saw it with her old man, but was willing to go again if she and Pixie and I all went together. I'd heard about the movie and the savory method the star of the movie had of devouring a cock.

"Promises, promises," I teased back. "I'm ready anytime you are."

"Deal," she said.

I'll never know if this would have been the night. With perfect timing, my house phone rang. I answered immediately. It was Johnny, the tow truck driver.

"A Trailways just rolled near El Monte on the San Bernardino Freeway. Too big for my truck to handle. They won't let me in over there, but I know you got ways. Gotta be a big one man. Don't forget who called you first."

"Johnny, thanks. Get some more details and call me right back. I'll get right on it."

I forgot Melina was there. It was nearly two a.m. I called Pixie and Jo and woke them up. I gave them the name of the truck stop where we would meet. I'd catch up with them. I was leaving as soon as I got Johnny's callback. I ran to the bedroom, took out a sock from my dresser, and pulled out one of my cash bundles. I knew if it went well, if the case was good, I'd need cash. The street would be blocked off, so we weren't going to the scene of the accident. We'd be going to the hospital. Cash was the key to get past guards who kept bad guys out, and blocked attorneys and/or their runners from getting to accident patients.

I was still dressing when Johnny called back with details after listening to police radio calls. He didn't have much more—just that there were six bodies or more thrown clear of the bus, and that the accident had happened not long before midnight. I was slipping shoes on, zipping, buttoning simultaneously as I made my way to the door, and caught a glimpse of Melina on the couch looking a little lost.

"Cuz, stick around and have some peanut butter and ice cream. I gotta run. Big bus crash."

She looked disappointed.

"Honest, if it wasn't this big, I wouldn't go myself." Maybe it was true.

Melina got up from the sofa.

"Good luck, Cuz." She kissed me on the lips. I didn't want to walk out with a hard on, and didn't linger.

"Are we ever going to do it?"

"Maybe," she said.

"You putting me on, Cuz."

I switched on the answering machine, and ran toward the door.

I pushed the button, and waited four seconds. The elevator was slow. I took the stairs, and got my own car. No time to waste.

I listened to the handheld police band radio to keep abreast of the buzz. It took me an hour and change to reach the truck stop where I was meeting Pixie and Jo. With normal traffic it would have taken twenty minutes from my apartment. On the radio they said that the freeway was closed in both directions a mile on either side of the accident.

Jo's car was the only one in the front parking lot. This being a popular overnight spot for truckers, the side and back lots were jammed with big rigs. I didn't know if it was because of the food, the modestly priced showers, or the lot lizard I glimpsed making her rounds. I pulled in, and joined them inside.

The double doors opened to a small vestibule. To the left was a small market, less kitchy than Cracker Barrel, and more practical and ugly. To the right was a long counter with tall stools that had seen more than their fair share of use. Several of these stools were occupied by blue-jeaned men with five-o'clock shadows, drivers nursing coffee. The counter bore plates of fragrant food, and tall thermoses in need of filling. Behind the counter was a coffee station, a mirrored wall of pies, a flat top grill, and swinging doors to a kitchen. A sleepy looking waitress sat on her side of the counter, smoking a cigarette and turning the pages of a newspaper. Another waitress was circulating. The dining room was a large space, but it had been roped off, and the lights were off. A sign suspended on the rope said 'Please wait to be seated'.

The area open to seating was the booth aisle parallel to the counter. It was easy to spot the girls sitting shoulder to shoulder at a booth set with four orange and red placemats covered with dancing pancakes. A small pitcher promised cream; and a bowl in the center of the table was half-filled with sugar cubes. They had chosen the first booth by the entrance, against the window overlooking Jo's car. Coffee steamed in front of them. Two mugs were face down on the empty side of the booth where I slid in.

I wasn't dressed up, but out to look accessible, clean cut and smooth. The girls were in what I thought of as their business wear, which was halfway between sexy college girl and respectable secretary. I was a little relieved that Pixie hadn't shown up in what she wore to body shops, but Jo had probably made her change. I put the police band radio on the table, and turned it on. I turned the cup in front of me upright, and waved a dollar. A sharp-featured waitress in a pink polyester uniform and white apron snatched the dollar and filled my cup. Her dull brown hair was piled impossibly high on top of her head, and on top of all of that hair was perched a little paper cap. She had little shiny brown eyes that were bloodshot, and a wide red-lipsticked mouth that looked like it never stopped talking.

"It's been a little slow. We usually keep a full house all night. Want anything else, hon?"

"No thanks, Doreen," I said, reading off her name tag.

Doreen snatched up the fourth placemat and mug.

"Then if you don't mind, I'll just grab this and set it over here." She moved the mat to a bare table that had recently been bussed, and pivoted back to hand me a breakfast menu. "No use cluttering up your table." She surveyed the condiments and salt and pepper shakers.

I handed the menu back to her. The pie wall looked interesting, but I'd already indulged in ice cream. I got a beep, and glanced at the number. I didn't recognize it.

I wanted Doreen to go away but she kept on.

"I'd recommend the pie," she said. "Of course we do serve everything on the menu twenty-four hours a day, so if you prefer dinner or breakfast since it will be dawn soon, we can do that. When you're on the road, you should be able to eat whatever you want whenever you want. That's our motto. Now did you want anything else? We can fix up something special, it don't have to be on the menu."

"Not unless you have news about that accident I passed," I said. "Otherwise, all we'll need is a little privacy."

"I'm sorry. I do rattle on. I'll go check on my other customers. And about that bus, let me see what I can do."

She moved across the room to the only other occupied table, chattering away. Behind the counter, the other waitress opened another pack of cigarettes.

"Have you heard anything else?" Jo asked softly.

"So far, all I know is the bus rolled. It wasn't due to weather. The freeway in both directions will be closed for hours."

"Before we leave, I'm hitting that shop for a couple extra rolls of film," Jo said. "And cassette tapes."

I picked up the police band radio. "Batteries too. This thing eats batteries like there's no tomorrow."

That reminded me that Pixie and Jo would need money to grease their contacts. I gave them each fifty dollars for the shop.

Pixie yawned. Jo waved the waitress back over, and asked for a carafe of coffee for the table. Doreen brought the coffee and set it down with impressive finality.

"So you were asking about the Trailways accident in El Monte that killed tonight's traffic. Is that right?" Doreen asked. When she saw she had our attention, I saw her teeth.

"Yes."

"Well, I'm not saying I know or don't know the how or why of it," Doreen said. "I don't know nothing first-hand, but if there's one thing I do know about truckers after working this place for twenty years, truckers know everything that goes on the road they drive. And I do like a good yarn. Every good yarn has a hero, and we got one on the bus, or I'm a monkey's uncle."

"For God's sake, get to the point!" Pixie snapped.

"I don't have to tell you squat, young lady," Doreen said, about to huff off, and take the coffee with her. Pixie's hand snaked over to the coffee urn, and there was a little tug of war.

I glared at Pixie, but spoke to Doreen, "No, please, go on, I want to hear."
Doreen relinquished the carafe, and stood still with her arms crossed.

"Tell me about the hero," I coaxed. I handed her a ten dollar bill.

She brightened. She was full of her story, and a little pique could not stand in the way of her it. "Well the way they tell it, the bus had rolled off the road, and it just sat there a couple of minutes. Some witnesses pulled over to try to help. They tried to get in but they couldn't. The people inside were wailing and screaming, and no way out. There was bodies all around who had been thrown out. Then from inside, someone busted out the glass in the back emergency door. Then the first out was a bloody mess, carrying somebody, and lying them out on the some twenty, thirty feet away on the pavement, and went back in. Some people came out on their own. Every few minutes another would crawl out, and along with them, the hero I was talking about would stagger out with another busted-up passenger. There were broken arms and legs and head injuries all over the place, and then here comes the hero again, carrying another and other. For everybody else, it was each man for himself, except that hero carried out eight people who would not have gotten out on their own—including the bus driver."

"Well that is a good story," Jo said quietly. "Do you have the name of this paragon?"

"No idea. Now, a bunch were tossed out the windows, and they all died. But that hero hauled out everyone too broken to go on their own feet. Ain't that something?" Doreen said complacently, and headed off to hand a menu to another weary customer who had walked in. The girls headed to the shop. Doreen returned, putting her hand over mine. She bent her head as if she were sharing some kind of confidence. "This ambulance driver is sweet on our Dutch apple pie. He comes in every chance he gets. So that's where I got this from. Six fire trucks, and he said the firemen didn't have to carry out any injured, because that hero already done it by the time they got there."

"Do you know which hospital they took this hero to?"

"Sure hon. All the injured were taken over to Garfield Hospital."

"Great. That's real close."

Doreen pointed out the pay phone booth for me, and I paid it a short visit to check the answering machine and make a quick return call. It had turned out to be Fernando, who was on duty with the Highway Patrol. He told me, "Nothing left of the bus but a smoking burned out hull, lying on its side. I'll get you copies of the manifest."

Out in the parking lot, I handed Jo and Pixie each a grand.

"Don't be afraid to use this. Jo, you know how hospitals are, so let Pixie tag team with you. Remember, no business cards, period. We can't appear like we're soliciting. It can come back on us and Jake. And it can get us thrown out of the hospital. Grease the guards with green." I winked at them.

"Are we going to fuck the guards?" Pixie asked with that giggle of hers. "Is that why we got to grease them?"

"Dumb butt," Jo scolded. "Get in so I can give you a briefing about hospitals." Jo got in the driver's side, and Pixie climbed in the passenger side, and they were off.

I got there first, and made a quick pass around the ER. It had been several hours since the accident, and whatever immediate fuss had been in the waiting room had been absorbed by the trauma team. It wasn't too hard to guess who had relatives inside. I never thought of myself as handsome, but my height and physique drew some attention. I could feel some stares and headed back out, waiting for the girls to arrive.

We were standing on the sidewalk by the public entrance to the emergency room. A siren blurted a single squawk, and the three of us jumped out of our skins.

"Shit, busted," Pixie said. She had turned white as milk.

Jo was holding her heart, but turned to face Pixie.

"We're not busted. We're not doing anything wrong." Her voice was confident, but trembled a little.

I took a step in front of the girls, and recognized the highway patrol car.

"Fernando?" I said. He was across the street at the wheel of his idling vehicle, and his window was rolled down. He was laughing.

He squawked again, in answer.

Pixie jumped again. Fernando laughed harder. I heard the drone of the dispatcher on his car radio warble on. The noise was fuzzy and static-filled, not something easily distinguished as words.

Fernando threw a wad of paper that hit me in my forehead. He shrugged an apology.

"What the fuck?" Pixie said, bending down and grabbing the paper. She drew her arm back to shunt the paper back at him.

"Give that to me," I said.

She tossed it at me, angrily, giving Fernando the finger.

I opened up the wad. The list of names was on two pages, thirty six passengers.

I gave Fernando a thumbs-up. He was still laughing and gestured back the hand signal for a phone. I nodded my head and gave a deep bow as if we were ending a match. Another indistinguishable message on the radio from the dispatcher caught Fernando's attention, and he responded to it, then inclined his head in as much of a bow as he could manage from behind the wheel, and drove off, still chuckling.

"What the fuck was all that about?" Pixie was indignant. "What a jerk."

"I take it that's your highway patrol guy." Jo said. "Funny guy."

Fernando was a long time karate student of Cosmo's, usually in the six a.m. class, and not too long with the highway patrol.

"Those are the names of everyone on the bus," I said.

Pixie groaned. "We'll be here all day. How many are on the list?"

Jo ignored the question. "As long as it takes," Jo said. "I'm getting coffee."

"None for me," Pixie said, "I gotta pee. I must have drunk a gallon of coffee. I'll be lucky if I don't piss on the floor."

We headed inside. We'd been here many times before. In fact, Jo and I had spent so much time in all the local hospitals, we knew the nooks where all the vending machines were stashed, and all the waiting rooms.

It wasn't standing room only, but it was pretty busy with the usual flotsam and jetsam of random injured, bored, sick, miserable people. No one comes to the emergency room happy. There was no line at the desk, and no one manning it.

I scanned the people seated in chairs, mentally crossing out small groups that had someone obviously wounded or ill. The family members waiting for Trailways passengers were the ones unaccompanied by injured people. They had a certain degree of agitation of a different type than those who were just waiting to be seen. I saw a beige little guy sitting down, and my eyes went right past him. He pushed out of his chair and walked over to me. He walked straight to me and was close enough to touch before I recognized him.

"Hey Mario. I guess you're here on a case. I had one, but it failed to pan out," hc said.

"Too bad, Hugo. Maybe you'll get the next one." I shook his hand.

"Anything I can do for you? You lead a charmed life. How is your lovely Jo?" he asked.

"I'm good," I said, staring at his eyes and hair, trying to figure out what color they were. Even when I was looking right at him, I couldn't tell. "Jo's around here somewhere. You should say hi."

"Maybe." He sighed heavily, "Looks like you got this one covered." He headed outside.

I took a stand leaning against the wall near the reception desk, and continued looking for a familiar face inside. I knew a lot of nurses at all the local hospitals, but none of them seemed to be around tonight. The front desk was set behind a wall and had a sliding glass window which was currently open. The area behind the desk was a hallway that had several doors and other hallways, through which there was some activity, but not very much. After a few minutes, I had seen four nurses, two doctors, and a couple of ambulance workers pushing a gurney. All were strangers.

Jo, trailing Pixie, returned with a cup of bitter vending machine coffee for me. I handed her the list of names.

We all looked at the list that Fernando had given me.

The names would help, but it wasn't like we had their photos or ages. It wasn't like we had names and pictures of their family members.

"The list is good if we had nothing else," I told the girls. "We're here and the injured are here in this hospital, so let's start from scratch."

"Most of the names are Spanish," Jo was happy to report. "Ay que hablar en Español."

"The bus was coming from El Paso. The families that would come to the hospital would be of those passengers that had family or friends in Los Angeles. The other families would be back in Texas."

"We're here to make a connection with the injured. Don't do retainers or try and get signatures. We seal it with friendship and trust, hand them some money if they need it, tell them we'll catch them later, and warn them there will be a swarm of runners and maybe attorneys coming to their houses wanting to get retained. Like I said make friends. There are no strangers. Keep your eyes open and you will be able to figure out who has an injured family member inside. Fernando will have a list of dead in the morning to update us, then we can plan the strategy for meet ups with them later. But for now, we're here. I want to focus on the injured."

A nurse had come to the desk. Another nurse I didn't know. She was in her fifties, with reddish brown lacquered hair, a sour expression and a nametag that spelled out 'Kathi.' I smiled at her. She glared back, and started going through papers.

"Now what?" Pixie said.

"Now we find a way in to talk to the people here who are connected to the injured." Jo said. "I'll find us a seat, and we can brainstorm."

"I still gotta pee," Pixie said. "And there's somebody in the john."

"Use it," I said.

Pixie minced up to the desk and conferred quietly.

Kathi got up. She called a second nurse in to take her place, and came through the swinging doors. She thumped on the lady's bathroom door. Someone inside said something, but I was too far away to hear what it was.

"Please," I heard Pixie say. Her walk was more of a desperate dance by now.

The second nurse let them in the inner area, and walked off. Kathi came back to her desk. When she sat down, I could see behind her, the door to a bathroom near the assessment rooms. Pixie came out of it, looking much relieved. She looked at me, and I waved her on. She disappeared down the hall into the forbidden area where the injured were waiting for doctors.

The nurse looked at her watch, got up, and headed toward the bathroom. In case she was on the hunt for Pixie, I had to do something to distract her. I walked up to the desk. I slapped the call bell with my palm and called, simultaneously, "Nurse?"

She returned to the desk, and sat tiredly.

"Kathi? Can you tell me about Gonzalo Gonzales? I have been waiting a while. Has he been taken to a room?" It was the name of one of the injured. I knew he would still be in Emergency. It takes them hours to get them upstairs into a room, if a room is called for.

"Would you write that down?" she said, shoving a piece of paper at me.

As I scribbled the name, another nurse came up and called out, "Chad Rogers."

There was a stir inside the emergency room, and a young man leaning heavily on his pretty companion walked up to the swinging doors. An intern pushed out a wheelchair.

She buzzed the intern back through, and he wheeled, his companion following.

"We're shorthanded tonight," she said. "What was his name again?"

"Gonzalo Gonzales."

I heard the electric doors open, and a young couple walked in with a crying baby. The young mother had dark shadows under her eyes, and was wearing a muumuu. The father was wearing worn jeans and probably the t-shirt he'd gone to sleep in. I stepped aside.

"I can wait," I said. "You're busy."

In a corner, beneath a wall-mounted television with a table underneath, Jo had staked out a station for herself. I could see that Kathi across the room at her desk had a view of the television and was bearing paperwork on a clipboard while talking with the couple. The seats facing the television were filled, though everyone was paying more attention to their misery than to Captain Kangaroo's genial discourse. Jo and her things were stretched out taking as much space as possible on a two-person couch, catty-corner from where her massive purse was occupying a chair. I lifted the purse on to the table, and took the seat. The hard metal bars of the chrome frame cut through the thin square cushion.

"She's in," I said.

Jo cast a skeptical look at the doors. We were stuck on the wrong side, and until I could get us in, there wasn't much we could do.

"They're so calm," Jo said. "Their family members could be dying in there."

"My guess is that the families of the deceased haven't been contacted yet. These are probably people who got called, directly. Tomorrow will be harder." I didn't tell Jo that tomorrow probably meant handling the families of the dead, because she knew.

I kept an eye out for someone I knew, but didn't see anyone. I got up to stretch my legs, and spent an hour or more talking to a couple of families. After I came back, I gave up the chair to one of my new friends, and fell asleep on Jo's lap, my knees hooked over the side of the chair.

"Wake up, Mario!" I heard Pixie's voice, but woke to the strangest sight. I was groggy, and blinked my eyes a couple of times, trying to clear my head or vision, and succeeded in doing neither.

Holding hands with Pixie was the ugliest woman I'd ever seen. She was barely covered by two green cotton hospital gowns—one facing front, one facing back. Her biceps, triceps, and deltoids strained the sleeves. She was barefoot and had at least size sixteen feet, and long, muscular bony legs with a good coverage of dark stubble that needed the attention of a razor or possibly a lawn mower. She did have a thick head of long black hair, easily the prettiest thing about her. I groaned, and managed to get my legs unhooked from over the side of the chair. My joints popped and complained, as I drew myself to my full height. I found this paragon to be a couple inches taller than me. That doesn't happen often. My driver's license says I'm six feet five.

"Mario, this is Taffy Garcia. You remember Taffy, right?"

"Sure," I lied, shaking her hand. I squinted up at her face and tried to remember. She didn't look like a Taffy to me. I wondered how I could possibly have forgotten anyone who looked like she did. She was like a Bubba, albeit one heavily covered in Maybelline face paint, including Day-Glo red lips. It was hard to believe I could have met Taffy before and forgotten her.

Jo stood up and shook Taffy's hand too.

"I couldn't believe it was you," Pixie gushed, "I hardly ever see any of my family from the old neighborhood." Pixie gave Taffy a big hug. Taffy and Pixie embraced, and did some squealing and some improbable-looking hopping around that made Taffy groan in pain. The flapping hem of the thin cotton gown also revealed that Taffy really was a Bubba, at least according to nature.

If Pixie was calling her family, then this was one of the corner girls. I struggled with the memory and came up with the mental image of a younger, much slimmer version of Taffy, with a blonde pageboy that was a wig.

I hadn't missed a grimace cross Taffy's face.

"Maybe you should sit down," I said.

Taffy looked down at the chair and at the hem of the gown.

"Don't think I can. They took my clothes," she apologized.

"So what happened?" Jo asked.

"Taffy was aboard the bus," Pixie said.

Jo frowned, and pulled out the list. "I don't see the name..."

Pixie handed Jo the retainer that Taffy had already filled out.

"There you go."

I looked over Jo's shoulder and saw Taffy scribble Zita Garcia on the signature line.

"Taffy was my working name, but these days I go by Zita. And I remember you Mario. You were just a kid. You sure grew up. I remember you were Nana's favorite person." Zita gave me a big hug with her right arm, lifting me completely off the ground. I heard the right sleeve ripping around her bicep. I noticed the bandage on her left arm.

"You'll never guess what happened," Pixie said. "You remember that story we heard about the hero who carried everyone out of the bus? That was Taffy."

"No shit," Jo said. "Can I shake your hand again?"

Taffy looked modestly down at her size sixteens. "I only did what needed to be done," she said. "I only got the ones who couldn't get out by themselves."

"Yeah, but carrying out seven people—you saved their lives."

"If I'd waited for the fire trucks to arrive, we'd have all been crispy critters,"

Taffy said. "Six fire trucks came, but by the time the first one arrived, the bus was engulfed."

"That's so amazing." Jo said. "Maybe you'll get a medal." She pulled out her trusty Sony cassette recorder and started taping. "Don't worry Mario," she whispered in my ear, "I have ten pounds of batteries in my purse."

I gave her a thumbs-up.

"I already have a couple of medals," Taffy admitted, "Before I got booted out of the military."

"That's a story I'd like to hear," I heard myself saying. Maybe it was tactless, but it was true.

The composition of the room had changed. The seats were just as full, but mostly with different occupants. The couple with the crying baby were still waiting, and there was now a line at the desk. The sun was up.

"Zita!"

"They're calling you," Pixie said, unnecessarily.

A nurse and an orderly came out, both calling for Zita. The orderly was pushing a gurney.

"Here I am!" Zita called out. They were already heading in our direction.

"Why did you go?" the nurse scolded. "We've got you a room."

"This is my baby sister," Taffy said.

"Nice to meet you," the nurse said, "But you are really not supposed to leave the emergency room on your own."

"I've already got fourteen stitches," Taffy said, rubbing her right arm. "Isn't that enough?"

"This is about that bump on your head," the nurse said. "Didn't the doctor explain?"

If they suspected a head injury, it would be a better case. "You should go upstairs," I suggested. "The doctors know best."

About the time we managed to talk Zita on to the gurney, I realized that we had become the target of all eyes. I heard Zita's name being whispered all around the room. One of the distressed families I'd made contact with came over. An older man introduced himself as Fritz's father, and the little old woman with him as Fritz's mother. Fritz had a wife too, but she was inside with Fritz. The little old woman grabbed Zita around the neck, and burst into tears.

"You saved my son," she wailed. "I can't ever thank you enough."

It didn't take long for all the family members to converge on Zita, in various degrees of hysteria. This didn't sit too well with the orderly and nurse trying to wrangle their patient. No sooner did they pry Fritz's mother loose, than the Smith family took her place.

"Go ahead," I said to Zita, "We'll get their names for you. So you can get together at a better time."

Pixie got Zita's room number from the nurse. Jo leaped into action, and started taking names and numbers. The recorder kept recording, for good measure. Jo liked to cover all the bases.

"This is Zita's little sister," Jo pointed at Pixie.

"It's a quarter till six, Mario." Jo stopped writing long enough to remind me of the time. "When we're done here, we'll go to the office and man the phones till you get home."

"That's a plan," I said. "And I'll call Aunt Carmen and make sure she gets Lainey to school."

I said goodbye to Taffy/Zita Garcia, and headed off to Cosmo's for a class, and breakfast with Fernando at the diner.

I want to believe we would have scored a bunch of clients with or without Taffy but where this case was concerned, he was like a skeleton key. Just as the military had, his family had dumped him over the cross-dressing. Now that he was a hero, his clothing choices mattered not at all.

For the next few days, Pixie became a fixture on the couch of Taffy's hospital room. In spite of the concussion, Taffy made the rounds of the injured in their rooms, though the nurses made him use a wheelchair. Pixie pushed him from room to room, accompanied either by Jo or me. The nurses smiled at him, and didn't even question us. He introduced us to six of the injured passengers he had carried out. The seventh one, Gonzalo Gonzales, died on the operating table. Taffy got us in to meet the grieving widow.

The only person whose palm got greased was Taffy, though I did send Johnny a gift basket. Fernando was more interested in being a regular sparring partner and getting a free breakfast doughnut than getting paid.

On the second day in the hospital, I spelled Pixie as she went down to the cafeteria for breakfast. I gave Taffy five hundred dollars. He was shocked—and delighted—and promised to call me in twenty-four hours to check-in just in case we needed more help.

Within five days, we had twenty-one retainers. I also signed the first four families of passengers killed in the tragedy. By the end of the month we signed the families of the other four fatalities. No one had come out of the accident uninjured. We had the entire bus except for four undocumented passengers who were afraid to make a claim.

For that matter, most of the clients we signed were here on visitor visas or illegal. Either way, it was no big deal. They had a right to compensation regardless of their legal status in this country.

Jake met me at the juice stand. His smile was so big that I could see every tooth in his head glint from a mile away. He reminded me of a 1950 Buick Eight.

They were still in view when I sat across from him, and while he talked. I don't know how a man can talk and keep smiling like that, but he managed it.

"One day you are talking wanting to get bigger cases, and like magic, you get this monster bus crash! You are a magician."

"It was teamwork," I said, exercising my own teeth.

"You're magic, Mario. I'm so proud of you."

I put the cup of my carrot juice to my lips to the tune of his glorification. I took my time drinking, and let him glorify me without interruption. I drank slowly, then finally, during a pause, set down the glass.

"I figure twenty-five[6] thou now, and what do you think my bonus is going to be?"

Jake didn't break stride. "Trailways will have huge limits of coverage. We need to build up the damages of each person, not just the medicals. And for those that died, we need their ages and professions. We will calculate their rate of income: what they did for a living times their life expectancy." Jake went on and on.

I interrupted.

"Jake, my bonus. How big?"

"Big, kid, very big. You know I'll take care of you."

"A hint, Jake."

"You know I can't guess. I have to know exactly what the case will be before I come up with a figure."

Jake had a method. I trusted him, but his caution did not satisfy my questions, and was an irritating rock in the promise of my $25,000 shoe. I had no choice but to live with his careful watchfulness. I couldn't get his promise in writing because I'm not a lawyer. I knew as long as he lived, his word was good. I loved Jake, I loved my life, at least for the rest of the day and night.

"And what about the twenty-five?"

"Walk back to the office with me. Let's get through some of the paperwork."

Jake paid me sometimes two, sometimes three times a week based on what I brought in but twenty-five thousand in one whack was big. The number was

---

[6] $25,000.00 in 1973 had the same buying power as $139,132.35 in 2016

one that I had just plucked out of the sky, and as such, it felt like big money. Maybe I should have given him a bigger number.

Back in his office, he made an announcement over the new case before he called seven paralegals, and assorted secretaries into Jo's office. He set Jo to conducting the team, and she managed with a vengeance. I saw the glint in her eye that she was in her element. Papers, orders, pens, and skirts were flying everywhere.

"Come on," Jake said. We left them in a beehive of action and went into the solitude of his office, where he shut the door.

He sat down and pulled out his big book of checks. There was no sound in the room but the buzz of the forced air, and the scratching of his pen. I think both of us were holding our breath.

He put the check in my hand. Twenty-five thousand.

"We'll see what the bonus is when we close."

I love this business. For a while vengeance was the farthest thought from my mind.

I felt like a million bucks. I took the check to the bank, then went home and wrote two checks of my own. Pixie and Jo were still busy at Jake's office, and I could not contain my nervous energy. I hadn't slept in days, and hadn't had anything but coffee since the diner in El Monte.

I sat down at a big table at the Pacific Dining Car. Maurice brought me the phone, and I dialed from the table.

"Let's put on the feed bag," I told Jo. "You two meet me at PDC."

"We're done with everything we can do today," Jo said. "We had so many people on it, we got everything ready at the speed of light. There's nothing to do here until we get on with the interviews of all of the clients."

"Bring your appetites."

I called Maurice, the head waiter, back to the table to retrieve the phone and explained.

"I want a feast, Maurice. This is a celebration. It's business, but it's big business. This is the first time in days we've come up for air. We've been living on crappola coffee and now we're finally in fat city. I want the girls to remember this for the rest of their lives. They'll hardly put a dent in it, but I want them to carry the leftovers home, and eat for days." I handed him a hundred dollar bill. "I want the girls to feel like they're queens for the day. It will just be the three of us, but I want everything to come in courses. Fancy as shit, Maurice. Are you up to it?"

"It's what I live for," Maurice grinned, with a glint in his eye. "I'll be the butler and have a troupe of servers."

"In that case," I said, finishing the sentence by handing him a handful of twenties, "Some incentive for your troupe."

He disappeared to the front to confer with the maître d'.

I was feeling no pain, seated at the table when the girls arrived. Maurice ushered them in like rock stars. I stood as they entered, and the wait staff helped them into their chairs. The girls were flustered by the extra attention, and cute, and a little overwhelmed. Maurice and three servers minced in with food with more pomp and circumstance than the royal heads of Europe received. They delivered cheese plates with grilled toast as soon as the girls were parked in their chairs. The only thing missing was solid gold plates.

The girls set to with gusto.

"Where's the menu?" Jo asked.

"Nevermind the menu today," I said. "Just enjoy yourself."

Maurice brought out crab cakes, shrimp cocktails, sautéed scallops with lobster sauce, and grilled artichokes. We devoured them family style.

We talked about our big successes, and plans.

"We're going to have every one on that bus," Jo said. "One hundred percent."

Maurice brought the salads before we were done.

"Don't throw that away," Pixie said, hanging on to her plate.

"I'll package it just for you," Maurice promised.

He filled the table with mixed green salad and a tomato salad, mostly for the girls. Jo forked into it happily, and sipped her white wine.

"What's next?" Pixie asked.

"Veggies. I asked him to serve in courses."

"No, I mean with the case."

Jo paused between bites of tomato. "We'll meet with the few holdouts, and get their signatures. Then we'll get their histories, you know, the paper chase. Don't worry, I've got a plan."

"I'm pumped," Pixie said.

As I had requested, Maurice brought the vegetables together as one course, with plenty of fanfare. Pixie made eyes with the servers, who were on their most formal behavior, and oozing consequence and deference simultaneously. They filled the table with spinach three ways, asparagus, and broccoli, with hollandaise on the side with three kinds of bread in baskets, and butter. Then we chased that with the main dish of filets and lobster tails.

Dessert ended like the meal had begun, with one of everything. I ended up with the succulent chocolate soufflé. Pixie, who has a conventional sweet tooth, polished off the hot fudge brownie sundae, and Jo nibbled at the edges of the apple tart. Maurice packaged up four leftover desserts.

The table was cleared away, with nothing on it but Irish coffees.

"I can't move," Pixie said.

Jo pushed back from the table to stretch out her legs.

"One more thing," I said.

"No more food," Jo begged. "I'm in danger of exploding as it is."

I shook my head and tried to look serious. It got their attention.

"No more food."

I pulled an envelope out of my pocket.

"Oh God," Pixie wailed. "We're fired. I knew it was too good to be true."

"Put a cork in it," Jo said. "Don't be such a retard."

I put the two checks I'd written earlier on the table face down, and slid them simultaneously to Jo on my right, and Pixie on my left.

They were silent, in disbelief.

"Just taking the opportunity to thank my best girls for jobs well done."

They stuttered out thank yous but were mostly speechless. That's an event in itself. I think Pixie said, "Ka-ching."

I had planned for us to feast and celebrate together at home, and was happily anticipating that.

"Thanks, Mario," Jo said. "This is amazing."

"You earned it," I assured her.

"I feel bad that I have to go home," she said, with obvious regret.

"Me too," Pixie said. "I mean, I have a date. Taffy and I are going to that movie we were talking about, you know, Deep Throat."

"Is that a good idea?" Jo asked.

Pixie shrugged. "Taffy's a switch hitter. Why not?"

The wait staff escorted the girls out and handed over two full grocery bags each. As promised, they would be eating it for days. As for me, I swallowed my disappointment, paid the bill, handed Maurice another hundred, and headed home alone.

I let myself in to my apartment. Just because the girls had bailed on me was no reason to be glum. I was still over the moon with Jake's check. Despite the ending, the spontaneous food fest had been a blast. I was tired, and home in my great apartment, and it was time to chill. I pulled off my clothes as I walked through, took my time in the shower, worked up a lather, and made myself happy even without the girls around. I wasn't quite satisfied, but at least I was plenty exhausted. I'm not sure if I rinsed, and I know I didn't towel off. I did manage to set the alarm to five for Cosmo's and barely made it to the bed before I collapsed.

It could have been minutes or days later. The next thing I knew there was a mouth on my cock. For half a second, I was thinking it was Pixie and I was back at Aunt Carmen's. But Pixie didn't go that deep.

I wasn't in the dark. It wasn't Aunt Carmen's. The wobbly drunk night light was on in my bedroom, light streamed from the en suite bathroom, and there was plenty of LA night light shining in the window. I could see Melina in all her naked glory. She had been truly blessed by nature. I tried to pull her up, but she was pistoning her mouth on my cock like there was no tomorrow. Linda Lovelace had nothing on her. For a few seconds, I couldn't do anything but lie back and feel the hot sweetness.

But I'm a big guy. It's not like she had a chance of winning a physical competition. I sat up, hooked a hand around her thigh, and pivoted her so I could return the favor. She squealed, and doubled her efforts. I'll probably get complaints from the neighbors.

I don't know how long it took, but I didn't get any more sleep. I'd been waiting for Melina long enough and was making up for lost time.

Eventually, we came up for air.

She mumbled something. I presume she was too exhausted to use more than one syllable, but I was too far gone to know what she meant.

"Someone for you," Jo said. She was sitting in my office, typing up cases of the day. I had been in the kitchen getting something to drink.

I took the phone. Jo went back to typing.

"Mario Luna," I said.

"You're a lucky stiff, Luna."

I recognized the annoying voice of the detective.

"How so, Sanchez?"

"You're off the hook. The District Attorney is satisfied that the death of the assailant was a matter of self-defense. No charges will be made against you."

I laughed out loud and hung up while he was talking. I grabbed the glass of ice water. Downed it in one swallow.

"Who was it?"

"Nobody," I said.

But I was as pissed off as I was relieved. For months that asshole detective had been looking for evidence so they could charge me for killing that bastard that killed Tanis and shot me. I hadn't even intended to kill him. I didn't mean for him to go over the edge. If I'd had a choice, I would have beaten the shit out of him, but left him alive.

It was a few days before Sanchez called back.

I didn't hang up, and Mike Sanchez played it like I had never hung up on him.

"Your shooter was a transient from El Paso, Texas."

"Is that so?"

"No doubt he was a bum just after the money."

It was hard for me to buy this, and I told him so.

"That's just stupid," I said. "Tanis and I were on the second floor of the motel. Why wasn't he looking for prey on the first floor?"

I was thinking that Carson must have hired him or had someone else hire him to take me out. I didn't share my thought process with the detective.

He was never satisfied for long. In a few days, he beeped me again. I dialed from Jake's office where I happened to be when I got the beep.

"What's up?" I asked.

I had to give it to him for being persistent. Every time I talked to him, he probed to see if I knew anyone who wanted me dead. I wasn't a snitch. My heart kept telling me it was Carson, but my mouth told the detective squat. I felt like I wasn't giving anything away, but maybe Sanchez guessed I was holding something back, even if it was only my own suspicions. It's not like I really knew.

"I have nothing to add, detective. Let me know if something new comes up." My brain sent beautiful pictures of Tanis for me to remember.

I was at home, making daily calls when Monica beeped me. I happily interrupted my routine, and dialed her on the office phone.

"My co-worker Isabel was in a wreck," she said immediately, with no greeting.

"Tell me more." I took out my pencil and started taking notes. I filled out a Rolodex card for my records.

"She works with me. She was at Safeway and crashed into a car that made a left turn in front of her. She wants to sign up right away so she can go see a doctor. She's all banged up."

"Broken bones?"

"I doubt it. She went to work anyway, but she's black and blue and hurting."

We arranged to meet in my car in the Safeway parking lot. When I saw Monica came out with her, I couldn't help watching. She resembled an actress out of a James Bond movie. She had a jeans ass right out of a magazine. When I was a kid paging through Playboy Magazines, I'd imagined girls like Monica. Monica, even fully clothed, was hot.

She crossed that parking lot and kissed me through the open window of my car. Her friend followed, and sat in the passenger seat. We shook hands.

"I'm Isabel."

Twenty minutes later, Isabel stepped out of my car with Jake's business card and a copy of the retainer she had just signed, and a business card for a medical facility to immediately go over and get checked out. Before she stepped out of the car, she took Monica's cue, and leaned over to give me a light kiss, and thanked me. She and Monica went back into Safeway.

I waited for Monica to come back to the car. For the second time that day, I watched her through my windshield as she walked out of the market in my direction. She moved like a cat. She never stopped smiling all the way. I handed her a fifty.

"Thank you," I said, "I appreciate the business very much."

Monica took the money, put it in the pocket of her Safeway smock. She gave me a flirty look over her shoulder and flung her hair.

"I get off at five. I have no class till seven. We got time to get it on if you come over."

It was not an unappealing suggestion. I reached out to touch her face, and returned the smile with one of my own. "I'll be there at five thirty."

Monica beamed. "I can dig it."

"What about your roommate?" I asked.

Monica shrugged.

"She doesn't get off till nine. And even if she's there, I got my own room, and a door that locks."

"Is it soundproof?"

"No, dude, but no problem. My roomie likes to listen in."

We were going to dinner at the Tower on Sunset and Vine, and Melina was perched on my bed all dressed up, passing judgment on my clothing choices. I had no intention of leaving my closet in the condition hers always was. The spare bedroom she'd outfitted as a giant clothes closet was closer to empty than full but looked like a cyclone had struck. I already changed clothes twice to suit her, and she still wasn't happy. I stripped back down to my shirt-sleeves, and hung up the jacket she'd thumbs-downed.

"Fuck it," I said.

"Men wear either a suit or sport jacket and tie to the Tower. If you show up without a tie or jacket, they loan you what you need to wear. You don't want that. Those ties and jackets haven't been washed for years. You have a bunch just hanging there in your closet." She walked past me and picked out another jacket and tie.

"Put this on."

I shrugged into the coat. "The Pacific Dining Car is the most expensive restaurant in downtown Los Angeles. I don't see why we can't go there. I can wear whatever I wish and I like their steaks. They don't give a shit what I wear, as long as I have the money to pay the tab. What's the big deal with this Tower place?"

"It's the place to go for business." She looked me over critically. "Let me help you with the tie."

She stood in front of me, looping the tie around my neck. Even in high heels, she had to look up at me. In under two minutes, she had knotted and draped my blue tie perfectly.

"Where did you learn how to do that?"

She slapped my chest.

"You think you're the first man I've dressed? Let's go. Our reservation is in thirty minutes."

She turned away but I grabbed her by the waist, and picked her up so our lips touched.

"You're so fucking strong," she whispered into my mouth.

It was not the first time I had taken Melina to dinner, but in this fancy place I was glad she took charge.

"This building was the first skyscraper built after LA rescinded the ban on buildings taller than thirteen stories. It's won all kinds of awards."

I don't know about architecture, but Melina was right about the Tower's dress rules. Every male but one came in in a coat and tie. I saw a coat being offered to the one guy who had arrived coatless.

She went back and forth with the wine steward about Merlots. All that wine talk was Greek to me. Finally the two agreed on what we would be ordering.

"Order a steak for me," I said putting the menu down on the table.

"I'll order a Steak Diane," she said with gusto.

I had no clue what Steak Diane was, but I'd had every steak available at Pacific Dining Car so this better measure up.

Our table for two was against a window overlooking Hollywood and Hollywood Hills. Thousands of lights twinkled across the night. It was beautiful.

Melina signaled the sommelier. She did the honors of sipping the wine first and signaled the steward to serve.

I said, "To us."

We toasted.

Melina smiled. Our glasses clicked.

"To our friendship," she said. She moved a glass, and her bag fell off the table. It was a little sequined thing. It fell with a hard thunk.

"To friendship," I said. I sipped, and picked her bag off the floor. It was heavy.

She looked agitated. She fidgeted in her seat.

The bag was much heavier than you would think a little shiny woman's handbag would be. I put it on my lap.

"Mario," she said, warningly.

I unsnapped it, and looked down at the gun grip poking out.

Chapter 7
February 13, 1973
Big Time

"Really?" I asked. "Here? At the fucking Tower?" After she'd made so much fuss over my dressing to the nines, she brought a piece.

She flushed.

"Give it back," she said.

"An ivory Beretta? Who the fuck do you think you are, James Bond?" I laughed.

I could see the wheels in her head turning as she changed her tactics.

"How do you think I got the gun permit to carry a concealed weapon?" Melina said. "You can't get gun permits unless a Chief of Police or Sheriff issues it. I had to drive north from Los Angeles until I found a police chief that was horny for me. Anyway, I sucked him dry eleven times over a course of six weeks, and he got me the permit. I bet I'm the only one in history to get top marks for fellatio during weapon training and target shooting classes."

"You're putting me on."

"Would I do that?"

She held up the glass again.

"To friendship," she said.

I took another gulp of wine.

I wished she'd put this curiosity about Carson to a rest. As if my thoughts had conjured him up, she asked again.

"So, when are you introducing me to Carson?"

I ignored her question.

"Stop mentioning that asshole's name to me!"

"Sorry, already. I figured that your suspicions were done since you told me what the detective reported to you about the shooter being a transient."

I ignored her defense. "No more talk about Carson."

"*Ad infinitum,*" she muttered.

"I heard that," I said, glaring at her. Enough was enough. "I may not have eight years of law and Latin under my belt, but I had ten years working for lawyers, and I understand that gibberish. Keep mentioning that S.O.B.'s name and I will show you what infinity really means."

Melina could not meet my eye. I think she wasn't regretful about mentioning Carson, but *was* embarrassed to have pulled out her lawyer Latin to use on me as a weapon like I was some kind of illiterate baboon who wouldn't recognize it, and that I caught it.

"I'm sorry," she said. She put her hand out for her loaded purse. I closed the flap, snapped it shut and handed it over.

"When I'm after something, I'll do what's necessary," she said. "Whatever is necessary."

I figured it was best to ignore the whole thing. "What are your long-term plans?" I asked her, "Speaking of Latin, are you planning to practice law?"

"I don't think so."

"After all those years of school?"

"I plan to keep active. I'll take any ongoing credits I need to stay in good standing with the state bar. I'll pay my dues so my license stays active. It's not like I'm going to throw it away."

"So what are you doing for money?"

"I have money in the stock market. I still have cash reserved from what I received from my parents' insurance and the sale of the house. When I jaunted around Europe, sometimes I kept bar or worked in shops. It was a fun way to fit in, make some friends. The trip didn't dent my savings."

I always wondered what she did during the day. I kidded her about sitting around on her ass watching television, and hitting the gym on the first floor. She was too young to settle for such a boring life.

"Stock market?" I said, "How does that work? I mean, I know about the stock market and public companies, but I know zero about buying stock."

She gave me a quick education on buying shares of stock and turning it over, buying low, and selling high. She talked about buying seasonal stocks like Disney and selling the stock in summer when the prices jumped. The talk made me excited. I had a lot of money in the bank, just sitting there.

"Stocks are a sideline. What I really want to do," she said as she ate her main course, "is build a huge Mexican market."

"Like the one your parents had?"

"Way bigger," she said, with a gleam.

"What do you have up your sleeve?" I asked her. "You look…mischievous."

She shrugged, grinning.

"I own the property. It's huge. Big enough to build something like…"

She gazed up as if there was a picture of this market painted on the ceiling tiles.

"…like a Safeway."

"Is there money in that?"

"Big money," she said. "No one has a huge Mexican market like I'm talking about, one with food products from Mexico and a meat department with cuts of meat popular with our people. It's a niche."

"So what do you like best, buying and selling stock or opening a market?"

She stopped eating. Her eyes met mine. "I like both. How much money do you have Mario? Maybe we could be partners?"

"Sure," I said carelessly.

Melina took me to meet her stock broker, Mr. Robinson, at his private office. At her suggestion, I deposited twenty-five thousand[7]. Their friendly chatter informed me that Melina was good friends with him.

I figured Melina had some serious bucks. I wasn't worried over the twenty-five thousand. I would hate to lose it, but if I did, I'd just have to make more. The one thing I didn't like about this whole stock business was how it was really a form of legitimate gambling. I'm not really a gambler, unless it means gambling on a sure thing, like my own venture. Because if it is my venture, I'm in control. I know exactly how hard I'm going to work.

Robinson explained that what I had chosen for a type of account had risk. I waved off his cautions.

"If Melina says stock is the way to go, I'm in."

She reached for my hand and put it up to her lips.

"You'll be fine," she promised.

I dropped her off at the apartment, and met up with Jo and Pixie at Jake's. Then my team went to sign a case that had just come in.

"So are you fucking her?" Pixie asked.

"None of your business," Jo said, then added, "Are you?"

I laughed. "I have plenty to go around."

Pixie reached over and patted me between the legs.

"Let me get it ready."

I slapped her hand away. I hate to walk in to a new client with a hard-on, and Pixie thought it was funny as hell.

---

[7] $25,000.00 in 1973 had the same buying power as $139,132.35 in 2016

We didn't work together lately unless it was a big case with multiple clients. This case wasn't that big—but it did involve two families in a VW bus that had been rear-ended by a drunk driver in a sports car.

We signed both families. After that, Jo and Pixie were caught up for the day.

In this business, you never know when something is going to come in that can't wait. There were a lot of Carsons out there trying to sign cases, so we never wasted time.

I drove us back to Jake's. Pixie sat in the front and Jo in the back so she could ready the day's paperwork, and we could just drop it off at Jake's.

Melina drove like a European, or so she told me. She didn't have much regard for speed signs, and zipped around in her 1963 Jaguar XKE roadster. It was red, of course. The seat felt about the size of a go-cart and was so low to the ground we were looking under cars instead of at them. While it was sort of fun and zippy, I had nowhere to put my knees. I felt like a squatting duck. I looked over and noticed instead of her usual short skirts, she was wearing lemon-yellow coveralls.

"I don't know how you talked me into this. Whatever this surprise is that you want to show me, you could just have easily have told me, and let me drive in a real car."

"This is a real car," she said, zinging through traffic, and whipping around a huge cement truck. I held my breath, and saw my life flash before my eyes. Sand flew up, and tires squealed. We might have even driven under a couple of cars. I'm not sure. I shut my eyes at one point.

"Fuck, Cuz, you drive crazy," I said, wincing as she zoomed past a pickup, and crossed in front of a lane of traffic to bounce down an alley off Sunset toward a fence, and a construction zone.

"Dude. Don't be a wuss."

"Where the hell are you going, anyway?"

She screeched to a stop, and was out of the car before I could untangle my legs. It was April, and the weather was temperate enough for the top to be off. She untied the scarf she'd had over her curls, and jammed it into her pocket. Without waiting for me, she walked up to the chain link gate blocking the alley, and swung it open.

I took a moment to examine the surroundings. We were near Echo Park. The construction up ahead was clearly a commercial building. I walked past the DO NOT ENTER signs, closed the gate, and joined Melina.

"So, what is it?"

"My new market," she said. "The build has been going on for nearly a year. The construction should be done in a month, according to the head of my crew."

"Hold on," I caught her by her elbow. We jerked to a stop. "You lied to me."

"What? What are you talking about?"

"All that shit you told me about the market you were going to build someday. It looks like someday happened a long time ago."

"I did want to build a market. It's something I wanted to do for a long time."

"So why didn't you just say that it was already underway? You started on this before you even went to Europe."

"I don't know why you're so hot under the collar. It's just a lot to explain. Besides, I'm showing you now. And it's clearly not finished yet."

It looked damn close to completion to me.

A handsome guy in a yellow safety hat walked up and gave Melina a familiar hug, and flashed a mouth full of white teeth. He was tawny, and Mexican.

"Hola Señora Marron," he said, and started rattling off details about the construction. He put his hand out to me. "Señor Marron?" he asked.

"Mario," I said. I was still feeling pretty irritated. We shook hands, and he tipped his hat, leading us through the construction zone. Mr. Handsome's name was Harry Chavez. A kid from the construction crew ran up with a pair of hard hats and an orange coverall for me. I clambered in. It was too tight to fasten, at least six inches too short, and gave me a distracting wedgie.

Melina saw my difficulty and grabbed the lapel, thinking to help. She tugged hard, trying to get the seams to meet in the middle. It didn't budge.

"You're a tall drink of water aren't you?" she said, under her breath, and put her hand on my bicep. She didn't seem to be complaining.

There was a large paved parking lot full of construction machines. Chavez gave us the ten cent tour. He led us through some heavy ply plastic hung from the ceiling, and over rubber mats. Electric doors had been installed, but weren't hooked up. Thick gauge plastic crosshatched over the surface of polished terrazzo floors beginning inside the vestibule. The inside racks had not been installed so there was a clear view of the side and rear walls. They were blocked out for butcher counters, display cases and refrigerators. The whole north wall was for cooked meats, a kind of deli. The south wall was for raw meats to be curated by Mexican butchers. The east wall was going to be set up for a vast produce area. Chavez pointed out the cases that had been installed, but it was Melina who got excited talking about the Latin products she intended to sell. She pointed out a seating area in front near the entrance where shoppers or employees could eat.

The crew took me for Melina's husband, and were all working toward my approval. I kept a somber mien and let them suck up, and show off their work. They assumed I knew everything, and I wasn't saying anything to prove them wrong. Melina hung on my arm, beaming. Every so often she would burst out in excitement over some unique detail in her planning. She pointed out a second floor suite of offices. We walked through the back area which was a small warehouse, including refrigerated areas.

Then we were back in the little car. Melina reached into her glove box and pulled out a pack of Marlboros. She ripped open the pack, tapped out a cigarette, and put it in her mouth.

"When did you start smoking?" I asked.

"Only sometimes," she said. "Sorry about the confusion with the construction crew. I said you were my business partner. They just assumed the marriage."

"No harm done," I said. "I had no idea you were leading a double life. So what's next? Is this your con? Are you about to hit me up for money?"

"It's not like I'm a builder. The thing is, now that I know you a little better, I made some assumptions too. Do you want to be business partners in this venture?"

"All this time I thought you were sitting on your ass," I said. "I have to think about it." I had a whole lot of uninvested cash, and I'd been waiting for a chance to put it to work. The market sounded like a good idea. But I didn't want to be taken for a sucker. This sounded almost like one of Carson's get rich quick schemes—except he wouldn't have had a building to show for it, only grandiose plans and nothing tangible.

"Tell me about your plans. The mark up on grocery stores isn't very much. I know this because I had a client with a small grocery store, and he always complained there was no money selling food."

"It's not going to be the usual Safeway. The Spanish-speaking population is huge and growing. That's our clientele. We're selling Mexican and Hispanic branded products, and we're going to have a bilingual staff. We're going to have an in-store deli and hot food. My dad's store was a matchbox next to this, but he made a lot of money because he had a lot of business, mostly Mexicans and Latins from other countries. And when this one gets going, I have a business plan to spread all across California. So, are you in?"

I'd put my money on the line if Harry gave me the go-ahead. There wasn't anything Harry didn't know about business.

"Let's go see Harry," I said. When we swung by her apartment to pick up her papers, I called Harry to check if he could see us. Harry knew business law better than Jake or anybody. Plus I hated to distract Jake from all the accident cases I'd channeled in his direction.

Harry gave me a big hug when he saw me, and greeted Melina as if he knew her. I introduced everyone at Harry's office to Melina.

We sat on a sofa across from Harry.

"Melina is a lawyer. She is building a market that I want to partner in."

"Let me explain," Melina said. She told Harry about her experience in the market business, shared a little about her education.

"How big an investment are you planning?"

"When the market is complete, I'll have a total investment of five hundred thousand dollars."

"Is that including the fair market value of the land?"

"Yes."

"Is there a mortgage?" Harry asked.

"No, it's free and clear," replied Melina. "Up to now, I have paid cash to cover all the construction draws."

Harry was impressed. Melina probably knew it as well, because she was smiling.

The lawyer in Melina came out as we cut the deal. I would invest two hundred fifty thousand in cash[8] to buy half of her investment and own half the business.

We were at Harry's when I wrote her a check.

"I didn't think you had that kind of cash," she said.

"Right. I bet." I was kidding. Maybe. I thought I saw guilt flash across her face so maybe not. "You know everything. You had free range of my house. You

---

[8] $250,000.00 in 1973 had the same buying power as $1,391,323.53 in 2016

couldn't resist looking at my bank books." I know how snoopy Melina is. I've caught her looking through my wallet, my bathroom cabinet, and going through my groceries. It didn't matter. What do I have to hide?

Melina gave Harry one of her big smiles. "I would never do that. Tell him, Harry."

Harry wasn't buying into her cutesy act. He looked over the top of his glasses at both of us, and back down at the pages spread in front of him. "All investments involve risk. But I think this is a good investment for you, Mario."

I took Harry at his word, and told Melina, "Thanks for letting me in to the deal."

"I am getting back half the money I have invested," Melina said. "I think you'll be the perfect partner." She turned to Harry and said, "I want to run things. You make sure I run things."

"Fine by me," I poked her gently. "You know I'm a pushover. You can control the action if I'm your partner."

All I knew is that the investment would leave me with less than twenty thousand in the bank, not counting the money I had in the brokerage account with Mr. Robinson. I would own half the market, including the building and land. I would take on fifty percent of the responsibility of future debt. Melina would be paid for her services as general manager of the market for a salary that the two of us would agree on. The bottom line is that we would split fifty-fifty whatever profit was left over after expenses. Even with my terrible math I had no problem understanding this.

It took more than a week to get the paperwork together. Harry worked with Felix Billingsly, the accountant who had handled my IRS problems when I got out of prison and during my probation. These days he took care of filing my tax returns. He was a wise older man Cosmo had recommended. Somewhere along the line, Melina had her tax guy work with Harry and Felix. Soon the deal was done. Melina was going to handle the day-to-day, though I had veto power if there was something I objected to behind the scenes.

"I have no problem being a silent investor," I said.

"As the Chief Operating Officer, I will be paid to manage and supervise." Melina said, "I'm good with it, and I have nothing else to do, unless I choose to go into law, and that's not going to happen. And you are not a silent partner, dummy. Everyone knows we're partners."

"I didn't say secret partner. I said silent. Silent means I wouldn't be involved in the day-to-day operations."

Felix warned me that I would probably owe taxes at the end of the year unless I could document a whole bunch of write-offs. He told me to save every receipt I got in case he could squeeze them in as business expenses. I was making a lot of money, and I also had the two hundred fifty thousand to deal with that Harry had given me at the end of 1972. Felix would worry about it when the time came. By now, I wanted in, and that desire had nothing to do with Melina and everything to do with the project being a profitable venture. To think I would own half of that giant building. I kept pinching myself to make sure I wasn't dreaming. I believed Melina was doing me a good deed. She didn't need me.

Stocking the store was going to cost a bundle, but Melina said not to worry about it. When she and the accountants talked about the mechanisms of how the purchases of produce and goods would be part of operating capital, my eyes glazed over. I know she said she had no plans of touching the money I had given her. But that was her affair. It was none of my affair how she spent her own money.

Melina and I were sitting on her sofa, enjoying a bottle of red at her pad. It was afternoon, but the drapes were drawn. She had three candles lit on the coffee table.

"You took me to your broker, gave up half your market project. Why are you doing this?"

"So I can be the boss," she said.

"Yeah, right," I kidded. "You're a control freak. I almost forgot."

"I'm going to make us rich."

"I already feel rich," I said.

She snuggled on my lap.

"I have wanted to put together the market deal ever since my dad was shot. I'm sorry I didn't explain better that the project was already underway. I just wanted you to see it with fresh eyes. I've always wanted to get the crew back together, all the people who used to work for him. It was like an extended family. I miss that."

"But why me?"

"I have no other family," she said. "Ever since that day you announced yourself my Cuz at the hospital, you're it. You're my friend, my family and I trust you. I want you as my partner.

"But why me?"

She shook her head, exasperated. "Honey, never mind. We're partners. We're happy. And we have our freedom. You paid for half the business. Enjoy it."

She bit lightly through my jeans and I got hard; she blew warm, moist air that penetrated the denim.

"Is it my turn, Mario? Or is it only you who gets satisfied during sex?"

I spent half the night convincing her otherwise. I forgot all about investments and markets, and lived a bout of desire and wine and food and sex that was mystical.

Good thing I had Jo and Pixie working cases.

"I need to get back to work. My team is doing great, but I need to be available and around for them."

For at least two weeks, my head had been in this deal with Melina, and not in my real bread and butter. I had been in a fog, caught up in the excitement of the new deal. After I missed four consecutive days of working out at Cosmo's, I saved so much transit time, I decided to work out at home. I cut back my Cosmo workouts to once a week. I didn't want to waste unnecessary time going back and forth when all I needed to stay in shape was that one class a week and using the gym daily at my apartment.

My first day back in the grind, the girls and I did signups together.

"What's up with the secrecy, Mario?" Jo asked, as I turned into the Echo Park alley. "Is this a new client we're handling?" She pulled out my day planner, and my black book, looking for notes on a case referring us to this area. Of course, there were none.

We got out of the car, and walked up to the chain link gate. I could already see progress in the few days since I had last been there. The machines had been moved around the lot; the parking lot was getting black top. A temporary roofed structure had been erected over the uninstalled refrigerators, showcases, appurtenances and fixtures, as well as locked shipping containers. The odor of tar and asphalt was heavy. Harry Chavez, the general contractor, saw us coming and crossed the lot to greet me by my first name. He gave us hard hats. He cautioned us to be careful, and I know he watched the girls as we walked away from him to the store. Electricians on scaffolding were working inside installing light fixtures into the tall ceiling. The empty building was a huge shell. It reminded me of a covered football field except for the terrazzo floor.

"What is this?" Jo asked again.

"My latest investment. It's going to be a twenty-four hour Mexican-style market. I have a half-interest."

Jo and Pixie were not speechless.

"Holy fuck!" Jo said. "You own half of this? Amazing!"

"Fucking amazing," said Pixie, taking my hand. "Can we get a discount shopping here?"

"You'll have to ask Melina."

"Are you still sleeping together?" Pixie said. I thought I heard jealousy, which was unlike her. She probably still missed the convenience of having me down the hall at Aunt Carmen's.

"Not sleeping, no." It's true we didn't sleep together overnight. We split to our own apartments after we were done with talks or sexual encounters.

Jo took my other hand as we walked through. Painters were priming the walls. Carpenters were putting up partitions for various working and storage areas. The girls had questions about where things were going to be, and I pointed out the details I recalled. I met Jake there early one morning and showed the place off. Harry came out one afternoon. Cosmo met me there at noon before we had lunch. My friends patted me on the back and told me it was wonderful and beautiful. Pixie brought Aunt Carmen out. She was as proud as you might guess. In spite of everyone's congratulations and best wishes, I doubted they guessed at the potential, not even Harry who had spent hours putting the deal together for me with the accountants and Melina. They would understand better when they saw how the store would galvanize the Mexican community. I was positive the market would make a killing, and that this store was the first of many.

We took our banker, Martin Keating, out to lunch at the Tower on Sunset and Vine. At least it wasn't my first time there. I wasn't thrilled at the highbrow location. There are plenty of restaurants I prefer more, but Melina said it was the place to go since we were courting him for the market. In the car, Melina explained, "I've banked with this guy for years. I want to give him the market accounts. We're going to hit him up for a credit line for the fixtures and merchandise. It can't hurt for him to see we're solvent."

"I've been wondering how we were going to swing it."

"I've already talked to our suppliers, and have a pretty good idea of what we need. It helps not having a mortgage."

"I won't be impressing anybody. I'm down to twenty-five thou in the bank, twenty-five thou in stocks, and twenty thou in cash. That ain't much."

"The two hundred fifty thousand you paid me for your cut is already in his bank, plus my own accounts. He will be happy to take care of us. Don't worry. It's plenty. Don't forget you own half the building. Equity talks."

We arrived first at the Tower, and were seated. A waiter brought us water and a wine list even though it was early enough for their brunch menu. We asked for coffee, and explained we were waiting for a third. There were already a number of businessmen with a head start on their three martini lunches. I knew Melina knew her way around, and she trusted her banker.

I wanted to keep my head clear for the meeting, but Melina liked to fuck with my mind. I don't know why she'd want me off my game. We were on the same side of the fence in this transaction.

"It's funny, Mario, how you just lie back and get pampered. Do you ever ask a girl if she had an orgasm?"

"I don't ask. A girl's pleasure is obvious if you know where to look. When I was a kid, Pixie gave me lessons on what gets a girl off, and the signs that she did."

I always saw my partner through her share of the fun, though her question threw me for a loop.

"Why throw this at me right now?" I asked her. "You want me to ask if you came, like some teenager?" Why would she want to throw me off my game? I guess growing up with a con artist like Carson taught me caution.

She shrugged and sipped her wine. "Ask or don't, I don't care." She dropped the subject. "Martin's a good banker," she said. "I bet he's already pulled your credit report."

I still felt like defending myself. "My assets don't all show up. If all my cases settled today, Jake would owe me, at the minimum, a million bucks in bonuses. I've never sat down to come up with the actual figure."

"Don't count on that money until you have it in the bank and the check has cleared."

"I have a lot of money coming. I got nothing to prove it, but Jake's word is good as gold."

Martin Keating arrived exactly on time. I assessed him as he walked up. He seemed fit for his age, and some years older than Melina. He was a middle-aged man in his fifties at least, his hair cut short. He wore an expensive looking navy blue suit, white shirt, and blue tie. His shoes were dark blue.

Melina and I both stood up when he reached the table. When Keating saw Melina, his face brightened. Melina stretched her arm out to shake his hand, and he pulled her up, and smacked her full on the lips. He lunged at her a little, and grabbed her in a big bear hug, except I saw his hands roaming down to cup her bottom. I found myself crossing my arms across my chest. Melina extricated herself. I was the first to sit. I was 10 years younger than she, and I couldn't begin to count how many women I'd had. I wondered how many men Melina had been with. Keating was obviously one of her conquests.

"My business partner, Mario Luna," Melina introduced me, and with her one free hand, smoothed out an imaginary wrinkle in her flawless dress. She sat down. Martin had a death grip on her other hand.

Keating was pleasant enough. He tolerated my introduction, but through it, his eyes were glued on Melina. He continued hanging on her hand after he sat down. I wondered if he was going to make Melina eat one-handed. I examined what I felt. It was closer to annoyance than jealousy. I did not feel possessive of her but he was holding her hand much too long. The hug and kiss were not what I would expect from a banker. Our stock broker Mr. Robinson was a big shot too, and had known Melina for long time. He had kept a professional distance.

Melina cut through the small talk, and explained what we needed. He seemed amenable. He talked about different options available to us, and interest rates, dead boring stuff. He finally let go of her hand when they brought the salad. We didn't sign papers then, but met the next day at his office to get the paperwork underway.

"I'll help you put a package together. I should have no problem getting it through loan committee."

"Does that mean yes?" I asked like a dummy.

"Probably," he replied. As in the day before, his eyes were on Melina. Melina smiled at him like he was Santa Fucking Claus.

I tried to look like a serious businessman, and let Melina do all the talking. A day would come when I would be doing all the talking, but she clearly had this bozo in the palm of her hand. I sat back and listened and learned.

Business was booming. Pixie, Jo, and I met each day. I took advantage of that meeting often being at my home office. Jo was waiting for me when I got home. I never locked the door.

"Hey gorgeous. You beat me," I said.

"The kid's mom won't sign yet. I didn't push. I ran it down to her, told her to keep taking the kid to the doctor, advised her not to speak with the insurance adjuster unless she had a lawyer with her, and made it a point that it didn't have to be our lawyer, but a lawyer she trusted."

"How badly hurt is the kid?" I asked.

"I think he's going to be fine. He's home. They kept him at the hospital for two days. He's banged up, but not too bad. The whole time I was there talking to his mother, he was playing."

I learned long ago the golden rule: Don't push. Don't push a door, don't push a client, don't push a meeting, and above all, don't push to get a signature on a retainer. And never tell the prospect not to shop for a lawyer.

"You did good, Jo."

I kissed the top of her head, and sat beside her on the sofa.

"And where is Pixie?"

"She's handling a good one over at ELA Hospital. Bus shut the door on a lady, and moved a block with the lady stuck between the doors. Lady got dragged until people screaming in the back of the bus got the driver to notice what was going on, and he stopped."

"Ouch," I said. "Is Pixie up to a biggie like this?"

Jo looked at me with surprise. "I wouldn't have let her go by herself, sweets. We started together. She's going to close it."

"Of course," I replied. "You taught her well."

"She's not there quite yet, but she's a fast learner."

"Do we have time for a quickie?" I asked, pulling her close.

Just then, the door opened.

"It's me," Pixie announced in a happy voice. "I got a big one signed!" Her high heels clicked on the entry marble floor. "Anyone home? Is everyone decent?"

"If we were naked, would you have not come in?" Jo asked.

"Fuck yes, I would have come in. I got the bus lady. I'm so fucking good."

"Come over here," I said opening my arms from my sitting position on the sofa.

Pixie dove to her knees and into my arms.

"I'm proud of you," I said.

Jo reached over and patted the top of Pixie's head.

"Mama is proud of you too, sweets."

We started off rolling around on the couch and floor in a heap of blankets, and cushions, and clothes everywhere, and ended up eating a huge bowl of buttered, salted popcorn, watching Colombo, and drinking rum and Coke.

Before she left, Pixie went into the bathroom, took a three minute shower, and gargled, hoping to hide the rum scent from Aunt Carmen. Jo took what was left of the rum home to her husband. I took a long shower.

In the two weeks it took for the loan to go through, I kept busy with cases. Time flew. Time did not fly for Melina. She was over every day, pacing and anxious. I kept telling her that work was a better way to pass the time than wearing a hole in my carpeting.

"I've done everything I could do," she said. "All the chores that depend on the loan are piling up. I am not touching one thin dime of my money to move ahead, so that fucking Martin better hurry up and wind this up."

"So what else would you like to do?" I asked her.

"I'm going to the building to spend a few hours driving the crew crazy, then I'd like to...shop," she said. She tore off somewhere for the rest of the day to come back later with armfuls of department store shopping bags. I guess she was well on her way to filling up that empty bedroom of hers that she'd outfitted as a giant closet.

I've mentioned how impossible it is to call out on a car phone. But as far as receiving a call, it rang maybe once a day. With only two lines available for all the car phones in Los Angeles, that was a lot.

On Monday, that call was Pixie.

"I'm in jail," she said. Her voice was calm.

"What!"

"They told me I'm going to be booked. I was arrested at General Hospital."

"What!"

I pulled over to the side of the road. Everyone in the area with a phone in a car could hear one side of the conversation. Pixie knew this and was careful.

"What jail are you in?"

"LAPD, downtown."

She did not mention the charge. I didn't ask.

"I'll have you out of there before you have a chance to pee," I promised.

I stopped at a pay phone and called Tony, the bondsman that had bailed me out when I was seventeen, who had referred me to Jake. He said he would call his man who worked that jail, and get her out pronto.

I beeped Jo, and waited at the pay phone.

A couple of guys came up, and wanted to use the phone.

"You have to wait," I said in an unfriendly voice.

One of them looked me up and down and walked away, and gave me the finger. The other one said, "I'll fucking wait."

Jo called right back.

"Pixie is in jail. I'm running over to LAPD on Los Angeles Street."

"I'm at the office. I'll meet you there."

By the time I got to the jail, Jo was already there, and Pixie was out. I hugged them both.

"I paid the bondsman," Jo said.

"Let's go to Jake's," I told them.

They nodded.

"What's the charge?" I asked.

Pixie said, "Soliciting."

We were walking to the cars and I had a thought. This was Pixie. I had to ask.

"What kind of soliciting?"

"Patient Soliciting. What kind did you think? I haven't done the other kind since I was almost eighteen, and moved in with Aunt Carmen, and they expunged my juvenile record. So shut up about that."

I laughed, and she punched my arm.

"It was a setup," she said. "I did not hand out a business card. I was talking to a prospect. I was invited to speak to her by a relative who was with me. Cop walks up and arrests me. And guess what? On our way out, I see Carson. He waves at me and smiles."

Initially, Jake was worried.

Carson was a problem who had cropped up before. My problem. As soon as Jake heard Carson's name, he blurted out an uncharacteristic mouthful of profanity ending with "that son of a bitch." He believed Pixie. Needless to say, I shared his belief that Carson was responsible. He called a friend of his who specialized in criminal cases. His name was Jack Fino.

The next morning, the three of us went to see Jack. His office was not far from Jake's. Pixie told him the story. I handed Jack two grand in cash.

"I promise you won't even have to appear in court," Jack told us. "Someone has it out for one of you, or all of you. I'll handle it."

Pixie gave Jack a big hug, "Thank you Mr. Fino. I really owe you for this."

I wanted to remind Pixie I had just paid Fino two grand, so she owed him nothing, but I held my tongue.

I took off in my car and headed to Carson's house. His car wasn't there. I came back in the afternoon. His car still wasn't there. In the early evening, I made another pass, and he had come home. I did what I had done several years back: I shouldered the door to let myself in. The idiot still didn't have a deadbolt. This time he was in the living room. I punched him, and heard his nose crack.

"You set up Pixie, motherfucker."

He was on the floor.

"You always blame me for everything," he screamed in anger. "I've been waiting for you to come accuse me about you getting shot and the girl, but you never showed. Now you are here. What the fuck for?"

"If you had me shot, you wouldn't be bringing it up now. But this chicken shit stuff is right up your alley. You don't like competition. You figured you'd scare Pixie out of the hospital for good." I reached down, picked him up off the floor with one hand. I was going to punch him again, but he didn't raise a hand to defend himself. I dropped him instead. His nose was a red mess.

I headed for the door, but stopped before I opened it. "Quit fucking with me and my team unless you want me to keep paying you visits. The next time it's going to hurt."

After about two weeks, I got a call from the bank.

I was escorted in by Keating's secretary and found Melina already in Martin Keating's office. They were laughing hard about something. Martin came around his desk to shake my hand. That he noticed me at all was a change.

"Good to see you, Mario. Have a seat."

I sat next to Melina.

She smiled broadly. "Martin got us the credit line. No mortgage. It's unsecured except for a UCC filing on the equipment we are buying for the store."

I looked at Keating.

"Thank you. You are very kind." I could not have been more sincere.

"Martin is a trooper. He's smart. He knows we're going to do fabulous, and because we do, he will too. The money we make will be banked here."

I agreed.

"For sure!"

We moved to a conference room where I signed my name too many times to count. Melina signed as many times.

Martin handed Melina a checkbook.

"You know the drill. These are temporary checks. Let the new accounts know what you want, and they will order for you."

Melina explained that when we wrote a check from that account, it would be a loan against the $300,000 credit line[9]. Every month we only had to pay interest on the outstanding balance. As we started making money, we would pay down the credit line. I never borrowed, so this was new to me. I was glad it was Melina who would be taking care of this.

We left the bank and went by the market, touched base with the general contractor, and checked out the progress until it was too dark to see. Melina wanted to go to El Cholo but it was too late, so we settled for the Pantry on 9th and Figueroa, a 24-hour restaurant that was always busy. It was late, but I felt like eating pancakes and two sides of bacon.

"I have a question," I said.

"Ask away."

"Wouldn't being a lawyer be as great as owning a market or markets? I mean, you put in all that time going to school. And with the market, there's so much other stuff—all those employees, vendors, so much other stuff to deal with that just seems like busy work."

She frowned at me. "You know the market was my dream. So shut up already."

"That's no answer," I said.

Melina bit into her bagel and cream cheese.

"So why did Martin give us this line without having to put up the building?"

Melina munched away and between bites, replied, "It's a good loan. Banks want to make good loans."

"Any other reason?"

"I get this feeling that you are jealous of Martin," she said, staring at me from across the table.

"Why would I be jealous?" I felt surprise.

"Good question," Melina said. "No reason. If you want to know if I fucked

---

[9] $300,000.00 in 1973 had the same buying power as $1,669,588.24 in 2016

him to get the loan, the answer is no. If you want to know if I ever fucked him before, the answer is yes."

The way she said it, I had to laugh. "I knew it," I said, taking a sip of the hot coffee. "I could tell. I knew back at the Tower, when he gave you that touchy-feely bear hug and played grab-ass. If I had been jealous, hon, you'd have known about it then." I laughed again.

"It was long ago. Martin is cute. Five years ago he was even cuter. Anyway we became friends. If you really want it all, I've even been to an orgy with him, twice."

I stopped eating. What came out was stupid, and I didn't mean to say it. "Why did you go to an orgy with *him*?"

"Five years ago, I was in school. My money has always been at his bank. He's a swinger and so was I."

"I meant why go to an orgy at all?"

"I just told you, I was a swinger. Group sex was in. It's still in. What's the big deal?"

"Tell me about the orgy," I said, and called the waitress for more coffee. "I'm just curious, and I've got all night."

I hadn't thought about "swinging" or that there was an official term for what had been going on with Jo and Pixie and me for a while. What happened with us was just, I don't know...natural. I don't know that I'd feel the same way about an orgy. I remember pictures in magazines going way back from when I was a kid. I always thought it was weird to see all the men and women naked and getting it on, even the pictures of a couple doing it. For me, the turn on was the girl. I didn't know anyone but Melina who had ever told me they attended an orgy, not even Pixie. Where we came from, I seriously doubt there were orgies going on, but you never know.

"I was in a swingers' club," Melina said, wiping her mouth, crushing the paper napkin into a hard ball, and tossing it on the dinette. She waved her coffee cup to get the waitress's attention, and didn't say any more until her cup was full.

"My sociology professor had seen the swinger club ads in the free weekly, and wanted us to do research and write papers on our studies. I remember the assignment was during a chapter called 'Deviant Sexual Behaviors.' A bunch of us went to a couple of those meetings together. Safety in numbers, you know? They had a bunch of party games. Free rounds for the first guy to make his date come at the table. First one to give the emcee their panties. A wet t-shirt contest. Treasure hunt for the biggest and littlest nipples. Stupid shit. We were all supposed to be observing like real urban sociologists. The club met once a week in a neighborhood dive bar, drank beer, played their weird games, and exchanged numbers." She swigged her coffee. "It was mostly couples. There was a weird sicko dynamic. There were some loser single guys who signed up just to score. And with the couples, it was always the husband who joined, just to get some strange. The wives would join reluctantly to placate their husbands, but after a while, they'd let down their guard, and turn nympho. The husband would turn jealous and the wife would be saying, 'Get it on.' Most of those couples ended up on the rocks. If they had been happy and satisfied in their re-lationships, they'd never have been into the swingers' club to begin with."

"I never pictured you in a swingers' club."

"I never joined," Melina said, grinning. "The club was all sickos. It was sad, and depressing."

"So, you weren't really a swinger."

"You know that group of sociology students? We came up with our own club. All of the benefits, none of the sickos."

"How'd you do on your paper?"

"I got an A. But I didn't do it on the club. I wasn't going to have the same paper as everyone else."

"So, the banker. Was he in the sicko club or the class?"

She sat back, thinking. "I don't know if I should even say."

"No worries. I don't want to know. I really really don't want to know."

"In that case," Melina said, "I'll tell you. His wife had wanted to join the swingers' club, and they joined and she dumped him. I felt sorry for him. I brought him with me a couple of times to the sociology class swingers meeting. He's really very shy."

"Shy?" I asked. "Remember how he kissed you when we met that first time at dinner at the Tower?"

"Shy about getting naked in groups, Mario, not normal stuff. Don't worry about the small stuff, Cuz. Martin is just my banker now. More importantly, he's my friend. He proved it by giving us this loan with practically no conditions."

I looked around at the people in the diner. Everyone seemed focused on the food at their tables. No one seemed to be paying attention to our naked swinger talk.

I nodded in agreement. "You're right there. So that was it on the orgies?"

"Cuz, you are so horny."

"And what are you?" I asked.

"Horny as all fuck," she replied, a little too loud.

"Did you ever go to another orgy after that?"

"I did."

"Tell me," I urged.

"Let's get out of here, go home, get in bed, and I'll tell you," she promised.

We met at my apartment at two in the afternoon. Melina heard me come in and knocked on the door. Jo brought two pizzas. Pixie brought pasta and salad from a joint she favored. We threw everything on my dining room table, and filled up paper plates. Melina declined the food.

"I'm going to El Cholo later," she said, but hung around to talk.

"Carson is at it again," Jo said.

Melina looked up and asked, "Carson, your old friend? The one you won't introduce me to?"

I stopped chewing. So did Pixie. She said to Melina, "There's only one Carson."

"Carson is doing what?" I asked. I put down my slice. "Tell me all."

"I was at Pete's. He said that Carson offered him double what we pay him."

I wasn't worried about Pete. Pete and I were rock solid. All Pete needed to do was call me. He knows I'd match whatever he was offered, for sure.

I said, unnecessarily, "Carson won't pay for a case that turns out no good."

Pixie shoved aside her plate. "He's such an asshole. Like he can't get his own fucking contacts. He knows it's going to piss you off. He has to know."

I turned to Jo. "So, how did you leave it with Pete?"

Jo said, "I signed the case at the shop. I matched Carson's rate. Pete said it wasn't necessary, but I did what you would do. I matched it. Carson is full of bullshit, but I couldn't take a chance."

"Good girl," I said. Pixie was now our go-to on body shops. The body shop guys loved her. Who could blame them? But I was glad that Jo had handled this.

I said, "That means the others are going to hit you up the next time you're there."

"No." Pixie said.

"Excuse me?" I asked.

Pixie stared. "Please don't go over there again. One of these days that asshole will be waiting with a lead pipe or a gun."

"She's right," Jo said.

I put my arms up, like I was in a holdup.

"Don't worry."

I did not tell them about when I drove to Carson's. I don't know how they figured out I'd been paying these visits. They would have argued, but there was no point in wasting our breath.

I parked my car a block away. Like a burglar, I pulled the screen from the open window and let myself in. The smell of weed permeated the air. The room was dark, but there was a streetlight shining in the window bright enough that I could make out three bodies on the bed. Conveniently, Carson was on the edge. Considerate of him.

I put my hand around his neck.

I saw the gleam of his eyes when they popped open and the awareness and shock in them when he recognized me. I eased my hand open enough for him to gasp a breath.

"Mario, man. I want to talk to you."

"Not a sound," I whispered, tightening my hand, and pinning him to the bed with my other hand and knee. "You got nothing to say that I want to hear. Keep fucking with me, asshole, and one of these days, you won't wake up. Stay off my turf." I smelled something stronger than pot. "Your girls will not be happy that you pissed the bed."

The two girls didn't move. They were still asleep or passed out. Carson sat up.

"Don't move," I told him. "Just stay there, and shut up."

I left through the front door.

I loved the fact that Melina had the reins on our market project. She spent two weeks doing the hiring. I'd get the news of her day when we met for dinner or shared an after-dinner coffee or wine. How the evening went reflected her daily success. Sometimes she came in droopy, highly disappointed that one or another of her dad's former employees couldn't be found. Sometimes she came in perky, after she'd found another employee who greeted her with open arms, and quit their job on the spot to come in with us.

Sometimes she'd leave a message with the doorman, who would tell me when I came in that Miss Melina had taken a sleeping pill. She'd see me in the morning.

She made a few executive decisions, like not to open for twenty-four hours a day. Being open from eight to midnight would lower costs. Twenty-four hours might happen one day, but it could wait till we were established. She wasn't going to be on the floor, so she had a manager and two assistant managers. Once we were operating, she'd know how much of a crew there would have to be to stay open at night on top of the crew who stocked the store, and how much business it would take to break even. Melina at work was not the playful Melina I knew elsewhere. Even if I had the time to help her, she would never have allowed it. She was preoccupied and hurried. She was even in a rush when we sat together at night. Sex, when there was any, was quick. I knew it wasn't good for her. She faked it, then got pissed off when I accused her of faking.

As the grand opening neared, the two Mexican newspapers in Los Angeles published laudatory articles about Melina. They talked about rebranding the old store she had grown up in, and ran a historical series on her father's store that led to her finding and rehiring a few more of the people she remembered working there. Another series talked about the investment she made with her friend to bring regional Latin American cuisines to everyone who missed their homes. They talked to her about being the daughter of immigrants. The LA Times wrote a great article about the store becoming the center of the Latin community; and Melina insisted I be there for a photo shoot. She purchased a one page ad in the LA Times, LA Examiner and LA Opinion announcing the grand opening on May 5, 1973.

She decided to make a thing of it, and have a ribbon cutting ceremony. After she invited the district congressman to the grand opening, the city councilman's office heard about it and called in. The ceremony mushroomed. The Mayor of Los Angeles was there along with almost all of the City Council and many of the county supervisors, all cultivating their Latin constituency. Melina dressed me in a new suit. She was dressed to the nines, and I couldn't keep my eyes off her. All the politicians talked, community leaders talked, then she and I both cut the ribbon, each of us holding one side of a giant scissors. She was so happy that she was glowing like she was lit up by candles. I had a big knot in my throat.

Aunt Carmen came to the opening. I gave her a shopper badge with her name *Carmen Luna* on it, and a personal tour up the stairs to Melina's office, and through other areas of the store the public could not go. She was bursting with pride. Her hands were clasped, and she was holding them to her heart; her eyes were wet with tears.

"I am so proud of you, Mario."

A bunch of her friends arrived, and I left her with them, showing off the parts of the store I'd just shown her.

We watched the crowd of shoppers surge in to every department. I got buzzed to a case and left two hours after the ceremony. I heard that it was a huge success and it was busy until closing time at midnight. Melina called me a number of times throughout the day and stayed late to train the managers and assistants. She adjusted schedules, and monitored the security cameras.

I could not help but compare the work involved in regular retail to how I made my money. My occupation seemed so much easier. That store had so much to keep track of, and so many people doing it.

Life fell into a routine. I ran the stairs for thirty minutes, then religiously worked out for thirty minutes every morning and was finished by dawn. I did my usual work with Pixie and Jo, and went by the market daily. Melina was always there. Before the end of December, our credit line at the bank was paid in full. Our proceeds had paid back the debt, and we had over a hundred fifty thousand in cash[10] at the bank. Melina was getting a payroll check for her work, just like everyone else. Because we had not made a draw, I hadn't made anything yet, but I wasn't worried about it.

Business with Jake was booming. Jake paid me as always. Some of my bonus cases settled. I was feeling no pain. My accountant told me that for the IRS, Niley's expenses should be tied to a business. I met with Niley and gave her the option of working as my secretary. She wasn't interested, but she wanted to start up a gift basket business at home. I had Harry incorporate Niley's Baskets, with only a thousand in working capital. I bought an old house from an estate for pennies on the dollar, put a couple thousand into it, making it livable, and gave Niley a deal on the mortgage. Even with the extra I put in, the house was half the going rate. I gave it to her at cost so I wasn't out anything, and it was a steal. With them settled in an old house with a garage workroom for the baskets, the kids had plenty of space. Pixie and Niley had gotten to be good friends, and were able to come up with some regular thank you baskets designed especially for the body shops, but most of Niley's business was welcome wagon type and holiday stuff. A big boom came when Niley started putting together the Mexican baskets to order to be sold at the market. That were a really hot item. Niley's Baskets had a small booth where a clerk took special orders. The baskets were packed with small special order items we carried from Hispanic countries. We gave Niley the items at cost, and she paid a small rent for her booth. Before the year was out, Niley had paid off the house, and was sending my accountant a monthly tax flow statement.

At the market, upstairs there were a few general offices for security, marketing, and business. Melina's office at the market was also upstairs, but it had

---

[10] $150,000.00 in 1973 had the same buying power as $834,794.12 in 2016

a private entrance up a metal flight of steps at the back of the building. It was shiny and new, but already stank of cigarettes. There were a couple of empty ashtrays scattered on end tables around the sofa, and on Melina's desk. One wall was glass and overlooked the entire store. From the first floor, like a detective's interrogation room, her glass wall looked like a mirror.

She and I were standing, admiring our success, the view, and our checks. It was May of 1974, twelve months after opening the store, the day we took our first draw. Melina lit up her Marlboro, took three puffs and set it down to burn out. She handed me a check for four hundred thousand dollars and showed me a check payable to herself for the same amount. I signed her check and she signed mine. We looked prosperous, and we were. The store was bustling. Counters lined two sides of the store. The dining area by the front window was full of patrons having lunch. The remaining wall was the fresh produce area, which we took great pride in. The inner aisles were roomy, and stocked with regular items but also a lot of imported items, and our own brands with bilingual labeling.

I looked at the check.

"Fucking unbelievable."

Melina slammed my stomach with her fist, then rubbed her hand as if my stomach had hurt her.

"Washboard abs," she said, nursing her hand. "What do you mean unbelievable? You doubted me?"

"Not for a second," I said. I grabbed her right off her feet and twirled her around once, twice, three times. We kissed, and without another word, I pulled down her slacks, I peeled off my jeans and took her right there on her sofa where she received everyone who came to see her.

"It's been so long, so fucking long," she sighed.

It was fast, but it was fucking fantastic. Or fantastic fucking. Either way works for me.

"Wasn't it you that said there was no money in selling food?"

"You're dreaming. I said no such thing."

"Thank you for being such a great partner."

I walked over to the small refrigerator in the corner of her office and opened a bottle of wine. We drank to our continued success.

"Thank you for being who you are. You're a fucking genius."

"Fuck genius," she said, "I worked my ass off."

"The split should be in your favor."

"A deal is a deal," she said, "and besides, I got paid very well for my work."

"Our accounts are solid right now. Martin is so fucking happy. When I made the draw, he volunteered that he's ready to spring with the entire amount we need to build another store."

We looked at each other.

I grinned, feeling reckless. "Okay, let's go for it."

It was a Friday night. Jo was busy with her family, and Pixie was off somewhere with some one night stand. Melina had told the front desk to warn me that she'd taken a sleeping pill. I didn't feel like twiddling my thumbs so I dropped in to Casey's. The Irish pub was packed with well-dressed business people and tourists. I walked up to the bar. I was standing behind a much smaller guy. I don't know what he ordered, but it was tall and pink and had an umbrella in it. Maybe he was with a girl. It was a girl's drink.

He turned around, and I saw his mouth fix on the straw.

"Hey, long time no see, Mario."

"Hi dude," I said, shaking his hand. I drew a blank trying to come up with a name. His face was definitely familiar. We were still shaking hands, much too long, when his name came to me. Of course.

"First time I ever ran into you outside of a hospital emergency room,

Hugo."

"Yeah," he said. "Hazards of the profession."

"Can I buy you a drink?" I asked

"I have it covered," Hugo said. "We should do this again some time. Good to see you, man."

I scratched my head over that one, wondering what we should do again. Run into each other by accident? I wondered what he meant.

He walked into the crowd, and I turned to the bar.

"Believe it or not, this place was built in 1916 as a bathhouse," the bartender was telling a tourist. "But it was rebuilt in 1969, so we're really only a couple of years old." With a flurry of silver tools and magician's moves, flipping and tossing bottles and performing sleight of hand, he mixed the tourist's drink that he called a "Nutty Irishman."

Dark paneling was waist high, and the upper walls were forest green. There were booths and tables, and the captain's chairs that ringed the tables had leather seats dyed a color between Guinness and chocolate. The bar was all dark polished gleaming wood, and looked to my untraveled eyes just like an Irish pub should. The wall behind the bartender was mirrored glass, glittering and a foot deep in mixologist potions. I doubt there was a single brand of whiskey they didn't have at least three bottles of. I spotted Patricia sitting at the bar nursing a glass of white wine. I ordered the same, and joined her. It felt like my lucky day.

"I haven't seen you for a while," she said. "I used to see you at the car wash every week."

"I've been busy," I said. "But I have been thinking of heading in your direction."

"I've been meaning to thank you," she said. "Thanks for letting me know when you moved out. I got your old place." She grinned at me.

I couldn't help making a face. She laughed at me. Her long blond hair was straight, and parted in the middle, contrasting with a healthy tan. I'd forgotten how pretty she was.

"No, really," she said. "When you moved out, I bought the duplex for a song. It was on the historic register and your old landlord had no idea what a gold mine he had. My off-again on-again boyfriend and I had an estate sale, and sold everything in it, then took the building down to its original wood. That place was built of solid mahogany. We restored it, polished it up, and put in a couple of antiques. Now I rent it out each month for more than I paid for it."

She laughed at my surprise.

"Are you still at the carwash?"

"Yes," she said, "But I bought in. Vinny who owned it moved on."

"He died?"

"No, he got married and moved to Burbank. His new wife didn't like the carwash thing. I think he moved on to gas stations. Anyway, now I'm paying myself to be head cashier. For now, I'm half owner of the carwash. I'm buying him out. I won't be joining any country clubs, or buying diamonds, but I've got some rental revenue coming in now, and I'm not hurting."

"Very impressive."

"So what's up with you? I saw you got written up in the LA Times as a hero rescuing some girl from a car wreck," she said. "To you and your car wrecks." She toasted me. Our glasses clinked and we sipped from each other's glasses with hooked arms.

"I've moved to a great new apartment closer to Casey's. Work out of my new apartment with two hot girls. Got a great new investment, and got some stock. In fact, would you like to check out my apartment? If I had etchings, I'd offer to show them to you now." I batted my eyes.

"Sounds great," she said. "I'd love to."

I ordered us a couple of Reubens to go.

She stood up and bent her elbow and put her hand on her waist. I took her arm, but first I backed off and surveyed her short skirt and perfect legs. I whistled. She took a step and winced.

"Something wrong?"

"To be honest, the heels hurt my feet after a whole day of standing at work," she said.

"I know somewhere you can take off those shoes. Care to check out the pad, beautiful?" I asked.

I pulled to the front of the apartment building and the door man ran out to greet me. I gave him my car keys. Patricia pulled in behind me in a VW.

"I'm impressed," she said looking up at the building.

"Johnson will park your car and get it for you when you leave," I said.

I always took good care of Johnson and the others who worked the front desk.

"Sure thing, Boss," Johnson said. "Boss, I have a message for you." He waved me to the side and whispered in my ear. "Miss Melina said she took a sleeping pill again, so don't wake her. She'll see you in the morning."

I didn't mention that the desk had already delivered the message earlier. The timing was strange for Melina. It wasn't midnight. It was early for her to leave the store before closing on a Friday night when so many people spent their paychecks on their groceries. I left Patricia admiring the view from the living room's panoramic windows as I poured us each a glass of chilled wine. My glasses were new and carved of Irish crystal. We talked at my kitchen dinette over Reubens and fries served on fine china.

Patricia could not say enough about my apartment.

"The doorman is a nice touch," she said.

"The market downstairs and the workout room ain't too bad, either," I agreed.

We caught up on the developments in our lives. She told me she had an open relationship with her boyfriend, and that she was in school part-time, working toward becoming a professional designer.

"If that's what you want to do," I said. "But you have the looks to be a model, I am sure."

She laughed.

"Thank you," she said.

We went into my living room and cuddled on my two person lounge chair.

"I have to use your bathroom. Which way is the ladies?"

I pointed her toward my hall. Patricia wobbled a few steps on her stiletto heels, heading away from me. I watched her retreat, like a king on my throne. She took a step out of one shoe, and then the other. Her stocking-clad feet sank into the deep pile of my carpeting. I could hear her sigh, across the room. She left a trail of clothes all the way there, and returned naked.

"Do you like what you see?" she asked.

I sat up in my chair. All of me was at attention.

The lights were off. The glow from the windows cast a sheen outlining her curves. I felt my heart racing as my body responded. Her curves cast a shadow on me. I wanted to describe how she looked to me but words failed.

I stood. I drew her in to my arms.

She looked up. "You are so tall," she said.

"Is that a problem?"

"Not at all," she said. She put her bare feet on top of my shoes, stood on her toes, and tilted her face up.

I met Patricia again, the next week at Casey's Pub. It was completely by accident, but I had gone in hoping she would be there. She was at the bar drinking shots. That surprised me, because she usually just nursed a glass of wine. But three shots were lined up in front of her, and a stack of bills were between her and a man seated to her right. I surmised she had made a drinking bet. She was looking in the mirror, and saw me coming up behind her. She didn't turn around, but gave me a huge smile, then put her finger up for me to wait a second. I stopped, about a foot behind her. She nodded at the guy next to her. He looked at his watch, and nodded back. In quick succession, she downed all three shots. The guy next to her looked at his watch, frowned, smiled and shoved the bills in her direction. She accepted them happily, and spun around to me.

"Thanks man," she said woozily to the guy at the bar.

"Three shots in under a minute," he said. "If I hadn't seen it with my own eyes, I'd never have believed it. Are you up to driving? Looks like you might need a ride home."

"I'd take you up on that offer sport, but my ride is here." Patricia pointed at me.

Sport frowned. "Maybe next time," he said. He met my eyes with a certain degree of good humor, and started scanning the crowd for another girl to get drunk. His eyes widened when I took Patricia's arm.

"Let me guess," I said. "He dared you to drink three shots in a minute. You thought he was gambling about drinking. He was really hoping he'd lose the bet, and those three shots would get you so drunk, he'd score without trying."

She nodded her head, and then grabbed her forehead.

"Wheee," she said, "I'm drunk."

"So, I'm your ride tonight?"

"Hell yes," she said, hopping off the bar stool and wobbling on her high heels. "You got here just in time. That was the fastest twenty dollars I ever made." She hiccupped, and said to nobody in particular, "I can too hold my liquor."

"What do we do about your car?"

"Took a taxi."

We walked toward my car. I followed her pace, which was slow and unsteady. I was paying more attention to her footing than I should have been. We were stepping off the curb when lights flashed, half blinding me, and a car whooshed by. It struck me a glancing blow in my shoulder, knocking me off my feet, and bowling Patricia over in a ball. Some guy on the sidewalk took off on foot after the car.

"Did you see the plates?" I asked her.

I helped Patricia to her feet. The traffic was pretty busy, and plenty of people had come over to help.

Patricia's carefully pinned hair had come down on one side, flopped over her ear. Her knees were skinned, and the heel had broken off of one shoe.

"Didn't see a thing," she said unsteadily. "I don't feel too good. Rain check on the date? If you don't mind, I'll just take a taxi home."

I offered to drive her, but then the guy who'd run after the car returned. He was an off-duty cop, a young guy. He was dressed casually, and in good shoes.

"I'd never have thought you were a cop."

"It was an Impala," he said. "I got the first three numbers."

We exchanged cards. His name was John Smith. "I don't know if I'd file charges," I said, "but I'd sure as hell like to know who that was."

Smith said he'd get back to me. The next morning, I was sitting in my office, making my usual daily follow-up calls. Smith called, wanting to know if I wanted him to pursue the case.

"Give Detective Mike Sanchez the details and let him worry about it."

I figured it was just a drunk driver, and didn't want to take time from a busy day to chase some drunk who was having a bad day. I thought I might see if Sanchez also got the feeling that someone was out to get me. Jo saw the bruise the next day. My shoulder and my whole side were bright purple. I tried to pass it off as nothing, but it looked worse than it was. She dragged me to the emergency room to make sure nothing was broken.

Jo and Pixie had already gone home, and Melina was down with one of her sleeping pills. The beeper call came from a phone booth. I returned it immediately, expecting it to be from one of my tow drivers or a body shop. The phone rang a couple of times, then someone picked up.

"Hey Mario. It's Freddie Rocha. Remember me?"

"What's up Freddie? Good to hear from you man." Of course I remembered him. We'd gone to school together. He was a loyal member of Pélon's school gang back then, and probably now.

"Hey Mario, I heard from Pélon. He wants you to see him up in San Quentin."

Chapter 8
May 15, 1974
Auld Lang Syne

Jake sent one of his two-year attorneys with me. The attorney, Jeff, called the prison in advance to let them know his firm was considering filing an appeal for Pélon.

Pixie had known Pélon almost as long as I had. She was excited about the visit and chattered the whole plane ride there, her first time on a plane. She was wearing a revealing little sundress that Pélon would be sure to appreciate, and had a long sweater to put on in case the authorities objected to it. Jo didn't know Pélon personally, and was working on her own, back in Los Angeles.

Jeff joined us in the airport rental car. As we rolled down Main Street just before we got to the parking lot, he explained a little about attorney privilege.

"Because you're with me, you get to be in the attorney visiting room. Attorney privilege is broken by the presence of other people," Jeff explained. "You should know that the court can legally compel me to share anything discussed with my client, if there's someone else in the room with us. So don't say anything in front of me and Pélon that I can't repeat to a judge."

That effectively stopped Pixie's stream of chatter.

Jeff's warning worried me a little. I couldn't think what it might be, since I hadn't seen Pélon in a long time. I wanted to find out about Carson, but I didn't want to bring Jeff into it. Freddie had said it was urgent. I knew Pélon had stuff to share that he would tell only Pixie and me. I was a little worried, wondering if my record would prevent me from being able to see him but it proved to be no problem. Pixie had so many arrests that she couldn't count them, but except for the action Fino was handling, they were all juvenile offenses.

We didn't wait long. We were warned there would be no contact allowed, not even handshakes. Jeff would be the only person who could pass documents to the prisoner. The lawyer visiting room was a grim looking institutional room furnished with stainless steel tables and attached stools, each having room for four. Two other tables were occupied. Everyone spoke in a low voice, but there was not actual privacy.

Pélon was all smiles as he was escorted in by a guard. I had pictured that he'd be in ankle chains and handcuffs, but he wore no restraints. It had been a while since I had seen him. He was as fit as ever in his prison jumpsuit. He'd always been slight; he was little and muscular, and scary in the way a pit viper is scary. As a kid, I'd likened him to a rabid Chihuahua. Now he was more like a pit bull. He had some new jailhouse tattoos peeking from the end of his sleeves, and scribed into his neck. He hadn't bothered to cut his hair or beard in a while, and, though it is a little hard to explain how he manifested this, he looked a little crazy. It was as if he was like a rubber band that had been stretched a foot farther than it could go, and was giving off energy on the verge of snapping.

Pélon and Pixie flirted for a second. The authorities had made her put on her sweater, but it hung unbuttoned to the hem, and she might as well not be wearing it. In the sundress, her breasts looked fine, and Pélon clearly appreciated the view.

A lawyer needs a reason to visit an inmate he does not officially represent. I don't know what was in the stack of files Jeff brought, but Jeff and Pélon passed pages back and forth. Jeff winked so I'm guessing it was for show.

After five minutes of lawyer-speak, Jeff got up from the table. He walked over to the guard and asked to use the restroom. After the guard let him out, he came over to our table and reminded us that there was to be no body contact or passing of anything to the prisoner. He returned to his vantage point.

"Make it fast," I urged Pélon. "Jeff left us so we can talk freely, but he won't be away for long."

"Mario, you know you're my brother. We hear 'bro' all the time, but you really are my bro. I would give my life for you. You know that I will only tell you the truth." It wasn't necessary for him to remind me, but I nodded. It's true. We went back to childhood. The three of us in the projects where we grew up: Carson, Pélon, and me. We'd been The Three Musketeers.

"Carson claims he wasn't the one who planted the pot in my car."

"I believe him," Pélon said. "I heard on my end that it was Vago's crew. Not that he should have brought them in on your gig. That was wrong of him."

Pixie's lip curled at the mention of Vago. Pélon and his brothers had always protected the corner girls from Vago's crew.

I started to object, but Pélon ignored me and continued. "That's not all. Carson had nothing to do with the shooting. He didn't order it. He has no power."

"I have come to the same conclusion, just because he was always quick draw with the lies, but nothing with guns. You sound convinced. How do you know?"

"I heard you were shot. Pissed me off. I sent five soldiers over to take him on a ride. My boys worked him over. My boys left him out there in the desert, but came back convinced he didn't do it."

I thought about the cop's theory that the shooter was a transient who saw us and came up to the second floor to rob us. I thought about the cop's alternative theory of it being a gang shooting. Pélon was right that it could have been Vago's gang. That would be nothing to let the detective in on. I'm no snitch.

"Give Carson some slack. He's worried you are going to kill him. I'm not saying you can trust him, or rely on him, but I believe he didn't do it. I think he feels loyalty to you and me, but he has his weakness. He's got all those sisters of his, and Vago knows it. If Vago wants anything out of Carson, all he has to do is threaten one of the girls, and Carson is going to cave. Carson wants out, but there's no way out for him. He's terrified of Vago, and just as terrified of you. He's scared for his sisters and he can't protect them. Five sisters. The poor shit."

I know Carson, and I know the kind of gang soldiers Pélon sent. Carson would have spilled the beans if there were beans to spill. He's lucky to be alive. If Pélon had been on the streets, he would have done it himself. I wondered why Carson didn't have better locks.

I nodded. "Okay bro, I believe you. But if this fool fucks with me or my business, I'm going to fuck him over."

"Fuck him over. Just don't kill him. He's not the one who shot you and your girl."

I didn't mention to Pélon that Carson stopped being a suspect in my theory of the shooting sometime back. I didn't believe he was sharp enough, or that he would get involved in a murder. Like me, he had always skirted trouble when Pélon and his gang were up to no good. Carson was a fucking asshole, but he wasn't a murderous asshole. He didn't hire anyone to shoot me or kill Tanis.

"We put some cash on your account for commissary and cigarettes," I said.

"Good man," Pélon said. "I can use the money."

"There's something else," I said. "Did you hear about my new partner?"

"Sure did, man," Pélon said. "My ma and your aunt are better than a news service."

"Her name is Melina Marron. She's got a problem."

"Spill the beans."

"Her dad was robbed and shot by two brothers. The Vicario brothers. One of them is still locked up. He's here. Bruno Vicario. He might be up for parole."

"You want him to go away?" Pélon asked. He sat back in his chair, and gave me an impish grin.

"Nothing so drastic. I just don't want him out," I said. "And I don't want anything to come back on you."

Pélon frowned a bit. "No worries, dude."

Jeff started toward the table. I hadn't noticed him come in.

I still held Carson responsible for the pot being planted in my car. Even if he had not put it in the car with his own hands, he had hired Vago and his crew to fake PI cases and brought him in to a crooked racket encroaching on my legitimate business. It wasn't even so much that he was stupid, but that was a stupid choice. Between a legal hard way or an easy way that bordered on criminal, Carson would always take the easy way.

On the plane, Jeff dozed off in a seat in front of us. I gave Pixie the window seat. We had raised the arm rest between us and had a blanket over us both. There wasn't much we could do, but there was a little fondling.

"Feel better?" Pixie finally spoke.

"A little," I admitted. I wondered if I would ever find out who was behind the shooting. I wondered if I could accept that it was a random thing. Somehow, a transient looking to rob someone to buy drugs that turned in to a shooting and murder just didn't seem like the answer. I dropped off Pixie and Jeff at

Jake's and headed to the market. I walked past at least three security guards. One of them was posted at the foot of the stairs to Melina's office.

He tipped his hat to me as I approached the stairway.

"Hello Buzz," I said. "I take it Melina is upstairs?"

Buzz was a heavy-set former football player, former cop, and head of security.

"Yes sir, Mr. Luna. Miss Marron has been up there for an hour."

I took my time going up the stairs. It's open on the railing side, but the other wall is a framed gallery of pictures and newspaper articles about the store, a mix of news articles and paid advertising. Some of them are yellowed with time, and show Melina's parents, and a few show her as a little girl. I look through them every time I climb these stairs, wondering if Melina has a stash of newspaper articles about the robbery and her father's murder.

I knocked on her door, opened it, and found her alone in her office. She was absorbed in the papers on her desk, and looked startled when I came in.

"It's just me," I said. "No worries. Nobody could get past Buzz. You should relax."

I glanced down at her desk and saw pages of figures.

"Are you sure you're getting paid enough to do this?" The rows of figures made me shudder.

She looked up at me without getting up, and we kissed.

"I have it covered," she said, pushing the papers aside.

"I saw Jo at your apartment today working alone," Melina said, "She told me you went to San Quentin to see a guy. Pélon."

I dropped on a chair facing her and watched her light up a Marlboro. She took a drag. A few days ago when she had told me it was the stress of the market that had her smoking again, I wondered if maybe I didn't know as much about her as I thought I did.

"Why did you go there?" She took another drag on her cigarette.

"Just a little investigation," I said. "I was checking up on Carson."

"But he's not in jail," Melina said. "How can somebody in jail tell you—"

"Grapevine," I said, avoiding a direct answer. "Still wondering about who shot Tanis and me."

"Did you get your answers?"

"Some answers," I said, and told her a little about the trip.

"Do you feel better?" she asked. "Did you learn what you needed to know?" She ground out her cigarette after the third puff.

"What I feel is I don't want anything to do with that asshole Carson. Once a snake, always a snake."

"I told you from the get-go that this friend of yours had nothing to do with your shooting."

"If I had believed he really had something to do with murdering Tanis, he'd be dead already."

"Easy, pal, this is me. I'm not your enemy."

"You don't know him. Carson will do anything he thinks he can get away with. He knew about Tanis and me. He saw us together a day before we got shot. I had reason to believe he was involved even if he wasn't holding the gun."

"The cops concluded that it was robbery by a transient."

"They don't know shit," I said. "You are naïve." I told her, "You have no idea what Carson is capable of. I don't get why you are defending him. You don't even know him. He is crooked. He is sly. He is small time. I only see or hear about him these days when he's trying to poach my cases. I've known him some twenty-odd years and don't know how far he'd go to get rid of me as competition. What makes you so sure he's innocent?" I realized it sounded like I was jumping back and forth about whether or not Carson was involved in the shooting when deep inside I knew he wasn't. I just knew in my gut he knew more than he was telling. Plus Melina had a way of getting me to erupt in more ways than in bed.

She shrugged. "The cops didn't think he was the doer. And your friend Pélon told you so. You just said so yourself. I'm just playing devil's advocate."

"Quit it."

I believed Pélon, but Melina's stubborn defense of Carson put me on edge. I knew she was expecting to eat with me, but I left. I didn't mention that I'd spoken to Pélon about Bruno Vicario. There was no need to bring it up. I picked up two steak burritos to go, got in line like everyone else and paid. I looked up to the second floor at the mirrored wall to Melina's office. I raised the burritos like a trophy, wondering if she was watching, and headed for the parking lot.

Back at my apartment, I answered the ringing phone. It was Jo calling from Jake's office. She was going home. She had turned in one case and was hanging on to a so-so case she had just signed that she wanted to discuss with me tomorrow.

I turned the stereo on and crashed on the sofa in the den. The TV was on but muted. I turned on some 'Los Bukis'. The Latin band was one of Melina's favorites. I didn't get any beeps or phone calls for the two hours I sat there dozing and listening to music. At five, I beeped Pixie. I could have gone to Casey's or called another willing female friend, but I wanted Pixie.

"Are you tired from the trip?" I asked.

"No way."

I hesitated but not sure why. "Do you feel like coming over?"

"Of course. Are you okay?"

"I need you, Pixie."

Her tongue in my mouth woke me.

"Pixie is going to make you feel better," she whispered.

I followed her to my bedroom where she undressed me and gave me a vigorous massage. She started with my head, and neck, then worked her way down my back, calves and feet. I fell asleep while she was working on me. When I woke up, she was in the den watching a rerun of *Match Game* and drinking a beer.

"When did you learn to do a massage like that?" I asked, coming out of my room and buttoning my shirt.

Pixie beamed. "I wasn't just a waitress. I tried a couple of things before I was working with you and Jo. I tried being a masseuse. I even took lessons. Aunt Carmen didn't like the hours. I tried selling vacuums too, but couldn't make any money."

"I didn't know you could do a massage like that. That was great. For real."

"Boss, I'm here for you." Pixie was lying on her stomach, with her arms folded, her head resting on her palms. Her feet were up in the air. Her empty beer sat on a coaster on my coffee table. She looked like a high school kid.

"You absolutely revived me. I'm going to work out for an hour. I feel that good."

"Cool," she said. "I'll go get you something to eat. What would you like?"

I corrected her. "Get us both something to eat. Your choice."

She hopped up, tossed her beer bottle, and was gone in a flash. By the time she returned with two bags of Chinese, I was drenched in sweat. I let her in.

I showered quickly, and made it to the table before the food had cooled. We chased it with ice cream for dessert. Mine was capped with peanut butter and whipped cream.

"If I ate like that, I'd be so big you wouldn't want me," she said.

"I love you no matter what you look like," I said, and fed her spoons of my ice cream mixture.

"That's a nice thought," Pixie said, "And maybe you even believe you believe it. But if it was true, you wouldn't always be saying how Jo and I are so hot."

Pixie left at one in the morning. I would have liked company all night, but Pixie wanted to be home in the morning to take Lainey to school. Aunt

Carmen was always there, and loved being needed; but it made Pixie feel guilty that she turned so much to my aunt for her daughter's care. After Pixie left, I waited. I expected Melina to come over. She usually did drop in when she left the market, but she never showed. She didn't call, either. It was strange that Melina didn't call or come by. I wondered if there was something wrong.

I peeked in my refrigerator and pulled out a bottle of cold champagne. Barefoot, I walked with it to her apartment. It was late, well after one. I had no intention of waking her if she was asleep. I knew she put in some long hours, but she was something of a night owl too. She might very well be awake.

She was at home.

A Spanish ballad was playing.

Melina was not like me. Her door was always locked. I put my fist up to knock, but the sound of voices interrupted me. They were barely audible, but I was there, at the door, and could clearly hear what was conversation and what was music.

Melina was laughing. I heard a man's voice. He wasn't laughing. What he was saying or doing was making her laugh.

I stood there for a second with my hand raised, frozen, then it fell to my side. Maybe it was a minute or two. The sound of the voices behind the door roused some strong emotion in me, though I couldn't say what it was. It came as an unpleasant surprise.

It was probably the banker Martin. Maybe it was the head of the construction crew. I was curious.

I couldn't possibly be jealous.

I walked back to my apartment and put the champagne back in the refrigerator. At least I hadn't popped the cork. I walked into my bedroom in the dark and threw myself on sheets that still smelled of Pixie. Pixie was beautiful. Jo was beautiful. Patricia was beautiful. Melina was beautiful. Would I want to wake up every morning and find one of them in my bed? Which one? Why should I choose?

I blamed Pixie's massage for relaxing me so much that I slept too late to work out. It was already nine. I was showered and dressed and working when Melina dropped in with two cups of coffee.

"Are you alone? Can I come in?"

"Hey stranger. I missed you." I extended my arms out. I watched her place the two cups of black coffee on my desk. She came around and kissed me deeply. I wrapped my arms around her waist and moved down and cupped a cheek in each hand.

She sat down across from me.

"You wouldn't believe how busy it was yesterday."

"Keeping banker's hours?" I asked her. I looked at my watch. Not that I am policing her work schedule, but she would normally be at the market at this time of day.

"I had a manager opening today, so I'm not running late."

"Good. Take it easy," I said.

"If I take it too easy, it will be a long time before we make another dividend."

"In that case, drink up and go."

She laughed.

I could not help but wonder who had been the man in her apartment just hours ago. Did she fuck the man with the mystery voice I heard? It was none of my business.

"I missed hearing from you last night," I said. "Did you get in late?"

"I did get in late and I had company after I got home. How about you?"

"Since I left you at the market, I was home all afternoon and all night. Pixie came over and gave me a massage like I've never had before. I had no fucking idea she was so good at it."

"Lucky," Melina said, reaching for my empty cup. She took it, and turned to go.

"Big hands, big cock," she teased, patting my hand. The cups, both in her other hand, clinked together. "Wish I had time. Gotta run to work. I'll call you later. Maybe we can get together tonight after I get home."

"Sure," I agreed. I got up to kiss her. I wanted to ask her who her company had been but let the opportunity pass. Melina, the mystery girl in my life, liked her secrets. She claimed she told me everything. I had come right out and told her Pixie was here, that she gave me a massage, but Melina kept a lid on her secrets. She was a tease.

Johnson normally worked night shift, but he also logged as much overtime as he could get. After Melina left, I called downstairs to see if Johnson was working this morning. I lucked out.

"No rush, but can you come up for a little bit?" He readily agreed.

When I let Johnson in, I had a fifty all ready for him. He had to work two days to make fifty bucks.

"What's up, Bossman?"

I wanted to know if it was the guy from the construction crew. I wanted to know if it was Martin the banker.

I explained what I needed. An hour later, Johnson asked me to join him in the security office. I came right away to get there while he was still alone. I didn't know the guards' names, and dubbed them all Security,

"Here you go, Bossman. Sit down and watch this."

Johnson fast forwarded the Sony U Matic video recorder that the security cameras recorded to. It was the same model we used at the market, the latest thing in security. Each tape held an hour's worth of video, and the security team at the market painstakingly logged hundreds of these tapes daily, and recorded over them at monthly intervals. I expected we did something similar at the building.

Johnson played what he had found: the man who came to see Melina.

My heart stopped.

I recognized him instantly. The fucker was all dressed up. What the fuck was he doing there? Carson was the last person I'd have expected to see in my own building, and certainly the last person I'd expect to see at Melina's door.

I watched in disbelief. Carson stood in full view of the camera while the security guard called Melina to announce him.

"You okay, Boss?"

I got a grip on myself. "Sure, what else you got?"

"Here is the shot from your floor. The visitor entering Miss Melina's apartment at twelve-thirty a.m."

The next recordings he played were Carson leaving Melina's apartment, and then walking through the lobby, then out the front door at a quarter after three.

What the fuck!

I handed Johnson a hundred.

"You took care of me already, Bossman. No need."

"Take the money my friend."

I had no thoughts at all, but my emotions were churning. I could feel it, but had not yet processed what I'd seen. I ran up the stairs to my apartment. I fell into work like it was an anesthetic, focusing on the two beeps I needed to answer. One was a case I had to handle myself; the other one, I called Jo to handle.

On my way to the client's house, the image of Carson smiling at the security camera played continuously in my head. I turned up the volume on Neil Diamond, and tried singing along. Nothing blocked the disgust I felt at the thought of him behind Melina's door.

I tried to use my mobile phone all the way to my destination, but everyone kept beating me to the mobile operator who connected the calls. At least the phone was a distraction. I cursed in frustration.

I signed the client, Carlitos Pepper, in record time. I used his home phone to call the medical facility I was recommending, and arranged for him to be seen right away. His car was at the towing yard, but his wife was home. She would take him to the doctor.

"I'll call you tonight to see how it's going. You're going to hurt, but you can only prove it if you keep seeing the doctor."

"I understand."

Mrs. Pepper embraced her big hunk of a husband and said, "My poor Carlitos. You could have been killed."

He nodded in agreement.

"No worries," I told them both, "This lawyer is good. He'll make that asshole pay for running into you."

Carlitos' car had been hit by a big truck. Carlitos could have been killed, but he just had bruises. Fearing it would explode, he managed to get all three hundred pounds of himself out of the wrecked car but it didn't.

I was at my desk, and Jo dropped by with a new retainer and my mail. She dropped the stack on my desk.

"You got a letter from Pélon."

"Already? Read it to me."

Jo grabbed the letter opener and sliced the envelope. She unfolded the small sheet of lined paper. Only a couple of lines were covered. Pélon had never been much of a writer.

"Dear Mario," Jo read. "Just writing to thank you for the smokes and for bringing Pixie. She was a sight for sore eyes. About that other matter, I heard the guy you were talking about got into it with a dude in the yard, and then got caught with a shiv in his bunk. He won't be out any time soon. I could use some more smokes."

She looked at the back, and examined the envelope. "That's all." She dropped the letter on my desk.

"Mail him cash for commissary. He's never asked before, but I should have done it long ago. Let's do it every month." I scribbled a note thanking him. I told him that the dude situation was enough as is, and said how great it was to see him again.

I met Pixie at Olvera Street in downtown Los Angeles. Cielito Lindo Restaurant had great food. Jo arrived thirty minutes later. The girls were in tiny skirts that made them look hot, but I was distracted by the tapes I had seen.

"I signed it," Jo said as she sat down.

"Good girl. I got the one I went after too."

I was pleased that the beepers were silent. I felt broody, and didn't want to sign up anything else today. I needed Jo and Pixie around me. As we dug in to our favorites, I looked between Jo and Pixie. I had a ton of acquaintances, but nobody to talk to about my personal issues. Jo and Pixie were really the only friends that I confided in. Melina was a stranger that I'd only known for a handful of months. I had confided in her. Why I had dumped my whole soul out to her was a mystery. Internally, I was a pressure cooker. I had gone from a simmer to a boil about Carson's sneak visit. During the hour we spent at Cielito Lindo, I had a couple of starts and stops, but couldn't bring myself to share what I had witnessed. We left the restaurant with the truth still hanging on the tip of my tongue. We went to my apartment in three cars, and left them at the front entrance where Johnson would attend to parking.

I entered the elevator with the girls, one on either side of me. The floors flew past, but all I pictured was Carson. It could have been anyone else, and it wouldn't have mattered. But fucking Carson. Unbelievable! Why would Melina be around Carson? She obviously knew him. But how? That must be another fucking Melina secret. Maybe she'd known him all along. She'd brought him up time and again till I wanted to puke and never once said she knew him. The bile of rage burned the back of my throat. It tasted of betrayal.

Tonight, the thought of my fantastic round bed with its beveled mirror headboard was depressing. If not for Melina, I'd never have gone to the wholesale store. I'd never have gotten the bed. The girls sensed something about my mood, and joined me in bed. They were Melina's opposites, as frank and honest and open as Melina was treacherous and duplicitous. I tried to focus on them, but Melina's trickery and Carson's shadow haunted my head.

"Are we taking the day off?" Pixie was all smiles. I tried to match her gaiety.

"If we get beeped, sweets," Jo said, "we stop and take care of that business, then come back and finish this business."

Pixie frowned. "Jo, you're a party pooper!"

Later, when Jo headed for the shower, Pixie stayed in bed with me, trying to coax the truth of what was bugging me out into the open.

"Baby, what's wrong?"

"Nothing," I told her. I tried laughing but the sound came out broken.

Pixie rolled on top of me.

"You're not getting out of this that easy," she said. "I knew something was going on yesterday when you called me to come over. Today, it's even worse. So you tell me. What is it?"

I shrugged, I kissed her.

"Nothing is wrong." I lied.

She headed for the shower when Jo came out. Jo went through the same routine, in typical direct Jo fashion.

"What's up, boss? Something's on your mind."

I denied it, but no one was believing me.

Later in the living room, with Bob Dylan blazing through my stereo speakers, the three of us sipped red wine. We were a sight for sure. I was barefoot in boxers and a t-shirt. Jo had a towel wrapped around her. Pixie was wearing black bikini panties with a halter top. That's when they double-teamed me.

"Are you going to tell us what's wrong?" Jo asked.

"Nothing is wrong. Why do you two think something is wrong?"

"I know something is wrong," Pixie said, holding her wine glass up to her lips.

"Is it you and Melina?"

I gulped what was left in my wine glass.

"Nothing is wrong that won't get fixed."

The sex and now the wine had put a damper on my emotions.

"I have an idea," Pixie said. "I'll go out and get us some weed. That will be the cure for whatever ails our boy."

I considered Pixie. She wouldn't be getting high much because my aunt would smell it.

"Wait," Jo said. "I have some at home. 'Nando smokes it when he has pain. He gets it from an old army buddy, so it's pretty safe, and it'll save Pixie from cruising the park looking for a dealer. I can check in at the house, and come back and spend the night if you want."

That was something new. Jo never offered to stay over.

Pixie said, "I'll call Aunt Carmen and tell her I have to go north on a case, so she knows to get Lainey to school in the morning."

Normally I would not have gone for this, but I was feeling injured. I knew it was a bad idea, but it felt great that both of them cared enough.

"I'll work out for an hour till you get back," I said, getting up.

"I'll shower," Pixie sang out from the bathroom. "And maybe Mario will get lucky again."

During my workout, I thought of Carson and Melina. I switched from my normal workout and punched the bag. I pictured Carson and got a lot of steam out.

"Poor bag," Pixie said. "Who is it?"

I didn't tell her, and tore into the bag some more.

A little after midnight, the phone rang. The three of us were back in bed. Sheets were scattered everywhere. The comforter lay in a lump on the floor across the room, along with several pillows. The room smelled of marijuana and sex. Pixie had lit candles around the room, on the dressers, window sills and nightstands. The flickering light and scent sustained a mood. The light glittered and danced, playing with shadows. We were more intoxicated by the sex than the smoke.

When it rang, I reached over Pixie to answer the phone on the nightstand. It was Melina.

"Hey," she said. "Your door is locked. It's never been locked before. What's going on?"

I was high. I felt good and mean.

"Yeah. I'm busy. Have a good night."

I laughed and hung up.

"Where were we when we were so rudely interrupted?" I asked.

The phone rang again. We all looked at it. The girls didn't say a word.

"Don't answer it," I said.

Pixie looked in my direction, waited till it quit ringing, and took it off the hook.

"Good girl," Jo said, and continued what she was doing.

I woke up marvelously with four hands massaging my body. I stretched and so did the tool between my legs.

"Hey," I heard myself say. "Why are you guys dressed?"

"Showered and dressed," Jo said. She was first off the bed.

"Take me just a minute to get naked," said Pixie.

"No way." Jo said, slipping into her heels. "We both have to get home, do what we have to do, and get ready for work."

Pixie kissed me. "Go back to sleep. It's only six."

I sat up. "I get up at five."

"Not today," Jo said. "Thank you, boss. It was a spectacular night." She bent over the bed to kiss me on the lips. "It was fun."

"Loved every minute," Pixie kissed me again.

"That weed was good. I don't feel hung over at all," I said, jumping out of bed, bare ass naked, my dick bouncing, still erect but on its way down.

I put on my gi, and did three hundred sit-ups in a fast whack. I punched the bag for fifteen minutes. I went in the hall, took the elevator to the top floor, got off, and the fifty reps of running the whole staircase had all my muscles burning. By the time I jumped in the shower, I was already drenched. I resolved to get up at five tomorrow and resume my normal drill to banish the guilt trip for missing the routine. The best workout was of course at Cosmo's but the drive there and back was a waste of time. I sparred on the weekend with Fernando. For now, it was enough. My karate skills were as sharp as ever.

I read my paper at the Pacific Dining Car having ham, sausage, scrambled eggs, three glasses of milk, and two pieces of whole wheat toast smothered in peanut butter and strawberry jelly. I read the LA Times almost every day, but not the news. I liked reading the classified ads. Miscellaneous for Sale. Business Opportunities. Personal Ads. I read every ad in those sections.

By nine, I was back to my apartment, sitting at my desk, and listening to the tape of Jo's most recent retainer. I hadn't been home for ten minutes when I heard the front door open.

I heard the familiar voice and kicked myself for leaving it unlocked.

"Is anyone home? Are you decent?"

"I am never decent," I said.

I forced a smile, knowing she was seconds from inviting herself into my office. The sex, the workout, and the food had taken off the edge. They'd pacified me, at least superficially. Though the anger was hidden so well that I couldn't believe how calm and cool I appeared, I was as curious as ever to hear how Carson ended up on the security tape, and in her apartment. The thing that kept me from asking was the need to find out if she'd volunteer the information without prompting.

I watched her place two cups of coffee on my desk and drop into the office chair Pixie favored. It was fabric, had a knitted throw folded over the back, and had a relaxed angle. Jo preferred the more expensive upright leather office chair; it was sleek and supportive with no frills. This was a duplicate scene Melina and I had played many times before, but it was like the funhouse mirror version. My emotions were all distorted. I could see that up to now, I'd been naïve. I grew up in the school of hard knocks and wasn't usually so green. I didn't like being taken for a patsy.

I reached for the cup. "No kisses this morning?" I made a sad face.

Melina got up. She smoothed her skirt in a way that emphasized her curves. I wondered if she was trying to manipulate me. She hustled quickly around my desk, hugged and kissed me passionately. I wasn't immune, but the thought crossed my head that either she or I was a performing monkey. As suddenly as she had done it, she was back in the chair, sipping her black coffee. Definitely performing.

"That's two days since the grand opening that you are still here at this hour."

"The assistant is doing his job," she said. "Let's see how it goes."

"You're a slick operator."

She smiled. "Thanks baby."

I wanted to tell her that was no compliment. I thought about ignoring her coffee as I wished to ignore her, but instead chugged the molten coffee and put down the empty cup. On top of the coffee I'd had at PDC, it burned like bile. I felt confident that I would soon get to the bottom of this.

"Let me get you more," she said, smiling.

I put my hand up. "No. I have had enough."

Her eyes met mine. Where I used to see vulnerability, I now saw cunning. I could see the wheels moving in her lawyer-brain.

"So tell me, why did you have the door locked last night? Why did you take your phone off the hook?"

I held a smile. "I was busy."

"Well, tell me, what was going on?"

"I was having an orgy."

"Oh you fucker, why didn't I get invited? Who was here? Anyone I know?"

The only reply was my steady smile.

She came up behind me. I remained seated, my back to her. She kissed the back of my neck, her arms around my chest, then one hand moving down to test my interest.

"They drained you. I've never seen you soft like this."

I wanted to tell her she was the one who had turned off the heat.

"Got to run. I'll be in touch."

I swung my chair around to face her. She kissed me.

"I'll take you to a real orgy," she said, "A banquet room filled with bodies doing everything imaginable to each other."

I shrugged. Call me selfish, but I wasn't interested in other men being in the room.

"Don't forget your cup." I handed the mug to her without getting up.

I did not walk her out. Her appearance put me on that powder keg again. I listened to the door close as she left. The anger came out of hiding. I slammed my fist on my desk. The sound was loud, and hard. Everything rattled. Nothing was broken but me. I got calmly out of my seat, and went to the den, engaging violently with the bag until my arms hurt. I don't how long.

I was saved by a beep. It was a new case. I decided to handle it myself. I took a cold shower, and was out the door within ten minutes. I locked the door behind me.

Margaret Lopez was thirty-four. She was single, lived with her sister Janice, a former client. Janice was off at work. I knew beforehand that only Margaret would be at home. I knocked at the front door, and she opened it, revealing herself to be a big girl with a pretty face. She was at least two hundred pounds, and of average height, which to me is quite small. She seemed shy. I tried to put her at her ease. I like women, regardless of size.

She told me about the case. The accident had happened last night. A car made a left turn in front of her. Her car was a mess, but she had been able to drive it home. The other car had not been towed either. The cops showed up, but asked them to exchange information, and said that a police report was not necessary.

"A police report is always good to have, no matter what. The cops were either busy or lazy. No worries. You have a good case."

Margaret said, "I don't have any bruises and nothing's broken. I know Janice went to the doctor two or three times a week. I don't want to do that. I'm trying to get a job and I just don't have the time."

"The only way you can recover something more than the property damage will be from the doctor," I said. "You need to prove you are hurting. Doesn't matter that you don't have any broken bones or bruises. Maybe you don't hurt now, but you never know. Tomorrow you might."

I could see that Janice had pushed her to call me.

"I just don't want to do it," she said stubbornly.

"No sweat. If you have any problems getting them to pay for your car repairs, call me. I'll get the lawyer to handle it for you free of charge, but you shouldn't have any problems."

"Sweet, Mario. Don't be mad."

I got up. "Don't be silly. I'm glad I met you. And listen, if you start hurting and decide to see a doctor, beep me, and I'll fly over here." I kissed her cheek.

"Janet never mentioned you're so tall." She looked up at me.

"It's a bitch finding clothes that fit," I said.

"I bet."

Margaret walked me to the door, and said, uncertainly, "If you think I should do it, I will. After all, I made you come all the way out here."

"Only if you feel like you need to. Now, we've met. We're cool. We're friends. If you hear about a case, let me know. If you need something personally, beep me for sure."

The PI business is crazy. Some days we are inundated with calls. Not all calls lead to cases. Not all cases are good cases. A good number of them are the fault of the person calling us. It didn't matter to me when a call fell through without a retainer. I liked the action. I liked being busy. Besides, every contact made is a contact, after all.

Some days it is slow, especially when the weather is good. We were lucky to get one or two cases in a day.

I checked in with Jo and Pixie. They were at my home office.

"On days like this, I wish I had a crystal ball so every morning I knew how busy we were going to be."

"Pixie is asleep on the couch," Jo said.

Nothing else was coming in.

"Wake her up, and go home early," I said.

"But it's just afternoon."

I urged her to go home. Imagine if we could plan our days instead of killing time waiting for a beep or a call.

After leaving Margaret's, I had dinner at Casey's with two virgin lemonades.

Johnson was working. He took my keys to park my car.

"Ring me if you see that guy on the tape come in tonight or any night."

"You got it, Bossman. I'll let you know even before I call up to Miss Melina about letting him in."

I handed him a twenty.

"Bossman, no need. You've given me plenty already."

"Always take the money," I said, walking toward the lobby. I stopped and turned his way just as Johnson was getting in my car. "When Miss Melina comes in, let her know I took a sleeping pill, and I'll talk to her tomorrow."

"Yes Bossman."

I laughed all the way up the stairs. Once inside my apartment, I locked the door, and laughed again. "Fuck the bitch."

I had told the girls that I would handle anything that came in. Nothing came in. That gave me too long to think about Carson and Melina.

At twelve thirty, there was a knock on my door. I was in the den watching television. I ignored the knock and the two calls I got on my house phone right after. I figured Carson wasn't coming over tonight.

With less than three hours of sleep, I woke up at five filled with energy. Maybe it was hostile energy, but it fueled my full workout. I hit the shower, and was dressed by six thirty and headed out the door on my way to the Pacific Dining Car.

Melina was in the hallway, naked.

"Asshole, you didn't take a sleeping pill. What the fuck!"

She reached up to poke my chest with extended fingers.

She was laughing, and pulled me toward her apartment. I caved. What can I say? She's a bitch, but she's a hot bitch. We fucked like pissed off animals. And yeah, I was still pissed off. Maybe it would have been a good time to come out and ask about Carson but I didn't do it. I wasn't wearing rose-colored glasses any more. After the angry sex, she thought we were all fine. I could fuck her from now till Christmas, but I would never trust her the way I once had. I wanted to see if she would tell me on her own. I wanted to catch him when he came back. The curiosity was killing me, but I held on. I'd had enough of Carson. Carson has been warned for years to stay away from anything connected with me. Melina was no great love of my life. She was a fucking partner. She was my business partner.

For the next couple of days, I visited the market and had lunch with Melina. We talked about the next market. She had two real estate brokers looking for property in Montebello close to my old neighborhood. There was a surge of redevelopment in the area. The property was more high end than the rat hole I grew up in.

"That's quite a drive from here," I pointed out.

"We're going to have more places. We will train good people like I'm doing here."

As disgusted as I was with her as a human being, I liked the money I had already made with Melina. I had my money back on the market with a big profit. The stock broker she'd introduced me to had doubled my original twenty five thousand dollar investment. I was on a roll, but I had no control.

I'm not passive in anything. In my life, and in business, I control the shots. Even at ten years old when I hustled karate business for Cosmo, it was all me. I was the key to the business, just as Melina is now. If something were to happen to Melina, how would I run this place, much less a chain of places like she planned? What if we ran into bad times, and the other markets didn't perform because Melina wasn't around to operate the store like she does in this one?

And where did that fucking Carson fit in?

"Want another burrito?" she asked.

I didn't hear her.

"Hey, are you here or somewhere else?"

"I was thinking of the expansion you are planning. You're a real operator." This time I meant it as a compliment. Maybe.

"Thanks babe."

We parted ways. She returned to work at the market, and I returned home to work my calls.

Things fell into a routine, but the situation had changed. I didn't trust her. It had not dawned on her that I wasn't thinking with my cock any more. The door wasn't always unlocked, and sometimes the phone was off the hook.

She rang me and told my answering machine that she was home.

I picked up.

"You're here early," I said. "It's only eleven."

"I've got the manager training another manager. When we've got them both up to speed, then we can decide which one will run the next store."

"Okay," I said. "Goodnight."

A day or so later, I got the call from Johnson that made all the difference in my world. You hear about careful people walking on eggshells. You never hear about when the eggshells break.

"The man is here, Boss."

No superhero could have dressed and gotten out the door as fast as I did then.

I took a post by the elevator door. Just as he stepped out, I pushed him. He went crashing to the back of the elevator and slithered down to the floor where he sat in a slack-jawed heap. I followed him inside. The elevator door closed, and I pulled the emergency switch to stop it from moving. The fucker had on a blazer and sporty shoes. His clothes looked brand new. HE looked brand new. Hell, he looked like a prototype of himself, like a magazine cover that had been airbrushed.

"Mario," he said.

"Motherfucker," I said.

Chapter 9
June 6, 1974
The More Things Change

"What the fuck are you doing here?"

"Melina–," he said. He was still on the floor propped up like a Chatty Cathy doll.

"Yeah, what's up with that? What the fuck you got going with Melina?" I reached down, grabbed his hand and jerked him to his feet. "I want answers and I want them now. If you play games, I will fuck you up."

"Long fucking story," he mumbled.

"I got all day, motherfucker," I said. "Sing."

"She wants someone offed in prison. She called me. I'm just a fucking go-between."

I didn't need to be a mind reader to know who she wanted hit. She'd be after that Bruno Vicario, the robber Pélon had fucked up to screw up his parole hearing. I knew she was scared that he was getting out. I didn't tell her I'd handled it. Anybody who came up out of the old neighborhood knew if you're smart, you don't talk about your gang connections–not if they were the kind who were in prison, and on a first name basis with death.

"So what are you, motherfucker? You into murder for hire now?"

I shoved him against the elevator wall.

"Stop fucking with me, Mario. You can't keep doing this and think I'm not going to get even."

"I'm really scared asshole. Go ahead. Take your shot!" I dropped my hands to my side.

"Fuck it," Carson said. "I'm no match for you, and we both know it. What the fuck makes you think I'm the one after you? There's enough business in this town for both of us."

"After me." I said. "What the fuck are you talking about? Who's after me?"

Carson swallowed hard. His complexion went from gray to white. I thought he might puke. He knew something he wasn't saying.

He shook his head from side to side, and shut his eyes. "Look man, I just want to bury the hatchet," he said.

"I know you, man. The only place you'll bury the hatchet is in my back."

"That ain't true, Mario. You and Pélon are all I got."

"Motherfucker, you ain't got me." As hot as my words were, I knew what he was talking about. We had been kids together, Pélon and Carson and me. I could no more kill him than I could cut off my right hand. Ok. Maybe the baby toe on my least favorite foot.

"I was just going to tell Pélon. She'd pay him to off Bruno Vicario. She'd pay a shitload," Carson said. "And she's hot in bed."

I knew Carson hadn't answered my question, but I followed his topic.

"No need," I said. "Pélon's already gonna keep Vicario fucked up. He's never getting out."

"Wrong." Carson was out of breath. "Pélon wants the job. The job is good money."

"Both of you are fucking crazy." It pissed me off. Of course I knew Melina would have been happy for Vicario to get dead. But I hadn't seen any reason to put Pélon on it. I knew Pélon would do it in a heartbeat, but I was hoping he'd keep his nose clean and get out some day. It pissed me off that Carson would dangle this carrot in front of Pélon. You don't tease a shark. They get a whiff of blood in the water, and it is irresistible.

Someone was knocking on the elevator door. I lowered my voice. "How did you meet Melina?"

"I tried to sign her at Queen of Angels. You got there first. I gave her my card, then I backed off, I swear. I tracked her phone number through the hospital, and I called her a few times, because she's a hot chick. We got to talking. She asked me over to talk."

My mind raced. The pounding on the elevator door got louder.

"Open the fucking door!" It was Melina.

"Who is after me?" I could see he was not going to give it up that easy.

I punched him in the stomach, not that hard. He made a harsh wheeze, slumped down the wall again like his bones were gone, and ended up back on his spot on the elevator floor again. He never could take a punch. He moaned a little, and I knew he was done for tonight. He gagged, and tossed his cookies. I reached down, grabbed him by the back of his collar and lifted the sorry son of a bitch's face out of his own vomit. He mumbled something. I'm not sure what it was. It sounded like "*thanks,*" through a face dripping puke.

"We're going to talk about this," I said. "It's not over."

Carson nodded, without opening his eyes. His hand came up. He flashed me a peace sign.

I pushed the emergency button. The door opened. Melina's face was as red as a tomato. She punched me once, twice, three times as I walked toward my apartment. Kitten punches. Fucking pussy.

"He's all yours," I said.

"You're a fucking asshole!"

I looked back and waved goodbye. "Ditto. Bitch."

I locked the door, turned off the lights, got undressed on the way to my bedroom, and crashed. I had no problem going to sleep. The confrontation had cleared the air. Nothing was resolved, someone was out to get me, and I felt great. Human psychology is weird as shit. I woke up at five, did my routine and was out the door at seven headed to the Pantry. I felt like eating pancakes, and the Pacific Dining Car didn't have pancakes. Johnson was not on duty so I had no one to ask if the asshole was still there or had left. I wanted to know what time he'd left.

Carson had said Melina was hot in bed. I hadn't analyzed if I was pissed off because she was fucking someone I know, or just because she hadn't told me about it, or if it was because specifically it was Carson. On my way to the Pantry, I remembered how she'd said she got a gun permit by blowing a cop. She always used sex as a wedge to get her way. If the cop story was true, why wouldn't Melina do the same with Carson? Carson was actually good looking. He'd always been able to get any girl he wanted. It wouldn't take much effort on her part to use sex to kick start what she wanted, then offer him green to get it done. I drove home from the Pantry figuring I'd work there until a case came up that I needed to handle. I brought the classified ads with me. There were several listings in business opportunities that had caught my attention and I wanted to call and inquire.

I had just sat at my desk when the phone rang.

"We need to talk," Melina said.

"No good morning, or fuck you or something?"

"We need to talk. Either you come over or I'll be there in a minute."

I didn't move. If anything was going down, it would be on my turf. Then she walked in. If Melina had a bad night, I sure couldn't tell. She looked radiant in a suit, dressed as if she were going to court and not the market. Of course she always dressed well, but the suit caught my attention. Her ass caught my attention, but I did not get up. She waited for me to, then sat, as usual, in the chair Pixie favored.

"No coffee? No kiss?"

"Let's skip the bullshit, Mario. What you did last night was dark, and stupid, and beneath you. You're a fucking bully."

"Oh, so you came to complain about how I treated your boyfriend? Or are you here on his behalf to let me know you're suing me?"

"Skip the bullshit."

"What you are doing with Carson is darker and way below what I figured you for. I'm not a lawyer, but I know that soliciting another human to kill someone for you is pretty fucking dark. So don't you go accusing me of being dark. I'm not a murderer."

"Wait a fucking min–,"

"Shut the fuck up, Melina."

I think that stunned her. She sat back in her chair and raised her hands as though giving me leave to continue.

"We are partners in a business that I don't know one fucking thing about. If you get sent to prison over some stupid stunt like this, I'm stuck running the market or markets you plan to open. I'm not going there. I'm done being your partner. Go back to your apartment, and think about how you are going to buy me out because that's exactly what has to happen. I'm fucking out."

"You're a fool," she said. "I told you from the beginning I was looking for a friend, not a steady boyfriend or fiancé or husband."

"I don't sneak around my friends. I face my friends, even my opponents, head-on. I don't care who you fuck, even if it's Carson. And by the way, he says you are really hot in bed. The fucker is a blabbermouth. Be very fucking careful. I don't want to be anywhere near you when things explode. I'm not going to jail a second time for shit I had nothing to do with."

Melina laughed. "Nothing is going to explode."

"In that case, congratulations. Bring me an offer. You don't need me as a partner. You don't need anybody. You used me in the beginning because it cut your risk down to half of what you had invested, but you have the money back now. The building is free and clear of mortgage and the credit line is paid off. Thanks for the opportunity. You did my investment proud, and I appreciate you for bringing me in. Now, I want out."

Melina looked at me with a mean look I'd never seen before. "You're a total fucking fool, Mario. You bet your ass I will buy you out. I'll be in touch."

I stood. That meant she had to look up to me. "Next time you come in here, bring me the offer," I said. "No other reason for you to come back."

"Just like that, you're even tossing our friendship. You're an asshole for sure." Melina stormed out of my office, and seconds later out of my apartment. The closer on the door probably stopped it from slamming.

The instant she was gone, the indecision set in. I walked into the kitchen and fixed coffee, and wondered if I had made the best move. But there was really no choice. Going to the cops and snitching was not an option. I had to write off being her partner. If she got implicated, I could be implicated, and that couldn't happen. There was no other choice, but still, my heart was heavy.

In the afternoon, I got a beep from Harry's office. Melina had told him we'd had a falling out. She'd given Harry an offer to buy me out. So I headed over there.

Harry got up and came around his desk to give me a hug.

"Harry, how do you feel? You okay?"

"Fine, fine. Just a little under the weather." Harry cut to the chase. "She's offering two hundred fifty thousand, all cash. I don't have it in writing but she's ready to proceed."

"What do you think?" I asked.

"She told me that you each netted four hundred thousand from the business. Not bad. But partnerships can be trouble, son. If you are having problems, better to get out sooner than later. As for the amount she's offering you, it's entirely up to you. I have no recommendation. You've always been smart." Harry chuckled. "I still remember the first time you came in to this office. You walked out of here with a hundred dollar bill and a promise to work on how you'd get me PI business. You were all of fourteen then. And I had no idea how well you were going to make good on that promise."

We both laughed. The last ten or eleven years had seen a lot of changes.

"Tell her I'll take four hundred thousand. If she doesn't have it all in cash, I'll take a promissory note and give her a year to pay me."

Harry nodded his approval.

Two days later I turned over my hundred shares in the corporation to Melina in exchange for three hundred thousand in cash.

I had come in to his office to deliver a check, but Harry flat out refused to take a fee from me, even though I insisted. He had a juicy cough. His office manager Barbara poured him a cup of herbal tea while I was there, and offered me some.

"Honey and ginger," she said. "With a squeeze of lemon, and a little ca[11]yenne."

"Only if you have some too," I said.

She served the tea in three mismatched office mugs that I remembered drinking from ten years before. I tried the tea, and it was surprisingly good.

Harry and Barbara had both gone silver, and I'd never really noticed. I guess it had happened gradually. They both still came to work every day. I was struck by the passage of time, but then so were they, since they couldn't stop referring to past clients we'd signed, and me as a kid.

"If you hadn't given me that big check, I could have never made this deal," I reminded him, after Barbara padded off with the empty mugs.

---

[11] $300,000.00 in 1974 had the same buying power as $1,535,876.62 in 2016

"I didn't give you that money. You earned it my boy. Now, take what you have and make more."

Harry hugged me before I left. He was so much smaller than he had been when I had met him. I could feel his bones. He smelled of eucalyptus. There was something about him, a frailty that I'd never noticed.

It would be the last time I would see Harry alive. That night he died of a heart attack. When I got the news, I cried like a baby and without shame.

Harry's funeral was the next day, on a Friday. Cosmo closed the entire day. Jake knew Harry was a man I treasured like a father, and he shut the firm out of respect for a man he barely knew.

Jo and Pixie accompanied me to the cemetery. Jake was there with a group of his attorneys from the office, including Jeff who had gone with me to San Quentin to visit Pélon. I saw Harry's two children who were there with their families. They were in their fifties.

"My dad loved you very much." His son Roger hugged me.

"I haven't seen Dad much since I moved out of town, but I've heard about you for years. I feel like I know you." Harry's daughter looked nothing like him except that she had his caring eyes. She was little and slim, and hugged me so tightly that I was afraid she would break. "You're so tall, Mario. My dad said you are a karate master."

Cosmo was right there, and he agreed. "He is."

I had tears in my eyes as I introduced Cosmo. I should have realized that they'd all met at some time in the past.

"I remember you," Roger said. His sister nodded.

"You were always across the street."

I introduced Jo and Pixie. We stood in small groups and talked. We had been standing for a long time when Jo got my attention. She inclined her head, pointing out a figure who stood at a distance, alone, dressed in black with a matching hat.

Melina.

I stiffened. What was she doing here? I realized she'd been transacting my business with Harry, so maybe she'd found out that way. She saw when I noticed her, and approached.

We hugged, stiffly, strangely formal, and without the heat of sex or anger.

"I'm sorry for your loss, Mario. I know he was a dear friend of yours."

"Thanks," I managed to say. "Thanks for being here to pay your respects."

"I didn't know him that well, but he was also my friend," Melina said.

I introduced her to Harry's son and daughter. She'd already met Cosmo once during his first visit to the market.

After the funeral, at Harry's house, I met attorneys I had never seen before. Harry had a lot of friends. I saw the attorneys who worked for him, and asked about the practice. It turned out they had a standing arrangement with Harry to take over the practice. It wasn't all attorneys; Harry's son and daughter had children with families of their own. It was hard to picture that Harry had been a great grandfather.

I was relieved that Melina didn't attend. Being around her made me uneasy. My feelings must have been obvious because Jo and Pixie avoided bringing up the topic of Melina. They weren't usually so sensitive. It was so fucking stupid to feel like this, but I guess regardless of what they actually do, people can't help how they feel.

I got home early. The emotion had drained me. I declined offers from Jo and Pixie to come over. They wanted to keep me company but I wanted to be alone. I opened a bottle of 1969 Chateau Mouton Rothschild. I remembered when Melina chose it, when she had stocked my wine cupboard. I opened the bottle. I had to let it breathe. I had to breathe, too. I poured a glass, and sat on my couch, in the empty, quiet room.

The phone rang. I picked it up. It was Melina.

"Let me come over and keep you company, I know you feel devastated."

I never replied. I just sat there, hesitating. Honestly, I wasn't thinking at all. I barely had the energy to hold the phone. My right arm lay across the arm of the couch, receiver dangling, and I was tucked into the corner. The next thing I knew, someone took the receiver and hung it up. She was standing there.

Melina.

I don't know what I felt, seeing her. She sat herself in my lap, knees on either side. She put her arms around me and hugged. For a long time I did not move, nestled in the corner of the couch, surrounded by Melina. But then, something inside my chest eased a bit. I hugged her back. My feet were squarely on the ground. I wrapped my arms around her and stood, carrying her up as I stood. She straddled my waist. I did feel devastated. My resolve was too weak to fight the circumstances. Or her. She poured herself a glass, and handed me my untouched glass.

We finished a bottle of wine and began another. We talked of Harry. She told me what Harry had said about me. I told her my side, how I'd met him, and everything after that. In the morning when I woke up at my usual time, Melina was there. She had never spent the night in my bed. I felt instant anger at myself, for my lack of resolve. But then I felt only pain. I was heartsick and in mourning.

The instant I glanced at the clock, I felt the room move, like a rocking boat. I only moved my eyes. I did not usually drink, but I recognized the most terrible hangover. Maybe I was strong enough to take punches from the best fighters and not show pain, but against a hangover, I had no defense. I was miserable. It was five in the morning, time to work out, but my twisted guts were as dark and gamey as the sky was outside. There was no way I could get up.

My hand was on the end table on the clock. Melina reached for my arm and pulled me next to her.

"Five is too early after four bottles of wine," she said.

"What?"

"Sleep," she whispered.

My guts churned. The room swayed. I didn't want to think about anything. Not Carson. Not murder. Not Harry. I just wanted to fall asleep, and stop the spinning. Melina turned on her side. I held her from behind, and cupped her breasts, our legs entwined. I passed out.

It was almost noon when chatter from Jo and Pixie woke me.

"How long you been here?"

"About an hour," Jo replied. "Why?"

She put a cup of coffee on my end table. I looked at it with mixed feelings, none of them good.

"Was anyone here when you came?"

"Nope," Pixie replied. "Why?"

"What are you, a parrot?" I was too sick to laugh. "I'm going to die," I said.

"You just need cuddling and a massage," Pixie said. She undressed and went to work on me. Jo left and came back with three different kinds of massage oil, then undressed, and helped Pixie revive me.

I was flat on my stomach. Pixie's hands were slick and fragrant over my back, but the voice in my head was furious. How the fuck did I leave down my guard? What the fuck did I let Melina come over for? She might be a squeaky clean woman, but the kissing and fucking was like Carson's leftovers. No, it was the other way around. I had been there first.

I thought of Harry. He had been around long enough to finish my deal with Melina. I was glad he had seen for himself how I had profited by that start-up money he had paid me. I would miss his advice in the future, but I could still hear his voice in my head.

I kept an eye on business opportunities in the classified ads. I found an apartment building with twenty units in walking distance from my aunt. The neighborhood was great. The apartments were rented. Randy, the real estate broker who had the building listed, was not much older than me. He explained the process of buying real property, escrow, title insurance. The math took some thinking, but I was getting better.

"With twenty tenants, do I need a management company?"

"It's up to you, really," Randy said. "You can probably make do with a manager who lives in the building in exchange for free or partial rent for managing."

A week later, I signed an offer to buy the building for $175,000. The seller came back with a counter offer of $200,000. I signed a take it or leave it offer of $185,000 all cash. The seller accepted.

Aunt Carmen was delighted with my purchase. She was still doing her birthing classes, and had taken little Lainey on as an apprentice doula, but that did not take much of her time. She appointed herself the manager. She would oversee the property and collect the rents. She had been an accountant for years. I thought it was a good idea, and hoped the change would do her good. I know she had spent her life as a nurse-midwife, but hoped she would stop the baby deliveries, and all the commotion at the house.

When escrow closed, I stood in front of the building admiring its curb appeal. I was so fucking proud standing there, alone, and feeling fantastic.

The building had six one bedroom units, ten two bedroom, and four three bedroom units. Pixie wanted one of the three bedrooms and planned to hire a live-in that could sleep in one bedroom and be there all the time. It took her some time to get someone that passed her, and especially my aunt's, vetting. She had never paid rent before. My aunt wouldn't accept anything from her so all the good money she'd made was just sitting in the bank. My aunt retrofitted the apartment with new carpet, new tile, new appliances, and a total paint job. The place looked great.

"Are you planning to do this to all the apartments?" I asked her. My wallet was hoping it was only for Pixie.

"We can get higher rent if the apartments are fixed up. As people move we'll take a look and decide what to do and what not to do."

My aunt was smart. I would have done the same. I figured I could learn the apartment business. I already had gotten down to how to purchase a building. I expressed my gratitude to Randy, who was teaching me the ropes and prospecting other properties even when the listing was not his, so he could get his half of the six percent. My broker had something to show me every week.

The next building I purchased was a block away, from the same seller who had sold me the twenty units. This building had fifteen units, needed some work, but looked great from the curb. I trusted the broker and I made the decision to buy it without mentioning it to my aunt. I wanted the weight of responsibility to be on me. I don't know why, but I just did.

My broker pleaded that I not pay cash. He'd work the loan for me. The seller accepted a hundred forty thousand.[12] I put up a down payment of forty thousand and the loan company gave me a loan for a hundred thousand with payments that would easily come from the rents. The broker didn't want my cash sunk in a couple properties; he wanted me to make loans, so I could buy more properties. I went along with him. I was learning. When I closed escrow, I picked up my aunt, and took her to the building. We both stood out on the street and looked at the building, filled with pride.

Jake was staying true to his word. The cases that settled for more than three thousand, he gave me a bonus on. The big cases took a long time; it took a year or more for the biggest cases to settle. But I loved it all. I loved Jake, I loved Jo and Pixie. I loved my life! It wasn't just the money. Oh, it was the money, but not really the money. It was like a fucking dream. Money opens a lot of doors.

---

[12] $140,000.00 in 1974 had the same buying power as $716,742.42 in 2016

In July 1974, I opened escrow on eighty units in Pico Rivera. It was not the greatest neighborhood, but it was a great building. The seller had problems with the law over something, and needed to sell. My broker worked it so I paid $500,000 for the building. It was a steal. I put $200,000 down and the loan company approved my loan for the balance in less than a week. I couldn't believe my luck. My aunt would never be able to manage this building from home. My broker engaged a management company to take care of everything in exchange for a monthly percentage of rents collected. When escrow closed, I took a look from the street. Four buildings, all mine. I was on a fucking roll.

I never met Melina on the stairs, but saw her occasionally in the hallway or lobby. We were cordial. We even hugged, and exchanged light kisses and pleasant talk. Melina opened the market she had planned in Montebello. She mentioned in passing she was about to open one in East Los Angeles in my old neighborhood. I wondered if Carson had advised her on that one.

I hadn't thought much of Carson other than wondering if he was telling the truth that someone was after me. Even if it was true, a year had gone by and I was still kicking ass, having sex almost every night with someone different, and enjoying my life.

My favorite people were my Jo and Pixie. I loved them. Every month I gave them extra money. Of course, they earned it signing cases. I was getting my bonus money now, so I needed to share with those that helped me make it possible. Business was good, but it wasn't booming. There were too many Carsons out in the field. My contacts stuck by me, but there was so much competition these days that everything was becoming hot. Though hospitals were now on the lookout for familiar faces, Pixie was good at getting around the guards. Jo was willing to give it up, but she didn't have the patience to negotiate with fools who wanted to trade sex to get in to the wards where the accident victims were being treated.

Even with a family member, it was difficult. When the case was worthy, I showed up. I almost always got what I wanted, either by standing tall over the chumps, or by greasing their palms with money.

Johnson kept me advised about Carson who had not been back, at least not on Johnson's watch.

My morning routine had not changed. I hit either the Pantry or Pacific Dining Car for breakfast. Once in a while I drove over to the Hilton for breakfast. It was actually closer than the other two, but parking was a hassle and it was crowded with hotel guests. A couple of times, I picked up some good looking tourist chicks even without trying very hard. I craved sex like any guy, but no matter how occupied I got with strangers that visited my bed, I loved being with Jo and Pixie. I made it a point to enjoy them as much as possible.

As usual I ran up the ten floors. As I walked to my door, Melina was waiting for me.

"Hey stranger," I said.

"You're the one who wants to be a stranger," she accused with a harsh laugh.

"What's up?"

"Can I talk to you for a few?"

"Sure, come in."

We sat in the living room. She brought no coffee. I didn't offer anything.

"Look, I just didn't want to ask you to do anything illegal. I know you don't want to know," she said, "but for what it is worth, that matter I wanted to handle with your friend in prison, I didn't go through with it."

"Smart move," I said.

"I paid," she said, "I didn't want Carson or the friend in prison mad at me."

"Don't tell me." I said, my voice firm. "I don't want any part of that. I don't want to know."

"Carson is calling me asking me for money. He says his friend in prison needs a loan."

I shook my head.

"You paid once. They know you'll pay again."

"It's not the money. He's not asking for much."

"How much?"

"Two thousand."

I shook my head. "I told you Carson was trouble. He's an asshole." When we had been kids, it had been me he'd hit up for loans. I had no idea what he spent it on, but I assumed back then it was probably loans for dope. I had been able to put an end to it, but doubted Melina could.

"I don't think it's Carson. It's Pélon or whatever his name is."

"That's not Pélon's *modus operandi.* You still defend Carson," I said getting up. "Are you still fucking him?" I stared at her.

She got up too, stared back, and said, "I fucked him so I could get him to do what I wanted at the time. You know that. What's the big deal? And no, I'm not fucking him."

I was actually getting pissed. "And what do you want me to do?"

"Tell them to stop. Tell them to stay away from me. I'll give them the two thousand, but they need to leave me the fuck alone. I don't have time for this. I don't have the stomach for this."

Melina was visibly shaken.

"How much did you pay them when you called the thing off? I shouldn't the fuck ask, but how much?"

"Ten thousand," she said.

That fucking Carson. I didn't even know if they were in cahoots. I didn't know if Carson was fucking over Pélon in prison, or if Pélon in prison was still working people. Probably both.

I said, "I'm not in touch with either of them." Just because I felt sorry for him, I sent Pélon monthly cigarette money, but that was nothing. If he knew I sent it out of pity, he'd be pissed off. He was probably regularly fucking up Bruno Vicario.

"I wasn't sure. I'm sorry to have bothered you. I'm just afraid."

"You have guns. You know how to shoot. Why be afraid?"

"I only fear what I don't see coming," she said.

I smiled. It was definitely a lecherous smile. I was feeling lascivious.

"What's in it for me if I try and help?" I heard myself say. Maybe I was being an ass, and maybe it was because I could see Melina was getting hot. Maybe I wondered how far she would go.

She started unbuttoning her blouse, her eyes on mine. A smile crossed her face. There was a challenge there, lustful and raw, and promising and lewd. There's nothing hotter than a woman like Melina backed into a corner, and bargaining. I looked her over. She was as beautiful as ever, and I could see she knew it.

"Fucking won't make me do more or less for you," I told her.

"Fuck you," she said.

It was a furious fuck. It started with her bending over my desk, moved to the floor then to the bedroom where we furiously got it on. There was no conversation, only squirms, sweat, and deep breaths.

Melina was a bitch, but she was a special bitch.

The morning after, I drove to Carson's house. I didn't break in. I knocked once, then knocked again.

Carson was in his boxers. He looked hung over. A pretty boy wreck.

"What the fuck you want Mario? It's nine in the fucking morning!"

I pushed him, gently. I stepped inside, and closed the door behind me. Carson was five feet ten inches, and he had to look up at me. I poked his bare chest with my index finger four times, hard enough to throw him off balance but still remain standing.

"Stay the fuck away from Melina. She's not your fucking bank."

"I am fucking sick and tired of you coming over here to my house and messing with me. You better stop this shit!"

I didn't want to do it, but I punched him in the stomach. He went down on his knees, and started coughing. No puke.

"Do we have an understanding?" I asked.

He looked up at me, and raised his right hand, giving me the finger. I grabbed one finger and twisted, just hard enough for him to scream. Nothing broke.

"Cocksucker!" Carson said.

"Do we have an understanding?" I repeated.

"Yes. But you better go see Pélon. The two thousand is for him."

"Go to the lobby. Tomorrow at the apartment, the guard will be holding an envelope for you. It will have your name on it. That's the last two thousand. If it was up to me, you wouldn't even get that."

"I understand," Carson said. "Mario, it ain't me. Pélon sends me these messages. All I'm doing is delivering. I don't say no to Pélon."

"She gave you ten grand for that shit you were arranging. That's a lot of bread, motherfucker. Leave her the fuck alone. Tell Pélon to leave her the fuck alone. I'm not going up there anymore, and he can say goodbye to his cigarette money. She's my friend, and nobody shakes down my friend."

"Okay."

"Carson, please don't push it. I don't want to come back here again. If I do, there won't be any conversation. I will kick your skinny ass. I will bounce you off every wall in this fucking place."

"Okay."

I drove back to my apartment. I hated myself, but with Carson there is no other way. He'll lie low for awhile, and come back and do what he wants.

Jo called in.

"Are you okay?" I asked.

"Sure, I'm fine. It's 'Nando. I'm sure he's going to be fine. It's some kind of chest cold. He's had it for days. I think we did too much on the Fourth of July."

"Go, baby. Do what you gotta do. You can call me here. If I'm not here beep me. You know the drill."

I hung up the phone. I couldn't remember a time when Jo had been out of commission for as long as a day. Her husband 'Nando had been taken by ambulance to the VA Hospital in Westwood with respiratory problems.

I hadn't seen 'Nando in several years. He was a pretty darn good artist. I had two paintings he had given me, but I never had the canvases framed so they were in a closet.

I returned a call that turned out to be a case. I drove to Hacienda Heights, and was in and out in 30 minutes with a signed retainer. It was a good case but not a big case. I'd been spending too much time fucking around with my real estate sideline, and ignoring my bread and butter. I wanted big cases, bus crashes, truck cases. I was doing nothing to advance to bigger cases.

Pixie called me on my car phone, and she got through.

"Fuck, I can't believe I got through," she giggled. "This fucking thing is always busy."

"Easy," I said. "You can't use that language on the air. Everyone is listening and the mobile operator will cut us off."

"Sorry everyone," she said, "I'll be good. Anyway, I signed the one I've been working since yesterday. I'm going to Jake's to drop off the retainer."

"I'll meet you there."

I was proud of Pixie. She had come a long way for a girl who'd gotten her

GED as an adult, not too long ago. She had learned to evaluate a case, and she scrutinized police reports when they became available. Jo called me aside earlier this week, and made me listen to Pixie's call to the investigating officer on a case to tell him off for not clearly reporting our client's version of the accident. This was something that Jake's personnel did on a case, but once in a while, we got really involved and followed it up, especially if questionable liability was involved. Jo was proud of her as well and reminded me all the time that Pixie had had a great teacher, namely Jo.

I had been with Marsha's answering service for years. I only used the answering machine on the home line—or maybe if I needed to record a call. I was touching base with the answering service as I did every so often, waiting for the owner to pick up.

"Mario, I sold out," Marsha said, "Your timing is perfect. I've been meaning to call you. I'm tired of dealing with the overhead. I'm stashing the few bucks I have left after paying all the bills, and going over to 24-Hour Service. You gotta move over there. They have the best service and they specialize on bridging calls."

"I'd never leave your company," I told Marsha. "You're the best. So if you aren't going to run your own any more, I'll go where you go, if you can set everything up the way we've got it." We talked it over and she promised to mail me the paperwork.

Years ago, the answering service would do everything possible to keep a caller on the line while I answered my beep, then I would be cross connected to the person calling me. I got suspicious that the exchange was eavesdropping on my calls but I had no proof. Anyway my business cards had my beeper number and home number.

"Let me know when you start over there."

"Deal," Marsha said. I figured she would get a commission.

Late in the afternoon, I stood at my office window looking out over the panorama that was Los Angeles. In a way, it did resemble a patchwork blanket. The clouds hung low, and were a dismal gray. Randomly, a glare would light up the clouds as if a giant firefly were trapped inside. On the ground, I could see palm trees thrashing in the wind. I knew something was coming. When the rain finally broke, it was tremendous. Unusual. LA drivers are desert drivers and know nothing about driving in the rain, especially in bad storms. As bad as that sounds, it's great for business.

Johnny the tow truck driver called, and gave me details of a lady taken to ELA Hospital with bad injuries. Her husband, who was also hurt but not that badly, gave Johnny the go-ahead to contact me. While I was on with Johnny, two more beeps came in. It occurred to me that if I had a big crew, I might send them out to all the hospital emergency rooms on days like today. But days like today were far and few between. Hospitals had started looking closely in emergency rooms, trying to catch lawyers soliciting.

Fernando, my highway patrol buddy, was working the freeway by Magic Mountain. He beeped me about a truck that had lost control and slammed in to the back of a car. A chain reaction resulted, involving more than 15 cars. It was just Pixie and me to handle it all, but nature doesn't care about that. It wasn't just the big pile-up. The flow of calls continued. I had not heard from Jo, but given the possible seriousness of her husband's situation, I wasn't about to ask her if she was coming back today.

I sent Pixie to ELA Hospital to handle the call from Johnny as quickly as she could. I made a recording on the answering machine saying that I was in the field, and would return calls as soon as I was able. I suggested that if I didn't call back immediately, they leave a message on the machine. Then I headed to the big one to invent a way to talk to the injured. I wouldn't go to the scene. When I got to Denny's Restaurant to meet Fernando, he handed me a list of names of accident victims that had been taken to the hospital.

"You want coffee?" I asked.

"Always," he said.

I didn't order food, but paid the waitress for coffee for me plus the plate already sitting in front of Fernando. The restaurant was loud, and full of people sitting out the storm. It wasn't particularly close or convenient to the accident, so I had no expectation people involved would magically appear. Fernando dug into his food, and promised to call me back when he had details about all the other cars involved in the crash, and the fatalities. He handed me the information about the truck driver–a huge cross country hauler–and the owner. The insurance limits would be good.

On days like this, I realized I could make a fortune if my car phone were reliable or if phones were portable. I had to carry rolls of dimes and quarters in the car for the pay phones. Sometimes the trouble was finding a pay phone, especially in remote areas. This Denny's had one phone.

Two hours later, I was making calls from Sparks Truck Stop. Not only was it near the hospital that had received at least seven injured parties, it also had a bank of several phones. When Pixie walked in, she should have looked like a drowned rat, but instead, she looked as sexy as ever. Her hair was wet and slicked back. Her high heels could not have been more inappropriate for rain, and the bright, thin cotton dress she was wearing clung wetly to her every curve.

"Hey boss," she said, as she sat down. "I signed the husband and wife at ELA Hospital." She grinned at me, patting her hand bag where I assumed she had the retainers and information.

"If I didn't love you so much, I'd marry you," I said, "or, I'd eat you for dinner."

"Oh boss, eat me, please," she giggled.

I gave her the names and addresses of three drivers who had not gone to the hospital but whose cars were smashed bad enough that they'd have some kind of injury. Pixie plotted out the addresses using her map book, and gobbled down a hamburger.

We walked out to the rain. It was still pouring. She got in her car and I got in mine.

I got home after midnight. The tape was full. I listened to thirty minutes of calls, most of them duplicates of beeps I'd already handled. I made note of calls to make in the morning. At one thirty as I was coming out of the shower, Pixie came in, drenched.

"Can I shower?" she asked.

"Put what you can in the dryer," I said. "You should have some clothes here," I heard myself say. I realized Jo should have clothes here too. Suddenly, I felt terribly guilty that I had not reached out to Jo to check on her husband. Pixie was already in the shower, so I walked in the bathroom.

"Did you talk to Jo today?"

"No, have you?"

"I'll beep her."

I beeped her once, then again. No call back. Guilt turned to worry.

Pixie came out of the shower wrapped in a towel. "I washed my pussy really good," she said. "Just in case you get interested."

"Have some peanut butter," I said. "Sit over here." I was in the kitchen.

"What else you got? How about ice cream?"

"You know where it is. Bring some out."

Pixie sat at the table in her towel and doled out a bowl of ice cream. She offered me one but I declined. She topped the ice cream with Hershey's Syrup, peanut butter, a crumbled churro leftover from Cielito Lindo, and a handful of salty beer nuts, and commenced eating.

"Jo hasn't answered my beep. I'm worried. You know she answers her beeps no matter what."

"Let me call the VA Hospital," Pixie said, picking up my house phone with the really long cord. She dialed information, and got connected to the emergency room, who connected her to an emergency hospital operator. It was a circus trying to get through at night.

"'Nando Webb," Pixie said into the receiver for the sixth time. "I need to talk to Jo Webb, his wife. She's been there all day and night."

"We don't know that," I said.

"She would have reached out to us if she hadn't been there."

I nodded. "You're right."

"I'm her sister," Pixie said. She put her hand on the phone. "I think we're on the right floor."

I took the phone from Pixie.

"Hello, this is Mario. I'm Mrs. Webb's brother, I need to know how her husband 'Nando is doing, and I need to speak with her. Can you page her?"

After ten more minutes of back and forth, and being placed on hold, my anxiety increased.

"Maybe I should run over to Westwood to see what's going on," I told Pixie.

Pixie nodded in agreement.

Just as I was about to hang up, Jo's voice came on.

"Mario? Is that you?"

"I've been trying to reach you. You've been there for hours. How is he?"

Jo was crying. Jo never cried except when she was happy, but Jo didn't sound happy.

"Jo, what's going on?"

Chapter 10
July 8, 1974
The More They Remain the Same

"'Nando's gone. He left me, Mario. I can't believe he's gone."

"I thought it wasn't supposed to be serious."

"They couldn't save him." Her voice broke.

Jo did not sound like herself.

"I'm here for you," I said.

"He had a terrible case of pneumonia. Mario, he just passed away a few minutes ago. I don't know what to do."

"Don't do anything. Pixie and I are on the way. We'll see you there!"

If I were a drinker, I would have taken a triple shot of one of my hard liquors to ease the pain I felt. I felt helpless. There was nothing I could do to ease Jo's grief.

"'Nando passed away," I told Pixie. "We have to go."

"Oh my God, no," Pixie said, running to the dryer to get her clothes.

Minutes later, we headed out to Westwood.

A week later, 'Nando was given a military funeral like I had only seen in the movies. The flag was draped over his coffin with flanking guards of honor. He was saluted with a volley of shots and drumming. The ranking officer handed Jo a flag, and shook hands with Joanne and Kevin, Jo's kids. Fifty white doves were released following the priest's prayers. It was beautiful, but my heart was crushed for Jo. I rarely thought of how tough her life had been up to now. I'd met her after her husband had lost the use of his legs, after she'd already adjusted to being the wife of an invalid. They had made it work. She had never once complained, or said a harsh word, not against her husband or God, or fate. At thirty-three, dressed in black and edged by her kids, she looked twenty. She was a beautiful woman. Her eyes were hidden by dark glasses that matched her dress and shoes. The most tearing moment for me was when 'Nando's service dog raised his front legs to the coffin and howled. Skip howled like his heart was breaking. Joanne and Kevin walked over to the German Shepherd and stroked his beautiful fur and took him by the collar. The dog lowered to all fours, and walked with the children back to their seats beside Jo.

Melina was the first in line to hug Jo, and pay her respects. I saw Jo hug her tightly.

I've always hated funerals. It didn't matter that we were all destined to die. It is just too sad to be borne. I couldn't help remembering Harry. His loss was still fresh. And now this. When I hugged Jo, I found I couldn't let her go for a long time. My eyes and face were wet with tears. Some were for all of us. Some might have been for 'Nando. Some were for Harry. I looked at those two brave little kids with tear-stained faces who would be going through life fatherless, and I couldn't help but think of how my aunt had raised me on her own. It could not have been easy; and that is what Jo was facing now.

"I love you Jo," I whispered to her, "I'll have your back for the rest of my life."

"I love you more," Jo managed to say.

Life goes on. After the funeral, Jo took off for thirty days. To give Jo space, we had not been over to visit. Pixie and I handled everything, but we lost a lot of cases because there's only so much two people can do. There were no big storm days. Sometimes, we teamed up and went out together. Not a single day went by without a very long talk with Jo on the phone.

"'Nando was so protective. The house is being paid off by the mortgage insurance he took out when we bought the house. He had an insurance policy from the Army, and another policy I didn't even know about. I'll have his military pay and benefits, so I'm set, thank God. Joanne and Kevin will have the money to attend college."

Jo had two older sisters who were married and local. She didn't see them much because of Jo's hours. Her mom was alive and well. Her father had passed away when she was a little girl.

"What are you going to do about your kids? We can adjust your hours." I made the offer but it was hard to picture Jo respecting office hours. "You know I'm here for you. Get a live-in to help out. I'll take care of it for you," I offered.

"No need," she said, "My mom is moving in next week. The kids love the idea. I love you Mario, you're so sweet. But I got it covered. Really. Thanks to you I have more than the insurance money. I've managed to save these last few years."

"I'm anxious to see you, and so is Pixie."

"A few more days and I'm back." Her voice was stronger than it had been for weeks.

"Take all the time you need," I said again, though I was looking forward to her return.

"Are you kidding? I'm ready, I'm ready."

Pixie was at my apartment when Jo walked in.

"You look fucking fantastic!" Pixie said.

And she did. She had never been heavy, but now she was as trim as a model.

Pixie got to her first. They hugged.

"I'm so sorry I was off work for so long." Jo hugged me. "I'll make it up to you."

"Baby, I love you and don't think like that. There's nothing to make up."

Pixie drove us to the Hilton. It was my normal daily routine, except running later than usual. It was already nine thirty when we sat in a comfy booth.

"How about Joanne and Kevin?" Pixie asked before I could.

"They're going to be okay. They understand that people die. They were so close to 'Nando. I know they miss him. I know having my mom around is going to help."

"Here's the deal," I said. "Make it a point to run home and have dinner with them and your mom, no matter how busy we are. Surprise them. Pick them up from school. It's okay. We'll manage."

Jo teared up.

"Baby, please don't cry," I said.

"I'm good, sweets," she said.

Pixie was sitting on her side of the booth, and they hugged.

When we got around to eating, there was nothing wrong with our appetites. I ordered sides of bacon, ham, sausage, steak potatoes. We had omelets. "No room for pancakes," I said, patting my stomach.

"This will hold me until tomorrow," Pixie said.

"Yeah, I bet," Jo kicked in.

I looked at them sitting there across from me, empty plates still on the table, coffee cups drained. I put both my hands out over theirs. I thought they were going to break down again. "We're going to be fine." I said.

I had decided to slow down a little after the purchase of eighty units, but my real estate broker still hounded me with deals.

"Mario, this place is a killer deal. If I had the money I'd buy it in a heart-beat."

I really didn't want to purchase anything right now. I wanted to lie low for a while, and maybe acclimate, get a feel for whether or not real estate was going to work for me. Since I'm no math whiz, I wanted to sit with the management company, and get an analysis of what my income was, how much was left over after the note was paid, and their fees were paid, and Uncle Sam got his share. I wanted to sit down with my aunt, and see if what we had was a reasonable revenue. But Randy did know exactly what buttons to push to perk my interest in a deal.

I took down the address and promised to drive by. The unit was located in Alhambra, close to my aunt's house and my two buildings in Monterey Hills. Randy knew I went for curb appeal. It was a great building. Actually, buildings. Sixty apartments, three buildings. Two pools and all sorts of amenities, including a spa. The next day I went to see it up close. Within 40 days it was mine.

This time I stood in the street to check out my buy with my aunt, and Jo, and Pixie. I felt a knot in my throat. I was getting too emotional. I'd have to work out harder in the mornings. Maybe that would bring back the rough in me.

Part of Jo's salary was still paid by Jake's office. I matched it, plus I gave her something extra for each case she signed on her own. The extra was just that. She received a salary to be on call to work wherever I needed her. In her first five years, the extra did not amount to much because she was sitting in the office. That was when I was doing almost all the retainers. The volume was low compared to the present. Now she made more on the extras than she did on her salary. That was perfectly okay with me. She earned it.

The small office Jake assigned to Jo when she started working was the same office she presently had. Sometimes the three of us met there instead of at my home office, especially if a client came in to see us. For the client meeting, we used one of two conference rooms, or we could just pick an office that was not occupied at the time.

Jo and I were waiting for Pixie and going over accounts. Rachel, Jake's office manager, came in with a book in her arms. Rachel was probably in her fifties. I knew she'd been with Jake a long time, maybe even since the beginning. She wore her sandy-blonde hair pulled back in a bun, and a pair of no nonsense glasses, but had the kind of face that you knew if she took off the glasses and let the hair down, she'd be someone you'd want to look at. Her manner was always brisk and efficient. Not much got past her.

"Mario," she said, "I have the active case list Jake asked me to prepare for you."

"You're a doll."

She handed me the three ring binder.

"Very nice of you Rachel. I owe you."

"Nonsense, you owe me nothing."

I glanced inside.

"This is just what we need, Rachel," I told her. I don't know what I'd been expecting—perhaps just a list of cases, *x vs. y,* one after the other, single-spaced. Instead, Rachel had given us copies of a form, one case per page. Each page had the case's important dates—the date of the accident, when they had signed, the date of any meetings, court dates—the names of the people involved, and a few pertinent details about the accident. The records were organized, and would be easier to work with than the jumble on the unindexed Rolodex.

It was a big book, but not as big as it could have been. Until Jo started, I had kept a Rolodex of every case I ever signed. Now, we were all busy working, not paper pushing. I kept putting off straightening up the list, knowing I'd eventually get to it, and today I was doing just that. The list of my cases that had not settled was a list of money in the (future) bank, and while there was no way to guess what it would be, I was tired of having no clue or even a range of what was coming. Through Jake's notices, my accountant kept track of the cases that had settled for the IRS. As far as I was concerned, they were history.

"Hang on a sec," Jo said.

She left to make a copy of the original binder's contents. She enlisted a couple of secretaries, an intern and a paralegal who split the copy job on several mimeograph machines, and one cup of bad office coffee later, she was back, with two binders.

We went through the packet of cases, and took out the ones that weren't mine or Jo's or Pixie's.

What I wanted to do was impossible. It was speculative. There was no way to know with any certainty what the remaining case list would bring. Still, I had been at this a while, and had been watching the outcome of a lot of cases. I had a ballpark guess of what the case would settle for. It was tricky and close to impossible. I gave Jo estimated lowball and highball numbers, and then she developed a formula so we could come up with a range. We were only looking at cases that would settle for more than three thousand dollars, so we reduced the stack of cases we were examining to only those where I was entitled to a bonus.

"The black binder is Jake's," she said. "The red one is ours."

After we pulled all of Jake's cases, and all of the settled cases, and all of our small cases, I double checked to verify. We both were surprised how many big cases we had coming. We'd been very busy these past few years, busier than I'd realized.

The intercom rang out.

"Melina Marron on line three," the receptionist announced to the entire office.

I picked up.

"Can't talk long," I said. "Working."

"Fine. It's not a social call. Just telling you, catering is in. The baskets are out," Melina said. The call was short, and crisp and to the point, "I was just giving you a heads-up. We're switching the booths for the baskets to be part of catering. Baskets compete with our in-house."

"Thanks," I said, hanging up. I might have slammed down the receiver.

"I recognize that tone," Jo said. "That's not a happy boss."

"I'm not happy," I said. "That was Melina. Niley's out of work."

Jo frowned. "That will be next on the list. First, let's figure out what Jake owes you."

Jo penciled in figures for the number of injured, deaths, and code letters for various things such as damages, medical care, pain and suffering, loss of income, punitive.

"Don't worry about the numbers yet," she said. "Let's keep it modest, and just adjust the formula as the case nears settlement."

She worked on the list as I took calls. Pixie beeped, and I sent her out on a second client. Jo and I kept working the list until Pixie returned an hour later with two retainers, and a pound of corned beef, sauerkraut, mustard, deli bread for sandwiches, and a huge box of doughnuts for the staff who'd helped Jo make copies earlier.

The three of us sat down around the office's kitchen table, ate Reuben sandwiches we'd thrown together and crisped up in the toaster oven, and had a powwow about what to do about Niley. I didn't even know if she knew that her business connection with the market was gone. I didn't know if she wanted to try to continue her gift basket concept on her own. I knew only that she did really well during holidays, and just managed to cover her bills the rest of the time.

I did not know her well. We'd only met a few times. Sometimes I could barely look at Niley, and others I could hardly look away. When I looked at Niley, I saw Tanis. Tanis had been slim and tall, with the darkest brown hair with strands of gold mixed in. She'd had creamy pale gold skin, and straight dark brows, perfect features and red lips, and oh, those bedroom eyes. She'd worn her hair long, but in public it had always been in some kind of chignon. To look at Niley was to see Tanis through different eyes. Niley wore her hair short, and glasses hid the eyes. She was not as tall, but just as slim; her hair was shades lighter, with more gold strands. Her brows were just as straight, just as bold as Tanis's had been. Her coloring was paler, more cream than gold, but still, when I set eyes on her, all I could see was the shadow of her sister.

The next day, Niley drove to my apartment to have lunch with the three of us. Pixie brought lunch from La Posada, one of our favorite Mexican restaurants. As always the standing order was to purchase much more than we planned to eat. We almost always gave a plate to Johnson and the guard in the lobby, or the other person who worked when Johnson was not there. I never knew the guard's name. Everyone just called him Security. I liked to have a spread at the table. The girls could take home leftovers if they wished.

"Gosh, do you guys eat like this every day?" Niley asked, chewing away at a crunchy taco.

"When there's time. We're just one big happy family. You can join in when you feel comfortable." Jo said, passing a warmed bowl of taco chips to Pixie, who was sitting next to her. Pixie dumped half the bowl on her plate. I declined them, and Niley took a few before she placed the bowl back in front of Jo. The girls centered the warm cheese dip and chilled fresh salsa strategically between them and ate like there was a competition to see who could empty the bowls first.

"Did you get blown away when Melina cut you off?" I asked.

Niley frowned a little. "Not really. I felt it coming. Baskets are seasonal. And I could tell something had changed. It was just a matter of time. Some good came of it. I bought a car, paid off the house, saved a few bucks and got lots of experience."

"So now what?" Pixie asked. She had eschewed the rest of the meal, and was going to town on cheese dip and salsa.

"Maybe I'll let the live-in go, and just stay home. I have four kids."

"I have two," Jo reminded her.

"And I have one," Pixie said.

I ate while this was going on, but I had noticed something different.

"Niley, what happened to your glasses? Are they just for reading?"

She blushed. "I have contacts now."

Pixie got up close to see. "I can't tell."

Jo gave Pixie a swat. "Back off silly. Leave Niley be."

"You look great, Tanis," I said. Then I was shocked at myself. "Fuck. I'm so sorry."

Jo glared at me, and patted Niley's hand. "He does it all the time. He's always calling me Pixie or Tanis. He's even called me Jake."

That was a flat-out lie, but Pixie and I let it pass. As lies go, it was pretty good. My aunt was always calling me Pixie or Lainey.

That brought out a shy smile. "I do that with my kids all the time, especially when I'm mad. Sometimes I just yell, 'hey kids.'"

"Niley," I pronounced her name carefully. "You looked great with glasses too, of course, but just different."

"Mario, that five hundred you give me every month, it's too generous of you to keep giving it to me. When I was working, I told Jo to tell you I could do without it."

"I told him," Jo said. "That's what you do around here. You tell Mario, and he does exactly what he wants."

I fake-glared at her, but I appreciated her efforts to relieve the tension.

Jo rolled her eyes, and rephrased.

"You tell the boss, and he does what he wants."

"Better," I said, turning toward Niley. "It's a good thing I didn't stop it. You need it now."

"With what I get for the kids, and that five hundred, I can almost make it. I may have to give up the car. It's paid for, but I owe insurance every month. Maybe I can find something else to do. Maybe something part-time just during school hours."

"Come work for me," I heard myself say.

There was no reaction from Jo or Pixie, but we'd already talked about it. They continued to eat as though I'd said nothing. Niley stopped eating, and looked at me as if I'd grown a third head.

"Really? Doing what? Or...it doesn't matter what, really." She was flustered.

She seemed insecure. I wasn't sure she could handle the work. I'd never seen how she was around people.

"You could sign retainers, like we all do. Sometimes, when the weather acts up, we have more work than we can handle."

She nodded, and said with a burst of confidence, "A job would be great. I'd feel better if I were earning that stipend." There was something about her, just a flash, and it was gone. I realized what it was. I saw Tanis. There was so much of Tanis in Niley that it hurt. I didn't need to do this. Niley was getting five hundred from me. It didn't need to go further. And there was no telling if she would take to the business in the same way as Pixie and Jo. "If you come to work for me, there will be a possibility that you'll make more than that. The five hundred is an obligation. It's for Tanis. It doesn't count, Niley."

I focused my attention on my plate.

"You're amazing," she said, her eyes on me. My eyes were on the burrito to keep from seeing Tanis in her face. I wasn't sure this was such a great idea. Pixie and Jo and I were more than just a team. I didn't know if adding another person would change our dynamics.

Marsha had moved to the other service. Everything worked without a hitch. Our new business cards had a toll free number that rang the twenty-four hour service. When a call came in for one of us, the operator asked the caller to hold on. I—or Pixie or Jo—would be beeped. SOS in numbers meant the caller was on hold, so we immediately called the displayed number. The service would connect us to the person on hold. It was swift. It was good for business. For the person calling us, the experience was the same as if we had secretaries screening our calls and we were in the next room.

I had promised Marsha a monthly bonus if she personally looked after my account so there would never be a single mistake and that all calls would be answered by the second ring. In the new service, Marsha was the day manager, and she made a deal of her own with the night manager that relieved her.

At midnight I got an SOS, and called the service.

"I have Carson on the line," the operator said.

Chapter 11
September 18, 1974
Hooks, Lies, and Stinkers

I wondered how he'd gotten this toll free number so fast, and why he had not called me on my home line.

"Put him through." I was reclining on the couch with a bowl of ice cream. The old black and white movie had been interrupted by a commercial that was better than the movie. Some crook had stolen a bunch of wallets, then Karl Malden cut in, hawking American Express Travelers checks.

"Hello?"

I heard Carson come on the line, and turned the sound down. The TV crook reminded me a little of Carson—not his looks precisely, just the expression on his face as he dropped his loot on the couch. It was a little smug. A gotcha look. I gotcha and you can't do shit about it, sucker.

"What is it Carson?"

"Ease up, guy. You're not old enough to be going through a change of life."

He laughed.

"What do you need from me? It's almost one a.m."

"I got this great fucking deal for you."

"Not interested."

"Mario, the lawyer I work with told me if you come over to see him just to talk, he will pay you five large, whether you like what he says or not."

"Not interested."

"Don't be stupid."

"Wrong, Carson, you're the one being stupid thinking there's a chance in hell I'm coming close to any deal you got, much less getting involved in it."

"It's not my deal *esé*."

I should have hung up but I didn't. Five grand is a lot of money for me to turn my nose up at. "What's the lawyer's name?"

"Oscar Cooke, spelled with an e."

"Why would Oscar Cooke pay me five thousand bucks to come over, and why doesn't he call me himself?"

"Hey, he'll call you."

"If it's true, give him my number. The toll free you just called. Not my home phone."

I was sure there was a big catch to this, but five large is a lot of money. I bet Oscar Cooke wanted me to send him business. I'd been approached before, even by attorney friends of Jake. I never mentioned this to Jake. What he doesn't know won't hurt him. Besides, I always brush off the offers, usually by phone. I turned down an offer for lunch from one, and an invite to go clubbing from another.

I hung up, and turned the movie back on.

Karl Mauldin's nose was back on the screen when I received the second SOS of the night. I called the service. The caller was Oscar Cooke.

"Mario, pleased to meet you even if it's by phone."

I cut to the chase.

"Why pay me five large to talk? What's the catch?"

"No catch, except one."

I knew it. "What's the catch?"

"We go to lunch and talk about some ideas I have."

"I never heard of you. Do you do PI?"

"My main business is criminal work. Ever since I met Carson a couple years ago, I've had a small PI department."

"Is PI what you want to talk about?"

"Mario. Come over. Have lunch. Let me run it down to you. When you leave, I'll hand you five thousand green."

I said, "Let me be honest, Mr. Cooke. I'm real happy where I am. I have no plans of moving."

"Nothing is forever," Oscar said. "Come on. At least think about it, sleep on it."

There was a pause. I hesitated. "I'll think about it. But I must tell you, I'll be taking advantage of you if we have that lunch, and you give me the money. I'm not moving."

"I got it. Let's talk in a day or so. I'll call you."

It was one in the morning. I wasn't tired at all. I missed my nights with Melina. She was a bitch. But she was a convenient bitch.

I poured a glass of wine, took a sip, muted the television and turned on Neil Diamond.

No way would I leave Jake I had so much money sitting there in future bonuses. Not to mention, I loved Jake. He was family to me. Fuck Oscar Cooke.

It was too late to call Jake and ask him if he ever heard of him. Oscar said Carson had been with him a couple of years and that he had a small PI practice. No fucking way would I work close to Carson for any amount of money. No matter how good the deal was.

It was one fifteen when I looked up Niley's phone number in my Rolodex.

A sleepy voice answered. "Who is it?" she said.

"Niley, I don't know why I'm calling you at this hour. No wait. I don't know why I'm calling you at all. It's Mario."

"Mario, it's okay."

"Listen, this afternoon, when I called you Tanis—"

"It's okay. Really." Her voice got kind of thick and emotional. "It's probably the biggest compliment I've had in my entire life. I was the smart sister, but Tanis was the beautiful one. And you don't know how much it means to me that you loved her. Her husband was a shitheel, and you...well, you were her knight in shining armor."

"I never knew she felt that. I just knew she liked to keep her independence."

"She called you Papi Grande."

There aren't many times I'm surprised or left speechless. I mumbled something. I'm not sure what. I sure wasn't expecting to hear that nickname in this lifetime. I think I said something like *I'm sorry I woke you.*

"No, I'm glad to hear from you."

"Really?" I closed my eyes and Tanis images played in my brain. Tanis or Niley. I was getting them mixed up. And yet, not. They were so different.

"Yeah, I am. You were so close to Tanis. You and I have never really talked much."

I had always let Jo handle everything with her.

"I'm sorry about that. I miss Tanis very much."

There was a long pause. "I miss her too."

"We can talk again soon."

She laughed. Where Tanis's laugh had been husky and sexual, Niley's laugh was like bubbling champagne.

"All that matters is that we're friends now," she said. "We're all friends. Please don't be sorry."

"I'm not sorry. I've never been unsorrier about anything in my life," I said, meaning it with all of my heart. "Good night, Niley."

"Good night, Mario. I'll look forward to seeing you soon."

It was Niley talking, but I heard Tanis's voice.

I went to bed, tossed and turned. It was three in the morning. What the fuck was wrong with me? It was Carson bugging me. His fucking call. Why couldn't he just stay away? I knew why. In his heart of hearts, he thought he was still my bro. I'd never understand how he kept burning the bridges between us, then thought they were still there. And it was too early to call Jake to ask about Oscar Cooke.

I turned on the bedside lamp, got up, walked to the office, got my Rolodex and brought it to bed. I dialed. Not Carson. Not Cooke. I dialed Niley.

"Hey. Guess who?"

I heard a little laugh.

"I had this feeling you might call back. I don't know why but I did. I got up, showered and got dressed. I was lying here waiting."

"Are you serious?"

"Yeah, serious," she said, "Want to go out for an early morning breakfast?"

I hesitated.

"Want me to come over?" Niley asked.

"Do you mind?"

"I'm on my way."

"How about the kids?"

"You forget, I have a live-in in this big old house." The quiet laugh.

"I'll tell the guard to let you up. The doorman will park your car. Are you really coming over, or am I dreaming?"

I paced my whole apartment. I got in the shower and let the water pound me for a long time. I was wide awake.

Why Niley? I'm using her. Am I using her? I don't know. I closed my eyes. But isn't this what I do with every girl I take to bed? Is this how it's supposed to be? I remembered when Melina accused me of thinking only I had to get satisfied during sex. She made fun of how I'd lay back and get pampered. She point-blank asked me if I ever asked a girl if she had an orgasm or if I just fell asleep or jumped out of bed to the kitchen, afterwards. Although when I was a boy, Pixie had taught me how to tell when a girl was having an orgasm, I did not always pay attention. When I was with a girl, I wanted to think I had done her justice. Maybe I was spoiled rotten by most women I had gone to bed with. I had a big dick and I lasted a long time. I knew I had something to offer. I didn't know who was doing the using, them or me.

I turned on the radio, and sat on the couch. I shut my eyes, not paying attention to the station's playlist.

Then Niley was there. I opened my eyes, and drank her in. She couldn't have gotten more casual. She wore jeans, her blouse tail wrapped around her waist, her belly button not quite visible. Her hair was still damp from a recent shower. She was slim and petite. The top button of her blouse was unbuttoned, baring the upper curves of her breasts. She'd left her underwear somewhere else.

As though we'd known each other forever, she went in to my arms. We just stood, her arms around my waist. My arms around her. I wanted to pick her up and kiss her, but I didn't.

"Thanks for coming back," I whispered.

She looked up at me. Her teeth gleamed. Her dimples twinkled at me, seeming somehow important. It was like they giggled and danced, proclaiming her Niley. Maybe Tanis's face had been pure sex. I could see now that Niley was pure joy.

"Can I get you a drink or anything?"

She shook her head, still looking at me.

"Do I remind you of Tanis?"

"I'm sorry I called you by her name yesterday."

She shook her head. "It's okay."

"But I see you now. I see you, Niley."

I picked her up, cradled her and walked her to my bedroom. There was no objection, no conversation. She turned off the bedside lamp, but there was enough light coming through windows for me to see her and her me.

I kissed her for a very long time. She tried to reciprocate, but I gently pushed her back every time.

"Relax," I said. This was not about me. This was about her. I kissed her entire body, forehead to toes. On her skin, she was wearing Joy.

When we made love, it was unrushed. There was drive, but no force; urgency but no haste; compulsion, but no contest.

"You're beautiful," I whispered in her ear. "You're beautiful in your own right."

Sometime before dawn, I melted into the bed. I never woke at five in the morning, nor at six. I didn't go to breakfast. I was out. The phone rang and rang, but I didn't answer, I heard it, but I didn't even open my eyes.

It was eleven when Pixie and Jo woke me. They were having a pillow fight, jumping on the bed and falling back. My body bounced.

"What are you guys doing?"

I looked for my bed partner of the night before. Where was she?

"How long you been here?"

"Thirty minutes," Jo said. "Pixie and I arrived in the same car."

"When you got here, was I alone?"

"You were alone. She left you with the tremendous smell of sex." Pixie sniffed three times, including once under my armpit. "I smell sweat and body fluids." She sniffed the pillow. "And Aramis. And Joy. And Prell shampoo. You don't have Prell. Why?" She looked like she was about to smell my cock, so I hung on to the sheet. She settled for rubbing her nose on mine. "Had to be Melina," she added.

She was probing for details. I didn't enlighten her.

"Boss, you got anything to say?" Jo asked.

"I want some of that coffee."

It was a good thing I didn't have a hangover. No drinking had been involved. I jumped out of bed filled with energy, and ran to the kitchen to the percolator that was blasting out coffee fragrance.

I had peanut butter with the coffee.

"How can you eat that this early?" Jo asked.

"Like this." I demonstrated. I put a full spoon in my mouth.

"We never fucked with peanut butter. Are you game?" Pixie and Jo looked at each other.

"Put it on the to-do." I said, saluting both with my cup.

The girls were dressed for work. I ran to shower with my coffee in hand. Drinking coffee in the shower while lathering up and not spilling any is an art form. I didn't linger. There was too much work to be done. And I had a call to make. Jake would be at the office by now.

"Any action?" I asked.

"Got some calls," Jo said, "Love this exchange. They are good about holding the caller until we answer. We have a couple to work for this afternoon."

"Good," I said, dialing Jake's office to ask about Oscar Cooke. "I'll catch up to you later. Stay in touch," I told Jo and Pixie.

They left.

Jake picked up. "I know Oscar Cooke," he said, "He does criminal work. He'll handle anything, big or small. That bondsman that no longer sends me any business because I'm buried in PI has become an additional source of business for him."

I thought about Tony the bondsman who had referred me to Jake when I got arrested.

"Is he like your pal, your friend?"

"Not at all. We just know each other. Why do you ask?"

"Apparently Cooke's been doing PI for two years. Carson sends him business. Last night I got a call from Carson, then one from Cooke. He wants to meet with me. He'll give me five thousand dollars to have lunch with him."

Jake chuckled.

Before he replied, I went on. "For starters, I'll bet he's after some of the action you are getting. I'm not going to do it, first because you're family; and second because I don't want to be within a hundred yards of Carson."

Jake chuckled again. "Go to lunch. Hear him out."

"Just like that?"

"Mario, I love you like my own son. My home is your home. I never want to see you leave, but nothing is forever."

"Those were Cooke's exact words when I said I wasn't interested."

"You're smart. Follow your nose." Jake said. And then, as if he thought better of his own advice, "But don't leave me."

He finally said what I wanted to hear.

I knew my future bonuses could amount to a million dollars in the next few years even if I never brought in another case. For sure I wasn't going anywhere. He knew that and I knew that, but I had to say it aloud.

"I'm not going anywhere," I said, then hung up.

My next call was Niley. By now, I didn't need my Rolodex.

"Hey lady. You abandoned me?"

"You were sleeping so soundly. I didn't want to wake you."

"Sorry I dragged you out here last night."

"I'm not sorry," she said. "I had the greatest time ever."

"For sure. Did you really have a good time or are you just saying that?"

"I loved every moment."

"Hearing that makes me feel so good."

"Did you get some sleep?" I asked.

"Yeah, but now I'm up and around."

"I haven't had a thing to eat. How about lunch?" I knew I was being manipulative but it didn't matter.

"Tell me where. I'll be there."

"How about I pick you up?"

I took her to the Marisol Restaurant at the golf course in Monterey Park, a great place overlooking the San Bernardino Freeway, minutes from my aunt's house and two of my apartment buildings.

The hostess walked us to our table. Walking in, I looked at this girl, and felt like I was the luckiest person in the world.

"You're such a fox, Niley."

She smiled. "You look pretty good yourself."

"Want wine or a drink?"

"Sparkling water. I'm sorry. I'm not much of a drinker."

"Great," I said. "I drink but I hate the hangovers. I don't drink that often."

During lunch we talked about the kids and the live-in. They loved the live-in, Delores, who had an old car that she used to take them to school and pick them up. Delores was a grandmother in her fifties who had applied to work in the basket business, but Niley took her home to nanny full-time instead.

Niley gave her free board, paid her forty dollars a week, and kept the refrigerator full. Delores's daughter and grandchildren had moved to rainy Seattle, and she filled the hole in her life with Niley's family.

"Do you have a steady friend or friends you see?"

"I occasionally go out on dates, but the relationships can never get too serious. I have four kids," she laughed a little. "Who would want to inherit four kids? I'm a package deal."

I know I wouldn't, but I liked this girl.

The waitress brought our food. Niley had gotten a bright-looking fresh fruit salad, with melons and citrus, grapes and cherries of different colors. A couple of finger sandwiches rimmed the plate. Girl food.

My steak was big, perfectly browned, and rare. When I cut into it, the juices ran, and it smelled like a backyard grill. The steak knife that came with it was hardly necessary. It was like slicing butter. I was hungrier than I'd realized.

I'd had an appetite for more than food, though.

"A beauty like you with the sex drive I experienced last night can't be idle for too long."

My conversation was to the point as always. Niley didn't seem to mind. I saw no blush. Only dimples. She was turning out to be as frank as Pixie.

"I have a cool vibrator," she admitted. "Actually, I have two. And you're right, I don't go idle for very long. It's like the older I get, the hornier I get. But now that I have the four kids, I won't just go to bed with a guy to get off. It's just too complicated. Most guys only look out for themselves anyway."

I think I may have blushed. Last night I had really focused on her. For a few seconds, we held a stare across the table. Melina had said how pampered I was. How selfish I was in bed. Melina had wondered if I ever asked a girl if she came. I hadn't asked yet. Pixie had taught me well. I'd have sworn Niley had been satisfied several times over. I never thought I needed to ask. But...

"I need to ask," I said. "Did you come when we did it? And don't lie. I can take the truth." I smiled.

Our eyes held.

"Mario, I came six times last night. You are unbelievable."

My beeper went off. She heard it go off. It wasn't quiet. The problem was I was hard.

"Niley, I have a problem. I need to get this, but I can't get up right now."

I looked down.

She understood. She laughed aloud.

Minutes later, the service sent out another SOS. I ran to find a pay phone in the restaurant. It was Jo.

"Took you long enough. Are you driving?"

"Sorry *Boss*. I had to wait for my flagpole to go down. It took five minutes."

She paused. I could hear her wheels clicking. I waited for her to say something sarcastic, but the urgency of her news made her decide against it.

"There's been a terrible train wreck. Overturned train cars. Lots of people hurt, and maybe dead. I heard it on the radio news. It happened a couple of hours ago in San Bernardino."

I'd never had a train crash case. If we went to the scene, they would run us off. We would have to find the hospital or hospitals near the crash.

"Beep Pixie. Both of you meet me the Marisol Restaurant at the Golf Course in Monterey Park. I'll make some calls." I dialed Fernando. The good news was that I reached him easily. The bad news was that he was at home, off today.

"I heard about it," he told me. "I'll get the details for you. Call me in one hour."

"I'll make it good for you," I promised.

"No sweat," he said. "I know you will. I'll keep Saturday open."

I went back to the table.

"That took longer than I thought it would. Is everything okay?" "Train crash in San Bernardino."

"Oh that's terrible."

"Yes, it is, but someone has to represent the victims. We're taking a shot at it. Jo and Pixie are on their way here."

Niley said. "Can I help?"

Chapter 12
September 19, 1974
And Baby Makes 3

"Are you game?"

"You bet, I'm game, boss."

The injured were taken to a hospital in San Bernardino and Riverside. From Marisol Restaurant, the drive to that area was a good hour. Fernando told me the train was coming from El Paso, Texas. On the bus crash, I'd gotten the twenty-five thousand front money from Jake, but I had no idea how much there might be for this case.

Jo and Pixie arrived together.

"We left my car at Jo's house," Pixie said.

We talked over the circumstances of handling the accident. We knew already from car crashes, it was hard to get close to the injured in the hospital, but it could be done. In terms of proximity, it was easier to talk with family members than with the injured. I had to think about reaching family. We had three categories of passengers: those from LA, those from El Paso, and those from somewhere else. Easiest to reach would be those who were coming home, who had family here. Their families would be at the hospital within hours unless the passenger had no one. Family for the others might be back in El Paso Texas, or anywhere, really.

"Niley will shadow me at San Bernardino Hospital. You two head out to Riverside. Beep me through the exchange. I'll try and answer right away."

"I'm not even sure you will appreciate what you will see from this point on," I said to Niley as we entered the ER entrance.

"I can handle it."

I grinned and kept walking. Niley kept up. My mind had switched to business.

The San Bernardino Emergency waiting room was not full yet. There were three persons, a young woman and two young men who might be her brothers, sitting together talking. I took my chances and walked over to them.

"Hi, my name is Mario. This is Niley. Are you here on the train tragedy?"

"No," replied the young lady. She pointed at a couple, a man and woman across from them. "They are."

The couple was in their fifties. They look distraught but were not crying.

I extended my hand to the man. "Hello sir, my name is Mario, and this is Niley."

The man shook my hand, then shook Niley's hand. The man stared for a moment at Niley. Even in times of distress, a pretty girl opens doors.

"My name is Pepe Ramirez. This is my wife, Berta."

We shook hands.

Their English was understandable but broken. I switched to Spanish as we took a seat next to them, Niley next to Berta. I sat to Pepe's right.

"You speak good Spanish," Berta said with a little smile.

I said, "Thank you. I can switch to English if you prefer."

"Oh no," Pepe said, patting my knee.

"Who got injured?" I asked.

"Our sons Ramiro and Pancho. We were at the station waiting for them in San Bernardino when we heard that the train crashed into a truck and derailed. They told us to come here, not the crash site."

"I'm so sorry," I said. "Do you want me to check if Ramiro and Pancho are here?"

"They are here. We have not seen them, but they are here. No one has come out to tell us anything. The receptionist said they are on the list here, and that someone will talk to us." Berta was on the verge of tears.

I saw Niley put her arm around her.

"Look, I know this is not the time," I dared say to Pepe and Berta. "I am not a lawyer, but I do a lot of work for a lawyer that is a specialist in bus and train tragedies. No matter what, you got to figure the train company will hire lawyers. Your sons will need a lawyer."

To my surprise, Niley said, "Without a lawyer, the train company may try and take advantage of your sons. How old are they?"

"Old enough to make up their own minds, but I like you," said Berta. "They haven't even talked to us."

"We'll wait with you," I said. "Can I get you some coffee? A Coke from the vending machine? I have lots of change."

"A Coke," Berta said, "Please."

"Coffee for me," Pepe said.

We brought their drinks and sat down again. Berta started chatting with Niley like Niley was a long lost Ramirez. They talked about kids, and exchanged recipes. I could tell Berta was talking to keep from thinking about her boys.

Pepe pointed out a group who had just come in.

"Those people were at the train station when we were getting the news. Those two, the ones in blue and red, I believe they have daughter and son-in-law here."

"I'll be right back," I said, thanking him. I walked over and made contact with the distressed couple, Alma and Tomas Flores. After a few moments, Tomas said he needed to call to their son-in-law's parents, but Alma clutched at him, and begged him not to go anywhere. She was frail, and shaking and even I could see she was coming apart.

"Please, stay here with your wife," I said. "I can do that for you."

Tomas opened his wallet, and pulled out an old heating and air business card. The back was covered with a dozen phone numbers in tiny print.

"Third one down, that's the Pedrozas. That's Marco's father. They don't know about the train crash yet. But it's long distance. They're in El Paso. It's going to be expensive."

"No worries," I said. "I am happy to do this for you."

Alma's left hand was clutching Tomas's left. I reached out and took their right hands, folding them all together, and holding them like that for a second. For an instant, I could see the effort he was making to be strong. Tomas teared up, then his backbone kicked in. He put his arm around his wife. She buried her head in his blue work shirt.

"Take it easy. I can handle it."

I found the pay phone, and called the Pedroza's. As I was talking, I jotted down their name and number in my little book.

"I'm so sorry," I said to them, after explaining there had been an accident. "We have limited information, but we are at the hospital now, and Marco is with the doctors. Tomas or I will be calling you back as soon as we have more news for you."

I took the opportunity to beep Jo.

It took only a minute for her to call me back.

"We are with families of the injured," Jo said. "We've met two families who have been told their loved ones did not made it. We have their phone numbers and addresses."

"We're in the same boat, pretty much," I said. "We've met two families. The parents of two sons who are injured. The parents of a couple who are injured. I've talked once to the husband's family in El Paso. That might be our way in to El Paso families."

Jo said, "I think we're going to be good. These are for the most part, poor people that can barely speak English. The insurance company will chew them up for lunch if they don't get help."

I remembered when I had told Jo that years ago when she started working for me. I remembered when Jo repeated it to Pixie. We weren't coyotes, but on this case we *were* soliciting. I wanted to think we were doing it for a better cause than Jake's bank account or mine. We weren't handing out business cards, and we weren't leaving a paper trail.

Alma and Tomas came over to sit with us. I returned Tomas's phone card. As the emergency room filled up, we made more contacts.

We were there for hours. We were there when a doctor came out and told Alma and Tomas not to worry so much; the worst injured were treated first, and their daughter and son-in-law were not among the first to be treated. That news did not go over well with the Ramirez family. We were there when they brought the news that Ramiro had rallied. We were there when they brought out the news that Pancho had not. Berta was hanging on to Niley like she was her long-lost daughter. We stayed there until Ramiro was brought to a room with two broken legs, broken ribs, and months of healing ahead. I accompanied Pepe and Berta to the chapel to be told about Pancho. The tears I cried with them were real. Niley was crying too, but she was so shaken I realized she was remembering Tanis. That grief was still raw.

Jo and I touched base on the phone a couple of times. By dawn, we headed home to pack. Before I dropped off Niley, who agreed to meet back in San Bernardino, I took note of a motel by the hospital. Pixie and Jo would go straight to Riverside near the hospital they were working out of.

I packed and hit my sock drawer for a pack of money for the families who might need our help.

I called the motel, and secured a couple of adjoining motel rooms in San Bernardino near the hospital. Pixie and Jo made their own arrangements in Riverside. For the next four days, we stayed among the families. We had very little sleep. The rest of the world had not come to a stop. Our regular stream of beeps came in on other cases, but we had to postpone the interviews. It was on days like these that I missed having an office staff or extra personnel. I thought about having my aunt come in to be available in the office, or calling in a temp, but it was just a passing thought. We would manage. This case was too big to leave it. And the drive was too long to head back to Los Angeles.

Niley and I became really close. We worked the hospital together each day. She never stopped to eat, and would be exhausted when we'd finally head for a couple hours respite at the motel. I would kiss her at her door; then we'd both go into our separate rooms. We kept the adjoining door open, though.

"Hey honey, I'm home," I'd say, a minute after our goodbye, unlocking my own door, and coming in.

In those four days, living out of two suitcases in a tiny room, getting close was inevitable. I figured we had to make the best of each day. She had those four kids. I knew we would never be serious and it wasn't just the four kids. It was me. I can't imagine being tied down to one woman. Certainly not now.

But Niley was growing on me. As soon as we got to the motel, we'd hit our phones. She'd call Delores, and talk about the kids, and if it was the right time of day, she'd talk *to* the kids.

I'd usually order take out to be delivered to us; then I'd call Jake. He was excited on the phone as I gave him progress of the signed retainers we were accumulating. Then, while we were waiting for the food to be delivered, I'd handle as many non-train messages as I could squeeze in, making appointments four days in advance. At some point, I'd squeeze in a shower. When the food got there, we'd usually eat in her room. They both had tables, but mine was the makeshift office, covered in paperwork. I'd brought in the IBM Selectric typewriter that lived in the back of my car.

On that first day, Oscar Cooke called me three times. I called him back.

"I'm out on the train crash. We can talk when I get back," I said.

"Have you seen Carson out there?"

"I haven't seen him."

"He's out there somewhere with one of my boys. I wish you could work together."

"Oscar, there is a history. I'm never going to work with Carson."

"When you're done Mario, call me. Or I'll call you for that lunch."

"Sure," I said.

"If you have anything extra from that crash, let me in. I will outbid Jake or anyone else. I hear you really know how to cherry pick."

"Oscar, you're wrong. I don't cherry pick. I take the good, the bad, the small and the big case. No matter to me. I sort it out later."

"I get it," Oscar said.

No doubt Carson and his big mouth were using me to advance himself.

On the morning of the fifth day, before heading home, Niley and I converged at the parking lot of the Riverside Hospital where Jo and Pixie were waiting for us. Jo had parked but I had just pulled up in the driveway perpendicular to a heavy utility truck, with no one behind or in front of me. It was too soon to do a final count, but we had twenty-three signed retainers for injured passengers, and two retainers from decedents' families. One was the family of Pepe and Berta, the first couple I had talked to.

"We're going to get double this," Jo said confidently.

"What do you think?" Pixie asked Niley with a friendly little push. "You're lucky. You got the boss teaching you."

I winked at Pixie, Jo then Niley. "Have you had breakfast yet?" I asked.

"Continental," Jo said. "Powdered eggs."

"Cardboard bacon," Pixie said. "Yum. And we could have used that coffee to cut paint."

"We too," Niley said. "Only it was doughnuts, or toast, and coffee, standing in the office of the motel."

"Save your stomachs, then," I said, looking up to see a black sedan pulling in this section of the hospital lot. "We can have a big spread of real food when we're done with this."

The car pulled closer. I saw Carson riding shotgun. Of course, we'd have to run into him.

"Time to leave," Jo said with a sidelong look in my direction.

Carson was in the passenger side of the sedan. A huge man was driving. This must be one of the boys Cooke had been talking about. When he stepped out, I realized he was taller than me, and buff. Okay, buff was an understatement. I see the occasional fit person, but don't see too many people taller than six feet five inches. His arms were huge. His hand was like a Thanksgiving turkey. I wondered where he found clothes to fit. He was so loaded with beef, he moved like he had a thigh rash.

"Hey," Carson said, nodding to Pixie and Jo. He knew Pixie from our childhood, and Jo from running in to her on the job.

"Bastard," Pixie said, almost smiling.

Carson smiled back, and did his fake tip-the-hat shtick. It was probably the nicest greeting he'd gotten all week.

"Who is this?" Carson pointed at Niley.

We all ignored the question.

The knuckle-dragging man-monster who had been chauffeuring him lumbered to his side. I gave him a quick once over. I hoped that I don't come across that way. Like someone who could be in a circus. Or a zoo. Or maybe on Saturday night wrestling. I would have worried more if he'd been agile.

"You hired a bodyguard?" I asked, knowing this was Cooke's man.

"Why would I need a bodyguard?"

"Things happen," I said, "When you stick your nose places it shouldn't be."

"So, how did you do?" Carson asked.

"We did good," I said.

"Oscar says he'll pay heavy for whatever you got."

"Told me the same thing on the phone. Got to run."

I nodded to the girls, wanting them out of the way. I could sniff the violence in the air, though I wasn't worried about myself. Niley had my papers secured in her bag.

I started for my car. The four of us were in two cars. Niley was already standing by my passenger door.

The big guy stepped in front of me. He poked me with his index finger on my chest. That should have infuriated me but I'd grown up on the discipline of karate. This guy had nothing. He could have taken me down if he'd poked my solar plexus, but he was into intimidation and had already shown me he had no skill.

I looked up. Not too far up, but up.

"Easy Fink," Carson told the ape. "Don't mess with Mario. He's good." The ape took a step back.

I almost grinned at Carson for warning his companion.

"That's the name? Fink?" I laughed.

"You got an attitude!" The big guy said.

"Yeah, I got an attitude, Fink. What are you going to do about it?"

"Mario, you don't want to fuck with Fink. Easy, we just drove over here to say hi."

"You're warning me, Carson?" I was surprised since Carson knew better, but then Carson played mind games. He didn't look worried. In fact, he winked at me.

By now the ape was mad. He started to poke me again. I saw he'd grabbed his keys, had them in his fingers like brass knuckles, pointing out. A big guy like this, I knew all I really had to do was stay out of his way and let him knock himself out. But they don't always learn a lesson that way. They think it's an accident. I needed him to know this was on purpose. I dodged to the side, and his hand slammed into the side of the truck behind me. One of the keys was stuck in the truck, and just hung there swinging in the center of a big dent. The ape stopped for a second to look at his turkey-sized hand that was looking kind of beat up. With a knife hand, I gave him a jab in the solar plexus. It would be five minutes before he would be able to draw a good breath. While he was bent over double, I braced my bent right knee against the truck. I put my hands together in a single fist over his head, and gave him a slam that bounced his head a couple of times back and forth between my double-fist and my knee. He staggered to his feet, looking dazed but lunging woodenly after me anyway. I doubt he had much experience with resistance.

I went airborne and kicked him square on the nose that was lurching toward me, followed by a direct kick to his stomach.

He buckled over, fell to his knees.

"Fink. Want some more?"

He was still out of breath. He shook his head. He was trying to breathe.

I met Carson's eyes. He seemed relieved, even happy. I wondered how much bullying he was living with. He was so pleased with the way this had turned out that I figured his life must really be fucking hell.

"Oscar's not going to appreciate this," Carson warned with a smothered laugh. Fink was on his knees, puking. "Oscar won't appreciate it," his voice lowered just loud enough for me to hear. "But I sure the hell do." Carson jerked the keys out of the truck. There was blood on them where they'd cut into Fink's hand, probably breaking some fingers. Fink was going to be out of commission for a while.

Carson turned toward his companion, and offered to drive.

"Hey Fink, I thought you were the man," Carson goaded him. "Let's go find some other emergency room," he suggested. "I think Mario owns this one."

The sedan creaked as Fink got in the passenger side. Carson waved goodbye.

For once, I waved back, then got in my car with Niley. Jo and Pixie followed.

The train case was overwhelming for Jake. It felt to me like a game of musical chairs. Jake put his personnel alongside Jo working overtime on the paperwork of each family signed. That was okay for him, but taking Jo out of the field made me short one person. I split the work; Pixie handled the interviews we had setup while away and I handled all the new business coming in. Niley was too new to work on her own, so she was still shadowing me. We worked through the day, lived on take-out, and ended up at my apartment after dark. It was a new experience for me to wake with someone, much less the same person in my bed several days in a row. We kept pretty much to the same routine we'd had at the motel, only in the morning instead of bitter coffee and cold toast, we'd get steak and home fries or fluffy pancakes dripping with butter and syrup, fresh squeezed juice either at PDC, or the Pantry.

Over breakfast one morning, I said, "I promise we'll talk about how much you will be making, real soon."

"I love working with you." She cut and demolished the last few bites of her steak. "I eat better when I work for you," she said. "It's just one of the perks. I don't usually treat myself to steak for breakfast, but I'm already prepared to skip lunch."

Niley worked with me nonstop, except that she took off when the kids got home at four. She'd be there for dinner and put them to bed at eight, then meet up with me wherever I happened to be. I suspected she squeezed in an extra shower when she was home, because she'd show up in clean clothes, looking fresh and smelling sweet. We'd work until we dropped, usually approaching midnight. There wasn't a whole lot of sleeping going on. When I got up at five to work out, she'd take a shower and start her day too.

By phone, I set up four appointments in El Paso: families of three who perished in the train crash, plus the Pedrozas whose son Marco had survived with serious injuries, including a brain injury he might or might not recover from. The accident families I was already working with had dropped my name to those I hadn't met yet. Word was getting around about me both in town, and in El Paso. That brought more phone calls, and not all of them train crash related. Nothing succeeds like success.

Pixie was working long hours in the field. She managed to show up between four and eight, while Niley was mothering her brood; I think they had arranged this among themselves. Normally I would have taken Jo to El Paso, but she had her hands full at Jake's. I talked to her on the phone several times a day. We exchanged progress reports, and talked about El Paso.

"Book Niley," I asked Jo.

"You got it, boss." Jo asked me a couple questions about when I wanted to get there, how long I wanted to stay, questions about reservations. Then she brought up Niley. "Does she know? About going to El Paso, I mean?"

"No, I haven't told her yet. But she'll go."

"Good," she said.

"She's learning," I said.

"I read some of her notes on Chavez," Jo said. "Not bad."

"Takes time. We're lucky to have her. I haven't even talked money with her. When I get back, let's discuss it."

"You got it boss," Jo said. "Too bad we didn't start her alongside Pixie."

"The timing wouldn't have been right," I said. "We were still grieving. And I don't think we had enough business to keep four of us busy then."

"Right now we could use six more," Jo laughed.

"Or just an extra you," I told her.

In the background, I could hear a commotion going on at Jake's. Male voices, female voices, tempers rising. Jo put her hand over the phone, and gave one of her ear-splitting sharp stand-to-attention whistles. My ear and I were glad it was muffled. It got very quiet on her side of the line. She returned to the phone. "Gotta go, boss," she said, "They need me to unravel some tangle."

"See you in a few," I said, "I have a stack of retainers to bring in."

She made an exultant noise that started off like a cheer, and was in the general neighborhood of a groan when it was fortunately cut off by the phone hanging up.

We were at Jake's. Jo was standing up waving around her new stack of retainers.

She called in the crew helping her, and said, "Got a new batch!" before she parceled it out.

One of the guys, a new one I hadn't seen before, whooped and said, "Fresh meat."

The bustle stopped like they'd all been frozen.

I thought the eyes were going to come out of Jo's head.

"No, Hamilton Burgette," she said. "No and no and no."

He still had a smile on his face and no clue what was going on.

"Excuse me?" He looked around, mystified. The cluster of people around Burgette inched away, as if he'd contracted leprosy, body odor, and bad breath, all in one fell swoop. "What's up?"

"Your job, if I have any say about it," Jo said tersely.

"My...hey, what's going on?"

"He doesn't understand," I said.

"He should. He shouldn't have to be told," Jo said, "If you have to be told, you're in the wrong profession."

I could see the guy thinking hard, trying to figure out what he'd said.

Jo took a step toward him. If it had been me, I'd have been poking him as I talked. Not Jo though.

"Never for an instant forget that every case is a tragedy. Even if no one dies, it is a tragedy. But here, this case, this so called *fresh meat*, this man who died is not some statistic. He is not some raise for you. He was not meat. He had a wife. Her name was Betty. Did you know that? Did you know that Betty was so broken up when he died that they found her wandering the neighborhood in the middle of the night, looking for him? They took her to the psych ward. She's in shock, maybe even a fugue state, and she's got amnesia, doesn't remember who she is because as long as she can't remember, maybe he's not dead. What about the kids? There are two kids who now may have to go to relatives, or might end up in foster care. That's your fresh meat, you son of a bitch."

The phone rang. She wheeled around and snatched up the phone. Burgette took the opportunity to dash out of the room, tail between his legs.

"Jo Webb," she said, in a voice warm enough to melt butter, as if she weren't glaring daggers in Burgette's direction. She nodded in response to whatever they were saying.

"Yes, Alma," Jo said, "I will be glad to look that up for you and Mr. Flores. I was glad to hear your daughter is doing so much better."

She sat down at her desk. We were alone again. I kissed the top of Jo's head. She had a phone in one hand and was writing with the other.

"Love you, Jo," I said, looking at my watch. If our current schedule held true, Pixie was going to be showing up at home shortly.

"Love you more, boss."

As I'd expected, Niley was gung ho about the trip. I'd never been to El

Paso, and I'd never been on a plane for a flight longer than an hour and change, the time it takes from Los Angeles to San Francisco. I was almost as excited as she was.

"My first time on a plane, boss," she said. "Jo told me what to pack. But I'm still kind of nervous." She'd thought we'd have to walk outside and climb stairs up to the entrance, but we exited the gate directly into the plane. She thought the jet bridge was cool.

This trip was serious business. Meeting families who have lost loved ones in any tragedy is never a pleasant experience, but we weren't with the families yet. All the way from Los Angeles, Niley and I were jazzed and animated. We joked on the plane like a pair of teenagers on vacation. A stewardess asked us if we were newlyweds, which made Niley roar with laughter.

"I'm just the office wife," Niley said, giggling. "One of three."

Niley was excited by the trays on the back of the seats; by the cunning little trays the food was served in; by the food itself, which was some kind of casserole, a couple of string beans, and a roll that had been packaged by Wonder Bread. She was entranced by the meal until she discovered the flight magazine tucked in the back of the seat. She was busy with the magazine until she found the airsickness bag. She wasn't at all airsick but shoved the barf bag in her purse, because it was so cunning. She loved the earphones that plugged into the armrests and she plugged the device in and out, and kept working the personal light and fan that was overhead. She remarked to me at least three times that she hoped we had trouble so she could try out that air thing that the stewardess had been demonstrating. She spent a long time in the bathroom, excited over every little detail, though she admitted she was scared to sit on the pot—what if she got sucked out of the plane, behind first? And the flush sounded like a rocket going off. She was as excited over her first plane ride as a toddler on her first visit to the playground.

Once on the ground and in the home of the first family we were there to see, the excitement disappeared. It was serious, and it was sad. Niley was very quiet, and let me do the talking; I could see that she was getting emotional. I wondered if it was hard on her. Tanis's death had not been long ago, and I think her own grief magnified her responses to the tragedy the family had experienced. When I offered condolences for their loss, Niley's compassion was immediate and touching. I was having a problem getting both grandparents engaged in our talk; the grandmother was having trouble with the kids. Niley picked up the smallest and fussiest of the several small children who had been orphaned by the train wreck, and walked around with him, bouncing and humming until he fell asleep in her arms. The grandparents were very touched by her taking care of the baby. They would have signed for that single minute of peace. I doubt they'd had a moment of relief since the accident had happened. She even put him to bed in his crib. I don't know if they noticed her eyes were brimming with tears when she returned to the room where we were talking.

Our hotel was in walking distance of the border crossing between El Paso and Juarez, Mexico. We took that walk, crossed the bridge, and went through Mexican customs without a hitch. It was early evening, and it was a hot summer night.

"It smells different," Niley said.

"What does it smell like to you?"

She sniffed the air. "Mexico," she said, laughing.

I knew what she meant. It was partly the feel of the hot night; I could definitely smell oranges, but also a unique blend of cooking aromas, grilling meat, roasting corn. It smelled familiar, and yet different.

We walked a block through what we believed was downtown, and were offered lottery tickets, tamales, tacos, and cones of ice. We saw a little girl with a mop of curly hair dashing around in tough bare feet and a faded blue dress. She was maybe seven years old. She ran up and tugged Niley's sleeve. She flashed a toothless, cheeky grin, and handed Niley a flyer telling her where she could go get a massage by the good looking *güey* on the flyer.

We bought and shared a slab of watermelon that was cool and sweet and sprinkled with spices, and corn that was grilled in spices and slathered in mayonnaise, and it was all unexpectedly delicious. I was handed no fewer than three flyers, one of them probably by the brother of the girl in the blue dress, advertising whorehouses where there were *chicas* waiting to do anything I could imagine. Niley and I laughed a lot at this. We talked about where our friends would go, and what they would want to do. Niley said from what she knew of Jake, he'd want to be served cold juice while his feet were rubbed; and I said Pixie would like a shot at that boy in the flyer, but only if his massages had happy endings.

We went in a bar. It was small, and there was actual sawdust on the floor. It had a lot of what tour guides call ambiance, and what Jo would say needed a good bucket of Clorox, some elbow grease, and a scrub brush. There were no soft drinks, and there was no ice. The dimly lit place was very popular, had a shoulder-to-shoulder crowd, and smelled of jalapeños, close-pressed bodies, and beer. The slow moving fan dangling from the ceiling only circulated the bitter scent of perspiration and cheap perfume, and yet, there was a certain charm. I ordered two beers. We were served two *Bohemias*. I took a sip and had to follow with a gulp of air. It was the strongest beer I'd ever had. It took my breath, but I didn't let it show. I smiled broadly. Niley did the same. We walked out a little later, and left the bottles practically untouched.

We went to curio shops. There were lots of them, and all with the oddest assortment of things. Niley bought small gifts for her kids, a whole lot of handmade wooden toys that operated with rubber bands and springs. I bought Jo and Pixie bracelets that were supposed to be sterling silver. I bought Niley one too.

We returned to the hotel, tired and drenched from the heat. The suite I'd booked for us to share had only one bedroom, but two full bathrooms, and a sitting room that had a couch that could be made out into a bed. After the sweltering night, air conditioning in the room felt as close to the perfect climate as I could ever expect in this lifetime. We set the temperature as low as it would go. I took a quick cold shower and could feel the heat coming off of me. Niley joined me in the tub.

She filled the tub with water then pulled me down to join her. The hotel's soap had a lackluster lather. I was disappointed, but not for long. Niley performed some chemical magic between the hotel soap and girly soapy things she'd brought along and got a lather going. Not just a little, but luxurious, dripping mountains of bubbles, an embarrassment of bubbles; buckets and cups, and bowlfuls of bubbles, so we couldn't see where the bubbles ended and the tub began. She lathered my upper half while I stood shin high in bubbles; and while I stood head to toe in soap, she worked over my body till I could have passed for the abominable snow man, if he'd had bubbles instead of fur. All on its own, my soapy dick tried nestling between her soapy breasts, among other places. We were one giant-moaning-groaning-slippery-slithery-slidey bubble. We didn't quite get it right, and had to practice, repeatedly, until we and the bubbles were exhausted, and melted across the terra cotta floor, and the water was cold.

We crashed hard on cool, crisp sheets. My night was completely relaxed, half a dozen hours passing in a perfectly comfortable dreamless instant. Niley had been on top of me, and I was deep inside her the last that I knew. The next instant, it was morning.

We got up, both of us a little taken aback by the water in the bathroom. I told Niley I'd just pay them for it, but she was aghast. As we rushed to get ready, Niley and I called for more towels. Niley even swiped some more from an unattended hotel cart in the hall and dropped an armful of sodden towels in the cart's laundry bag. I wonder what they said when they saw it, whoever opened that laundry bag. Niley used the stolen dry towels as reinforcements to dry the floor. It had never been so clean. But it was still a rush of dressing, and preparation. We had an appointment at eleven with another family.

I could talk about getting cabs in Mexico. I have stories. But this time it was easy. We caught one in front of the hotel. As soon as we were settled inside, and I had given our direction, I apologized.

"I'm sorry I went to sleep."

"Papi, I went to sleep too."

Her nickname hit me hard. Like Tanis, she had called me Papi Grande during the night. I guess sisters talk about things like that. I was thinking about Tanis again, and realized Niley was still talking.

"...you were deep inside of me, then I don't remember."

She kissed me. The taxi was old but the upholstery was clean. It smelled of lacquer and leather; it was sleek and cared for. More importantly, the cab had air conditioning, and the driver seemed to know where he was going.

I was a little shaken by the house as we drove up. It had been constructed of wood that looked to my untrained eye like unpainted fencing gone gray from exposure to the elements. Here and there, it had been patched with new wood, still green, and unpainted. The building was not large. It was a low flat structure, and had been well and closely attended by someone with mediocre repair skills. The roof could have used some more tile. There was a yellowed, cracked front window through which I could see a room, a center courtyard, and a room beyond.

The older boy introduced himself as he let us in the tidy little home. Inside, it needed a lot of repairs. The boy was of medium height. His hair was trimmed short, and he had grease under his fingernails. He looked older than his age; his face was careworn for a nineteen year old. Should I in my mid-twenties call him a boy? There was something sad about the cast of his eyes, and something manly about the way he carried himself. He had a gravitas that Carson would never have nor understand. If I had guessed his age, I'd have said in his late twenties, maybe even thirty. His name was Axel.

Axel provided us cool tea in mismatched cups that had seen a lot of wear. His sisters brought around a tray of homemade churros, dripping with crunchy sugar and fragrant with cinnamon. They were delicious. Niley barely touched hers. I was glad I hadn't brought Pixie who was pretty much about total instant gratification, especially where food was concerned.

We sat down on a sofa that had seen better days. It was centered in a tiny tiled den, slightly uneven, in a way that few American homes are. The small house was built in a square around an open center. We faced windows that were open to a courtyard. Someone had a green thumb. The plants out there looked lovely and cool. I'd been outside though. The plants lied. Several fans kept the warm air moving. The air was sweet and spicy smelling, but I dabbed my forehead with a handkerchief and looked forward to the air conditioning of our hotel room. On the other side of the courtyard, I saw what was probably a bedroom. Clothes hung on the wall on hooks, and on either side were what looked to be narrow halls to the bedroom, making the house a square. The kitchen was behind us: a sink, a tiny refrigerator, a small table, a vintage gas stove. Shelving held more mismatched crockery. I hoped there was at least a bathroom off of one of those halls. If not for the ceiling fan, I'd have thought this place didn't have electricity.

The Espinoza family had lost both father and mother in the train crash. Axel, the eldest, was nineteen. He had two younger sisters, Penelope and Calliope, and two brothers, Felipe and Lupe, all minors. He introduced them all, and let us talk long enough that we were charmed by his siblings. Then he sent the others out and spoke to us alone. He seemed very small and young and alone, but at the same time, he radiated responsibility.

"My parents were headed back to Los Angeles where they worked in a big house for a family there."

"How long have they been working there?"

"About five years." His eyes focused on the wall behind me as if there were a calendar carved there. "Yeah, that's right. Five years."

"So you have been the man of the house all these years?" asked Niley. "You poor thing." She got up from beside me, and sat beside Axel on the settee, holding his hand.

He nodded, wiping away tears. "Yes, but I graduated from school. I have a job as a mechanic. My brothers and sisters go to school. I don't make that much, but I will keep taking care of them. I won't lie and say we won't miss the money my parents sent home every month."

"You'll never get your parents back," I told him, "If the law could bring them back, I would make sure it would. I don't like to make promises, but I promise you will get enough money to be comfortable, and raise your siblings until they grow up. The attorney will make sure of that."

He signed a retainer for himself and on behalf of his brothers and sisters. I handed him five hundred dollars.

"Here is my phone number. Call me when you run out. When you get your settlement you can pay me back."

The young man hugged me, then he hugged Niley. His brothers and sisters rushed and tumbled in. They had not gone anywhere but to hide by the open door where they could listen. They came up to us to thank us more warmly than was polite, and hugged us and finished off the churros.

We walked outside into the day's heat. I took out a linen handkerchief from my pocket and wiped off the sweat.

"That Axel, he's some kid."

Niley agreed.

"It's times like this when I feel really good about the work I do," I said. I hailed a taxi, and opened the door for Niley.

This taxi did not smell of lacquer and leather. It smelled of old cigarette butts, and feet and sex, and it lacked air conditioning. The windows were open, but the hot air that blasted by was no relief.

I turned to look at Niley. We were both sitting upright, barely touching the back of the seat of the taxi, wanting as little contact with it as possible. It was certainly not as clean as the taxi that brought us to the Espinozas.

Niley raised both of her hands and put them on my shoulders, turning me toward her.

"You're such wonderful man. I'm so honored to be your friend and to be with you at a time like this. I am learning so much. I look at the poverty of that home we just left, and I feel guilty to think I have a house of my own, with electricity, a full kitchen, and bedrooms for everyone."

We met with two other families, got signed retainers both times, and arrived in Los Angeles at six in the afternoon. I drove Niley to the office to get her car. She leaned over and kissed me.

"Thanks Niley," I said. "You are doing great. I hope that you like this work and that you want to stick it out with us."

She kissed me again.

"Papi, I'm in for the long run."

"Take a couple days off," I suggested.

She got out of the car.

"No way. I'll be at work tomorrow."

As soon as I got to my apartment, I went straight to the workout room. I was exhausted, but the workout would help. I did two hundred pushups instead of three. I hit the bag, practiced dynamic tension, then took a shower. I came out revived.

I turned on all the kitchen and living room lights. It was almost eight. Too early to sleep, but I'd be wiped soon enough. I scooped some ice cream into a bowl, skipped the peanut butter and sprayed it with canned whipped cream. Good stuff. If I didn't work out, I would weigh a hundred pounds more than I do.

Cosmo lectured me all the time, but I love my junk food. Life without goodies like ice cream and peanut butter and whipped cream—and sex—is just no fun. I moved my ice cream whipped cream feast to the den, turned the television on mute, then put on Neil Diamond. I sat on the sofa. This is what I work for, I guess, the rare moment of relaxation, feeding my senses ice cream and Neil Diamond, relaxing in my lovely air conditioning in my clean skin on my new couch in my fantastic apartment. My Bose earphones radiated sound. My ears and brain tripped the light fantastic. My mind wandered here and there, but I couldn't help thinking of Niley, of how close we'd become while working together, first in the hospital and motel, and then afterwards working cases, and then in El Paso. I heard something that didn't come from Neil or my muted TV. I opened my eyes, and there was Pixie.

"Come here baby," I said, opening my arms. I couldn't hear her or me.

Pixie moved to hug me tight.

I took off my earphones, unplugged them, and tossed them across the room. Music filled the space.

"I missed you, boss."

"*Guapa,* I missed you too."

"You lie. You been having a good time with Niley." She playfully hit my chest several times.

"Baby, she's part of us now."

Pixie kissed me passionately.

"I'm kidding. Not about missing you, but about Niley. I want you to be happy. Is she the one?"

"The one? How can I have one if it means giving up you and Jo? You know how I am. Maybe I'll never be any more ready for one than you are."

Pixie got on her knees. She reached and pulled me out of my boxers.

"I want to devour you," she said.

I felt her warm mouth take me. I closed my eyes and lay back like the pampered man Melina had accused me of being, but then I returned the favor.

I had called ahead and asked if he had thirty minutes to talk, so Jake was in his office waiting for me. I was glad we didn't meet at the juice stand. Jake's office was much nicer than Harry's old office had been. There might be bigger firms, or firms with marble floors, and gold lined doors, and firms with hot and cold running secretaries and paralegals; there might be firms that had museum class art and furniture or command multiple floors of the fanciest skyscrapers in Los Angeles. Jake could hold his head high, and feel equal to any lawyer in the city. Jake might not have a hundred partners and associates, but the ones he had were damned good. Any man would be proud of an office like Jake had. The comfort went on and on; and the luxury stopped just short of being opulent.

"So what do you think of the train crash?" I said, grinning. I'd done a good job, and didn't care who knew it. I reached across the desk, grabbed the little silver "garden" and raked the sand in it with a tiny silver rake.

From across his enormous desk, I looked for Jake's response. The desk was shiny, immaculate, expensive, and impressive. On the legal bookcase behind him, there was a shelf of lawyer toys that looked like sculpture: a miniature silver gavel that had been some kind of award; a couple of silver dice that instead of spots had sayings like not guilty, plea bargain, beg, ask mama, plead insanity. A variety of silver balls in a variety of configurations that demonstrated various physics tricks like perpetual motion, magnetism, pendulum waves and the like. I'd played with all of them at some time or other.

"I love it. You are the best."

"I have a lot of money out already on this," I said. "I'm not sure how to work it. I know we have the bonus deal in place, but how much are you planning to front me?"

"How much do you want?"

I leaned forward. I was in a grand leather tufted chair, dyed red, and smelling of lacquer. There were two of these flanking either side of his desk, and a few smaller ones that sat against the wall like lesser soldiers standing at attention. Jake's clients usually sat here. He liked them to feel pampered and cared for and powerful and confident. The scent reminded me of something. I thought a moment, and remembered the air conditioned taxi. I smiled.

"This case is bigger than the bus crash, and we're still signing cases. We have eight decedents already. And I'm talking by phone to someone else in El Paso. I may have to run back there to sign one or more."

Jake was glowing.

"How about twenty-five, and the end piece like we have?"

As much as I loved this guy, I did not have a shy bone in my body about asking for more.

"I was thinking more like fifty. But because it's you, I'll be happy with thirty. What do you think?"

I had no clue how much Jake was worth. I never knew how much Melina had either, but I know she had a lot. Jake was big time. The truth is that I think he could buy and sell Melina.

He didn't even argue. He agreed without the blink of an eye. "I'll give you thirty.[13]" He opened a desk drawer, and pulled out his check book.

"I'd have taken twenty-five," I kidded.

"I'd have paid fifty," he kidded back.

"Next big one, I'll hold you to that," I said.

"Deal."

I felt my pulse rise. I bet I was blushing. He wrote the check out and handed it to me, then came around his desk and gave me a hug. He reminded me of Harry. Jake was not a hugger. The train crash really had him feeling good.

"You have a fabulous team," Jake said.

---

[13] $30,000.00 in 1974 had the same buying power as $153,587.66 in 2016

I nodded in agreement. "I sure do. And I have a new person."

"You mean Niley, Tanis's sister? I've seen her bringing in retainers. Jo told me who she was, but I could see the resemblance."

"Yes."

"Good for you."

I think I strutted all the way to the car. I turned on the radio. The sun was shining, and all was right with the world. Redbone was playing "Come and Get your Love." I could dig it. It switched over to John Denver and "Sunshine on my Shoulders" and when I got to the bank, The Carpenters were serenading me from "Top of the world." I heard The Carpenters' last notes, and went inside to make my deposit. I wrote a check for cash to recover the cash I had taken from my sock stash. It needed to be replaced or I'd run out.

I told the crew to dress up and summoned them to my apartment, said that we were going to Sunset and Vine to the Tower restaurant to have dinner. Pixie and Niley went along with it, but Jo suggested that we order pizza and pasta and have dinner at the apartment. I called back Pixie then Niley, and they admitted they preferred the apartment to the Tower. That was fine by me. So did I. I preferred not having to mess with a tie.

Jo arrived first so we could talk before the others got there.

"I spoke to Niley about her pay," Jo said. "She'll get one fifty a week with no specific promise of bonus money; I told her we all got extra, but that is up to you. I also told her we pay her gas and auto repairs, tires, the works. Same as Pixie and me. I filled her tank on your gas card, and got her an oil change at that corner car shop you like. I had them check over her car to make sure it's safe. They fixed something. They're mailing you an invoice so you'll see what it was."

"I'm okay with that. Don't let me forget to forward it to Felix after I look at it. Thanks for handling."

Pixie picked up the food and arrived next. Niley got there at seven.

Together, they set the dining room table. We passed around the pizza and shared three different types of pasta with three different kinds of sauces: Bolognaise, Alfredo, and Marinara. We had Cokes.

After dinner, I gave Pixie, Jo, and Niley each an envelope. Pixie and Jo got fifteen hundred dollars each[14]. I gave Niley a thousand.

I sat back down at the head of the table and raised my Coke can.

"And now a toast to you, Jo, Pixie, Niley. Thank you very much for your hard work."

"Cheers," we all said, and sipped away.

They cleared the table. We talked. Pixie suggested we play naked Twister. Everybody answered simultaneously, "I'm too full," even Pixie. After a while, I opened a bottle of red wine. Jo got out the wine glasses.

"No pressure," I said, "If you don't want wine."

Niley raised her glass along with Pixie and Jo. I grinned.

We had a couple of glasses and a couple more toasts. I guess we were all feeling a little happy.

Pixie whispered something sidelong to Niley, who started giggling hysterically. "You won't believe this but Jo was with me when it happened."

"What?" I echoed.

Pixie put her finger up, and finished her glass of wine. I poured her some more.

"Say when."

Pixie watched me pour to the top and never said 'when'. She sipped the full glass.

"Now," I said, "Jo was in the car with you when what happened?"

Pixie giggled. Jo snatched the glass from her unsteady hand and put it on the table.

Pixie said, "When you took that big ape down the other day in front of

---

[14] $1,500.00 in 1974 had the same buying power as $7,679.38 in 2016

Carson, I actually came in my panties."

We laughed.

"You are so dirty," I said, laughing.

"That's not dirty. How is it dirty? I didn't even do anything. It's natural, orgasms are natural."

"They are," Jo said, "but normally not provoked by watching someone getting beat up. And normally not announced as after-dinner conversation."

"I came too," Niley said, raising her wine glass. "To us!"

Niley and Pixie and Jo raised their glasses and sipped some more.

We all laughed. Of course, I didn't believe either one.

The offices of Oscar Cooke were located at the Crocker Plaza on 6th and Grand Avenue in downtown Los Angeles. He was located on the fiftieth floor. It was my first time to the high rise. I noticed a sign in the lobby about a restaurant at the top, and wondered if the restaurant required a tie and jacket.

Cooke's waiting room was a total class act. I felt like I was waiting in a museum or maybe for royalty or something. Everything was stone, and glass, and expensive, and new, from the marble floors to the pointy girl escorting me to Oscar's office two minutes later. Oscar's office was easily three times the size of Jake's personal office. Fifty stories up, the view was almost like from an airplane. It was amazing. His office was in a corner, and the continuous panorama from side to side was breathtaking.

When I first saw him, I figured Oscar to be in his sixties, a little older than Jake. Guessing ages is not my strong suit.

"Business must be good," I joked as we shook hands.

Oscar wore a three-piece suit, a tie, and a chain across his vest with a watch on one side of the chain and a knife on the other. I saw him pull them out to check each one before tucking each in its own vest pocket so only the chain showed. I don't know what impressed me more—the cut of the suit, or the fob.

He reeked of class, not in a boastful way, but with polish.

"Let's have lunch," he said. There was no time to sit.

On the way out, I smiled at the receptionist. She gave me a big smile back. I was sure she winked at me.

As we walked out the door, Oscar chuckled. "Her name is Betty. Broke up with her boyfriend a couple weeks ago."

"Pretty girl." I chuckled to myself. A pretty girl can be a disarming weapon. How well I know, since I use the same strategy all of the time. I didn't blame Oscar but wasn't about to underestimate him either.

We took the elevator to the top floor. The restaurant was elaborate, and elegant. China and silver shined like jewels, and the furnishings looked straight out of what I imagined was in Buckingham Palace. But it was the panorama of Los Angeles through glass that raised the bar. Just the view by itself put Melina's favorite restaurant on Hollywood and Vine to shame. I couldn't wait to bring my girls here.

Even though I was just wearing jeans and a sports jacket, no Maître D' came running with a jacket and tie. The guys already seated had suit and ties, but no one said a thing about the way I was dressed.

We were seated in a corner beside a window.

"Thanks for coming over," Oscar said.

My reply was a nod and a smile.

"I wish you hadn't tossed Fink around the way you did."

"That big ape?" I asked with a laugh. "He provoked it."

"Fink is not one to tinker with. He's hard for me to control."

"If you can't control him, why keep him around?"

Oscar ignored the question, but I didn't really expect an answer. He ordered a Chivas rocks with a water back. I ordered Pellegrino, cold but without ice or lemon and no straw.

Oscar smiled. "How did you do with the train crash?"

He was being so respectful and friendly that I decided no wisecracks. This was not Carson. I didn't know this man.

"Good. How did Carson do?"

"Carson signed six passengers with injuries."

"That's good," I said.

"It is, but I need more business, especially cases like train crashes. There's a lot of money in these cases." He cut to the chase. "What kind of deal do you have with Jake?"

I looked him in the eye.

"Oscar, don't ask me questions like that. I'm not going to tell you what's between myself, Jake, or anyone else I do business with."

"Sorry. You're a good man not to broadcast your business. I only wish you had given me a few of those cases. I would have given you five grand for each person that died, and top it off with a piece of the fees at the end of the case."

"Good to know," I said, as friendly as he. "I'm not a lawyer. I can't get a piece of the attorney fees, and you know it."

I smiled and he returned the smile.

"Let's eat," he said. "*Provecho.*"

"*Provecho,*" I said in kind.

We both ordered steaks. His was burned. Mine was still walking around.

"When I get the right criminal client case," he explained, "I make upwards of a hundred thousand. That's just for openers."

"Then why mess with PI?"

"PI is a constant. Big criminal cases are not as constant."

"Something has to be going right," I observed, looking at him. "Your office smells like money."

"I didn't say I was hurting."

"Obviously not," I said.

"Look, send me something, Jake won't even know it. I'll pay you green cash, no checks. You pocket the money. No taxes."

I laughed.

"No way, José. I went to jail for that very thing."

"I know," he said.

"You do?"

"It's public record. It's no secret. I checked you out before I asked you to come see me."

"You mean, you squeezed Carson for information about me?"

I laughed, but moderately, respecting the place we were in.

"I had an investigator check you out."

So far, he'd been a nice guy. I didn't want to get mad.

"So I passed your inspection?"

"You did. Come here to my firm. I'll cut you a deal that will make you rich."

"I'm not hurting either," I said. "If you checked me out, you already know I own nine apartment buildings. I have money in the bank."

As soon as I made the boast, I wanted to take it back.

"You should be proud of yourself. You've done well."

He concentrated on his food for a few minutes, but it was like a distraction. I think he was trying to come up with another angle. Finally, he spoke again.

"Send me some of the business. Not all. Just some of it. Tell me you'll consider at least that. Jake can't carry this load you are putting on him forever. It takes tons of money to run these cases."

That wasn't news to me. I'd heard there were expenses. But Jake didn't come whining to me that he was hurting. I wondered if the expense really was putting a strain on him. I'd have to ask.

Oscar was still talking, "...my PI practice is tiny by comparison and it costs me big time."

"Look where your office is located. Your rent has to be ten times what Jake pays." I grinned at him. "I got a place you can rent if you want to cut your overhead." I was kidding. I had no such rental, but didn't mind letting him know I had property. I could hardly have let his rental overhead pass.

"You got a point, Mario, but if you were a lawyer you'd understand. It costs money to finance a case until it settles. If it goes to trial it costs more. There is so much to it. But PI is worth it if there is volume. And I'm looking for volume."

I had coffee. Before I was done, my beeper went off.

Oscar had port followed by coffee. He pulled an envelope from inside his jacket pocket. "Here's the five large I promised."

"Not necessary, Oscar. I came here out of respect, even though I don't know you. You called me so many times, it would be rude not to have lunch with you. So, friends," I said, extending my hand across the table. We shook hands.

But Oscar was not done.

"Take the money. Don't be foolish, I made a deal to pay you for this visit."

I got up. "Thanks, Oscar, but no. I'm not obligating myself to you. And I can't do it to Jake. If and when Jake tells me no more, maybe, just maybe, we can make a deal. I don't want to badmouth Carson, but I have a long-standing problem working with him. As for Fink, I've only met him once and I've never worked with him, but if I did, I can promise you, I'd sure as hell have a problem with Fink." I chuckled a little.

We both stood and headed toward the elevator. When we reached it, he gave me a little shove.

"Then, let's leave it like this. We'll have lunch again, some time in the future."

"Of course," I replied. "I'll buy."

"Deal. I'll call you."

We stepped inside the elevator. It was rich looking, sparkling cut glass everywhere, even the benches. Spectacular, really. We were alone.

"I was wondering, how did you meet Carson?"

"He didn't tell you?" He looked surprised.

"No." My beeper went off again. I put my hand in my pocket and turned it off by touch. I would call back as soon as I was able, but I wanted an answer, and I didn't want a distraction.

"I represented that friend of yours, Pélon. Carson was going crazy trying to find a lawyer to send his cases to. Pélon wrote and asked me talk to him. I saw a clean cut kid, a little nutty maybe. Talented. Maybe not as talented as you, but he's got something. I cut a deal with him, and he's been with me ever since."

Pélon of all people. He was the last person I'd have expected to introduce them.

"How could Pélon afford a lawyer like you?"

"The court where Pélon was being tried for murder appointed me as his attorney. On murder cases, the judge appoints an independent attorney and the county pays a pittance. It's practically *pro bono*."

"Okay then, but if you're as good as you say you are, how come he got convicted?"

"It didn't matter. Nothing mattered. They had Pélon dead to rights. I was sorry to see him go away for so long."

We shook hands again. He got off on his floor, and I went down to the lobby where I took an escalator to the parking levels.

The crisis at Jake's was under control. Jo was back in the field. I dropped off a retainer, and joined Jake walking to the Grand Central Market to the juice bar. With only two tables in the small space, most customers ordered and took their juice with them. As usual, we sat, drank the juice, sometimes ordered a second drink, and talked about cases. I told him about my lunch with Oscar Cooke. I also told him I didn't take the five thousand.

"Smart move. Had you taken the money, you'd be on the hook, even though he said no catches. I don't say that because it's Cooke. I don't know him that well. But you know, there is no such thing as a free lunch."

"You are right, Jake. No such thing."

Jake was smart. He was put together in his usual suit and tie. Jake and Oscar were cut out to dude up that way. I had liked the dash of the three-piece suit that Oscar wore for lunch. I wondered if I should dress like that. If I did, would I sign more cases? Get more phone calls? I doubted it. If I dressed up every day it would be because I wanted to have a new look. I'd never leaned that way, mostly because of what I learned watching Carson in his cheap suits. Now I wondered if it was the suit I objected to, or something about Carson. There were other reasons I didn't walk around in a suit. My body was fresh from sweltering El Paso. It was summer in Los Angeles. I spent most of my time in the field. I knew from experience that in a suit, the heat could be brutal, if not going from air conditioned area to air conditioned area.

"So how did you leave it with Cooke?"

I shrugged. "I told him I wasn't moving over. I agreed to have lunch again if I pay the tab."

"Good boy."

"Jake, let me ask you something. You would tell me if I was giving you too much business, right?"

"That won't happen. I can use whatever you got."

"I'm not the only expense you have when I'm bringing in piles of cases. I see what it takes. The people that work at the office. It has to cost you dearly. Cooke implied it's just the tip of the iceberg, financially speaking."

"You're right. But, we keep a good pace settling cases. That provides the cash flow to keep moving."

I digested what he said. "But if settlements slow, cash flow slows, your overhead grows, then what?"

"You want the math? You always say you're terrible with math." He sipped the last of his juice.

"Not the math. I want the solution. My math is bad but strategies, I learn. Look at my apartments, especially the buildings that have mortgages. If I suddenly had a bunch of vacancies, I'd be hurting to pay the bills. I'd probably try some kind of lease with existing tenants. Offer some deal, free move in, or something. Start a whole new dynamic that wiped out the old way that didn't work. What would you do in that situation?"

"I'll cross that bridge when I get there. If I get there. Mario, we're fine. Don't worry. If I get to a point where I really hurt, I'll tell you."

"It's not me," I said. "I have no lack of confidence. Cooke was all but begging me to slip him cases. Said what you didn't know wouldn't hurt you. Or words to that effect."

Jake didn't seem surprised.

"By the way, I changed my phones to five button phones with my old line rolling over to a free line if the main line is busy."

Jake nodded. "Can't have too much phone access. Same arrangement I have, but I have a switchboard."

Technically I could have five calls coming in to my main number, answer the call and place on hold till I could get to them. If there were two of us on the phone, it got more efficient. The idea of the phone change was to work more efficiently at home. I even had phones in the bathrooms.

Jo and I had calculated the future bonuses. The low average came out to be a million dollars, though the top of the range, if everything settled at top rates, came out to be four million. And that was before the train crash. That was a hell of a future cushion to have out there. Knowing it was out there made me feel easier, even relaxed. It made me realize how I'd been working since I was ten, without a net. Now I had a net. It didn't feel bad.

"You've been really good to me. I never tell you this, but I do treasure your friendship. Thank you Jake."

We both got up and left the little juice bar.

Jake hugged me and, said, "I love you son."

"I love you too."

As I drove home, I wondered if he had money troubles he'd not mentioned before. I thought not. He'd handed over the up front for the bus readily enough. I was happy that Jo and Pixie were handling the field. Niley was home with one of her brood who was sick. She had called, conflicted, but I told her to stay home, take care of the kid, and get some rest while she was there. I always think that I hate to be alone, but I rarely am.

I hit the peanut butter, put on my earphones and Los Bukis with the television on mute. I fell asleep in the den. The phone woke me at eleven at night. The only light was from the television.

"Hey you," Melina said.

"Hey you, back."

I stretched and stood. I walked over to the TV and switched it off, looking through the windows at the panorama of nighttime LA. Lots of light in the city. Even if I wasn't on the fiftieth floor, even if it was night, it was spectacular. I leaned against the glass, looking out. Ten floors was not the Empire State Building, but it was a long way down.

"Ages since I've seen you," Melina said. "Don't even run in to you anymore."

"I was thinking the same the other day," I replied. "I've been very busy. I've been out a lot. I've been out of town."

"You want to come over? I have some great new wine."

"I was so tired today, I got home and went out like a light. I'm wiped."

"That sounds like you shutting me out."

I didn't feel like arguing. "I'll never shut you out. I may get pissed at you, but we're friends."

"That's all I wanted," she said. "Thank you."

I jumped in the shower, and wondered why I had not gotten any beeps. That was a long, quiet stretch. I figured that Jo and Pixie had instructed the service to forward calls to them.

I dried off, and walked into the bedroom as naked as the day I was born, turning off lights along the way. I switched off the light fixture, and saw Melina grinning ear to ear. She was sitting up on my bed, propped on pillows, legs extended, wearing nothing but a smile.

"Surprise, friend," she said. Her arms opened in invitation.

What a sucker I am.

I dove on the bed. She screamed playfully. We wrestled, and eventually stopped rolling around. Melina ended up on top of me. We spent a minute looking at each other, and got tangled in a kiss.

"Missed you, friend," she said.

"Me too."

It started romantically slow but we worked into a frenzy of deep passion and fury. I remembered her criticisms of my performance. I didn't ask, but I heard at least three of her orgasms before the end of my first go. Later, our bodies were finally idle.

"So you came over to get serviced," I joked with a laugh.

Her lips moved in a way that seemed like those were the only muscles she had left that were not exhausted. Come to think of it, her lips should have been exhausted too. She wasn't laughing.

"No one, I mean, no one, fucks me like you do."

"In that case, leave me a fat tip when you go," I joked again.

"You could make a fortune as a gigolo," Melina laughed.

"I'll keep that in mind."

She sat up and kissed me. "Gotta go. Big day tomorrow. Can we see each other more?"

Melina put on the robe that she must have come over wearing. Oversized hotel-style white terry cloth.

"Come over any time."

"What if you have someone over?"

"If I do, the door will be locked."

She kissed me, and disappeared in the dark.

Darkness has a presence, a stillness, a certain calm. When things move about in the darkness, tension swirls in the air. Turbulence stirs it up, and when you're properly grounded, jolts your senses like electricity, with a rush of adrenaline. So one second I was asleep; and the next my eyes popped open, all senses on, jolted, aware. Thanks to karate, I am a light sleeper, at least when I haven't been imbibing. I woke but didn't move. I don't know if it was something I heard, something I saw in the dark, or something I felt, but I could sense it moving toward me, in the dark. I knew something was here in this room with me, and I could feel it approach. My floors did not creak, yet I heard the creak of his steps as I saw a huge shape approach my bed. Something raised high over my head. Could any human be that tall? No, something was in its grasp. A weapon. A club. It was a fucking bat. It was already on the way down as I rolled to the right of the bed and off on to the floor in a crouch. Air moved softly past as it slammed the mattress instead of me.

I rolled to my feet, a foot away from him. His back was to me for a second, as he still faced the bed. There were no lights on, but with all my windows open, my bedroom is lit by the whole of Los Angeles. I could see he wore a mask. I wondered if I could be dreaming. He swung the bat but his reflexes were leaden. I was out of the way. He swung again.

"Who the fuck are you?" I screamed.

I was so pissed off. Who would dare do this to me, break in to my own space and come at me with a damn baseball bat? Whoever he was, he was big and slow. That couldn't be disguised by a scrap of fabric on his face.

"Fink, is that you, motherfucker?"

He swung again. I jumped back. The bat just brushed my stomach. Had I not dodged, he would have hurt me bad. I was bare ass naked, equipped with nothing but my senses. Now that we were face-to-face, I could see some details. He was about my height, heavyset rather than muscled. This was not Fink. I banked off the bed and wrapped my arms around his neck. The bat hit the floor. Good. A sleeper hold would be good about now, but he squirmed around and hit my stomach. He kept hitting me. His big hands hit my stomach, but not very effectively. I squeezed harder, and he kept hitting me. I pushed against him, got him an arm's distance away, and slammed his chest with a series of rapid punches and kicks. The sound of contact with his flesh was meaty, sickening. My foot made hard contact with his groin, once, twice, three times. My other foot encountered the bat, and I kicked it under the bed where it couldn't threaten me. He grunted with the force of each impact. He was a big guy but no fighter. I heard something drop heavy to the floor. Not the bat. I'd already gotten rid of it. I felt its weight, and shape as I kicked it hard under the dresser. I heard it slam against the wall. A gun. The bastard had brought a fucking gun in my apartment.

"Who the fuck sent you motherfucker?"

I should not have wasted the time and energy speaking. He got in two good hits at my face that connected. That pissed me off even more.

I crashed back on the bed, and I batted him with both feet. I felt his body shudder with the impact. I leaped up to jerk off his mask. It ripped but hung around his neck. I still couldn't see who he was. He flailed at me wildly a bunch of times, but only made impact once. I hit him in the face too many times to count. He hit the floor, searching for the gun. I kicked his head. Impolite karate.

Good real-life defense. Good solid contact. He groaned in pain.

The gun was against the wall behind my dresser. He was groping for it in the wrong direction. Good. Let him search for it all he wanted. I didn't need a gun. He lurched up and crashed on top of me, with the force of his body weight. The fucker was heavy. I rolled from under him. I jumped to my feet. He lumbered up and after me. I kicked him dead center between his legs, upwards to his testicles, hard. He screamed in pain.

I kicked him in the stomach. He moved toward the windows, away from the bed. I could see him better now. He wasn't moving so fast, and I'd hurt him, a lot.

"Who the fuck are you? Why are you here?"

I asked him, but he didn't answer.

He grabbed the thing nearest to him, lifted my vintage wooden valet stand, suit and all, and slammed it at me. I kicked it away, tangled in fabric and broken wood, and struck him too. He tripped and went falling backwards, his momentum driven more by his weight than anything I did. He fell back, slammed into the window. I heard the safety glass crunch. It was one of those slow motion moments, and I have snapshots of it frozen in my mind. His arms flailed in the air as he reached to grab something, anything. I reached for him, but there was nothing there for my hand to grab. He and the window frame were spinning toward the ground in free-fall. I stood there, frozen, still reaching for his hand to stop him from going back through the window, but he was already halfway to the ground. The hot breeze from outdoors flooded me as I wavered, barely managing to stop myself from following in his wake.

I hit the bedroom light switch and surveyed the damage. Everything was broken. The mirrors were crushed, the legs of the bed broken, the supports a crumpled mess, the sheets piled with glass tumbling down the incline of the smashed frame. The bedside lamps were on the floor, shattered. The Italian valet stand was splintered, piercing the new Brooks Brothers four hundred dollar suit I had never worn. I looked out the window, some distance from the edge this time. Ten floors down, the body of my attacker was splayed on his back, on some poor neighbor's demolished car in the well lit parking lot. He was, no doubt, dead.

The door to my apartment opened. The door creaked. I heard her voice first, calling me, and then I saw her. Melina was frantic.

"Mario, what happened? Are you alright? Mario! You're bleeding." She ran towards me.

Shards of pottery, splinters, broken mirror, glass and debris coated my bedroom floor. I had a hundred small scratches I noticed at once. I guess I was bleeding from some of them. I moved away from the window and blocked her. She gasped and hung on to me when she saw the missing window.

Moments later, Johnson and the guard from the lobby followed her in.

"Excuse me," I said. "I need to get dressed."

I brushed off as best I could and went into the bathroom adjoining my bedroom. I grabbed some jeans and a t-shirt from a clean laundry basket and pulled them on. I heard Johnson shuffling Melina and the guard from my room into the den. I grabbed socks and shoes and followed them, sitting down at my dining room table and picking glass off of the bottom of my feet. Fortunately, more was stuck on me than in. I managed to get the socks on.

"The cops are on the way," Johnson said. "Bossman, I'm at a loss how this crook got through the lobby and up here."

I brushed him off. "We'll get to that, Johnson. I'm still breathing."

Melina shook off Johnson and made a grab for me, around my torso.

"Watch your step," I said. "There's glass everywhere." I had tracked it with me into the dining room. Her cloth scuffs would not protect her feet from glass.

I stood, and carried her into the den. I tried to put her down. She would not let me go. She was shaking. I had never seen her like this. Melina, fearful.

"Baby, I'm glad you went home," I said. I kissed her forehead. "Go in the kitchen and take a spoon of sugar." My aunt had taught me that was good when you were scared.

When the homicide detectives arrived, they escorted me down to the parking lot. The coroner had taped off the area where the attacker had fallen. The attacker had flattened a BMW.

"Do you know this man?" asked one of the detectives. He'd introduced himself as Grizzaldi. He was older, stooped, had a grim aspect, and dripped suspicion. He was in plain clothes, but I'd have known him to be a cop. He almost made me miss Sanchez.

The parking lot was well lit, giving my first view at a thirtyish-year-old black man. He looked like a bouncer from a girlie club. He didn't have the intimidating look that Fink had, but then this guy was dead. My two hundred dollar curtains were between him and the car he'd flattened.

"I've never seen him before," I said. "He was masked."

"Got it," the coroner said, pointing. The torn, bloody mask was stashed in an evidence bag.

We took the elevator back up to my apartment. Melina was still there, still in her white terrycloth robe and slippers. The questioning went on.

"You should go home ma'am," Grizzaldi said.

"I should stay," she said. "I am his attorney."

"Honey, go home and get some sleep," I urged her. "I don't need a lawyer here now."

"Thanks, but I'll stay." I would say that she had recovered to some extent. Her voice was no longer shaking, nor was she. But she hadn't gone home to change. In her normal frame of mind, she wouldn't be standing in her bathrobe and slippers with a bunch of cops hanging around.

They questioned me over and over again, the same questions framed in different ways. "Anyone pissed at you that would order a hit on you?"

"Nope," I said. "If this guy had intended to kill me, he would have shot me when he came in. His gun is under my dresser. I kicked it there, when we were fighting. And he brought a bat with him. The bat is under the bed. This guy was here to hurt me, to scare me. I think if he meant to kill me, he'd have used the gun first."

"A gun would have sounded an alarm," Grizzaldi said. "We'll be the ones to determine his intent." He didn't like me having an opinion

"Sure, of course. That's just my opinion."

I stayed in the den. They went in my bedroom. I heard the tinkle of glass, and falling wood as they lifted up my ruined bed to get at the bat. At least the dresser was intact. But one of the detectives was cussing over cutting himself on glass when he reached under the dresser to get the gun. It was a .48.

"What the fuck happened in your bedroom?" the cop asked. "Start from the beginning. Top of the day, Wednesday. Or was it Tuesday night?"

"I woke up. It was well after midnight. I heard him creeping around and woke up as the guy was about to slam a bat down on my head. He missed. We fought. He went out the window." I abbreviated a little.

"That guy was big," the cop said.

"I can handle myself," I said. "I can defend myself."

"Where did you learn how to fight like that?"

I went over to the half of the den I used as my workout area, and opened a drawer in my weapon cabinet. I pulled out a big packet and handed it to him. Inside were a bunch of ribbons I'd won growing up. The trophies were at Cosmo's. There was a scrapbook too, which my aunt had put together, a hundred pages of me holding ribbons and trophies at some of the matches I'd won since I started karate at ten. The detectives thumbed through it all. I started to put it back, but then dropped it on the coffee table. I had already been asked the same questions by another detective. Might as well leave it out until they asked a third and fourth time. They're awful fond of repetition as an interrogation technique. Melina was taking coffee duty for me and the cops very seriously. I was on my third cup.

About three hours after the intruder dropped to his death, it was daylight, and there was still no word of his name. I asked Melina to call Jo. Jo would let Pixie and Niley know I had a problem. They would be hurt if they were left out. Already I had waited too long. I'd never mention this to my aunt unless she found out on her own.

There was a knock at the door. I started to get up, but one of the cops answered it instead. The visitor was Jake. His first time at my apartment.

"You okay, son?" Jake said. "Jo called to let me know what happened. I drove right over."

"Good to see you, Jake," I said. "You can come over any time. You don't have to wait for an emergency."

I gave him the summary version of what happened early this morning. The guy had broken in after midnight. Jake listened, then called his private investigator. Within thirty minutes, he had a full run down on the property owners. The girls had arrived by then, and checked me over. They were all emotional, crying over my injuries. They were crying over everything.

"I'm just glad you weren't here," I said. "Shouldn't you be happy? I mean, I survived, right?" That made them cry even harder, and cling. They kept crying and fussing over me. I'm not the subtlest of men, or the most sensitive, but I'm accustomed to them all being kind of mouthy and sarcastic, so even I knew they were really bothered.

The cops stayed till eleven, asking me a million times how I woke up the morning of Wednesday October ninth. Melina had left when the detectives left. I didn't know what to think of Melina who had stuck with me for hours when the cops were there. I had never seen her in fear, shaking, hanging on to me during a crisis. She hadn't been at risk at all. I hadn't realized she was so concerned with my welfare. I was touched.

The girls were still upset. I was in the den with them, away from the now boarded up window that was making them so crazy. Jake was in my office giving someone a terrible time. We could hear bits and pieces of his side of the conversation. Then his voice raised.

"I will sue the hell out of you!"

He rejoined us in the den and said, "I talked to one of the owners. They are going to move you to an apartment identical to this one where you can live until they repair this place, or stay there for good. It's your choice. Your landlords are arranging to have movers come in. You don't have to do a thing, or pay a thing. And you should be moved within twenty-four hours."

"Thanks, Jake."

"They don't want to damage their precious reputation for having great security."

We both looked in the direction of my thrashed bedroom. "That's some security," I said sarcastically. I thought of Johnson, and the security guy. I didn't want Johnson to end up as collateral damage. I'd deal with that later after the investigation pinned down the holes in security.

"They're looking into where security failed," Jake said. "Let me know if they don't come up with a great explanation. That's a lawsuit waiting to happen. And you have a hell of a lawyer, if I do say so myself, Son."

I put my arm over his shoulder, and said, "Thanks, Dad." I was kidding, of course, to make light of the attack, but I wondered if he knew how I felt about him. I knew he had my back. Where I grew up, that was pretty rare.

"My bed. My poor bed." I made a sad face. And I had just gotten that damn antique valet stand for my new suit. So much for dressing better. It was going to be a long time before I spent that much on a suit again. The girls huddled around me, dabbing alcohol and Bactine, and applying Band-Aids that I would shower off as soon as they left. I couldn't walk around with fifty Band-Aids stuck all over my skin, but putting them on me seemed to make them feel better.

Whatever it was that Jake threatened to do to the landlords, I'm not sure. Even my phone service was switched to the new apartment, located two floors directly above mine. As promised, the floor plan was identical. Except for the one that ended up in the parking lot, the window treatments that had been in my apartment were removed and relocated by the professional decorator who came in with the crew to accomplish the one-day move that Jake had demanded.

At first the beeps came in as usual, as if it were a normal day. Pixie ran out twice to sign cases then came back. Jo ran out to see a prospective client. Niley stuck it out with me. By seven that evening, I was in my new apartment that had never been lived in. It was weird because it was identical; it felt the same, but different. The only tangible difference was that the view was two floors higher, and the bedroom was practically empty. I decided to sleep on the couch until I decided whether or not to replace my round bed.

The attack left me curious about a whole lot of things. It bugged me that I had no clue how this asshole got through the lobby, and how he knew what apartment I was in. My phone is listed, but not my address.

I was calm, but my mind was rolling with questions. I wondered if this attack was connected to the shooting incident. I wondered if Carson was right that I was a target, that someone was after me. It had been maybe a year since he had mentioned it, but now I was wondering if it was true.

At different times, the *LA Times* and *LA Examiner* came to the lobby that night to interview me. The *LA Times* reporter was a pretty young girl. Johnson escorted her up to my new apartment. I'd given him permission to let her check out firsthand the old apartment they were working on. From her contacts at the police department, she had collected pictures of the huge opening in my bedroom, the covered body in the parking lot, and images of the caved in BMW. She also took some of her own. The reporter from the afternoon paper, the *LA Examiner*, also had the pictures. He wasn't as pretty, but I answered his questions just the same. Both reporters concluded that a super karate expert–me–had caught a burglar in progress and halted the robbery by tossing him out a window on the 10th floor of the Bunker Hills Apartments. I referred them both to Cosmo. I figured he'd get a big surge in business from the publicity. He wasn't leading classes so much these days, but he still went to work every day, bossed people around, and drank tea at his desk.

I made the front page of both newspapers. Normally I would have resisted the publicity. I had refused to cooperate when the papers had been interested in Melina's accident, when I had pulled her from her car. But this time, they'd timed it just right; I hadn't been to bed, and once in bed (or couch, for the time being), could not relax. I was too exhausted to fight off reporters. They'd bug me to death until they got the interview, so I caved.

When the reporters concluded it was a burglary, I agreed. Maybe it was. I was quoted as saying, "The police have it under investigation. I have full confidence in them. They will learn more when they are done with the inquiry." I sounded like a fucking politician, and there was as about as much truth in what I said as in our mayor's last election campaign.

After the interviews, I showed up at my aunt's place. It was damage control.

"Guess who came over?" I said, while she was feeding me a meal in the Monterey Park house. She was never satisfied I was okay until after she'd fed me. Her longtime beau, Señor Chapo, was there. I think she's been stringing him along since I was four.

"Who came over?" she'd asked. The three of us had already sat down. She usually set platters on the buffet, and we served ourselves heaping plates of Mexican rice, fajitas, carnitas, enchiladas, and roasted corn on the cob. I had just dropped in, so it wasn't anything elaborate. She always cooked like that. We had tall glasses of sweet tea.

I told her about the reporters. I told her there'd been a break-in and the robber fell out of my window. I made a big deal of describing the hole left by the missing window and frame, because there was a fucking picture of it in both newspapers. I didn't make too much of the robbery or the fight, but I knew there was no way she'd miss the news, especially when her friends started seeing the articles in the paper, and called her up. They were world-class gossips, and this was going to be as big a topic as when Ida's son went to jail for murder. Of course Ida's son was Pélon. He ran a gang, and he'd been tied to plenty of murders before the one they could prove, but that wasn't the point. The point was that there was no way she wasn't going to hear about it from somewhere. I had to break it to her in a way that wouldn't make her worried.

Local television and radio stations had picked up the story by Saturday morning. I avoided the interviews for television. How many times did I have to tell the story? It was just the day after, and the phone was ringing off the hook. Aunt Carmen had been one of the first calls. Niley was on the phone non-stop; I only had to deal with every fourth or fifth call. I kept hearing Niley answer the phone with variations of this speech:

"Yes, he is fine. He is right here, on the other line. If you leave me a name and number, I'm sure he'll call you back."

She'd mention the name, and when I was free, I'd give her a thumbs-up if I wanted her to switch it right over to me. Thumbs-down and she took a message.

Pixie and Jo were back and forth on cases all day. It seemed as if every source I knew, and every client I'd ever signed was calling to see if I was okay. Plenty of them just happened to have a case I might be interested in. I didn't turn them down. It turns out that tossing a bad guy out your window to fall off a building is pretty good marketing.

I didn't know it wasn't a regular call when Niley put her hand over the receiver, and said, "Another one for you."

I punched in the line, and took the call. It was Carson.

The phone rang, and Niley answered line two.

"I read the newspaper, *esé*. Be careful with Cooke," Carson said. "After what just happened to you, he'll be offering you protection. And I did not make this call, right?"

"If you say so, Carson. Thanks for calling."

"And don't be paying me any fucking visits like I did this. I did not do this."

If it weren't so serious, I would have laughed. "We need to talk," I told him.

"If you come over, bring beer and pizza, and leave that fucking chip on your shoulder at home," Carson said.

"You told me last year that it wasn't you that was after me. You said it like you knew who it was. I'm starting to believe you."

"I can't talk about that," he said. "Stay cool, man. Don't get dead. Don't trust Cooke."

There was no telling what his angle was. I didn't know if he was concerned, or if he said not to trust Cooke just to keep me off his turf.

As Carson had predicted, Oscar Cooke called.

"I'm sorry to hear what happened, Mario. I read about it in the LA Times. What is the world coming to? Are you alright?"

"I'm fine," I said. "I'm breathing."

"Let's have that lunch," he said.

"For sure," I replied. I was waiting for him to suggest a time and place, but he went another direction.

"If you have a problem with anyone and need help, let me know." Cooke said. "I know people."

As Carson had predicted, Cooke offered protection.

"Oscar, thank you, I really appreciate it, but I'm okay. A stupid, fat robber fell out of my window. I guess newspapers are hard up for news these days."

"I guess so," Oscar said.

"It's fucking shit that my relatives didn't need to worry over, but what's done is done. Look on the bright side. I'm not the one that went down ten floors."

"You got me there, Mario," he laughed. "I'll be in touch."

That's what I was worried about.

I don't know why I worried. He wanted to do business with me. My worry wasn't logical. If he wanted me to come over with him, why would he go after my life? I just didn't think it was Cooke. If Cooke thought muscling me would make me accept his offer of protection, then he was way the hell off the mark, and had no clue who he was dealing with. Who did he think he was, Al Capone? He's a fucking lawyer; that's it. So what if he ran around with some big monster-looking apes? Maybe that gets him off.

I waited till Niley had gone out for food, so that when I returned Melina's call, we would have privacy.

"Nope, staying here. Not moving back."

"You left me behind, two floors down," Melina complained.

"I have no intention of returning to the apartment where I had been assaulted. The landlord moved my whole phone service. They even moved my window treatments. I just don't want to move again, even if I don't have to do the moving. It's two fucking floors, Melina."

"So?"

"So how about you go with me to pick a new bed and whatever else I need for the master bedroom? I've been sleeping on my couch."

"Baby, I would, but I'm buried. I'm going back and forth to Hacienda Heights where I'm about to break ground on a new market. Martin talked me into a crazy hectic schedule. I've got seven managers in training, and they follow me around like my personal entourage. Only the best one gets the job."

"What, you can't take thirty minutes? Takes you longer than that just for lunch. I know your schedule."

"You don't know my schedule now till next July. It's grueling, baby. Don't get mad," Melina said.

"I'm not mad. You stuck by me. Told the cops you were my lawyer. I'll never forget that, really. If we go to court, will you wear the bathrobe?"

"Funny guy," she said. "Maybe you can pick up some work on The Carol Burnett show as a comic. That should pay for a new bed."

"Forget it. You know I can afford a bed. I'll just call Peter from that wholesale house. I still have his card, and he calls me back every week wanting to sell me more shit. If they don't have the mirrored bed any more, I'll just tell him I want the biggest bed he's got. I'll miss the mirror on my old bed."

"Dummy, get a glass company to install a mirror on the ceiling."

"Great idea, Melina, I'll do that."

"One last thing. I'm calling a locksmith to install a heavy duty deadbolt on your entry door. You keep the damn thing locked. I'm doing it at my place."

"Okay," I agreed, "How will you get in when you need service?"

"I'll have him make me a key."

"I feel used," I kidded her.

"Poor baby. Cuz will pay you back next time we meet. Promise." And she hung up.

I dug out Peter's card and called him.

"I need a bed. First choice is the round bed I had before. If you don't have it, send me the biggest bed you have on the floor," I told him. "King size. And sheets. How soon can you have it delivered? No canopy. I'm putting a mirror on the ceiling."

Peter promised to have it on the delivery truck before lunch.

I had to keep answering phones, but I was hard from thinking of what that promise of Melina's was going to mean. A couple of minutes later, Niley walked in with a couple of bags of food from Barragan's Restaurant on Sunset.

"Papi, you have to start locking the door."

I laughed.

"What?" she asked. But I didn't tell her why I was laughing.

I was answering phones right along with Niley, but there were so many cases accumulating that I decided to go out on two likely retainers. I'd just sent Pixie and Jo in two different directions, dealing with people who wanted to talk about retaining Jake. The cases were fender benders but as long as the accidents were real and our client was injured, visibly or just hurting, we signed the case.

I put on a new sport jacket for a change, ready to leave for ELA to check on the cases I had arranged on the phone.

"You stick on the phones then," I told Niley. "You sure you can handle?"

"Got it covered, Papi," she said.

The phone rang as I was going out the door. Before I got to the stairway door, Niley followed me out and caught up. Her face was pale.

"Better take this call," she said.

I went back in.

"It's Jeff from the office," Niley said. "Something terrible happened."

<h1 style="text-align:center">Chapter 13
October 14, 1974
Vigil</h1>

"Jake is dead," Jeff said. "Killed during a break-in."

My knees sort of folded under me. I found myself in an office chair without any real sensation of sitting there. It was one of those awful moments that happens and then suddenly, nothing else is ever the same. The world shifted on its axis.

"What?" I stammered.

"Lupe, the housekeeper, found the house broken into," Jeff said. "Let's meet. I don't want to do this on the phone."

When I told her Jake had been murdered, Niley looked like she was going to be sick to her stomach.

"Too many people dying," she said, collapsing.

I got her to her feet. I thought it wasn't so much Jake's death. It was any death, especially a murder. Niley hardly knew Jake, but she knew he was the foundation of my business. And my business was the foundation of her new life. I knew she was exhausted. We kept crazy hours, and I knew her sister's death was something she hadn't recovered from. Sometimes she seemed frail to me, like a china figurine that had been shattered and put back together again. I never knew if the glue would hold, or if she was really stronger than ever. Now was not the time to test it out.

"Listen closely," I told her. "Go in my bathroom and take a hot shower. I know you didn't sleep last night. Take one of those sleeping pills in my bathroom medicine cabinet, and go straight to bed. Pick anywhere. My new mattress, the couch, one of the recliners, anywhere you want. Don't answer another phone. I'll talk to Jo and Pixie when I have more to tell them. Promise me you'll do as I say. You don't have to talk to anyone, make any decisions, or have a thought in your head. All you have to do now is rest, and let me handle it. When you wake up, we'll all talk about it. We'll have a plan of action. Ignore the phone ringing, That's an order."

She agreed to do as I said. I was almost out the door, but I came back in and held her, then walked her into the shower, and waited till she got under the hot water. I was torn. I truly felt like I should bathe her and put her to bed; but someone had to keep going. I had to meet Jeff. I had to know what was going on, and how we were going to handle it.

We met at the Pantry, just Jeff and me. I don't really remember driving there or walking in. Jeff was already seated when I arrived. We ordered coffee and comfort food that neither of us felt like eating. Jeff and I both ate. The food was ashes in my mouth.

Jeff explained what had happened. Just before calling me, he had spoken directly with Lupe, Jake's housekeeper.

"She knew something was wrong immediately. She told me that every day, she had to enter the security code soon as she came in the door. It was always on. But today when she got there, it wasn't on." Jeff told me how Lupe had arrived at seven in the morning, her usual time. She screamed when she entered the kitchen and saw the family dog, Barkly, lying on the floor. The dog didn't move. When she screamed, no one came to see what she was screaming about. She was the only one in the house who was alive.

"Lupe dialed 911 from the kitchen phone. She waited on the line as the operator had instructed. Usually she delivered a tray with coffee, toast and orange juice to the master bedroom because Jake and his wife had coffee together in the morning before Jake left for the office. But Lupe did not fix a tray or go upstairs. The 911 operator told her not to leave the kitchen, but to wait there on the line until help arrived. The first police car was in the driveway within minutes. The cops made Lupe stay in the kitchen, and went through the house. They found Jake and his wife Michelle, dead. The second floor was intact. It appeared, at least at first glance, that nothing was taken. The security system was off. No one knew why."

"I'm shocked," I said. Grief hadn't hit me yet. What I felt was disbelief, and numbness. I had heard the words, and knew intellectually that Jake was dead. I was running on borrowed time. I'd have to keep busy. If I had free time, my mind would go there, and as soon as I thought about it, I'd be wanting to curl up into a ball somewhere. There were too many people depending on me to let that happen.

"Me too," Jeff said. "I'm having trouble getting my head around it."

"He came over after the burglary, you know, the thing that was in the papers. It was the first time he'd been to my place." I had no idea it was going to be the last. I guess people do that—focus on their last meeting.

"I've got an appointment. Let's meet back at the office in a couple of hours," he said. "The office is closed today. Everyone won't be there, but you should be."

"Okay," I said. "Listen, I've got a couple retainers I was going to sign, but now, I don't know…"

"Sign them," Jeff said.

Right or wrong, I was impressed with his confidence. I nodded. "I'll do that, then I have to check in with my team. I haven't told everyone."

Jeff continued, "The clients will feel comforted knowing they will be represented. And they will be represented. We will do what it takes to keep the firm alive."

So that's what I did. I don't know if it was legal, strictly, but I was still taking the cases to Jake's firm, so what did I, a non-lawyer, know? All I knew for certain is that when I went home to meet with Pixie and Jo to give them the bad news, I had two signed retainers in my pocket.

When I got home, Pixie wasn't there yet. Jo was.

"What the hell is going on?" Jo asked. "I signed my cases and called here and no one answered. I walk in and find Niley dead to the world in your bed."

"Yeah," I said. "I had her take a sleeping pill. Sit down."

Jo wasn't that good at taking directions. She liked to understand a job, grasp the objective, and do it her own way. But she heard the seriousness in my voice, and sat.

"Jake's dead." I didn't dress it up.

Her face went gray. All her motion froze. She came to a grinding halt. Before that instant, I don't think I realized that her hands were always busy doing something work related, often two or three things at a time. I never saw her sitting still. Yet here she was as still as if her own heart had stopped. Maybe I should have softened it up some. After all, she'd known Jake almost as long as I had. She worked part of the time out of his office, or at least she used to. She'd gotten close to him herself, in her own way. Like Niley, she'd suffered a recent loss that had fractured that tough façade of hers.

I guess people respond to these things differently. It still wasn't real to me. But Jo got it. She got it all right away. Maybe she was just more in touch with her feelings. The news broke her, instantly. The tears came, and her face crumpled. I reached to hold her, to offer some comfort and she shoved me away, and clenched her arms around herself, crying as if her heart were broken.

I knew it wasn't me she was rejecting, but the news. Still, it stung.

Pixie walked in, took one look at Jo, and punched me in the shoulder.

"What the fuck did you do to her?" She crawled on the couch beside her, and reached for Jo. Jo grabbed Pixie and broke down even more.

Pixie glared at me over Jo's shoulder.

I broke the news.

"Jake was murdered in his home. Last night or this morning. He's dead. His wife is dead."

Pixie's glare faded. She took the news in her own way. While she'd known Jake ever since he became my lawyer at eighteen, Pixie hadn't worked with him closely. They'd never been close. When she'd been arrested for soliciting at the hospital, he'd recommended the right lawyer, Jack, to represent her. He'd taken an interest in her case. That had been the extent of her contact. But she knew Jo had been close to Jake. Pixie shut her eyes, and concentrated on trying to comfort Jo.

I felt like a third wheel, droning on with the story of what had happened as Jeff had explained it to me.

"Now what?" Pixie said. "What else can happen? Tanis, Harry, 'Nando, Jake. You were almost on that list, Mario. What next? Who next?" She clutched at me frantically.

I put my arms around both of them. They both leaned into me.

"Now we roll with the punches, Babies. We got each other." Their grief spilled over me. That's when I felt it. I felt their loss. Their sadness. I felt the loss of Jake, the fucking, aching, bleeding hole his loss made in my life. The pain hit, and along with it, a fierce need to protect my team. Who am I kidding? It was no team. These girls—Pixie, Jo, Niley—they are my family, my life. I had to say something comforting.

"This isn't the time to talk business," I said, "but it's something I need to do right now. I've always been my own man. Lawyers like Jake and Harry depend on me, on us, for the business they have in their office. It's not the other way around. Please don't worry about tomorrow or the next day. Let tomorrow come. Whatever happens, we'll be okay. I have money. I have rents coming in from my apartments. I can and will take care of you, no matter what happens."

Life has its hard knocks sometimes. It can be bad when one of the supports breaks, crashing the roof in on your head. And it's dark, and it's hard to know where to turn. Jeff's optimism had shown me there was a light at the end. The problem was that now we were in the tunnel. It was on me to make sure we weren't stuck there.

"I have to go," I said. "I'm meeting Jeff back at the office. We're going to work something out."

They protested my leaving, but I had to go. I needed to be there if there were going to be decisions made. As I drove in, I thought about the situation. Jake had five lawyers in his firm. It was my understanding that they were not partners. Jake owned it all. Jeff was only a two year attorney. The others surpassed him in years and experience. Archibald Graves and Lorne G. Crutchfield had been with Jake since the time when the practice had been all criminal, and they were as old as their names sounded. Of the other two attorneys, one was a four year. His name was Tim Todd. The other was a six year named Ken Harvey.

When I got there, I found only a skeleton crew. Rachel was working, and an office worker Jo probably knew but I didn't. Jeff and I met in the larger conference room, minutes later we were joined by Graves and Crutchfield.

We shook hands and offered each other condolences.

Jeff took me aside, and said, "Archie and Lorne have a successor agreement that basically means they will take over the firm. The agreement was executed two years ago before I came on board."

We sat down.

"I hope you have someone manning the phones," I said. "I'd recommend putting three girls on it over the weekend. Preferably bilingual. I have people who will be calling in, wondering where they stand. You know the service is going to be overwhelmed by calls, even if you are normally closed."

"You're right," Archie said, rubbing his chin. "Money is going to be a concern though. Maybe we will just make it two girls." Archie was pale. His hair was white and curly where it grew around the edges. He was a stocky man with pronounced jowls, who had come from New York with his accent and his set opinions.

Lorne Crutchfield nodded, but I couldn't tell if he was agreeing with Archie or me. Lorne had an optimistic, weathered face, kind brown eyes, and a set of bushy black eyebrows that probably kept his lower half dry when it rained. He'd had white hair as long as I'd known him, and an impressive set of mutton chops. When he wasn't in court, he walked around in cowboy boots and a string tie.

I didn't know a damn thing about a successor agreement, but it appeared that although Jake had no partners when he was alive, he had his death covered.

Lorne said, "If no agreement existed, the clients would be put through a mess of red tape. The State Bar sometimes steps in and takes over the firm. That's a mess." I didn't know Lorne very well but he seemed like a good guy. I know that Jake liked him.

Archie's mind was still on the finances. He said, "I don't know how we'll be able to afford the huge case load we have unless we can start settling cases right away for the cash flow. We're going to work with Rachel on cost-cutting where we can."

"It's complicated," Lorne said.

Jeff was silent all this time. Our eyes met. I could tell he was in the same boat I was in. For all he knew, he could be out to lunch when they were done doing the cutting.

Archie continued. "Lorne and I are in position to keep the firm going for a while. Hopefully Jake's attorney who prepared the successor paperwork will tell us Jake provided for working capital. We'll have to see."

I stood. "Jake and his wife lie murdered in a morgue. We have no idea who the killers are. Even so, I am sure Jake would have wanted you to step right in and take the reins of the firm without delay."

The three attorneys nodded in agreement.

I had retainers with me. I put them on the table. "I assume you don't want more new business. At least not at this time."

"I don't think we can handle what we got," Lorne said. "Rachel gave us an idea of what you have been getting paid as cases come in. These expenses, well, we could never afford that."

I picked the retainers back up, folded them, and stuck them in my inside pocket.

He damn well knew it wasn't expenses. I was paid contingent on what I produced. Yes, it was a lot of money. I got paid sometimes as frequently as three times a week. I also had overhead. Almost every person who sent me a case was used to getting a cash gift from me.

I shook hands and gave Jeff, Archie, and Lorne a hug.

"We'll talk again," I said.

After this meeting, I was more anxious than sad, and uncertain of my next move.

I loved Jake, and I would grieve. It was a good thing that my heart and head weren't connecting yet. I had to figure out what to do. The only thing I had figured out was that there was no time for me to collapse. I had to keep it together.

I should have known better than to figure Jeff was going to be in charge. Jake was no dummy. He would have chosen the best successor for the clients and for the firm. When he had made the agreement, it would have been with the mindset that if the firm prospered, Jake's family would benefit. His wife, whom he'd probably figured to support, was also gone. I couldn't stop thinking about all the cases I had with Jake.

I knew that Jake had a thirty-eight year old son who was a physician in New York, and a thirty-five year old daughter married to a doctor in Palos Verdes; and that Jake had three brothers and four sisters. His wife had no living brothers or sisters. His children would be in the will to inherit whatever there was to inherit; and the attorneys would succeed the practice, rewriting the rules to suit them.

I wondered about all the clients I had brought in. Their names were in file cabinets that were stored in the file room. Some big cases too: the fucking bus crash, the fucking railroad crash. Where would all those clients stand? I didn't want to think of the millions in bonuses that would probably be evaporating like a whiff of smoke. Hundreds of names, hundreds of thousands of dollars. Personally, I wasn't hurting, at least not yet. But I thought of the million tied up in those pending cases Jo and I had figured before the train wreck. Now I'd be lucky if my life didn't turn out to be a train wreck.

Before I left the office, I made a call. I caught up with Melina at her Montebello market.

I didn't have to tell her. She'd already heard the news. The murder had already hit TV and radio.

"Oh Mario, I am so so sorry," she said. "I just don't know what to say other than how sorry I am. I'm here for you. I can come over right now, and be with you."

"I'm out," I said. "Come up after you get home. I want to talk some legal stuff with you."

She was very quiet for a few moments, then she asked, "Your bonuses?"

I was ashamed to say it. "Yes. I'm just so fucking mixed up. I lost my two friends, one after the other. Harry and now Jake."

There was a long pause. "I'm your friend, Mario. I will always be your friend."

I actually choked up. "Melina, thank you. Really, thank you."

I was going out the door when Rachel called me over. I looked at her for the first time. Behind the glasses, her eyes were bloodshot and swollen, and she had a hiccup in her voice. She took me into Jake's office, which was exactly as he had left it—except the shelf containing his collection of office toys had been cleared. There was a box sitting on the desk.

Rachel picked up the box and handed it to me.

"He started getting these when you began working with us," she said. Tears were pouring out of her eyes, but her voice was level. "Every time he'd order one, or get one as a gift, he would chuckle and talk about how you were going to love it. They're all yours."

She put the box in my hand. I felt its weight. It was surprisingly heavy, but then it was full. I numbly looked down at the collection: the rake and sand set, the magnetic gadgets and sculptures, the Newton's cradle. They were all there. I'd never realized Jake had even noticed me fiddling with them, but it was something I always did when I was over. I stood there holding the box, too choked up to reply. Rachel patted me on the back, and gave me a tremulous smile. "He loved you," she said softly. "This is what he would have wanted."

The murder had been on a Monday. By Tuesday, the news of the murder had taken over the front page of the of the two major newspapers in Los Angeles. The Mexican newspaper, *La Opinion,* had a big write up. If you flipped through TV channels, there was sure to be someone talking about it. It was all over the radio.

The phone rang once. I just looked at it. It rang a second time.

Already a hundred times today, I'd fielded the question, "What's going on with my case? Who's representing me? What about me?" For once I wanted to say, "Hey fucker, what about me?" But these were my clients, and they were worried.

The phone rang a third time. Wearily, I picked it up.

"Is that you, Mario?"

"Speaking," I said.

"How are you man?" I had heard so many voices today, I was hardly paying attention. My mouth was ready to drone on the script I'd been telling everyone. It took me a second for the voice to register in my ears.

"Fernando?" It was my highway patrol guy. The one who I sparred with at Cosmo's when there was the time. He was one of the few sources I had who didn't expect some kind of gift, unless you call doughnuts and getting regularly beaten up a gift.

"Yeah, man, I heard about your pal, Jake," Fernando said. There was a long pause. "If there's anything I can do, let me know, okay? I mean, I'll treat you to doughnuts next time we spar. And if you can't come in Wednesday, dude, I'll understand."

"I'm broken up over it," I admitted, "but I will let you know if I can make it to Cosmo's."

Automatically, I wondered if he had a case for me, and the thought almost made me laugh.

"I wasn't just offering condolences," Fernando said. "I just wanted to let you know I'm friends with the guy in homicide. If there are any developments in homicide, I'll inform you. If I were you, I'd be strung out over all this. Keep it together man. We'll get to the bottom of it."

"Thanks, man," I said. It was the first call I'd had all day from someone who wasn't looking for a piece of me. I regretted when he hung up.

Immediately the phone rang.

The phone had not stopped ringing, not at the office and not at my home. This was the first time ever I'd had second thoughts about working out of my apartment. Everyone in Los Angeles had heard or read about the murders, and every fucking one called me. The phone rang again. Second ring.

Without picking it up, I yelled at it. "Yes, I was attacked! Yes, Jake was killed. You want to know what's to become of your case? So do I! But I can't fucking tell you that. You want to know what's going on? Good fucking question!"

The phone rang a third time.

I took a deep breath, and picked it up. Before I said a word, they launched straight into their questions. "What's going on with you? First you're in the paper, and now my lawyer's dead. Who's got my case now?"

My yelling had brought Jo out of the bedroom. She was bedraggled looking. Her hair was a mess, her eyes bloodshot from crying, and the tip of her nose bright red. She'd had make-up on at some point in the day, but it had melted all over her face. She had nothing on but one of my t-shirts. I didn't say anything. Just sat there with some client's voice screaming in my ear. All I could think was that I'd never seen her look so beautiful.

She walked over to me, clicked on the answering machine, hit record, and transferred the client to the machine. She pulled the phone out of my hand. She had to tug; I was hanging on to it. You've got to understand that I'm a giant standing next to Jo but that doesn't matter to Jo. She pushed a phone line not in use, and dialed.

"This is Jo," she identified herself. "As of right now, pick up all calls on Mario's home line. No beeps. Take messages. No exceptions."

She tucked her arm around mine.

"C'mon boss. You need a break." She led me into the room where Niley and Pixie were already sleeping.

The new bed was quite high off of the floor. The mattress was wide, an Eastern King. There was plenty of room for all of us.

We'd been sleeping for hours: Jo, Pixie, Niley, and I. The phone rang. It was the security line. The lights were off, but unless the drapes were drawn, the room was never dark. The window was lit by a haze of reflected city light. I sighed, stared at the night sky, and picked up the security line on the second ring.

I whispered into the receiver. "Johnson?"

It was Melina.

I got out of the bed and spent a second untangling the long cord that could reach anywhere in the apartment, but was a pain in the ass to untangle. I walked to the hall outside of my bedroom with the phone balanced between my ear and my shoulder, and carried a wad of curly phone cord, unraveling as I went.

"I been knocking on your door for fifteen minutes. I was worried when you didn't answer. I came down to the lobby to have Johnson get you on this line. The other phone is going to the answering service."

In the hall, I pushed the bedroom door almost closed, and used my usual speaking voice. "I'm sorry. I crashed hours ago. Bad day."

"Want me to come up?"

"Sure," I said, "I'm not alone. The girls are here, but I'll open for you."

"I'm on my way up."

I didn't wait for her knock, but approached the door, and started on the locks. It took about the length of the elevator ride up to get the door unlocked, anyway. The locksmith Melina had sent had gone overboard, in my opinion. I opened the door wearing my boxer shorts, and nothing else. Melina was in jeans and a t-shirt.

"What? No bathrobe?"

Melina grinned, looked me up and down, and smiled. The smile did not reach her worried eyes.

"I see you dressed for company," she said, then wrapped her arms around me as I closed the door.

"You poor baby. I'm glad the girls are here taking care of you."

"Actually we're taking care of each other. The news hit us hard."

"I can imagine. Let's have a glass of wine." Melina walked toward the kitchen. She picked a red wine from my wine rack, expertly opened it, then set it down to let it breathe.

"Where are the girls?"

"In bed."

Melina smiled. There was innuendo in her expression.

I had to smile back. "No sex today. Believe it or not."

I pulled two glasses from the cabinet and placed them in the center of the table. We sat across from each other at the small dinette table in the kitchen, the bottle of wine between us.

"So you wanted to talk legal stuff," she said. "Tell me everything you know about Jake's firm and what is going on."

I told Melina about the first meeting with Jeff, then the second when I found out that Jake had made arrangements for the firm in case something happened to him.

"The new partners will say they can't afford you. They will say no to new business. Even if they had the money, no bonuses for you, because it could be construed to be unethical to pay you."

Melina picked up the wine bottle and poured wine into both glasses.

"The meeting was brief," I said. "They didn't mention the bonuses, not yet. But they did tell me no more business. They took a look at how much I make, and figured it out."

"Let's cut the bullshit. What Jake promised to give you is really a cut of his fees. He covered his ass by calling it a bonus."

"Jake's been paying me bonuses on cases that settle for more than three thousand. If his fees are three thousand on a fifteen thousand settlement, he gives me about a thousand."

"So he's been paying you twenty percent of his fees."

I shrugged. "I guess. It's never exact."

"You have a problem, Mario," Melina said, "but you probably knew this already. The problem is that you are not an attorney, so you have no legal right to claim a cut of attorney fees. You can't sue anyone for it either. You have nothing in writing, but even if you can prove that it was a verbal agreement by showing past payments to you, the law will not protect you because the agreement is probably illegal. I'd have to check."

I reached for the wine glass, and swirled it. Melina did the same.

"Tell me about the partners," Melina said.

"Graves and Crutchfield weren't partners," I said. "Maybe they are in this new arrangement, but they weren't before. I don't know much about them, except that Jake must have respected them. They are probably going to be your adversaries, but we can hope not. There's just one who is important."

"Who is that?"

"Jeff," I said. "He's the only attorney who speaks Spanish. There were plenty of employees who speak Spanish in the firm, but he is the only attorney who does. He is cool when he meets with clients, and he's patient. And something else, I always get good feedback from my clients who have had any encounter with him, on the phone or in person."

"Good to know," Melina said. "Anything else?"

"A while back, Jo and I penciled in real low numbers next to the list of cases that were pending. It's very hard to estimate the value of a case. You'll have to talk to Jo if you want the formula she used. We figured a range, but the low end was that I had about a million dollars coming. [15]That was if all the cases on the list settled, even if I never sent another case to Jake. And since we figured this before the train wreck, the estimation predates a lot of cases."

Melina shook her head. She raised her glass, and we toasted to Jake.

---

[15] $1,000,000.00 in 1974 had the same buying power as $5,119,588.74 in 2016

I didn't sip the good wine, I drank it.

"Easy, buster," she said, "This is not the time to get drunk, or to wake up with a hangover. You need to be together."

I nodded in agreement but held out my glass for more. She poured me just a little and poured herself a double.

"Unfair."

"I'm your elder," she said with a cool look. "Let me think about this for a few days. I promise I'll get involved. I'll help you somehow."

"Really?"

She put her hand over mine. "Listen, friend, I'm here for you." She shook her head and said aloud what I already knew, "You had to know that if something happened to Jake, you'd be royally fucked. Jake knew that too."

"Of course I knew. Jake and I had talked about it. But who would ever have imagined that Jake would be killed? It's unthinkable." Before I knew it, my eyes watered. I swiped at my face with my forearm, and sipped the wine.

Melina got up from her chair and hugged me. I remained seated.

"First things first. Jake and his wife will have a service and funeral. I'll be with you all the way. I'll go talk to them, even though I know I don't have a legal position. There may be a way. Let's see if Jake's friends are good people or assholes."

"You're right."

"Of course I'm right," she said, stepping away. "I got to run baby, but I'm two floors below. If you want to get off, come down and we can do it on my bed." I stood, and she kissed me, and held her lips on mine. "I love you, friend."

"I love you too."

I grabbed my robe, and walked her to my door, the elevator, then her door. I kissed her good night, and rode back up to my apartment where the girls were sleeping. Melina was still secretive. I had not trusted her enough to maintain the partnership we'd had, but there was no question how I felt. I had a special feeling for her, and I knew she had the same for me. She'd said from the beginning that she wanted friendship. That friendship included everything we had shared to date, giving ourselves to each other without catches or restriction. I guess now it would include her representing me to Jake's firm, or whatever it was turning into. I went back into the kitchen and put the cork in the wine. I rinsed out the empty glasses and left them in the sink. On second thought, I put the half-drunk wine in the refrigerator. Jo and Pixie liked to add it to their salad dressing.

I walked toward the bedroom, turning off lights as I went. I climbed into the bed as quietly as I could, not sneaking, but just trying not to wake them. They let me know they were awake.

"Melina is smart," Pixie said.

"For sure," Niley agreed.

"She has to be," Jo said. "Look at all the years she went to school."

I sat up. "Were you guys listening?"

"Yep, we heard it all," Pixie said.

I had to laugh, then felt instant guilt for laughing. Jake was at the morgue along with his wife.

I lay down, closed my eyes, and huddled with the bodies on the bed, mesmerized by the scent of female flesh and the feeling of being loved. Within minutes I was asleep.

I didn't go back to the office. Work was on hold. We had a massive backlog of messages to answer. I had no answers to give, so the backlog kept growing. Three days later, we still didn't have a date for Jake's services. Autopsies were holding everything back.

On Friday, Melina picked me up at the apartment. She drove. She wanted to talk about the meeting we were about to have, and wanted to show off her new gold Corvette. She had called Jeff, and he had arranged a meeting with the two partners that were taking over. I hadn't been back to the office, but this I could not miss. We—Graves, Crutchfield, Jeff, Melina and I—adjourned in the larger of two conference rooms.

Melina was dressed in a business suit. She looked professional, and capable, and every bit the equal, if not the superior of Graves and Crutchfield. I could see Jeff was more than a little intimidated. He shook Melina's hand, silently.

"Crutchfield," Crutchfield said, holding out his hand. Melina shook it.

"Archibald Graves," Graves said, with his hand out, "but you can call me Archie."

Melina shook his hand. "Archie," she said.

Crutchfield looked pained. "Lorne," he said.

"Good to meet you, Lorne," Melina said. "And you, Jeff." I noticed she had not volunteered her name.

She had already informed Jeff that she was representing me.

Graves and Crutchfield sat across from us at the big conference table. Melina sat briefly, then stood back up.

"I'm here in hopes that you are appreciative to Mario for the tremendous caseload you have. I'm here for you to help me work out something so that Jake's promise to Mario is fulfilled."

Graves looked upset. He pushed his chair back, and said, "But—"

Melina raised her hand and smiled. "Let me lay it out, then we'll discuss it further."

The table was both oval and rectangular, but without angles, did not feel as if it had a head and foot. They nodded in agreement. Jeff watched from what might have been a foot, but today it was more like the neutral sidelines. I wondered if he had any experience in arbitration.

Melina said, "There is a trail of checks written by Jake, especially in the last year, that when examined closely represents twenty percent of the attorney fees on cases that settled for more than three thousand dollars. In addition, there are countless checks to Mario as payment for services on cases he delivered to Jake. Mario understands that you are going to abstain on any new business. That leaves only the promise of paying Mario what Jake called a bonus when a case settles for more than three thousand dollars."

I could see Graves getting more wound up. It was like with every word she spoke, he got filled up with two or three good puffs of air. He held his tongue until she paused. She did not sit, but indicated he could have his say.

Graves said, "There is no way we can pay the attorney split of fees to Mario. He's not an attorney. And we may not have the money."

"But you can pay it to me," Melina said. "I'm a member of the bar in good standing. My dues are paid. Current. You can check if you want." She stared at them as she spoke.

I exhaled. I hadn't even realized I'd been holding my breath. I'd had no idea she was going to do this. I don't know what kind of magic I thought she was going to pull, but this strategy had not even occurred to me. I grinned at Melina's cleverness. If I'd had suspenders, I'd have stuck my thumbs under them and strutted around the room. I looked at Jeff. Jeff was looking serious, so I quashed the grin. But, oh, the cleverness of her.

Jeff was quiet.

Crutchfield said, "If we do that, we're all guilty of circumventing the rules. We would need client consent to share the fees."

Graves said, "Even if Mario went around and got all these signatures on retainers to include you, ma'am, it's just not the right thing to do"

"It's exactly the right thing to do. Are you just going to step in here and take over a gold mine and not give anything to the person that brought all these cases to this firm?" She impaled them with her eyes. "You can tell each other that you're doing it for ethical reasons, and you can lie and tell me the same thing. But we all know you're only doing it to cash in on Mario's hard work."

Crutchfield's voice did not waver. He said, "We know from our office manager, Rachel, about the checks Jake paid Mario, two, and three times a week. I would never want to admit they were in payment of cases he brought in, but it sure appears that way. And if this is correct, Mario has been paid, up front."

Jeff and I were the two silent dummies, just sitting there saying nothing.

"Jake made a promise," Melina said sternly. "Is the firm not honoring Jake's promise? His word?" She was tapping her pen on the conference table, but no one told her to stop. She was still standing.

Crutchfield said, "This conversation has become so frank, I suppose I can call you by your first name." He continued without her acknowledgement. "Melina, taking over this firm is not going to be easy. It's going to be a nightmare. Jake did not financially provide adequately for the successors to continue the practice as it has been for the last two years. No doubt he would have had no idea that the firm's case load would expand as it has. We just don't have any real capital to speak of. We are going to depend on the cash flow that settling cases will generate. We're not Jake. Jake had a great deal of capital. Jake invested from his own funds. He was worth millions."

I knew it, I thought. I remembered when I'd gone to him after talking to Oscar Cooke, when I'd been worried that I was bringing him too many cases. I could practically hear his voice now, assuring me that there was no trouble of that. I smiled a little. If anyone noticed, they would have no clue why.

The conversation was heating up.

"With the same frankness," Melina said. "If we don't cut a deal, it is possible, even probable, that you will lose every pending case that Mario brought in. All it takes is a substitution of attorney signed by the client. You know this."

"Is that a threat, Melina?" Graves barked.

Crutchfield's face wrinkled, waiting for Melina to reply. She didn't reply fast enough. I did.

I thought about Oscar Cooke. "I know a guy," I said. "He'd love to step in and take all the cases. He'd probably pay big money for the opportunity."

Melina sat down as soon as I started talking.

"More threats, Mario?" Graves said. His face was bright red. I thought he might have a stroke. Crutchfield's face was much the same. I looked over at Jeff. His expression hadn't changed. His color was good.

"I know a guy who will take these cases," I said, "but I will take the cases out of here only if you don't want them." I looked from Graves to Crutchfield.

"Do you want to keep the cases?" I asked, "If you do, are you going to see each case through to the finish line, no matter what? Because the one thing, the only thing, that matters to me is that the clients get a fair shake."

Melina opened her mouth to speak, but I reached over and tapped her arm so she would let the attorneys answer.

"Of course we want the cases. And we'll do a damn good job on them. We always have," Graves said.

"Of course," agreed Crutchfield.

"You're making a mistake," Melina said to me in a low voice. I could feel her eyes on me, but I didn't turn to face her.

"Is Jeff going to stick it out, or are you going to show him the door?"

Jeff didn't answer. I looked at Crutchfield, who was biting his lip. If I was right about reading body language, then Jeff was on his way out. The least I could do would be to help him secure his job.

"Jeff, you speak Spanish. You're good to the clients. There are so many that you will never be able to deal with each one personally, but you must try and do it. This is very important to me."

Jeff said, "Mario, you know I'm here all the time, even when the office is closed. If I'm here, I'll look after them."

I liked Jeff. I could see only sincerity in his face, but I pointed my index finger at him. "I will kick your ass if I find out that you neglected a single one of my clients."

"Won't happen," Jeff said.

I looked at Graves and Crutchfield. "If you can, Jeff, and I find out you neglect a single one of my clients, I will kick your ass."

Melina looked like she was having misgivings about what I might say or do.

"Don't worry, Melina. I'm not talking bloodshed. I'll let you beat their ass in court."

If I took these cases to Oscar Cooke, I'd have to go back to the clients, and tell each one that I had changed my mind now that Jake was dead. I'd have to tell them that the firm he left behind could not properly handle their cases anymore. I'd feel like a fool. I did not know how Cooke's cases went. I did not know if he cared as much as Jake. As much as Jeff. This way I knew if Jeff was around, the clients would have the support and maintenance that they needed and were entitled to. I didn't know if Oscar Cooke was trustworthy. He was a total stranger to me. Carson kept insinuating how bad the man was, and to be careful with him, not to trust him. No, I couldn't get Cooke involved with these cases.

Melina did not object further nor did she ask me to step outside to talk. I suppose she knew me well enough to guess that my mind was made up.

We were on our way to the apartment. The Corvette went fast, and hugged the road. Melina drove fast when she was upset. Of course, she drove fast the rest of the time, too. The silence was heavy, full of the words Melina wanted to say. I could feel her anxiety, but knew she wasn't going to say her piece unless I brought it up. We were almost home.

"Go ahead," I told her. "Say it. Say what you want to say."

"If you had let me finish, those bastards would have caved or at least given up something."

"I don't think so. They are scared to death about what's ahead of them. I deserve the fucking I'm getting for putting so much in to one firm. I know better than to put all the eggs in one basket, but that's what I did. I could have distributed the cases. I'm sure other attorneys would have given me the same deal as Jake. I just never tried."

"Had Jake lived, you would have gotten the money," Melina said.

"Yes, for sure," I agreed. "The truth is that when I started in this business, when I was just a kid who refused to talk percentages, I got paid for each case I brought in. With Jake, I got paid. Sometimes I got less than I would have asked for had I not had a promised bonus, but I got paid. So, I'm just not getting a million bucks or whatever in the next four years or five when the cases settle. So what? Fuck it."

"You say fuck it so easy. A million bucks payable over the next few years could buy you a bunch more apartments."

"You're right," I had to agree, "but I'm fucked."

We could have walked to the office. That's how close the apartment was to Jake's office—one of the reasons I'd rented it—the other reason being that I wanted to be close to Melina. The traffic was heavy, but no deterrent keeping Melina from driving as crazy as she could.

She steered the car with her left, and with her right hand, reached over and grabbed my dick through my slacks.

I turned to look at her. "Thank you friend. I know you're busy with the markets, and here you are trying to save my ass."

"You owe me," she said, and squeezed.

I felt it grow.

"You got it. Anything you want," I said.

She squealed into the apartment parking lot, pulling up to where we would usually leave the cars. I saw Johnson approach.

"Get out," she said. "I'll be back late. I'll call you. If the girls are there, you come over, and start paying your debt."

I waved Johnson off, and he returned to his post. I scrambled out of the car, barely. I was way too big for this car. I'd had one that the IRS had taken away from me. Maybe at sixteen, I was more agile then than now.

"I'm going to fuck you like a machine," I promised. Her face flushed, and she showed me her beautiful teeth before squealing out of the parking lot and back into traffic.

Jo drove us to the Pantry. Niley sat in the passenger seat and Pixie sat in the back with me. I told them what had happened.

"So Melina was not as good as we figured," said Pixie.

"Wrong," I said. "I stopped her from pushing it. Do you want to go find three hundred plus clients, and have them sign new retainers, ask them to substitute out Jake's firm then explain why the new attorney is better than what Jake left behind?"

"No way," Jo said.

Niley said nothing.

We all ordered breakfast for dinner. Maybe it was knowing that Jake was still in the morgue kept all of us from ordering meat. I still felt queasy knowing that my friend was in the morgue refrigerator.

Pixie, as usual, went overboard on syrup on her pancakes. Jo and Niley had salad. I had a Spanish omelet.

I forked extra salsa over my omelet, and said, "I don't know what we're going to do with new business, but here's what I want the exchange to do, starting tonight. If a caller is a new case, they take a message, no beeps. If a caller is wanting information on their case, it goes to Jeff. Jo, let Jeff know he's getting those calls from now on.

"Got it," Jo said, dipping a cherry tomato into her dressing that was served on the side.

"We're not doing any more client maintenance. Jeff has assured me that he's going to take care of our clients."

"He'll never be able to keep up," Jo said.

"He will," I argued, "He will, or I'll kick his fucking ass, even if he is a good guy."

"He's cute," Pixie said. I think she likes Jeff a little, even though she's only met him a couple of times in passing.

I cleared my throat. "If a caller wants to know if I'm okay after reading about the break-in, the exchange simply reads something you'll write Jo. I'm fine. I'm taking a few days off. If they are wondering about Jake's tragedy, the call goes to Jeff."

Pixie cut a huge wedge of her pancakes, and held it up, dripping syrup. She frowned and stopped eating in mid-bite. "That sounds like we're out of a job," Pixie said. "Now that I'm living in that great apartment you put me in, I can earn some good money hooking high-end stuff." She grinned.

I figured she was kidding.

"Not a chance," I said. "You're getting boysenberry syrup on my napkin." I reached over and shoved the fork into her mouth.

"Taste it," Pixie said. "It's fucking delicious."

I touched my finger to the drop of syrup, and agreed.

"I'm the last one to come in," Niley said quietly. Her salad was untouched. "I'm cool if there's nothing for me to do." She managed a quivery smile, and got a solid one back from me.

"No way," I said. "And eat your salad."

She looked down, took a half-hearted bite, and gave me another big smile. The smile was still a little on the wobbly side. Her sister, Tanis, had never been quiet. Tanis had been much like Pixie, loud and unrepentant of her speech.

"In two weeks, I close escrow on the Monterey Park apartment deal I made last month. You know the buildings in Monterey Park, Montebello and Alhambra. Right now I pay a management company to collect rents, and to rent out the apartments that are vacant. That's a big slice out of the rents. If something happens, and I throw this fucking business out of my life, do you object to managing the buildings I have? Jo will have to do the math, but I'm pretty sure that there's going to be enough left for you to make the same as I pay you now, and you'll probably have much better work hours."

Jo, Pixie, and Niley exchanged looks.

"Are you serious?" Jo asked.

"I'm serious," I replied. "I'm not sure that's what I'm going to do, or if it is a permanent solution, but it's an answer to any dilemma you may be having about losing your job. Not sure how I'll work the extras like you get for signing cases, but I'll give you a raise or percentage on new rentals or something. I can afford it."

"Gosh," Pixie said, sitting back. Her plate was empty. "Things can change in a flick of time, just like that." She snapped her fingers.

"So true," Niley said. She took a couple bites of her salad. I thought she looked a little less worried.

"Are you guys in till the end?" I asked.

"Of course," they all said. Well, I think one of them said yes, and another said why not, but they were all in.

"I'm going to see Melina tonight," I told them.

Pixie made a wolf whistle, stood up, did a little shimmy and gave me a thumbs-up. Three guys at the Pantry called out their phone number to her as we headed out. She laughed and said she was going home to her kid.

"I need to go home and spend some time with my kids," Jo said.

"Me too," Niley said.

I drove into the parking lot. Johnson took my keys. The girls headed off.

I wandered around my apartment fooling with the television, and putting on my earphones and listening to tunes. The truth is, hearing the phone not ringing and not getting any beeps was making me really anxious. I even lay down in the bed for thirty minutes but couldn't sleep. I got up and went into my office and started looking at the real estate figures, trying to figure how much would need to come in for the girls to get good wages, but the more I scribbled, the more I saw I'd really need Jo for that. I knew only that my account balances kept growing each month. Thank God I made these investments.

I was on the couch trying to get absorbed in music, and thinking about the non-ringing phone, wondering if I had a lapse in my business, how I would get my sources back if I abandoned them, wondering what lawyer I could go to who wanted cases, and could afford them. From now on, no fucking bonus promises. From now on, pay me up front. I want nothing at the end.

About one in the morning, Melina walked in. She slapped me playfully.

"Lock the fucking door, dummy."

"I left it unlocked for you," I lied. Then I got a good look at the see-through nightie she was wearing. "You came up the elevator wearing that?" I asked, knowing it must be true since she was standing right there. "You know the security cameras record everything. Just look at you."

She licked her lips. "Yeah, baby, look at me."

She took me by the hand.

"We're doing this in my apartment. The bedroom is ready and waiting. It's comfy. I lit candles and I'm burning some great incense."

I walked slightly behind her, looking at that fine ass that was clearly visible through the fine fabric of her gown. We walked down two floors. Once in her apartment, Melina's walk became a run to the bedroom where she dropped her gown and tore off my clothes with both hands.

She lay on her back, and spread her legs. "Okay machine, come do as you promised."

We didn't have sex that frequently, so it was hard for me to say that one time was better than another. But that night was fantastic. We went on for hours. For the second time since we met, we woke up in the morning together in the same bed. This time, we were in her bed. I finally did fall asleep for a while.

At ten in the morning, Melina brought our coffee to bed. She was wearing the nightie again. I took it off of her.

"Aren't you going to work?" I asked.

She sipped. "Fuck it. I pay good money to the managers. Let them earn their keep. I need a break."

We clicked coffee cups, lying there bare-ass.

"Fuck it. I need a break, too."

I'd be lying if I said that I didn't feel the pain of the loss of my future bonuses. I knew I was supposed to feel better about it with time, but with time, I was feeling worse.

I had hired a limousine for Pixie, Jo, Niley, Melina and myself. The limo had been Melina's idea, in case we had too much to drink at the after funeral bash to be held at the Downtown Hilton. The double funeral was on a Sunday, six days after the murder. The girls were solemn, but they all looked great in black. Melina was the queen in some designer label I'd never heard of, but that made Jo and Niley speak in awed whispers. Aunt Carmen had stayed home with Lainey. I could have hired someone, but she needed an excuse not to go. She was more upset over Jake than she let on, and part of that might have been concern over my future. The cemetery was elevated, and green. It looked over Glendale, views that were beautiful, but all I could think of was how neither Jake nor his wife could see them. I hoped they were aware of all of us coming together to bid them goodbye. The big crowd attending included many people I did not know. I expect there were a lot of lawyers. At the conclusion of the service, they released a hundred white homing pigeons. They flew up with a rush of pale wings that faded into a sea of clouds. Back when we'd been partners, Melina had twisted my arm to make me attend Hamlet, and I remembered one line now. "And flights of angels sing thee to thy rest," would be better spoken "fly thee to thy rest." Orchids were passed out, two for each of us, instead of the roses they'd had at Harry's funeral. Many more were here than had attended Harry's funeral, and that was big. Two orchids, one for each coffin. We approached the two coffins, side by side, and placed the orchids on top. The final goodbye to my friend Jake. I cried.

It was a relief that finally Jake was laid to rest. The limo carried us away but did not leave my feelings behind. I was devastated to have just buried my friend. The limo had a bar inside, and it was loaded. Trust Melina to find the wine. She poured a glass for each of us. I looked at the girls, my girls, sipping wine as we were driven to the Hilton. Jake's life was over, but mine was not. I took a deep breath and felt the air expand in my lungs. I sipped the wine. I saw the sun shining through the clouds. God forgive me, Harry forgive me, Jake forgive me, but I was glad to be alive, and I wanted them all.

We barely drank at the after-funeral event. A white-coated waiter filled our glasses, and moved on to the table next to us in one of the Hilton's event rooms. Nilcy, Pixie, Jo and I drank. Melina whispered that the wine was terrible, and said not to drink it. Obediently, we all pushed our glasses away. I had a chance to say hello to Jake's son and daughter. I'd met them both at random times, when they'd come around for the holidays, or Jake and his wife held their seasonal parties. They'd thrown quite a few social events. Their house had been designed for entertaining.

We were all relieved when the limousine took us to La Fonda, an upscale restaurant near MacArthur Park on Wilshire. The place used to be a theater, and the tables and booths are still set out that way. *Mariachi Los Camperos* were part owners and played there on a big stage. They're easily the best Mariachi in Los Angeles. After all day mourning Jake, the music was a welcome relief. Mariachi fills you with joy. Some of the ballads are killer, the crying kind, especially for all of us, fresh from a funeral.

They brought us pitchers of margaritas, tall glass pitchers sweating beads of condensation filled with happy juice. Melina made no complaint. We ate a bite here and there, interspersed between dozens of toasts to Jake. The plates were many and full. Hearty plates of chili rellenos, carne asada, flautas, ropa vieja, beans, and rice. As delicious as it was, we picked at the food. It was just not a day for eating, except for Pixie. I don't know where she puts it.

Niley who is always quiet was not quiet that night.

"I love all of you," she said, full of margarita, and holding up her refilled glass, sloshing a little over the side.

The rest of the girls joined in, raising their glasses, equally as enthusiastically.

"Amen," I said, clicking the glasses of the girls in the center of our large booth.

The music was bright and loud, and relentlessly cheerful, even when the words to the ballads were tear-jerking. The violins sang, the singers sang, we joined arms, and even we sang. Thanks to the musicians, my companions, or the margaritas, I mercifully lost track of time.

Thirty minutes before last call, we were served two pots of coffee and a selection of Mexican sweet bakery goods. I love churros, but after all the tequila, I passed. All of us drank coffee. It was closing time, probably a little after closing time before they herded us out.

The limousine delivered us to our apartment building. We were all still singing and humming one of the songs that stuck to us, *Cielito Lindo*.

Even in my tipsy condition (or maybe because of it) I couldn't believe how well Melina sang.

"Heya, Johnson," I said, as we swept in. Johnson opened the door for us, and I saw him hide a smile. Well. He tried to hide it but I saw, obviously, so he failed.

"Hello, Bossman," he said. "Celebrating?"

Pixie caught his arm, and whispered loudly, "Funeral."

Melina knew the lyrics, and kept singing as we walked through the lobby. My feet headed for the stairs, but the girls herded me into the elevator, singing along, humming through the stanzas and joining in during the refrain.

We ended up in my apartment. Melina was pretty well lit, and went straight into the bedroom, and flicked one of the new pottery table lamps on. She angled her head, looking up at the ceiling with a disappointed expression.

"What?" Jo, Pixie and Niley followed her in and stared at the ceiling.

"Nothing there," I observed.

"You gotta get that mirror over the bed," Melina said, flopping down on the mattress, and still looking straight up. The girls chorused in about the mirror. It was the first they'd heard of it, and they were apparently all in favor.

My clothes were all over the place. Everyone's clothes were all over the place. The last thing I took off was one sock. I wasn't sure where the other sock was. I looked on the end table, in the jacket pocket of my Brooks Brothers suit on the new-to-me vintage valet, and under the bed, then found it on my other foot.

"Are we drunk?" I asked.

"No way," Melina said.

"No way," said the others. I think Niley and Jo were already asleep, so the "others" was Pixie.

"I agree," I said.

I heard Niley groaning. I saw it was well after five a.m. and gave my spinning head a break, and ducked back under a pillow. It was close to noon when we started talking, all of us lying still to keep from jostling our oscillating skulls.

"Did we do it?" Pixie asked. "I don't remember."

"I don't remember leaving the restaurant," Niley said, "but we must have, because we're here. We're here, right? Not under the table." She hadn't opened her eyes yet, and one slim arm was bent to shade her eyes.

Jo didn't say anything. She just groaned, and ran to the shower. I think I heard her throwing up.

"I thought Melina was here," I said. I looked around, and didn't see her. None of us remembered much, so there was no telling what, if anything, happened. Typical Melina, to leave before morning. I couldn't remember if she'd been there when I'd said hello to five a.m. and ducked back into oblivion. Just thinking of her gave me a warm feeling. Not arousal, just a warm close feeling. I really loved that girl. But didn't I love them all?

Jo came out of the shower in a towel and gathered up everyone's clothes. I heard the washer start up. "I'm using cold," she yelled, "so there's still hot water left."

I shut my eyes for a minute until the shower was free.

"Is the room spinning, or is it just me?" I yelled. The water was hot, and wonderful, but the hangover was horrible.

"I don't want to see another margarita for as long as I live," Jo said.

Niley swallowed a cup of coffee, black, in one gulp. She seldom drank liquor. "Never again," she said.

"Oh come on, guys, a little hangover is no big deal," Pixie said.

"Fuck you," Jo said, holding a wet wash cloth on her face.

"Good idea," Pixie replied to Jo. "Fuck me. Come on, show me your dick, baby."

"Stop it, it hurts to laugh," Jo said, laughing.

"Kids, behave," I said.

"I'm so horny. I'm so sick," Niley moaned. "I need a man or something."

"You don't need something," Pixie said, lying still and making no move to back-up her mouth. "I'm here."

That's the kind of day we had. All talk. No action. We were all too hung over. I took three showers. No idea how many the girls took, but my hot water heater had a workout. They spent the day in wrapped towels. Good thing I had two and a half bathrooms and a shitload of towels.

Jo started organizing my clothes. The next thing I knew, the girls were into my things. They made as much mess as they straightened, and were pretty entertaining, as they tried on everything I owned. They found my two extra new suits wrapped in plastic. The third one was on the new valet. They got me to talk about when I bought them. I had gotten the sales guy at the store to spend twenty minutes with me until I learned to tie a new knot. In exchange, I bought three suits, 3 dress shirts and five ties. He was on commission so he was happy. The girls were happy that I spent twenty minutes showing them how to tie ties. They took rude, entertaining and very creative liberties with a huge pile of seriously ugly old ties I'd had for years. I'd been meaning to hand over the ties to Goodwill anyway.

Sometime in the early evening, the girls left. They'd been away from their kids way too long. I felt guilty, in a way. I wondered if any of the kids resented Uncle Mario for hogging their mothers. There I was, alone again. I went down the stairs to the weight room for an hour, ran the stairs for a half hour, and did a solo karate workout for at least another hour. When I came out of the shower after all that, I felt like I'd burned the hangover off.

On Monday, I had my early morning breakfast at the Pantry, and read my classified ads. The girls arrived in separate cars. I was dressed and ready, but not sure what for.

On her way in, Jo stopped off at the exchange. She handed me the long list of messages she had picked up. I scanned the names and messages. Oscar Cooke had called three times. His message said to call him back. Jack Fino, the criminal lawyer I had retained to handle Pixie's arrest for solicitation at the hospital, had left a message that he had heard what happened to me, and wanted to be sure I was okay.

There were a lot of referrals that were on the list that would turn into retainers if we followed them up. But I didn't know which lawyer I was turning to. Those calls were on hold until that was established.

"Fino was a nice guy," I said.

"And he was good. Got me off that charge without me even having to go to court. I owe him," Pixie said.

"You don't owe him. I paid him," I reminded her for the second time.

"I still owe him."

"What's the plan?" Niley asked. "What are we doing today?"

"We're taking it easy," I replied.

Jo glared at me. "Let's organize," she said, and dragged Pixie and Niley into my office. I'd had a whole wall of new legal type bookcases installed, with matching file cabinets. The shelves were empty. Their contents were still inside the dozens of boxes that cluttered the room. The movers had done the packing. I turned to Jo. She was busy unpacking books, muttering invectives against the movers under her breath.

"Call my aunt and get the management company contact information. Get a list of tenants in each building. They send my aunt a report every month but I never bother looking at it. Get us a current copy. And when you guys are done with whatever it is you're doing, you can go home. Take some family time."

"You got it, boss."

I dialed Oscar Cooke, and paced.

"We need to talk," Oscar said. "Just come over. I'll be here all day."

My mind was split where he was concerned. As Jake would have said, the jury was still out. That Oscar wanted me working with him made me feel good. But not if the motherfucker had been the one who ordered everything that's been happening. Who had ordered the attacker with the bat? Who had gone after Jake and his wife? And why? I certainly wasn't worth that much. If it were Oscar, would he do this just so that he'd be the beneficiary of what Jake was getting from me? I hated how the situation was making me so fucking suspicious. I must be giving myself too much credit. The services I rendered were certainly not worth killing a human being. But then, to a killer, what was the value of a human life? A killer didn't even need a reason.

This time Oscar Cooke and I met in his office. There was no lunch. I sat across from him at his desk in his fancy high-dollar marble office. In my karate years with Cosmo, I had learned to assess my opponent. How to get in his head in order to predict his next move. Usually the eyes telegraph where the next move would be. Karate was fast. Take the opponent down, fast. Cosmo had told me, time and time again, "Pull back. Study your opponent. Look him in the eyes. Dig your way into his head. Concentrate." I was applying all this to Oscar.

"You must be exhausted with all that's happened," Oscar said. He met my eyes, directly. Of course, as a lawyer, he would know how to look convincing.

"I am exhausted. I plan to take it easy for a while."

"Are you kidding me?"

I would never normally discuss my business with a stranger, but Oscar had a way of drawing me in. I didn't want to tell him too much, in the event he was the one in my life who was a stick of lit dynamite. I told him my decision to leave the cases at Jake's firm.

"You fool. I could have taken those cases." I could see he was perturbed.

I shook my head. "I'm not sending my team on a wild-goose chase to hunt down hundreds of people from here to El Paso with pending cases to get them to sign substitution of attorney forms and new retainers. I'm comfortable that the Spanish-speaking lawyer there will look after the people."

"Just like that?"

"Just like that."

I didn't tell him about the bonuses I wouldn't be getting.

"Are you telling me you didn't have a tail end deal on your cases?" Oscar leaned back in his chair and toyed with his pen. He eyes flickered down, then back to me as flipped it between his thumb and forefinger. He had thick hands and hairy knuckles. The slim gold pen looked like a toy in his blunt fingers.

"Even if I had an agreement, I'm not a lawyer, Oscar. It would be unenforceable, and skirt the letter of the law. I can't get in to my deal with Jake. I've already told you more than I would tell anyone I really don't know. Let's just talk about the present."

"I understand," he said, pausing and watching his own fingers on the pen. "What are you going to do with new business?"

I looked right at him. I waited till he looked up, and met my eyes.

"I'm not sure."

Oscar looked confused. He reached for his cigar box. He opened it and held it out.

"Cubans." He offered me a cigar that I refused. I watched him clip the end of the cigar, and then light it. His ashtray was made of cut glass, and sparkled in the light coming in from his window. It was probably lead crystal.

"I need to ask you something. And frankly, I don't care if you're offended or not."

The cigar was in his mouth now. "Frankness is good. Ask me anything."

"Did you have anything to do with the attacker that came at me in my apartment? Did you have anything to do with the killing of Jake and his wife?"

Oscar coughed and spat out the cigar. He reached to his lap gingerly, brushed ash of his pants, and picked up the cigar. "What the fuck are you talking about, kid?" He shoved the cigar back in his mouth, and looked shocked.

"Sorry, Oscar. I say what I think. I speak from the heart. I don't know how far you'd go to grow your PI Department."

Oscar's expression changed from surprise to a laugh. I watched his eyes, his expression. "I would never go that far."

"I needed to ask. Not that you would admit it if you had, but I needed to see your response."

He puffed.

"Did I pass?" He chuckled.

"I wouldn't tell you if you had or if you hadn't," I replied. I got up.

"Where you going? You just got here."

"I have to do a few things. Maybe we can talk business in the future."

Oscar got up and walked around the desk. "I look forward to hearing from you. We will work out something. Together we could build a huge PI mill. Bigger than Jake had."

No question that I had a product that must be very attractive. Oscar seemed anxious to tie me down. I was not anxious to be tied down, yet. I still didn't fancy working on the same team as Carson.

"I'll see my way out," I told him. "I want to chat with Betty a bit."

I winked.

Oscar winked back.

"I told you, she broke up with her boyfriend."

"Cool," I said. I opened the heavy door and walked toward the reception area. Betty was seated at the reception desk working on something. She brightened when she saw me.

"Bye, Betty," I said. "See you again, soon."

"Have a good afternoon, Mr. Luna." She smiled.

I didn't stop. I went straight to the elevator.

"I thought you guys were going home," I said to Pixie and Niley. They were there when I walked in. They told me that Jo had gone to pick up the paperwork from the management company located in Santa Monica. I had not been hands-on much with my real estate deals, but wondered now why my broker had recommended management across town from my apartments.

"We wanted to be here when you got back," Niley said.

"Just in case you need us for something," Pixie said. "Got to do something for the money you pay us."

"Are you sure you don't need something?" asked Niley.

I walked to the refrigerator and took out a Coke.

"I could use a massage. No sex, just a massage."

"You got it." Pixie took me by the hand and pulled me to the bedroom. Niley walked behind me, pushing with both hands against my butt as if I need help moving forward. We laughed.

I was on the bed naked and almost as relaxed as a man could be. Pixie had spent five minutes making good use of the massage oils Jo had bought recently. With perfect timing, the security phone rang.

"You have two detectives here to see you," said the security guard in the lobby.

"Have them come up."

I jumped out of bed, and rubbed massage oil off of me, then quickly put on a pair of jeans and a t-shirt. I smelled like a fucking flower, but there was no time to wash.

"What's going on?" Pixie asked, "I'm not done."

"Two detectives are on the way up here."

"What the fuck for?" Pixie asked.

"Ask me after I talk to them," I said, stating the obvious, "Put some clothes on, just in case." I looked over the girls. A shame to cover all that up with clothes.

"Just in case what?" asked Niley.

"They're not the fashion police. They're detectives. Put some clothes on," I said.

Pixie popped Niley with a towel. "Dress, dummy," Pixie said. Minus the towel, it was a credible impression of Jo.

Niley squealed when the towel made contact.

I went to the door and opened it. I had my fingers crossed that the girls wouldn't do anything too outrageous. I'm not being paternalistic or sexist here; normally I encourage them to be as outrageous as they want, but not in front of cops.

At first, one of the detectives was unfamiliar to me; he was thin, bronzed, and had salt and pepper hair. He had the start of a beard, like he had been working a long day, and a dry, sinewy look that some men get in their sixties or so. He had a slightly bowed posture. I recognized the other LAPD Detective. Mike Sanchez had handled and closed the case of the shooting of Tanis and myself in East Los Angeles. In hindsight, I realized how hard Sanchez had worked to clear me.

We shook hands. I asked them in to the living room.

"Moved out of Monterey Park," Sanchez said. "Nice pad." I think I remembered that he had a young wife and baby at home, but I didn't remember their names—if I ever knew them. Sanchez sniffed the air and looked around, then cast me a look that had a laugh in it. A married man laughing at a bachelor pad.

Pixie came in and gave them both Cokes that had ice chips dripping down the sides of the glass bottles. Both men forgot about me while she was in the room. I'd wiped off the oil. It looked like she'd put more on before she put on a tiny t-shirt that stuck to her skin. She was wearing short shorts. "It's hot out there," she said, smiling as if it wasn't almost mid-October. She walked into the office, then walked back through the room.

"I forgot to get Niley a Coke," she told me, and waved at the detectives both going into the kitchen and leaving. Both times they waved back. Seriously, if we could bottle Pixie, we would have some kind of weapon to use on the male half of the species.

"What's up?" I asked.

Both of them cleared their throats, and looked at the Cokes they were holding as if they didn't know how they'd gotten there.

"We're investigating the murders." Sanchez recovered first.

"You mean Jake and his wife?"

Both men nodded.

Grizzaldi said, "One day you kill someone by throwing him out a window. Oh wait, but before that you kill another guy by kicking him from the second floor of a motel."

Sanchez had cleared me of the motel thing. Of course, I'd been the victim.

Sanchez cleared his throat, and spoke over his partner, "I am not forgetting that you were the victim of a hit and run. That case is still under investigation. The Impala nearly ran you down. It probably would have killed anybody else, but you got off without a scratch."

"There was no scratch," I said, "but a hell of a bruise. My gal Jo made me go to the emergency room the next day to make sure nothing was broken."

"Get those pictures to me for evidence," Sanchez said. "It could be tied to this attempt also. You're lucky the incident was witnessed by a cop."

The older detective wasn't happy that Sanchez disagreed with him. I remembered him now. He had been in the parking lot when they scraped up the robber. He had been cocky and abrasive that night, and was just as cocky and stupid now. "And now these two murders."

"What's my connection to the two murders supposed to be?"

"You worked for the attorney. You tell us."

"He was a good friend," I said. "The best. I want to know who killed him, too. Stop this nonsense."

"Nonsense? I don't think so," said the older detective.

"Maybe you want to come down to headquarters and we can do the interview there."

"Fine with me," I said. "First I'm going to call my attorney."

I didn't know where Melina would be at the moment. On an impulse, I dialed Oscar Cooke. Betty answered. In two minutes, I was talking to Oscar Cooke.

"I have two detectives here asking me questions about Jake and his wife. They're insinuating a bunch of shit."

"Put one of them on the phone."

Sanchez looked at me and rolled his eyes.

I handed the phone to the cocky older one. He was quiet for a minute, listening to whatever Oscar was saying. I could hear his voice, but not make out the words. He went on for a minute or two.

"Hey, Oscar. This is Grizzaldi. I didn't know you represented this guy."

I had no clue what Oscar was telling him, but the longer it took, the more curious I got. It was another full minute before Grizzaldi spoke.

"Oscar, no problem. We can do the interview on another day. I'll call you and set it up. There or here or your office. You tell me."

Whatever Oscar was telling this asshole, the asshole was chuckling. "Sure Oscar, no problem."

He hung up.

Grizzaldi said, "We'll talk again when Oscar can be present."

Mike said, "Mario, we aren't focused on you, but we are interviewing everyone that had any contact with this couple. I also have the case open on the attacker that you threw out the window."

"He fell out the window. I tried to catch him," I said. "Not that I could prove it."

Grizzaldi said, "I'm sure we'll get it cleared up when we get together with Oscar." They left. The girls came out of the office, both of them looking angry.

"I just wanted to punch that Grizzaldi in the nose," Pixie said, "for talking like that to you. The other one was kind of cute."

I called Oscar to say thanks.

"I called you on an impulse. Sorry I didn't warn you. I didn't know they were showing up, but I did know you're a criminal lawyer."

"No problem," Oscar said. "This is routine. Don't worry about it."

"Oscar, I'll pay you like any other client. This is not a freebee. I don't expect that."

"Don't worry. Go check out what you said you needed to check so we can shake hands on the other."

"To be clear, cases have nothing to do with this criminal thing," I said.

"I got it, Mario. Don't worry."

I hung up. I should have felt better, but I was feeling more paranoid than ever.

Jo came back with the management company's records of tenants. She walked in in the middle of Pixie and Niley giving me a massage.

"You just missed the cops," Niley said.

"What happened?"

"You'll have to ask Pixie. I only eavesdropped from the office. Pixie walked through."

Pixie told her all about it.

"Is it going to be okay?" asked Jo.

"Of course," I said. I figured it had to be okay. After all, I didn't have anything to do with Jake and his wife's murder. The attacker who fell out of the window had broken in to my house, and he'd been packing not only a bat, but also a gun.

"So what did you bring me?" I asked Jo.

"I got everything from the management company. The paperwork includes all the details of the tenancy of each," Jo said. "Are you really going to fire them and let us do the management? Are we really giving up the business that put all of us here?"

I was lying on my back. Four hand massage is a great way to defer cop shock. I looked at Jo, and tried to stay too relaxed to think.

"I don't know what I'm going to do. I'm still numb from losing my bonus."

Since Jo had done the computation, she knew what bonus I was talking about.

"Poor baby," Pixie said, working my chest with oil.

Niley said, "Relax already." She had none of the massage experience Pixie did, and did something to my right foot that tickled something crazy. I pulled back.

"Niley be nice. Don't tickle me."

Jo was hovering over the three of us.

"You got the records. When you have a chance, look them over. I'll call my CPA to see how much cash I have left every month. I know it's heavy."

Jo frowned. I knew it was useless to tell her not to double-check all the figures. That's just the way she was.

"Between you and my CPA, we'll figure out what everyone's wages will be."

"Okay," Jo said. "I'll check what I got and if we take it on I'll be familiar with each apartment and how many tenants are there and what vacancies exist."

"Cool," I said, shutting my eyes to concentrate on the massage. I soon felt another set of hands on me. Jo. My first thought was how I am so fucking lucky. Of course, the shadow of my lost million popped into my head again, like that last guest who won't leave the party. Not always lucky.

I sent the girls home.

Before Pixie left, she beeped Carson for me.

"Wait for his call back," I told her. "Ask him to come over to see me."

Pixie's jaw dropped about a mile.

"You're going to see that asshole? For reals?"

"Can't avoid it," I told her. "There are things we need to straighten out."

I went into my office and got on the phone with my accountant. I was sitting on the desk in my boxers with my feet in the chair, and looking over the chaos that was my office. We talked over the new developments going on in terms of apartment management. I didn't talk to him very often but sent him a lot of work, so he had a full head of steam built up about various projects we were working on. We did not get through all of his questions. While I was on the other line, I heard Pixie take Carson's call. She waited till I hung up. Felix is a really nice guy, and I like him, but we do not speak the same language. I admit, I cut the accountant's phone call short. I said goodbye, and promised to call him back. Eventually.

As soon as I put the phone down, Pixie said, "Carson called back. He told me he'd come, but he said that you better not lay a fucking hand on him. I promised him that you're not going to hurt him. I promised you're not going to hurt him, so tell me the truth. Are you going to beat the shit out of him?"

"I'll try not to," I said. "Thanks baby. You can go home now."

"He's shifty all the time, but he's only mean when he's drunk off his ass. You know he's more likely to stay on his good behavior if I'm around. Are you sure you don't want me here when he comes over?"

"I'm sure."

She went around my desk and hugged me from behind. I thought of Melina when she did that. But it was Pixie who entreated in my ear.

"Baby, let me stay. I don't want to worry about you being with him. I don't trust him."

I laughed. It was funny because what can Pixie do to protect me? She's half my size. I slid from the desk to my chair, and wheeled around to face her.

She straddled me.

We were face-to-face now, but for good measure, I put my palms on either side of her face. She did the same. We looked like a couple of hippies doing some kind of yoga thing, or maybe like a couple of Vulcans off of *Star Trek* doing the Vulcan mind meld. Not that we ever saw any of Spock's girlfriends grind on his lap like Pixie tended to do on mine, but you know how they always cut out the racy stuff for TV.

"I can take care of myself, I promise."

"I know, but—"

"No buts. Go home, I'll be in touch."

On the phone, I caught up with Melina.

"You could have called me instead of Cooke. You should have."

"Maybe, but the cop knocked me off my game," I said. "He was getting nasty talking about going downtown to do the interview." I pictured myself going down there innocently for an interview, and getting arrested instead. I pictured the US Marshall putting me in handcuffs, putting me in a square barred cell while I waited to be printed and photographed. Fuck that. "He was talking interview, I was thinking I was getting lured down to the precinct to get arrested. So I called the criminal lawyer."

"Cooke seems to have juice with this Grizzaldi guy. If you got me, I would have told the fucker to get the fuck out of your apartment unless he had a warrant."

"Good thing that I didn't call you."

We both laughed.

"You won't believe this," I said.

"Tell me, fucker."

"Carson's coming over at seven tonight."

"No shit. What the fuck for?" Her voice got louder. "Are you going to beat him up again?"

"I went through this same conversation with Pixie earlier," I said. "I need to ask him some questions. That's all. No bloodshed on the agenda."

"So now you probably think he murdered Jake and his wife."

"Who's jumping to conclusions now?" I said.

"I am. He's a good kid," Melina said.

"We're the same age," I said. I don't know if I was jealous. I just didn't like her being as familiar with Carson as she was with me.

"Yeah, and you're both kids."

"Yeah, and you fucked us both."

The phone sat silently while we both held our tongues. No point in re-hashing old arguments.

"Why is he coming over?"

I believed she didn't really care why I'd invited him. She just wanted an assurance that there wasn't going to be any fighting. I know Carson as well as I know my own hand. I knew he didn't kill Jake and his wife, just like I knew he had nothing to do with my shooting and Tanis's death. I didn't need to explain my feeling that he knew something he wasn't saying. Months before I'd met Melina, I'd had a feeling of being followed. Maybe I'd been right then. Maybe I needed to pay more attention to my gut feelings. But I couldn't explain all that.

"He's coming over because we need to talk. I'll let you know more when I see you in person."

"I'm going to be real busy for the next couple of days. I'm working my ass off on the new market I'm opening, but I'm here for you."

"I love you, friend."

"I love you too, friend." She didn't hang up. She kept talking. "Please don't get in trouble. Don't beat up on Carson."

"How many times do I have to say it?"

Security called me when Carson arrived. I could tell Johnson was shocked. After security called, Johnson called too.

"It's the guy who saw Miss Melina," he said. He sounded a little nervous. He'd seen Carson's condition when he'd left the last time. "Are you sure it'll be okay?"

"Jeeze," I said, "Johnson, I promise I won't throw him out the window."

I was still hanging up with Johnson when I opened the door for Carson, who was right on time. He wore a suit and tie.

I was glad I'd put on jeans and a t-shirt. Just boxers would have been out of the question.

"You always dress up like this?" I asked.

We shook hands with no monkey business or wiseass remarks, almost like we were adults.

"Cooke insists I sign cases in a suit and tie," he said. "I was working when I talked to Pixie, so don't think I got dolled up for your hairy ass."

"The suit is nice. The tie's okay too."

I was sure he didn't shop at Brooks Brothers but I had to give him credit for graduating to a better tailor. He followed me to the living room. It was a little weird bringing him to my own turf after our last few encounters. Hell, it was weird bringing him over at all.

"Nice place," he said. "So you moved after the incident. I'd have stayed there to be on the same floor with the hot chick."

"The bedroom was trashed," I said. "What can I get you to drink?"

"You still drink beer like us home boys?" he asked.

"I got beer if that's what you want." I headed into the kitchen and opened the refrigerator. He followed me. I pulled out a beer, handed it to him, and shut the refrigerator door.

"What about you? No beer?" The chair was facing the wrong way, but he straddled it, facing me across the table.

"I had enough to drink after Jake's funeral to do me for the rest of the year. I can't handle the hangovers."

I watched him take a big gulp. I put a kettle on, and grabbed a tea bag and dropped it in a mug. Melina would have turned her nose up at tea in a bag. It was one of Jo's herbal concoctions, with lemon and ginger and a little cayenne. With enough sugar, it would be tolerable. It wouldn't kill me, and it would give me something to do other than twiddle my thumbs and watch Carson drink. He watched me make tea.

"Hey, I remember when we were kids. We'd pass the hat, and get some grownup to buy beer for all of us. You drank it then," he laughed.

"I did," I remembered. "Aunt Carmen almost killed me with guilt."

Carson gave me a sober look. "Aunt Carmen, she's got some serious mojo. I'd never have the balls to get on her bad side."

The tea kettle whistled. I turned off the burner and poured boiling water on the tea bag. I added a shake of ginger, and a squeeze of lemon, the way Jo always did. I added a shake of cayenne pepper, and put the cup on the table between us.

"Carson—"

"That's the name, don't wear it out," he said, sounding just as he had as a kid.

"Look, man, I owe you an apology."

"What for?" Carson looked surprised.

"For the shit I've been giving you about the bad shit that's happened to me," I said.

"I'm sorry," I heard myself say.

I looked him in the eyes. "After the drugs were planted in my car, and all the shit that happened to me, I never fingered you, but you were the logical choice. I figured you were pissed off I punched you out."

"I was pissed off," Carson said, "but man, not enough to rat on you like that. We were bros, man. Vago put the shit in your car behind my back, when you quashed our gig. He didn't give a shit you beat me up. He was pissed off when I told him Harry wouldn't take cases from me any more. All of those crashes he was in, he fixed them up. He piled his gangies in the back seat, and he made the bucks. It passed right by me into his pocket. He went ballistic when I said it would take me a while to meet up with a lawyer who played his kind of ball."

"I held you responsible because you brought Vago in. I was hurt, man. I turned you on to Harry, and taught you the ropes. And you made it dirty. You turned it into fraud."

"I didn't know it was wrong," Carson said. "I'm not bullshitting you. I knew zippo about consequences. Okay, I knew it was a little wrong but not how wrong. I got mixed up with Vago in the first place because I was trying to respect you."

"How do you figure that?"

"I was trying to stay off your turf," Carson said. "Even back then you covered a lot of ground. I felt like you had all of LA, not just East LA. The only place that wasn't your turf belonged to Vago. So that's how it happened. It's not like he'd ignore anybody working his streets. And then he wanted in. What could I do? Not shit. But Vago, he put that shit in your car behind my back."

"Old news," I said, "but good to know." I'd never had it out with Vago. I'd all but pushed Carson into Vago's posse. Carson was right. When I got called, there never was an accident I knew of where I'd think that was not my territory. The whole fucking city is mine. I felt a little guilty. I should have worked out a turf for Carson when we were kids. Drawn a line across the city, or some shit. Maybe none of this would have happened.

"Is that what you called me over here for?"

I shook my head. "No, the past is the past."

"Easy for you to say. You're not the one that got beat up," he said with a laugh. "This karate shit has gone to your head, but it was beautiful the way you took Fink down." He grinned. He started laughing.

Whatever I had doled out to Fink, Carson felt it was well-deserved. Of course I'd only known Fink for five minutes, and even on that short acquaintance, I could see he was a bully and a jerk.

"Tell me why you liked me taking down someone that is working with you."

"Sure," Carson said, "If I can have another beer."

I got up, and reached in the fridge. I handed him a beer and a chilled glass.

Carson laughed at the chilled glass. I stuck it back in the refrigerator and sat down again at my dinette.

Carson opened the beer and took a gulp. "Mario, why did you ask me here?"

"I want to know who is after me. I need to know. Last year you made it clear that you knew who it was. Who it is. Tell me what you know. It will not leave this room."

"*Esé*, I really don't know anything," he said, looking away, and then looking back at me, "Even if I did, but I don't, how would I know I can trust you?"

"I keep my word."

I was quiet. I watched as Carson enjoyed his beer. I put a spoon of sugar in my tea, stirred, and took a sip. It wasn't bad. It was pretty good, in fact, but tasted similar to what Aunt Carmen used to brew up for me when I had a cold.

Carson said, "Too many times I went after a case, and you had already signed it up. Eventually, Cooke got curious. I told him I knew you. And Fink is a shithead. He's as stupid as he is big. He got the idea I was sending the business somewhere else. I hate Cooke. I don't trust him. Of course I don't trust him," he laughed. "Remember Harry? Harry was so fucking good. Can you imagine anybody as good as Harry keeping a guy like Fink on the payroll? But

Cooke keeps him on. He looks spotless, but what kind of a guy keeps goons? A guy who needs goons. That's who."

"And you told him what about me? What the fuck did you tell him?"

"Nothing special. That we went to school together. That we grew up on the same block. That my mom and your aunt are good friends." He thought for a minute. "I also told him there was friction between us." He played with the bottle, for a minute, idly. "At first, I didn't think anything of any of this. Then one day, Cooke said something that stuck in my head. He said to me, *'If this Mario Luna guy wasn't around anymore, would you get the business he gets?'* That's what Cooke asked me. I figured he'd send Fink or one of his other heavies and scare you away or something." He grinned at me. "I didn't tell him you don't scare. And I didn't tell him you're badass." He sobered slightly. "I figured you'd handle anything that came your way. I never figured there'd be a gun involved though."

"And what else?" I asked.

"Nothing. That's all there was to it. I don't trust him. I'm not in on his inner circle, and don't want to be. He looks all shiny and upper class, but he's a mean bastard. I tried for a raise on what I'm bringing in. He got pissed off. He got Fink to slap me around. And Fink enjoys his work."

My gut had been warning me about Cooke all along. I was primed and ready to hate him.

"You were never a fighter, Carson, but I can't remember you taking any shit from anyone like that," I said. "You'd fight back when you were cornered. What happened? I don't give a shit how big Fink is. Why do you let him torment you, if that's what he's doing? And it sounds like that's what he's doing."

"I went through so many lawyers before Pélon hooked me up with this asshole. I'm tired of starting over. At least with Cooke, I know what to expect." Carson hesitated again. "And I've seen Fink go after families. I don't mention to either of them that I've got sisters. But they know."

"Do his office people take care of the clients? Do they cave, or do they try to make the most of the case, do the best job they can?"

"He has a good lawyer working in that department. Settles almost every case, and for pretty good money. Clients seem pretty happy with their settlements. I brought over the last couple of years. I don't get as many cases as you, but it's steady."

"When the burglar broke in, you told me Cooke would be calling and offering me protection. Why did you say that? Does he want cases so much that he'd order a hit or hits to get them?"

Carson thought, but only for a few seconds. "Not murder. At least, I don't think so." He shook his head. "I really don't know how we came to this. I mean, we were like brothers once."

"I don't trust you from here to the parking lot," I told him.

"Thanks," Carson said, finishing off his beer. "Have a heart, man. Be nice."

"I'm going to be better than nice," I said. "I'm going to let you get all the business I'm getting now, and take it to Cooke."

"What the fuck are you talking about?"

I walked to the freezer and pulled out a bucket of chocolate ice cream, a napkin and a spoon. I plopped it down on the table. I tossed Carson another beer.

"*Esé,* you eat ice cream like that?"

"Yeah, I love ice cream. Want some?"

Carson made a face. "No way. Not with beer. Beer is fine."

He leaned forward, his eyes bright with interest. Something in his face reminded me of the teenaged Carson, the one who'd wanted so much to find a magic way out of the poverty of our childhood. He'd wanted it so much that he'd always had some get rich quick scheme in mind that never worked. "What do you mean by giving me business?"

I had not thought about it deeply. I just decided on the spot to be done with petty cases. I had the apartment buildings I'd managed to buy. I had cash in my sock drawer and money in the bank. The real estate could support my team and me. I was not ready to look for a lawyer to work with. I was tired.

Carson stayed there for all of two hours, long enough to consume a six-pack. We shook hands on the deal, though it depended on Cooke.

Cooke wanted me. Why go sell myself and my skills to a stranger? Cooke had done his due diligence. He'd had me investigated by a private eye. He knew I'd been in prison and he still wanted me. How I felt about Cooke overall did not matter. If Carson measured up, and Cooke measured up, the clients would be taken care of, and that was my priority.

I felt good, having made a decision. I was still yet to sell Cooke on my terms. My position would be stronger if he didn't know how eager I was to close the deal. And I could trust Carson. Maybe not trust him the way normal people are trusted. Carson was a hundred percent trustworthy when there was no stress. He only folded when he got to the edge of his rope. I knew Carson would be completely trustworthy in this one circumstance not because he'd suddenly sprouted a backbone, but because our bread was buttered on the same side. He wouldn't let it fall face down. Carson would not snitch me out because he'd be shooting himself in the foot if he did.

Pixie had been my friend for many years. She had such a silly streak. Sometimes she was such an entertainer, there was no way I could resist her. She had a knack for making me laugh and feel good, even when I was down. I'm fine with being alone, but then, maybe not. Maybe I prefer not being alone. I expected her to call wanting to know what had gone down with Carson. I would have let her know the Carson event had played out as promised, without bloodshed. I might have let it drop that I was now alone. She might have offered to come over. I might not have discouraged her. But she didn't call.

Jo could have called. If she had, I'd have asked her over. After ten years working under the same yoke, Jo's more than my pal. I love her for her stubborn, reliable, acerbic, organized, crisp, unadulterated Jo-ness. But she didn't call. Maybe I didn't know Niley as well as Jo and Pixie. When I see her, even though I still see my beloved Tanis in her, I loved her for being Niley. But she didn't call. Instead, I plugged my head into music that made me think.

I thought about Cooke. I hadn't gotten into his head like I had wanted to. I wasn't sure I believed him. If he agreed to the proposal, I would not be around him at all. If he did have something to do with Tanis getting killed, and me getting shot, the attacker that came in to my apartment with a bat and gun, or the killing of Jake and his wife, I would eventually know. If he was guilty, I would not hesitate for a second to find a way to extinguish him like a bug.

I met with Cooke for lunch at the tower where the office was located. He was already seated in the restaurant, drinking wine. He got up to greet me. We shook hands. I sat down and he poured wine into the empty goblet beside my plate.

"You're all dressed up," he said with a smile.

"It's my new look." I smiled. I thought about Carson.

I was wearing a three-piece suit from Brooks Brothers. I felt presentable. Not bulletproof, but good.

"Coming to work for me, Mario?"

"No," I said, "I'm not."

I saw a muscle twitch in the side of his face.

"I thought you were here to cut a deal."

"I am," I said, "but I'm not part of the deal."

"If you say so." Cooke's voice was reluctant but polite. "But what I wanted was you."

"You can't have me. But I can fix it. I have…" I searched for a word that would cover it all, "a network. I get probably forty new cases a week of which thirty turn out to be good cases with insurance, collectable type cases. Some weeks it's more. It's a bitch keeping up and I've been doing this since I was fourteen."

Cooke's eyes bugged out when he heard forty cases a week. I thought he was going to start drooling on the table.

"What do you propose?"

"I will fix it so these calls I get all go to Carson."

Cooke interrupted.

"I thought you hated him."

Maybe I did hate him, but I hate him like a brother. I've given up fighting that he's family, as far as I'm concerned, but that was nothing that Cooke needed to know.

I said, "Doesn't matter how I feel. You must trust him, or he wouldn't have been with you for two years."

"You are correct."

If he was going to strong-arm Carson from time to time in the future, that would be something I'd settle with Cooke when it happened. If we made a deal and Cooke broke it, I'd deal with it when it happened, too.

"I don't know if Carson can handle the business he'd be taking over from me. I don't know if he can continue taking care of his own business that he's sending to you. That's not my problem. I used to handle it all myself. I have a team of three now, and they work their ass off. I only work when I want, these days. But this is the deal, take it or leave it. I will see that Carson gets my calls and he signs the cases with your retainers. I trained Carson years ago. He's smooth. He's cunning. Unless he's changed, he's good with people."

"Maybe he is but his volume is low compared to yours," Cooke said.

"That can change overnight."

"And in return, you want...?"

"I want you to hire Spanish-speaking personnel to run your PI department, as many as necessary so the clients are well taken care of."

"Okay. That's easy," Cooke said.

"You have to give Carson a budget. If he stops paying sources that I have been paying for years, the calls will dry up. That's up to you. If Carson takes care of my sources, he will become the man. The clients read the papers and watch TV. I'll tell them I'm taking time off after everything that has happened. It's true. I need to get out of this business for a while."

"What else do you want?"

"I'm not kidding about that fair deal with Carson. He has to front money to the sources. He can't do it on what you pay now. "

"I agree and I can do that and will. I want the business."

"Do you know what the business is? The majority are so-so cases that settle for fifteen hundred dollars, five hundred to you as fees, five hundred for medical care and five hundred for the client. You also get some heavy cases. Bus crashes. Train crashes. You know the heavy cases are your gravy."

"What's in it for you?"

"I want a hundred thousand dollars[16] up front. By check, not cash. I want another hundred thousand payable to me at ten thousand per month for ten months. If you don't get at least eighty new cases a month, you don't need to pay me that ten thousand payment. It's a wash. And no lies. Carson doesn't lie to me. You don't lie to me. If you sign the cases, I want the money."

I was examining the way Cooke studied me. I saw no objection in his reactions.

"What about fifty up front and one fifty in payments of $10,000 a month under the same conditions?"

"No way. The deal I propose is a good deal for you. I may never see that second hundred thousand if Carson slows down on you or you don't get him

---

[16] $100,000.00 in 1974 had the same buying power as $511,958.87 in 2016

some help. The first hundred is mine with no conditions other than I turn it over to Carson."

"You got a deal," Cooke said, "but consider this. I'll give you $250,000 today, if you come over and do this with me yourself. A quarter of a million. Consider it a signing bonus."

I shook my head. "You flatter me, Oscar. Thank you, but no."

Oscar extended his hand across the table. We shook hands.

"I'll write you a check as soon as we eat."

If Carson did everything he promised to do, limit his drinking and pot smoking, and work his fucking ass off, he could make big money for himself and for Cooke. It was a good deal all around. As for me, it was probably not as good of a deal. I doubted I'd ever see that second hundred thousand. But I wanted a change.

I left his office with a check, and went right over to my bank. I called my accountant and told him to find me a tax shelter so I wouldn't have to pay a bundle on taxes.

I called PDC, and had them cater a huge buffet; then called the girls and told them to bring their appetites. When the girls arrived, they were thrilled with the prospect of a spontaneous party. They ate. They laughed. They joked around. They drank wine. That's when I told them my plan. I didn't mention the money part of the deal. I fielded their questions, which were mostly about the new job, then before dessert, presented them each with checks for ten thousand.

"It's all yours," I told them. "Put it in the bank, spend it any way you want. It's a nice chunk of change."

"Oh my God, Mario," Niley said. "I don't have this coming. I haven't been here as long as Pixie and Jo."

"Take the money and shut up, sweets." Jo nudged her with her elbow.

"I've never ever ever had this much money at one time. I've never even seen so much at one time. I could waitress for three years and never see this much," Pixie wailed.

Then they were all crying. Sometimes I just don't get women.

"This Cooke must be fucking loaded," Jo said.

"I believe he is. That will be good for the clients. They will be taken care of. I told Carson I'd beat him to a pulp if I heard he was screwing the clients over."

Niley said, "You'll never know because you aren't going to take the calls anymore."

"I know I won't know, and you know I won't know, but Carson doesn't know."

"So we're out of a job?" Pixie said, pushing the check back in my direction with a quivering sigh. "Does this mean we're fired? Laid off? At liberty? I refuse to quit."

Niley eyed her check, but didn't put it on the table. "Unemployed, out of action? On the shelf?"

Jo had already put the check in her wallet. "You sad sacks can call it what you want. I'm calling it a vacation." She gave one of her big whistles.

"Not out of work unless you want that." I said, "You are going to run my apartments. Take a management class if you need it. When I find my next line of work, which will be more interesting and less boring than apartment management, you will be the first to know it. I'll offer you to come do whatever it is with me."

"Gosh," Niley said, "This is just too good."

"Fuck yeah," Pixie whooped.

"But is it fair to you?" Jo asked me.

"Of course it is. I'm paying an arm and a leg to manage the apartments. Paying that money to complete strangers who are way across town from the properties. Hell, Pixie already lives in one of the buildings. I may buy more."

"Wow, come to think of it, you're rich now," Pixie said with a certain admiration.

"I'm not rich," I said. "I'm just moving up. George Jefferson can eat his heart out. We're the ones having good times."

"You're rich." Jo disagreed with me. "And I'm so proud of you."

"Don't hog the pride, Jo. We are all proud of you," Niley said, "And it has nothing to do with these checks."

"I know," I said, looking at my friends seated across my dining room table.

"Pride isn't a big enough word," Jo said.

Pixie looked around. She got up and stood behind her chair. She took a deep breath, opened her mouth, and did a big *grito*, a Mexican yell that can peel paint, start earthquakes, and rally *criollos* in screaming range. She punctuated the yell by punching the air with one hand. Then Niley did a count down and all four of us did a synchronized *grito*. Well, we did about a dozen of them, each one louder and more raucous than the last, till we were all hoarse, and got a phone call from security wondering if someone was being killed again. Then we all sat around the table, laughing with our cracked voices.

After I hung up with security, Jo said, in what creaky little voice she had left, "Well. That's how proud I am. Of all of us. " Which got us started laughing again.

When we were settled, and after the decaf and dessert, and a brief discussion of various ways we could spend our dough, I told Jo, "In the morning, go over to the exchange. Meet Carson there. Get the lines moved over from management to us. My phone numbers will become Cooke's, so get me new numbers. Personally, I just need two lines. Tell Cooke keep the exchange, keep the business. Drop the exchange, lose the business. I already recommended that to Cooke but a reminder can't hurt. On the apartment business, by next Monday, send out letters to all the tenants. Have the letters hand-delivered. Let them know that checks should be mailed to a PO Box. Niley, you will get the box at a post office convenient to your house. Checks should be payable to me. By Monday, the management company should be out. Jo, if we need to pay them because of short notice, let me know. You have enough there to keep you busy," I said. "That's a lot of letters and a lot of delivering. Decide what is most efficient—outfitting one of the apartments in one of the buildings as a central office, or decide if you want to work here."

Jo had started off taking notes, but switched on the tape recorder. Niley and Pixie were looking a little anxious.

"My accountant says that key here is that we maintain a low vacancy factor in each building. Keep the apartments rented. We need to paint, and keep them clean and nice when someone moves out, and get it ready fast so we can show it to persons interested in renting. The exchange should have a toll free number that you can put on the "for lease" signs. You three work out who gets the beeps from the exchange when they have a tenant reporting a problem, and who buzzes over to show it to a new prospective tenant. Establish a resident manager at each building that we can give half off for being available to show the vacant apartments, but you need to get the call, then arrange the appointment with the resident manager."

I was just rattling on like I'd been doing this forever. After all, I'd grown up in an apartment that was a great example of how not to handle tenancy. Jo is rarely taken by surprise, but I could tell that Pixie and Niley were realizing this was not a handout job. They were going to be busy.

"Aunt Carmen has a list of painters and plumbers and handy persons that she used when she was managing the first apartment building before I turned it over to the management. It may be a good place to start. You need to handle repairs quickly and clean up quickly, and for sure you can't do that yourself."

Pixie said, "I'm so excited I think I'm going to come."

In the morning, I went out for breakfast, then came home and called my aunt to tell her about the management changes.

"You were smart enough to buy these buildings," she said. "You certainly are smart enough to make the management decisions. I think it's a good move. I'm not sure the girls can do it on top of what they already do, but if they need help, all they need to do is ask."

"I already told them to ask you for the names of the contractors/workers that you hired at the first building."

"I got the list right here," she said.

"There's more," I said. "I've buried the hatchet with Carson. I'm even lightening my load by sending business his way. I'm sure you'll hear about it from his mom. Wait till she calls you though, and you can sound surprised."

She laughed.

"Oh that is just wonderful. I'm so glad you boys have made up."

That was my whole agenda for the day. I actually found myself with nothing to do. I went in my closet and picked up after the arranging the girls had done. I went through Jo's organizational system in my office, and realized that they'd probably take the papers to a more convenient on-site office, as I'd suggested. I really had nothing to do.

I called Melina.

"Just say you are busy if you can't do lunch," I offered.

"Cuz, I'd cancel everything without notice for the opportunity to break bread with you," she replied, "but, can we do it in my office? We can have something made downstairs."

"Sure," I said. "I'll be there at noon."

By the time I got there, the conference table in her office was filled with Mexican dishes. I thought it was great, but then ten minutes after I walked in, one of the chefs from downstairs came up the steps and put a huge grilled porterhouse in front of where I was sitting.

I thanked the chef profusely, and as soon as he left, said, "Fuck, who needs to go out to eat with this kind of luxury at your beck and call?"

We hugged and kissed. She kissed me again before we sat down across from each other. I knew she liked sitting so we could face each other.

I started right in on the steak.

I said, "I haven't seen you in more than a week."

"I miss you too," she said. "What's up?" she said, "You didn't come over to mooch lunch."

I brought her up-to-date.

"Fuck, you are full of surprises. So why did you sell off your business? You didn't do it for the money."

She had filled a plate, but she was doing more listening than eating. She busied herself by spreading some guacamole on a tortilla chip. It always fascinated me a little to see her do that rather than dip them like everyone else did.

"Who knows," I said. "I was restless. I've been doing the same thing since I was fourteen."

"Carson must be elated."

"Not sure about that, but if he works, he'll make a lot of money. That, at least, should put a smile on his face."

"And what will you do?"

"No idea. But I put the girls to work." I explained about their conversion to management. "I'm thinking of getting away for a while. I'll get that interview done with the cops, and I'll get a passport, and maybe I'll do what you did after school. I know zero about travel to Europe, but I'll learn."

"Mario, that's a great idea!"

She seldom called me by my first name. It was usually friend, or Cuz.

"Oh how I wish I could go with you."

"Well, maybe you can meet me somewhere exotic when it's convenient."

"Deal," she agreed. "I'll make you a list of every place you should go. You gotta go to Italy and check out the frescoes."

That was textbook Melina. In control. It made me laugh, and she had no idea why.

"Sure, please do."

She could plan to her heart's content, but I knew I wasn't going to follow any agenda. I would explore just to explore.

The cops interviewed me for thirty minutes with Cooke there. I could see Grizzaldi was on his best behavior. He had a big case of hero worship or something where Cooke was concerned. Mike was another story. I had a feeling he was still trying to puzzle out the series of events in my life. Cooke and Grizzaldi wished me safe travels. Cooke was gracious and happy. He was already getting cases from the arrangement. He played it down, but he looked like butter wouldn't melt in his mouth. I knew it would work. Mike took me aside before we left.

"Watch your step, man. You got more than a string of bad luck."

"Is that a warning to stay on the straight and narrow?" I tried to make a joke of it.

"No, Mr. Luna," he said. "I haven't been a cop that long, but they train us that when there are horseshoes, to look for horses, not zebras."

I noticed he was calling me Mister, which was a step up from bonehead, or whatever it was he called me at first. "What the hell is that supposed to mean?"

"Sometimes the obvious solution is the solution," he said.

"Not helping," I said. "I don't know which side of that symbol I'm on, and I don't know if I'm the horse or the zebra or the donkey on the roof. So just tell me."

Mike laughed. "I talked to a lot of people who know you. I talked to people who testified for you when you went to court at eighteen. You had a hell of a lot of character witnesses vouching for you like you were some kind of junior saint. I met your aunt."

I stood straight, and glared down at him. "You leave my aunt out of this."

He shook his head, but not aggressively. "I can't. I'm completely helpless. My wife is expecting, and your Aunt Carmen Luna is the best damn midwife in the city of Los Angeles. We're taking a childbirthing class from her."

I couldn't help it. I groaned. "I must have sat through a million of those classes."

I didn't know whether to offer the guy condolences, or congratulations. I settled on the congratulations.

Mike said, "The point is that I've got an aunt too, but not one like yours. I'm developing what they call a gut instinct. On top of all those glowing testimonials about you, my gut instinct tells me there's no way Saint Carmen Luna raised a killer. So when I took an unbiased look at your situation, I was thinking maybe someone is after you. It is not a case of bad luck. Watch your back."

What he said made me think.

"Hang on," I said. I went out to my car, and opened the glove compartment. I handed him the Polaroids.

"What's this?"

"I took those photos the day before I was shot. I was on the way to meet Tanis. The guy in that pick up was tailgating me, and I got out of his way just before he hit the bug. I was late, or else I'd have stayed to get names. It was crazy at the time, but I had a feeling he was after me. More than a feeling. He was riding my ass, and he was pissed off something fierce. I think he was gunning for me, not the bug."

He took the pictures with a grin. "I always knew you were holding something back."

I shrugged. Maybe he could make use of them. I didn't mention the truck was stolen, but he'd do his own due diligence.

He looked at his watch, and went off to join his partner.

It's great (or ought to be great) when no one believes you and then suddenly someone does. I had told two people that I was getting paranoid: Tanis, and Jo. Jo was just too practical to make anything of my suspicions; and Tanis was gone. But this cop, Mike, had independently come to the same conclusion. I didn't know whether to be terrified or gratified, or both. I wish I could be skeptical like Jo, but I had been shot, Tanis had been murdered, and then Jake. How much more proof did I need? Only I had no clue who was doing it, or why. If the killer's interest was tied up with all my PI cases, he'd have somewhere else to look, now. Sanchez called back the same day, asking me to come down to look over new evidence. I came alone.

He and I were walking down a hall in the precinct.

"The interrogation room is free," he said casually, as we passed the security door, "or we can go to my desk."

He laughed at my expression, and continued into the communal room where his desk was parked. After working with well-to-do lawyers who spent thousands on furniture, I couldn't help but notice the difference between those and the old metal pigeonhole bought on some distant date by government dollars. Actually, I couldn't see that much of it. The surface was covered in stacked boxes and manila folders.

He sat down and offered me a seat.

"I'd rather stand," I said.

Sanchez opened a file and lay out several stacks of eight-by-ten black and white images.

"The Polaroids you gave me led me to this accident. The pick up that missed you hit the Volkswagen bug and a red Camaro. The driver of the pick up left before the police arrived. We never matched the prints. The driver is still in the wind, and the pick up was taken into impound. It was reported stolen, and was using stolen plates so records didn't do much good, but items in the vehicle were taken into evidence. Does any of this mean anything to you?"

Inside the folder were dozens of photos, some of the vehicle, and some of a variety of items.

This whole operation felt like a wild-goose chase to me. "This won't lead anywhere," I said. I thumbed through generic stuff you would expect to find in a glove box: an ice scraper, tire gauge, vehicle registration and a rubber band. There were also a couple sticks of Juicy Fruit, a hanging car deodorant, a melted chocolate bar, and parts from a couple different broken flashlights. The name on the paperwork meant nothing to me. There were photos, back and front, of business cards of several lawyers in a firm I was unfamiliar with. I thumbed through those too, and they meant nothing to me. The business cards were dented in the middle as if they'd been held together by a rubber band, probably the rubber band in evidence.

I handed them back.

"Sorry," I said.

The detective looked disappointed.

I had a mental double take, and said, "Give me those cards again."

I ran through them quickly, and found the one I was looking for. I handed it over.

"That's the only one in the lot who isn't a lawyer," Mike said.

I nodded. "I know this guy. Hugo Pliego. He's competition. He does. . ." I looked at the officer, and used the euphemism, "...client development for lawyers."

"He's an ambulance chaser like you," Sanchez said, satisfaction in his voice.

"Nothing like me," I said. "I can't imagine he'd be dangerous though."

"You think not? I'm not ignoring my only lead, especially since most of your troubles seemed to start after the day of this accident. All of these lawyers are tied up in fraud cases."

"Fraud?"

"They had people out there slamming on their brakes in front of new cars. That's fraud against the insurance company."

"I don't know anything about Pliego or his cases."

Sanchez said, "We believe he arranges them ahead of time. Hence his card in the pick up."

"I hate that," I said. "It gives us a bad name. But I still don't see how I'm connected."

"This may surprise you. There's a money trail between Pliego and the guy you threw off the balcony."

"Huh." That took me by surprise. I sat down on the chair by his desk. The rage I'd been living with since Tanis had been shot was absent. I was just shocked.

Sanchez said, "Unfortunately, we can't prove anything in your case. But we just brought him down for questioning in the fraud case. I'll let you know what turns up."

We shook hands. I turned my head and saw Hugo being escorted in, flanked by two cops. I looked at him. He looked at me. His face was expressionless, and I saw he was wearing cuffs. One of the cops grabbed his arm, and directed him in the opposite direction, in the hall that led to the interrogation room.

"You know, I've seen him at Casey's before. What kind of car does he drive?" I asked.

"I've already checked. Different plates. But it's an Impala. Same color, same year, same dent in the fender."

I met the girls for dinner at the Pantry.

"Coffee and chili all around," I said, "Plus whatever else they want."

Pixie asked for a Frito pie, but the Pantry was out of corn chips. "I'll settle for regular chili."

They got sides of shredded cheese, tomatoes, lettuce, salsa, jalapeños and sour cream for toppers.

"I love management," Jo said. "We got matching coveralls. What do you think?"

"Very nice," I said. Above the pocket was embroidered LUNA PROP-ERTY MGMT. The girls looked trim and polished. No cleavages, no miniskirts, no spike heels, no come-hither perfume. They were still beautiful, still hourglass, and although they looked untouchable, I had a feeling we'd all be touching before the night was through.

"I went to the police station today," I said, reaching for the salsa and Tabasco.

"I hope you didn't see that Grizzaldi," Pixie said, "I can't stand him. He pisses me off."

"What did they want?" Jo asked. She tossed Pixie a package of corn chips from the depths of her purse. Pixie grinned, crushed them, poured them over her chili and dug in. She added some cheese and green chili, and gave Jo a thumbs-up.

Niley seemed happy with what was on her plate. She didn't add anything.

"It wasn't Grizzaldi. Mike Sanchez called me in because they think they have someone connected with the shootings, a fraud case, and the hit and run on me."

Niley stopped with the spoon halfway to her mouth; Pixie dropped her silverware.

"Who?" Jo demanded.

"Hugo Pliego."

"No," Jo said in disbelief.

"They're trying to connect him with a fraud case," I said. "They brought him in for interrogation. I saw him there today."

"Which one is he?" Niley asked. "Do I know him?"

"He's that milk toast guy who's always at the emergency room."

"The one who's always buying us candy? I remember him," Niley said. "He doesn't seem like a crook. He doesn't seem like...anything."

After dinner, we all decided to meet at my apartment. I agreed to stop off for ice cream, and took orders. Pixie wanted rocky road; Niley asked for vanilla; Jo wanted Neapolitan; I got caramel ripple to round it out. Of course I got fudge sauce, brownies, cookies, peanuts, peanut butter, and cans of whipped cream, so everyone could get creative. I pulled up. The girls' cars were lined up in a row, with keys in the ignition. I followed suit, and picked up the grocery bag. It seemed peculiar that neither Johnson nor the security guy were anywhere in sight, but I supposed they were assisting another tenant. I let myself in, and took the elevator.

I was untroubled to find that the door was unlocked. Although I'd taken to locking it while I was gone, Jo and Melina both had keys. So I opened the door, and there was Hugo, with a .38 out and pointed at me.

Jo, Pixie, and Niley were parked on the couch with duct tape heavily binding their wrists. Johnson and the security guy were similarly taped, and against the wall behind Hugo. The security guy's ankles were also taped. Johnson's feet were free, but he'd been taped to a kitchen stool.

I couldn't believe bland, dull, unsuccessful Hugo was not only not arrested, but in my own fucking apartment holding a gun pointed directly at me.

"Welcome home, Mario," he said. "Surprise. Have a seat."

He gestured toward the couch with the gun. I looked that way.

"Might be a little crowded," I said, mildly. "Mind if I put this ice cream up before it melts?" I sounded as if finding a house full of tied up people were a normal thing. I thought a million things. If he was a foot closer, I'd kick the gun out of his hands. I could toss the groceries, or the gallons of ice cream. I could crack him on the head with the hall tree. Nothing seemed practical or fast enough while there was a gun pointed at me.

"Shut the door," he said.

I moved out of the way, and the door slowly closed on its own. There was no way I was letting him put tape on me.

He tossed me the roll of duct tape.

"Do it."

I looked at him.

"Hell no," I said.

He pointed the gun at Niley. I heard it click.

"Okay," I said, dropping the groceries. The paper bag hit the floor with a bang. Everyone jumped, including Hugo. His gun wobbled.

"Easy, big guy," I said.

The paper bag had split open, spilling out the jar of maraschino cherries, and cans of whipping cream. I stretched the tape out wide, and tried to pretend incompetence. Every second of delay was a second longer to think of a solution.

"Just fucking do it, Luna," he said.

The phone rang.

"I better answer it," I said.

"Not on your life," he said, "Not on her life." He put the end of the revolver against Niley's head. I could see she was shaking. Tears were pouring down her face. She closed her eyes. Beside her, Pixie looked flushed and frightened. Jo just looked pissed off. The phone stopped ringing. I couldn't push Hugo any farther. I could see he was getting nervous, and I still didn't know what the hell this was about. I wrapped the tape once around my wrists.

"Keep going." I made a couple more cycles of tape, and managed to rip it off the spool.

I didn't really need my hands free anyway. If I could get a little closer, I could easily get the gun from him. If he would just move it away from Niley,

I'd make a move. I wondered if talking to him would diffuse the situation, or maybe distract him.

"What's all this about, Hugo?"

"Don't take me for a fool. I saw you talking to the cops. If I'm going down, you're going down too. When you're out of the way, there will be more cases left for me."

Behind him, I saw Johnson move. He silently lifted the stool he was taped to. I shook my head. He better not try anything with the gun still pointing at Niley.

"Going down for what, man?"

"Don't act like you don't know."

"They said you were setting up cases. I didn't believe them."

"I'm not stupid," Hugo said. "I know you were after my cases. I had to defend myself."

"Your cases?" I was mystified. "I don't know your clients. I don't even know the lawyers you work for. That's how little I know of you."

"I've lost cases to you for years. People I had in the bag, who backed out and went with you."

"We've never had a client mention your name. Not one!" Jo yelled.

Hugo ignored her.

I stared at him. No client of mine had ever mentioned him to me. I'd heard clients mention Carson, but never Hugo.

"Fucking greedy bastard, sucking up all the Latin cases in LA. I thought you were taken care of. I knew with you out of the picture, I could do my job. But no, you're fucking bulletproof."

There were more than enough cases for all of us. I knew it. We didn't come close to getting them all, or even most of them. I could have hired three more girls and not put a dent in the cases out there. But I could see he wasn't in the mood to hear it. He probably wouldn't want to hear that he didn't get clients because he was fucking invisible, either.

"Bulletproof?"

I heard the word, and then it clicked in my head. "So you're the one who paid that guy to shoot Tanis," I said.

"Not her, stupid. She was collateral damage. Two thousand bucks, and he fucked it up. He was supposed to send you to the morgue, not the hospital. What do I care about some random bitch named Tanis?"

The instant he mentioned Tanis's name, Niley shrieked.

The door flew open, barely missing me. In stepped Melina, as naked as a peeled apple.

"What the fuck?" she said.

It all happened at once.

Hugo's jaw dropped. His brain must have stopped when he saw naked Melina. His gun hand did too, sagging to point at a couch cushion. I took a step forward and heard the gun blast. I got knocked back, slammed against the wall. Felt something hot and burning.

"Fuck." I'd felt this before. Now it just pissed me off. I stumbled forward.

"He shot you! He fucking shot you!" Pixie screamed.

"I know that Pixie," I said.

I saw the gun hand drop around the same time I understood that he'd just confessed to killing Tanis. A red haze covered my eyes, and I went off like a fire cracker. I kicked, and the gun went flying. I went after him. I struggled to get the tape loose, but I had wrapped it too many times, and now everything was getting slick with blood. I don't know what the hell I did. I was working on automatic. The room was spinning. I kicked and grazed him, and kicked again and made solid contact. My knees were feeling like limp spaghetti.

He was unexpected. He was a medium-sized guy, but little compared to me. I should have handled him already, but I had lost a lot of blood, and he was as slick as an eel. He kept slithering out of the way like the snake he was.

He saw me coming, and gave a nasty laugh.

"I don't need a gun," he said, and pulled a couple of knives out of his pockets, and held one in each hand. Switchblades. They snapped open. The creepy little guy was turning out to be a shithill of surprises. He jabbed at me with both knives. I felt his left slash my arm, but it was no deterrent. If I'd been thinking, I'd have just tossed him through the window. I wasn't fooled. He was trying to make his way back to the gun. I had no intention of letting him near it. I saw Niley jump up from the couch, and kick over my coffee table. She was hysterical.

"Stay out of it Niley," I yelled.

"Son of a bitch killed my sister!" she screamed.

Out of the corner of my eye, I saw Jo fling her arms over Niley's head, and hang on for dear life. The girls were all crying, but Niley was hysterical.

I kicked him again, knocking him away from the girls. I wasn't going to let him near them. He rolled away and stood up. I hit him a couple of times, but every time I made contact, he slashed me again. My arms were a mess, still taped, and greasy with blood. I didn't feel it though. All I saw was Tanis. He slithered under one arm, and pivoted and slashed at my shoulder blade. I raised both arms for a killing blow and he slipped through again, diving for the gun. He picked it up. Niley broke free, and started wrestling him over the gun with her taped hands. She was no match for him. He lifted her clear off the ground, the gun dangling from her encumbered fingertips.

"Son of a bitch, you're gonna die," Niley said, trying to get control of the gun, trying to keep from losing it.

Jo stood, almost dancing in place. She was desperate to do something to help Niley or me, but clearly leery of the gun. One of his knives fell, and slid across the floor. Jo saw it, grabbed it between her fists, and tossed it at Pixie who was closer. It landed on her forearms. Pixie cradled it, struggling to get a grip. It was sharp, and cut through her sleeves, but she managed to wrangle it between her palms. She shoved it into his side and jumped away, like he was a cobra.

He wheeled around, shaking the gun loose from Niley. He had the gun and one knife in one hand, and with the other was trying to pull out the knife jutting out of his back. He made a couple of small circles trying to get the hilt but couldn't reach. Niley was still hysterical, an unintelligible stream coming out of her mouth.

"Fuck it," he said, and pointed the gun at Niley. Instead of running away, she ran at him again. I rammed him, and he went flying back into the window. It shattered, but looked for a second like the crazed glass was holding firm. He flailed wildly for something to hang on to, and laughed as he realized he wasn't falling.

"You're not getting off that easy!" Niley screamed.

She came running from behind me, and rammed him in the gut. I managed to hook my fingers in Niley's jacket, and then shoved him, hard. The window gave the rest of the way, and he went crashing through. Then Security and Johnson were in the empty window frame, dragging Niley and me back inside.

"Easy Bossman, Miss Niley," Johnson said. "We ain't gonna let you go to jail for that piece of shit. He won't be bothering you no more." He looked toward Melina, then looked away as politely as he could. "Thank you Miss Melina, for cutting us loose."

"No problem," Melina said, still bare-assed, but standing there like a fucking queen. She'd cut everyone lose, and was still holding the blade in one hand and the gun in the other. She'd used one of the practice weapons that I kept on display. Her robe was probably in the hall. She didn't seem to miss it.

"I'm calling the police," Melina said.

"Get down, Mario," Jo ordered. "You've been shot. You're losing blood." She had gotten a clean kitchen towel and tossed it at me. I put it on the wound and pressed hard.

I sat down on the floor near the back wall. I was close to the edge, both the edge of the building, and my endurance, but didn't really feel like moving. My knees had gone from spaghetti to jelly, and if the room was spinning before, now it was a freaking tornado. Johnson and the security guard dragged me farther from the gaping hole in my wall toward the door, and then Jo and Pixie and Niley were all hanging on me, crying. I could hear Melina on the phone, rattling out directions.

I had my arms wrapped around all three of them. They were crying into my chest. I didn't mention that it hurt. I kept whispering into their hair, "It's over. It's over." We were all a mess.

"I can't believe that little squirt got everyone up here," I said, looking at my ruined window. "Son of a bitch."

"He followed us in," Jo said. "Then held a gun to Niley, made Pixie and me tape each other up. I managed to call security. Hugo hid behind Niley again when Security came in. When Johnson came in, he coldcocked him with the gun butt."

"Sorry, Bossman," Johnson said, hanging his head. I could see the bloody lump on his skull.

"No worries," I said.

By the time the ambulance got there, Melina had put on a robe, and the tape was off of everyone. Melina was running around, trying to fix everything for everyone. Johnson had stopped her from cleaning up so the cops could see the evidence. She was as white as her bathrobe had been, but now it was spotted with blood. She went over Jo, and Pixie and Niley, looking for cuts, and feeding them tea that no one wanted. The apartment looked about what you'd expect it to look like after a gunfight and a knife fight and a karate match. I was sure to hear from my landlords. I wasn't that worried. I knew of about a thousand other apartments I could move into if I wanted.

It was a through and through. The medics managed to stop the bleeding.

Whatever adrenaline or natural anesthetic that had kept me going ran out. It hurt like hell getting on the gurney. I had dozens of little knife slashes that felt like pinpricks, but the fucking gunshot was unbearable. Someone suggested that maybe I should go live somewhere on the ground floor. I laughed, and was out like a light.

Grizzaldi and Sanchez came to the hospital. I told them what I remembered, but I was under sedation, and had no idea what I said. Mike told me not to worry. They had listened to eight eyewitness accounts of what happened.

"Hopefully, this is the end of attempts on your life," Mike said.

Epilogue
January 7, 1975
Free

The hospital stay delayed my trip for two months. Ten weeks later on the day of my departure, Melina had a righteous fit when she saw that all I was bringing was a backpack of the minimum of stuff I felt I could get by with. I was still practicing half-ass karate workouts, but wasn't going to put it off any longer.

"I can purchase what I need on the road as I need it." I remembered the massive pile of boxes and trunks that had filled Melina's entry the first time I'd set foot in her apartment. There was no way I was setting out on a lighthearted free-spirit vacation and be enslaved to that kind of baggage.

Melina's hugs and kisses were so passionate I almost got undressed and took her to my bedroom. But there was no time. I had to catch the plane from LAX to New York that connected to a London flight. The traffic was awful.

Pixie, Jo, and Niley rode with me to the airport. I drove my car. they would look after my place and take care of the buildings, and take the car back. I left

Jo plenty of money in the checking account to pay my rent every month and anything else domestic that needed to be paid. The management rental account would be used for everything else relating to the rental units, including the girls' wages. Either Jo or my aunt could sign those checks. I told them they could not sign cases for Cooke or Carson no matter what, not if they wanted to work for me. I didn't want Cooke to get used to my team. I was still on the fence about how dangerous he was. I knew my friends and I would pursue future ventures. I just did not know what they were going to be. I wanted to clear my head. I needed to get away.

I stopped the car curbside in front of American Airlines. We got out of the car. Jo was the first to hug and kiss me.

"I love you," I said.

"I love you more, sweets."

Pixie wrapped her arms around my waist. I picked her up and our lips met. Her arms went around my neck and we kissed deeply. I put her down. Then Niley was crying.

"You've been so good to me and the kids. I love you so much." She wrapped herself around me. Cars were piling up, and honking. Drivers were yelling in our direction.

"I love all of you. Take care of my auntie. Check in with her often."

"Call us," Jo said.

"I will," I promised. "But don't wait on me. Make decisions. If you get really stuck, ask my aunt."

Even though I knew I'd be back, it broke my heart saying goodbye. We took so long I missed my flight. The trip to New York took a little over six hours. I sat in first class. I could hardly believe what was happening. I was just a young man that had come from the poorest of beginnings, and here I was taking a fucking vacation with a one-way ticket. I was flying solo, and the whole world was mine for the taking.

Author's Notes and Apologies to History

Dear Readers,

Some things need to be said. I am not Mario, though I have known several people like him. His life is not my life, but I have been to the places he has been, and know some of the people he knows. Names and personal details have been changed. This is fiction.

Money went much farther in the 1970's. A case that was valued at $100,000 in 1972 is $575,486.62 in 2016. I have included footnotes for monetary values to make it easier to see what the value of the dollar was relative to the year.

I took very few liberties with actual things. Smith & Wesson was not in the knife market until 1973, and its first knife was a Bowie knife. They actually didn't start selling folding knives till 1974. I could have written about another brand, but then it wouldn't have been a Smith & Wesson.

The Scared Straight program takes students on prison tours for a day. Our fictional judge took liberties with the concept. The first Scared Straight TV documentary was filled in 1978. Mario's federal judge took the law into his own hands slightly in advance of when the program was instituted.

In 1972, the 4th case to settle for a million was to Michael Metzger: 42 injured installing equipment at Ocean Salt Co. in the Long Beach harbor. His lawyer, Larry Booth, won. A jury returned a verdict of $1,398,000[17] on Dec. 4, 1972. To stay accurate to history, Harry's (fictional) case settles Dec 5, 1972, and is the source of Harry's gift to Mario.

---

[17] $1,398,000.00 in 1972 had the same buying power as $8,045,302.92 in 2016

About the Author

George Hatcher is an entrepreneur with a gift for business and storytelling. Whether he's traveling the globe as a consultant/strategist for lawyers in high profile wrongful death cases, running one of his many enterprises, or at home with Molly amid the birds and cats in California, he's always got his eye on the next project. He does a whole lot more than what is mentioned here.

A longer bio is on his website at: www.georgehatcher.com/bio/bio.html